ALL THE SHINY THINGS

A KATE REID NOVEL
BOOK 1

ROBIN MAHLE

HARP HOUSE PUBLISHING, LLC.

Published by HARP House Publishing
January 2016 (2nd edition)

(Original publication, September, 2013)

1

THE NIGHTMARE

Katie Reid made her way to the back of the plane through the pleasant smiles of flight attendants and chattering passengers. Lingering images of yet another unpleasant dream disrupted what had started out as a restful nap. When the metal cabinets in the galley rattled from mild turbulence, Katie instinctively gripped a handle to steady herself.

A flight attendant soon approached, displaying extraordinary balance, and placed a tray of clear plastic cups on the counter next to her. The water inside swished around in little waves. "Please, help yourself."

A nagging thirst had taken hold and Katie found the relief she'd needed. After the third cup, her tongue no longer felt like cotton still clinging to its boll, but the water did little to quench the unnerving images that were still forefront in her mind. The dreams, more like nightmares, had been the cause of many sleepless nights lately.

Katie returned to her assigned row and was now standing next to a man who blocked her approach. "Excuse me." He shifted just enough to allow her to squeeze back into the tightly packed row of seats.

"Are you okay?" Spencer sat in the window seat and was roused by her return.

"I'm okay; I just needed to get some water."

"You had another dream, didn't you?" His concern hadn't waned since they started nearly two months ago and seemed to only grow deeper.

The corner of her mouth tilted up, followed by a shrug of her shoulders. Katie's post-nightmare routine—leaping out of bed, eyes, full of terror—was becoming something of a habit to which Spencer had grown accustomed. Nevertheless, its occurrence during a brief nap was something new. It seemed her fatigue was crossing into new levels of desperation.

Overhead, the familiar ding and illumination of the seatbelt indicator signaled the plane's descent. The left wing tilted up toward the blue sky, high above the clouds to make the turn into Eureka. The jet engine groaned and a swift drop in elevation sent a shot of adrenaline through Katie's body. Her tolerance for flight had lessened significantly over the past few years.

When they boarded in Sacramento this morning, there wasn't a spare seat on the plane and that was after the sold-out flight from her hometown of San Diego. Traveling from southern to northern California could be as difficult as a cross-country flight and it wasn't over yet. They still had the forty-five minute drive to the suburbs where they'd planned to stay with Sam and her fiancé.

Katie hadn't traveled to these parts for almost three years and it wasn't something she relished. Sam's wedding was the only reason that she found herself on this flight, dragging Spencer along. Her dearest friend had chosen to make her home very near where the two had grown up and had asked Katie to stand next to her at the altar.

"I'm glad your parents will be at the wedding. I know you weren't happy when Sam invited them, but I think it's important that you work to mend fences." Spencer was all too familiar with their strained relationship.

Katie tightened her seatbelt and prepared for the landing, ignoring his comment.

Rio Dell was a small town and was even smaller when Katie and Sam were growing up. Everyone knew each other, and each other's business. So when Sam mentioned she had sent an invitation to Katie's parents, it wasn't a big surprise. Just her friend's all too transparent plan to get the three of them in the same room. It could, however, be a plan she might regret.

The wheels made contact with the runway and the drag pulled it forward, bouncing the plane along in a rough manner. Relieved that she had touched ground, Katie opened her eyes and released the death grip she had on the arms of her seat.

"Come on, this'll be fun." Spencer could always be counted on to lighten Katie's mood, even if his sardonic wit was a quality she only mildly appreciated.

"I'm looking forward to it." She returned an equally caustic smile as they deplaned. Sam's wedding was something Katie had been truly looking forward to, but coming back home, to this small town she'd been so desperate to leave, was at odds with that excitement.

In the baggage claim area, Katie spotted Sam in the distance and headed her way. Arms open and flashing her sparkling smile, Sam seemed thrilled at the sight of her old friend. Katie's eyes brightened in response as she was both happy to see her friend and grateful the journey was over.

"Oh Katie, it's so good to see you! How was your flight?"

"You know me, I'm not much for flying, but I'm glad we made it. It's great to see you too, Sam."

Spencer collected the bags from the conveyor and approached the two of them. "Hi, Sam, long time no see." The ensuing kiss on the cheek seemed a little uncomfortable for him.

"I can't tell you how thrilled I am that both of you could come," Sam replied.

"Are you kidding? I'm the Maid of Honor. I couldn't exactly miss this now could I?" Katie looked around for Sam's missing other-half. "Did Jerrod come with you?"

"Oh, he's driving around the airport, waiting for us to go out on the curb. He didn't want to pay for parking." Sam took hold of Katie's hand and pulled her toward the terminal exit.

With raised eyebrows, Katie turned to meet Spencer's similar gaze and whispered to him, "I told you he was cheap."

After some pre-wedding celebrations, the day had arrived. In the dressing room of the church, Katie watched the fluttering of people in and out as they assisted the bride on her big day. The other bridesmaids, most of whom were work colleagues, busily slipped on their shoes and touched up their hair.

"Katie, can you help me find my garter? I can't see it anywhere." Sam scurried around in search of the elusive item.

"Don't worry. I think I remember seeing it in the back of the limo. I'll go grab it." Katie returned a few minutes later, blue lacy garter in hand.

"I knew there was a reason I chose you to be my Maid of Honor." Sam pulled the garter up to her thigh.

"In fairness, we have known each other for nearly twenty years. That could be part of the reason, too. But, I can only hope you'll be half as good as I am when it's my turn." Katie smiled and grasped Sam's shoulders, turning her in the direction of the full-length mirror. "You look beautiful."

"Thank you for always being there for me. I could not have asked for a better friend."

Katie started to blot her eyes with her fingertips, careful not to smudge the makeup. "Stop it already. You're going to have both of us blubbering like idiots in a minute."

Sam's mom entered the room, took one look at her daughter, and nearly burst into tears herself.

"Okay, Molly, we can't have Sam messing up her beautiful face with tears," Katie insisted.

"I know, I know." Molly swatted at the air as if to brush away her emotions. "You've always been the sensible one. Never letting your emotions get the best of you. It's we Fields women who can't keep it under control."

Molly was right, keeping her emotions in check was something Katie learned from an early age. Her father had been an expert.

"Well, I'd better check on your dad to make sure he hasn't frightened poor Jarrod away with talk of what would happen if his little girl's heart gets broken. You know how he can get, Sam."

Molly left the room and Katie was once again alone with Sam. She wanted to tell her about the dreams and ask for her advice, but this was not the right time. It was Sam's day and she didn't want her to worry.

"You're very lucky to have such amazing parents. I've always thought that." Katie fidgeted with the long flowing train of Sam's gown. "I always felt like they were my parents too."

"Speaking of parents, you are going to talk to them today, correct?"

"I'm sure the opportunity will present itself." Her glib reply suggested otherwise.

The wedding planner burst through the door of the dressing room. "It's time, ladies. I've gathered the other bridesmaids. Let's get you down that aisle, Samantha."

The stunning bride took a deep breath, waiting for assurance from her childhood friend.

"Everything will be fine," Katie whispered.

THE CEREMONY BEGAN and the minister cited passages from the Bible that were broad and non-specific. He focused on the importance of commitment and trust for the long journey the couple was about to begin.

It was in those words that Katie began to search for meaning and the path of her own future.

Spencer was pre-law and she had been studying social sciences when they met. Since then, they've been practically inseparable. That was almost seven years ago. After college, they moved in together and here they were now, four years later. Katie thought she would be the one in the white dress at this moment, but Spencer's work as an intern at the law firm and studying for his bar exam seemed to consume most of his time. Katie didn't object. She supported him completely and had her own budding career at the Foundation that kept her occupied. Nevertheless, she looked forward to the day when Spencer passed the bar and could start his career as a trial lawyer. Maybe then, she thought, they would get married and start a family.

"Um, Katie?" Sam looked over her shoulder with wide eyes. "It's your turn." Her voice sounded just short of panicked.

Katie returned to the moment. "Right. Sorry about that." She approached the podium and unfolded the sheet of paper that had been neatly tucked away in the sash of her strapless champagne-colored gown.

As she proceeded to read Sam's favorite poem, Katie looked out among the guests and there they were. Her mother was slender and elegantly dressed with perfectly coifed hair—a vision for a woman in her late fifties. Her father was slightly plump, balding, and heavily lined, but had a gentle face and lacked the sophistication evident in his wife.

She locked eyes with her mother for a moment as a smile vaguely appeared on her mother's face. The moment vanished and Katie continued, unmoved and her expression, unchanged.

WITH THE RECEPTION in full swing, Spencer leaned in and whispered in Katie's ear as they sat at the head table. "You know, you're not supposed to look more beautiful than the bride."

She pulled away and lightly slapped his shoulder. "What are you talking about? Sam looks amazing. You shouldn't say that."

"Yes, she does. But you're the only one worth looking at to me."

"Boy, someone's hoping to get lucky tonight."

"Maybe, but we do have an early flight and I will need my rest." He held out his hand as the band began to play. "Care to dance?"

"Who are you and what have you done with my boyfriend?" She placed her hand in his and after a few brief turns on the floor, Spencer seemed to have his fill.

"I could use a drink. You want something?"

"Sure."

He immediately headed toward the open bar and Katie took a seat at one of the tables. Out of the corner of her eye, she saw a billowy white dress floating toward her. Sam dropped down in the seat next to her.

"My feet are killing me!" She slipped off one of her shoes and began rubbing her toes. "If I have to dance with another crazy uncle or distant cousin twice removed, I'm going to shoot myself! Honestly, I don't know why my mother invited so many people."

"I have to say," Katie began. "It was a beautiful wedding. I'm so glad you had it here. Remember when we'd drive home on school breaks and pass this place?"

"I sure do. I've never forgotten about it. There's something so majestic about the way this old hotel stands alongside the Redwoods. It's like it was always meant to be here."

Katie rose from the table for a look around. The ballroom glistened in the sun's setting rays that reflected off the river below. The windows filtered the light in such a way as to make those dancing on the floor look as if they were floating, their feet submerged in the twilight. "Ah, there's Jarrod. I'm sure my moves will pale in comparison to yours, but I shall do my best as the Maid of Honor to dance with the groom!"

~

THE WAIT STAFF FILED OUT, almost in unison, and began serving the entrees and the dinner got underway. Spencer searched for Katie as she was the only one of the bridal party not already sitting at the head table. When she finally came into view, he motioned for her to take her seat next to Sam.

"Where did you run off to?"

"Sorry, I lost track of time. I was just taking in the view of the river. My parents brought me here a few times."

"I noticed you didn't talk to them before they left the church. Are they here?"

"No, I haven't seen them. They must have decided not to come to the reception. I'm sure my father is busy with work and you know Mom. She'll be off volunteering for the latest cause. No time for socializing, I guess." Katie pretended not to be bothered by the fact that they hadn't even said hello, or goodbye for that matter, but she knew it was of her own doing.

The toasts were beginning and she swallowed the last of her wine in hopes of smoothing the edges before it was her turn to speak.

Sam's father stood up with his glass in hand and waited for the guests to fall silent. When he began speaking about the love he had for his daughter, Katie was reminded of the time she'd spent in the presence of that love. They had been her de facto parents up until the two of them left for college at UC-San Diego.

Katie waited for him to finish. "I'm almost up," she whispered to Spencer, blotting the corners of her mouth.

"Thank you, Mr. Fields." She took hold of the microphone. "Sam, we have known each other since the second grade and when you told me Jarrod asked you to marry him, I could not have been happier for both of you. I am so very grateful you found someone who makes you laugh and who holds you above all others. That's truly all I've ever wanted for you. Jarrod, I know you'll be good to her because if not, you'll have to answer to me and no one wants that, just ask Spencer." She paused for a moment to allow the pathetically few chuckles in the crowd to settle down. *Tough room.* "But in all seriousness, Sam, you're like a sister to me and even though we don't live on the same street anymore, you are always in my heart. I love you, and congratulations to Mr. and Mrs. Hansen. Cheers!" Katie dropped to her seat with a sigh of relief.

"Nice job, babe." Spencer leaned in for a kiss.

She was just glad it was over.

THE HISTORIC TUDOR-STYLE hotel sat perched along the banks of the river, adjacent to the Redwoods. Katie pulled back the curtains of their hotel room window to reveal the shadowy outline of the giant trees outside. Even in the darkness, she could see branches swaying in the breeze. Sam always told her she would get married here one day. Fortunately for her, she did. Sam's family didn't worry about money, which was a good thing because it took plenty of it to get married here.

"You ready for bed?" Spencer asked. "You must be exhausted after today."

"I am." She began a slow and seductive crawl onto the bed.

Spencer smiled at her approach, slid his hand around her long, delicate neck, and guided her to meet his slightly parted lips.

THE DRIED twigs on the ground cracked under the weight of her bare feet. Rocks jutted out from the cold and damp soil, sinking into her tender skin, making each step more painful than the last. Running as fast as her legs would carry her, the unexpected light blurred her vision

as they struggled to adjust. She traversed through the trees and realized that something was tied around her neck; it was a blindfold. She recalled yanking it off her face at the time of her escape. Over her shoulder, the shadowy figure quickly approached and soon everything appeared out of proportion. The trees seemed to reach up to the clouds. The silhouette loomed closer and larger as the giant trudged after her. His faceless head was shrouded in darkness and he was gaining on her, but she could not run any faster. The pain from her bloodied feet slowed her pace. He was right behind her now as the earth trembled beneath each step. An extraordinarily long arm and grotesque hand reached to grip her tattered t-shirt. She lunged forward and pulled her shoulder away from the scrap of fabric he managed to grasp. The force of the lunge caused her to stumble to the ground. The sound of cracking ribs filled her ears as she landed on a jagged boulder and a chilling scream clawed its way out of her throat.

"Wake up. Katie, wake up!"

She bolted upright in bed and reached for her side. One look at her hand and she expected to see blood, but there was none.

"It's okay, you're safe. You're okay." Spencer reassured her as they embraced. "It was that dream again, wasn't it?"

She peered at him with frantic eyes, still catching her breath. "Yes, it's getting worse and it's happening more often."

The dream had gotten worse. When it started a few months back, it was never intense enough to wake her. It started out as just someone chasing her and then it would fade away. But a couple of weeks ago the dream came to her more frequently, each time becoming more real and more frightening.

"Maybe you should talk to someone about this. Maybe it's just stress. You have been really busy helping Sam this past month or so. That seems to be when it got worse."

Katie could see he was struggling for an answer. Stress, she thought, was entirely possible. Juggling her bridesmaid duties from a distance as well as working on the upcoming fundraiser for the foundation, yes, that must be the reason. She squeezed him hard as a way of thanking him for understanding. "Maybe you're right. When we get home, I'll call Dr. Reyes. She works with the foundation and counsels some of the families. I suppose I could talk to her."

"I think that would be a good idea. Try to get back to sleep." Spencer kissed her damp forehead and turned to sleep again.

It was a Sunday morning in Eureka and the airport was thinly populated. Nevertheless, Katie and Spencer calmly but quickly ran through to security after having overslept. A few very tired-looking individuals stood ahead of them, but it wasn't as busy as Katie had anticipated. Still, it would be a sprint to get to the gate in time.

The flight was already boarding and Katie handed the attendant her boarding pass with Spencer following closely behind.

"See, there was nothing to worry about. We made it in plenty of time." His raspy voice couldn't conceal the previous night's celebration.

"Well if I hadn't prodded you along, we'd have missed it for sure." Katie shoved her carry-on under the seat.

Almost as soon as they were airborne, she noticed Spencer was already asleep. *Unbelievable.* She reached for her tablet and turned it on when the announcement to use electronics was finished. The airline charged a steep fee for wi-fi access, but boredom quickly set in and with a few hours to kill, she opened up a search engine and typed "treatments for stress."

Maybe this was all stress-related, but before she called Dr. Reyes, Katie would be armed with information. Several results were returned, including something called relaxation hypnotherapy. *Sounds interesting.* As her search deepened, other forms of hypnosis and treatments came up. However, after reading more about the idea of the relaxation therapy, she was warming to it and would bring it up to Dr. Reyes. Of course, Katie was unsure if the doctor was willing or capable of performing such therapy, having only ever known of Dr.

Reyes' work with troubled families and victims of abuse. The Advocacy Group, her employer, was involved in everything from victim's assistance programs to substance abuse clinics to community outreach. If Dr. Reyes couldn't help her, she probably knew of someone who could.

There was no denying Katie had a knack for research and she was always looking for ways to solve problems, be it her own, or others'. Katie had a desire to learn everything she could on a subject in which she had an interest. This was likely the reason her work at the foundation was so invaluable. Her caseload often involved detailed research.

An overhead announcement began. "Please turn off your electronic devices, place your seats in their upright positions, and stow your personal belongings. We will begin our descent into San Diego momentarily."

"Spence." She nudged him. "Spencer, we're getting ready to land. Wake up."

"Okay, I'm awake."

"How are you feeling?"

"Better; not great, but better."

THE PREDICTABLY COMFORTABLE weather signaled that they were home. The sky was still clouded, but by mid-afternoon, the sun would burn off the remaining haze that rolled in with the tide.

Their two-bedroom apartment was teeming with the odor of pent-up, damp sea air when Spencer opened the door. "I'd better open some windows." He pulled back the curtains to bathe the living room in light and lifted the old single-pane windows to allow the fresh air inside.

Katie headed for the bedroom and dropped her small bag on the bed. Immediately, she tossed her clothes to the floor and hopped into the shower.

Just as she stepped out, Spencer appeared with a cold bottle of water in his hands. "Here you go. Thought you might be thirsty. Oh, and Sam called your cell. Looks like she left you a message."

"Okay, thanks." She pulled on a tank top and shorts and wrapped her thick dark hair in a towel. The cell phone on her nightstand buzzed again, indicating a waiting message. Katie retrieved it and held the phone to her ear. "Hi, Katie, it's me. I just want to thank you for everything you've done for me over the past several months. You made my wedding truly the best day of my life. I'll tell you all about Fiji when we get back. Take care of yourself. Love you. Bye."

Katie smiled and pressed the *delete* button. "Love you too, my friend."

2

Their second-floor apartment was fairly close to Pacific Beach. The place was small but suited both of them for now. In fact, it was almost close enough to get a clear view of the ocean, if Katie turned her head just right while standing on the third step outside the front door, and peered through the alleyway of the condos across the street. Then, the view was perfect. The upside was that her commute to the office was brief, which was her destination now as she locked the door.

On arrival, Katie passed through the tall glass doors and into the lobby. The third floor was where she'd spent the past couple of years, in a cubicle with high walls that offered a veiled sense of privacy.

At her desk, she searched the company directory and found the contact information for Dr. Reyes. In a hushed conversation, she continued, "There's one more thing, doctor, what are your thoughts on hypnotherapy?"

"I've used some forms of it for assistance in addiction treatments. Generally, stressors in a person's life can cause a whole host of problems. I believe that's what we may be dealing with here and hypnotherapy may be of some use. But first things first, we need to get you in here to talk about your situation in an objective manner. How about next Thursday at 4:30?"

Katie examined her calendar. "Yes, that would be fine. Thank you, Dr. Reyes, I'll see you then." Just as she hung up the phone, she noticed Jennifer approaching. Only a few years younger than Katie, Jennifer was a touch naïve, but kind and hardworking. Katie acted as her mentor on occasion and they often worked together on fundraising events when she was in between cases.

"You're working with Dr. Reyes again? I didn't know they assigned you another case." Jennifer's eager approach to the job would likely wane as she got on in years, but for now, she had a relentless enthusiasm.

"Oh, that. No, it's not a case. I was just asking her about something I had researched online."

"Oh, I thought you were meeting with her."

Katie felt she had painted herself into a corner. She knew Jennifer wasn't the gossiping type, but discussing this with her wasn't an option. "I am next week. I thought that since we deal with so many cases of abuse, I wondered how certain therapy treatments were viewed, so I'm going to her office to discuss them."

Her colleague's expression suggested an acceptance of Katie's account and she didn't inquire further. "Great. You want to grab some lunch later? It's a beautiful day."

"Sure, how about 11:30?"

"Sounds good. See you later."

THE STREETS WERE full of tourists and workers jockeying for position. Employees who had neither the time nor patience to sit in overcrowded eateries during their too-short lunch breaks, instead opted for food trucks parked in and around Downtown. Meanwhile, the visitors sat down in open-air cafes, sipping wine and enjoying the scenery in springtime San Diego.

"Isn't Spencer supposed to get his results soon?" Jennifer asked as they headed out of the lobby and joined the masses.

"They're due to be out next Monday. He's been so busy working on research for the firm, I think he has almost forgotten about it. It's been months since he's taken the exam."

"I guess he'll probably work long hours too, once he's hired on as a practicing lawyer, right?"

"I suppose so, but I'm so proud of him. And besides, I knew what I was signing up for. He's got a long road ahead of him. I'm just hoping that I can talk Richard into using his firm once in a while, once he's offered a job, of course."

"Is there any reason to think they wouldn't present him with an offer? He's been interning there for what, like two years?"

Katie pressed the crosswalk button. "Yep. I can't see why they wouldn't, especially if I can convince Richard that the firm might be willing to take on some pro-bono cases once in a while. It would certainly prove Spencer's effectiveness if he could bring in new clients right away."

"Do they usually do pro-bono?" Jennifer asked.

"If Spencer has anything to do with it, they will. He'll want to do some good and help when he can, same as me." Katie stopped in front of the Greek restaurant. "Feel like Greek today?"

ALMOST THE ENTIRE week had passed without Kate suffering through another nightmare, but in the early hours of this morning, she awoke in a most violent manner. Spencer wasn't lying next to her this time to offer comfort, so she decided to walk down the hall in search of him.

The glow from the television bounced off his face like a strobe light as he sat in a near-catatonic state on the couch. Dawn had broken and a dull light filtered around the edge of the window curtains.

"How long have you been up?" She rubbed the sleep from her eyes.

"Since about three." He shrugged his shoulders. "Couldn't sleep."

Katie sat down beside him. "You passed. Don't worry, I know you did." She wasn't about to disclose her reason for being awake at this hour, not today.

"I wish I had the same confidence in me as you do."

"I'll go make some coffee." She squeezed his thigh and walked into the kitchen. "You want some toast?"

"Yeah, that'd be great. Hey, by the way, how'd you sleep? You're up awfully early."

She shoved the spoon into the coffee can and took a deep breath. "I slept all right. I just noticed that you weren't in the room and decided to come and check on you." She hated lying to him, but there was no way she would worry him any more than he was already.

Katie used the little silver tray they'd received as a housewarming gift to hold their coffees and toast as she brought them into the living room. "Here you are."

"Thanks." Spencer took a sip of his coffee. "So no bad dreams last night, then?"

"No. I tossed and turned little, but nothing that I can recall."

"Honey, come on. It's me. I know you're still struggling. I haven't said anything because I didn't want to pressure you. But it's clear you're trying to deal with something like emotions or stress. Have you thought any more about talking with someone?"

"I didn't want to burden you with more of this nonsense. You've been so anxious about your exam results and a few bad dreams seemed pretty insignificant."

"But it's not, is it? And it's more than a few," he said. "Your mind and your body are trying to tell you something. Whether it's to relax or change something in your life, I don't know. Have you been happy at work?"

"Of course; I love my job. It's been a little quiet lately because I haven't had an opportunity to work on any cases. Fundraising season, you know how that goes. If it makes you feel any better, I called Dr. Reyes. I told you about her at the hotel, right?"

"Yeah."

"Well, I called her and I've got an appointment for Thursday. I was going to tell you, but not until you got your results. I didn't want you to worry."

"But I do worry about you. I know I've been swamped at work and admittedly stressed about the bar, but honey, please don't keep things from me. I can handle more than you think." The toast ripped away at his bite. "Well, I'm glad you made an appointment anyway. Whatever's going on, we'll get through it. I'll just need a few more cups of coffee to help me get through today."

KATIE HAD WRAPPED up a meeting with a major contributor to the foundation when a call came in on her cell phone. "Excuse me, Mr. Wallace; I've got to take this. Jennifer will show you out. Thank you again for your generous contribution." She shook his hand and walked into the corridor. "Hey, babe, tell me the good news." There was a pause on the other end of the line and her heart jumped into her throat, fearing the worst.

"Yeah, well about that." He paused again and gave rise to impending bad news. "I passed!"

She was overcome with relief. "I swear, if you were here, I'd slap you for that."

He laughed on the other end of the line, that wonderfully contagious laugh she loved so much. She couldn't help but start laughing herself.

"It's one o'clock," she said, glancing at her watch. "How about I give the guys a call and get everyone together tonight for a celebration?"

"I would love that."

"So, what about your boss? Does he know yet? Do you think they'll offer you a job?"

"Don't know. I literally just got the news. I'm going to go tell him now. I doubt they'll offer me a job on the spot, but we'll see."

"Well, they'd be fools if they didn't hire the hottest lawyer in town. I'm so proud of you. Anyway, I'll get everyone together. Why don't we meet after work at Wayfarers?"

"Sounds great, honey. I'll see you later. Love you."

"I love you, bye." Katie stood in the hall, struggling to conceal the grin plastered on her face.

"You look like the cat that ate the canary," Richard said.

"Spencer passed the bar." Katie could hardly contain herself, even in the presence of her manager.

"Congratulations! That's wonderful news. Also, congratulations on getting a rather sizable donation from Mr. Wallace. That's no easy task." Richard patted her shoulder and continued on his way.

For the first time in months, Katie felt like a weight had been lifted from her shoulders. *Maybe Spencer was right, maybe I've just been too stressed.*

Wayfarers was packed, as usual. Luckily, a few of the guys were able to get there early and get a table for everyone. Katie mingled with their college friends and a few of the interns from Spencer's firm. Finally, Spencer arrived, late, but today that was okay.

She stood up in front of everyone and began to clink a spoon against her wine glass. "First of all, on behalf of my amazingly intelligent boyfriend, I'd like to thank you all for joining us on this special occasion. After years of studying, spending long hours as a thankless grunt in a law office, and passing, on his first attempt, the California bar exam, ladies and gentlemen, I present to you, Mr. Spencer J. Harris, Esquire!"

With raised glasses and shouts of accolades and applause for the man of the hour, Spencer and Katie's friends toasted his success.

"Thank you all and thank you to my beautiful Katie. Without her support, I would surely have failed not just the bar, but failed at life." He walked around the booth to Katie, knelt, and pulled a small blue velvet box from his pants pocket. Gasps could be heard from their surrounding friends. Katie's eyes grew wide and began to fill with tears.

"Katie, when we met in college, I had no idea that the five-foot-six brunette beauty who stands before me now would turn out to be my soul mate. You have supported me every step of the way and I know it hasn't been easy. I can only hope to find a way to repay you. I'd like to start by asking you to spend the rest of your life with me so that I can try. Katie, will you marry me?"

Without hesitation, Katie knew her answer immediately. "Of course I will."

He slid the diamond solitaire on her ring finger and raised to embrace her. "I love you so much, Katie."

Those were the only words that mattered and she knew they'd come from his heart. Most of their close friends attended UCSD with them and had watched their relationship grow. Katie showed off the ring to the other women, while the men congratulated Spencer.

"Did you have any idea this was coming?" Lindsey asked.

"No, none at all. Even at Sam's wedding, he didn't allude to any of this. Honestly, I had no idea."

"So long as you're happy," Amanda replied.

"Yes, I'm happy, very happy."

After a few rounds of drinks, the newly engaged couple finally had a moment alone as the others were occupied with their own conversations.

"I've been planning this for a while, you know," Spencer started.

"Really? Since when?"

"Since the day I took the exam, 5 months ago. I knew right then that if I passed, I would be able to provide you with the life you deserved. We can move out of that crappy apartment and buy ourselves a house. We can talk about starting a family. This is all I've wanted for us since we graduated. It about killed me at Sam's wedding. I wanted to ask you so badly then, but I had to wait. I had to know that I would make it as a lawyer."

"Spencer, I'd have married you, lawyer, or not. You know that, right?"

"I know. But this is what I needed to do first." Spencer looked over at their friends. "Well, it looks as though everyone's enjoying themselves. Don't suppose you're ready to get out of here?"

"You bet, let's bail." Katie stood up to get everyone's attention. "Hey, guys. Thank you all so much for coming tonight, especially on short notice. I think we're going to head out and do some celebrating in private." She winked at Spencer.

KATIE STOOD ON THE LANDING, searching her purse for the keys to the apartment. Spencer's arms wrapped around her while he kissed her neck.

"There they are." She opened the door and tossed her purse on the couch. "It'll be nice moving out of this place, so long as we find a house with a great big closet."

Once inside, they began kissing with a passion that seemed to be lacking recently.

"You know, it's only 9:00," Spencer glanced at the clock on the shelf. "Do you want to call your parents and tell them the news?"

"Let's see, it's 9:00 on a Monday night." Katie looked up and placed her hand beneath her chin. "Dad will probably be asleep on the couch after what I would guess to be his fifth or sixth drink of the night. Mom will be in her bed reading the latest self-help book. So, I'm thinking...no. Not tonight. I'll call this weekend."

"Okay. You know, sometimes I think you're harder on your folks than you should be."

Katie pulled out a chair at the dining table and sat down, feeling less amorous at the mention of her parents.

Rather than squander the mood entirely, Spencer went into the kitchen to open a bottle of wine and continued. "You had a good childhood, from what you've told me. You grew up in a great neighborhood and had family vacations, so I don't understand why you don't have a closer relationship with them. I think we've only been up there, what, like maybe four times in the past seven years?"

"You're right. I was given pretty much everything I wanted. The problem was that what I wanted was their attention, their time. My dad worked constantly to build up his business and I always felt like he kept me at arm's length, you know? I can probably count the number of times he told me he loved me on one hand. After a while, it seemed like the only things that really mattered to him were work and plenty of beer. And, Mom, well you know how she is, Mrs. Humanitarian. I had to help her with practically every charity event she ran. She always said, 'There are those far less fortunate than you, Kate. It's important to give back.'"

"Was she wrong?"

Katie sighed. "Of course not; she taught me the value of having a social conscience. I don't know. It's hard to explain. I love them both, dearly, but it's like I'm not really their flesh and blood, like they're detached from me."

Spencer handed her a glass as he sat down at the table. "Well, maybe it's time to change that. What's going to happen when we have kids? You'll want them to spend time with their grandparents, right?"

"Well, we've got yours." Katie grinned.

"Mine live on the other side of the country. At least yours are only a two-hour flight away."

"Three, more like."

"Okay, whatever, but you know what I mean."

"Yeah, I know. I'll call them tomorrow then, okay? I promise."

Katie held up her hand and admired her new ring. "You did a heck of a job picking this one out."

"Yeah, well, I know what you like." Spencer's devious smile gave away his intentions.

"Oh really? Why don't you show me, then?" Katie stood up, glass in hand, and began walking toward their bedroom. She stopped at the hall and looked back. "You comin', Mr. Harris?"

"Yes ma'am, soon-to-be Mrs. Harris."

SHE HID BEHIND A TREE, *hoping he wouldn't see her and tried to take a deep breath, but the cramp in her side made her wince in pain. The throbbing in her legs begged her to sit down, but she couldn't. And the birds chirped high in the trees. She looked up to see them, fearing they would give away her position. It was bright, too bright for her aching eyes. She had been in darkness but did not know for how long. Time seemed to stand still with no light to guide the senses. Everything around her appeared hugely out of proportion. It was as if she was in a land of giants, like the kind in the children's stories. The sound of leaves crackling made her spin her head. He was getting closer; she must run again. With each step, the cuts on her feet opened further and new ones formed as she trod over the broken branches and rocks on the forest floor. She could smell the rancid odor coming from the giant. He wasn't far behind.*

As she ran, his footsteps drew closer and the smell grew worse, nearly making her gag. She forced her legs to continue and pushed with every ounce of strength she had. Images of her parents flashed through her mind like a slide show; memories of them at the playground, at the beach, playing with her in the backyard. Everyone was so happy. She remembered happiness and love and this was what kept her running through the fear and pain. But it was not enough. She felt the hot stench of his breath on the back of her neck and his large fingers reaching for her shirt. She looked back for a moment and saw nothing but darkness.

A sharp pain pierced the arch of her foot as she lurched forward to avoid his grip. Her foot gave way as she tumbled to the ground. She looked up at the giant. His arms reached out for her. His great big hands clasped onto her shoulders and squeezed.

Katie's eyes flew open as she lay in a pool of sweat. Her heart raced so fast, she took hold of her chest as if that would slow it down. This was by far the worst one yet. Never before had he touched her. She could still feel a tenderness in her arms as if it had actually happened. Katie rolled off the bed and reached for her robe.

Shuffling into the living room, she sat on the couch and flipped on the TV. The clock showed 4 a.m. It did not matter to her what channel the TV was on; she only stared at it to fill her mind with images other than what she had just dreamed.

"What's wrong with me?" She closed her eyes and began sobbing quietly in the early morning hours, the day after her engagement.

SPENCER SHOOK her awake as she'd fallen asleep on the couch. A few hours must have passed.

"Did you sleep out here?"

She was startled by his touch but quickly recognized him. "It was a bad night; I woke up and came out here to watch TV. I guess I must have fallen back to sleep." Katie began rubbing her neck, stiff from resting on the arm of the couch.

"Do you want to go back to bed?"

"No, no. I'm good now. Let's have some breakfast." Katie started to rise.

"You stay here. I'll make it."

"Thanks, hon."

Not long after, Spencer returned with coffee and a bagel. "So, it was pretty bad, was it?"

"It was, yes, but it was different, too." Katie paused for a moment. "It caught me this time." She'd tried to explain to him before what *it* was but didn't really know herself.

"Oh, honey. I'm sorry. Why didn't you wake me?"

"Over what? Some stupid dream that won't leave me alone? So I have bad dreams, it doesn't matter." She wasn't angry with him, but it certainly was coming out that way. It wasn't anger at all, it was frustration.

"You know, you're right," he began. "It doesn't matter because you're going to the doctor this week and she'll figure out what's going on and you'll be fine." He was trying not to make a big deal of it, but was he doing it for her sake or his own?

"Thanks for breakfast. I suppose we've got a big day ahead of us, right? We need to start planning our wedding." She desperately wanted to change the topic and since they just got engaged, perhaps a conversation about that would help. And, the aroma from the coffee was beginning to help shift her mood. "We haven't set a date yet. When were you thinking?"

"Well." Spencer appeared barely able to contain his delight. "I was thinking Valentine's Day."

Katie winced. "Really? Isn't that a little—um—cliché?"

"You think so?" He spoke as if that hadn't actually occurred to him.

Now she'd managed to hurt his feelings, an unintended result from which she would have to quickly recover. "Never mind, if that's when you'd like to get married, I'm all for it."

"No, no. I didn't really think it through, but you're right. Valentine's Day is way too obvious. What about this winter, around Christmas time? Like around December 15th?"

Katie smiled. "Of course, that's perfect, but why then?"

"Seriously? You don't remember?"

She searched her mind for some recognition of that particular date, assuming it must have been important. "Oh right. That was the day we met."

"It took you that long to remember?"

"Have I told you lately how amazing you are?" She glossed over her obvious blunder.

Morning quickly turned to afternoon and Katie still hadn't given Sam the good news. With a quick break in her schedule, she picked up the phone.

"Oh my God, Kate, that's fantastic! First, he passes the bar, then this? It's really wonderful and I'm very happy for you both."

It was good to hear the excitement in her friend's voice. "Thanks, Sam. I'm sorry I haven't called you since you got back from your honeymoon. I guess I've been a little preoccupied."

"Don't worry about it. You guys are busy with work; I know that. And we only just got back a few days ago anyway."

"That's not what I meant, exactly." Katie felt compelled to say something, especially after last night. "It's just, well, I've been having a lot of trouble sleeping, and by a lot, I mean, for the past few months. I didn't say anything to you at the wedding because I didn't want you to worry. So, I thought it best to just see how it would play out. But it's been going on for a while now."

"Okay, now you've got me worried." Sam's tone was decidedly changed from only a moment ago.

"I keep having this, well, pretty disturbing dream. Disturbing enough to keep me from falling back to sleep on most nights. So Spencer and I agreed that I should talk to someone. I finally scheduled an appointment with a therapist for this week."

"Oh, Katie, I wish you would have said something. You know you can tell me anything, doesn't matter if it was my wedding day or not; you know that."

"I know. I should have told you and I'm sorry. But please understand that it was only because you had enough on your plate. I suppose, in the end, it's only some trouble sleeping, nothing that can't be managed, I'm sure." Katie absentmindedly pulled apart several paperclips and lined them up on her desk as she spoke.

"Well, I think that's the right thing for you, therapy, I mean. You're probably stressing yourself out even more because you're not getting enough sleep either."

"I'm sure you're right. You know, on the flight back after your wedding, I started doing some research on hypnotherapy."

"Okay." Sam sounded protectively cautious.

"I was thinking along the lines of relaxation hypnosis. The kind they use to help treat smokers, people who are afraid to fly...stuff like that."

"Oh, that seems like it might be useful. Maybe help you with the flying thing, too. What did your doctor say?"

"She thinks we should meet first so she can determine the best course of treatment."

"Sounds like you may have found yourself a good doctor. I know how you are, Kate. There's nothing wrong with being proactive, but I'm glad the doctor's taking charge here. She is the trained professional."

"I know. I know. So listen, let me know when you can fly down to help me find a dress. We've got time, so no rush, but I would like to start looking in the next couple of months. I mean, it's only March, so I've got 9 months to plan this thing; although, it would have been eleven months if Spencer had his way. He wanted to get married on Valentine's Day."

"Ouch, really? That's kind of cliché, isn't it?"

"That's what I said, but maybe it's just us. Maybe we're too cynical. Lots of people get married on Valentine's Day."

"I guess. I'll let you know when I've got a free weekend. Jarrod's been busy at work, but things have slowed a bit for me. Not much call for outsourced marketing firms. Most companies have brought their advertising in-house...it's cheaper."

"I hear ya. We haven't raised nearly as much money as we did last year. What is it that they say? 'It's the economy, stupid,' or something like that. Anyway, you let me know and I'll talk to you soon."

"Hey, Katie?"

"Yeah?" She waited for Sam to continue, but the line was quiet for a moment.

"Let me know how it goes at the doctor, okay?"

"Of course I will. Bye."

Katie knew the next call would have to be to her mother, but that could wait until she got home. It was not a conversation to be had at work. She would call while Spencer was out shopping for groceries tonight.

He was the cook of the house and always got irritated when she came home with the wrong type of steak or couldn't find some spice he wanted. So he decided to handle the shopping. It didn't bother Katie one bit. She was the organizer and the planner. It was what made her good at her job, and what kept her sane during his internship.

She tried to imagine herself being married, living in a big house, and having a couple of kids running around and she wondered what would become of her career. Quitting was not an option; she loved her job too much. However, with Spencer becoming a lawyer, it wasn't like he was going to be around much and someone would have to take care of the kids.

Katie began to wonder if he would end up like her father; working all the time. No, she thought. He was nothing like her father. He was loving and attentive and actually cared about what was going on in her life. Maybe it was too early to think about such things. They were both young and children could wait.

3

The appointment was scheduled for this afternoon and the time had almost arrived. Katie was working to finish the final few tasks of the day so that she could leave in time. The restless nights were taking their toll and she was ready to find out what was going on with her and prayed this was the right course of action. The desire to see an end to the nightmares and get on with her wedding plans and her life with Spencer was all that mattered.

"You're taking off?" Jennifer noticed the time as she passed Katie in the hall.

"Yeah, I've got a doctor's appointment."

"Oh, are you feeling okay?"

The girl always asked a lot of questions, which normally didn't bother Katie, but today wasn't one of those days. "I'm fine. I'll see you tomorrow, Jen. Night."

Katie left the office without any further goodbyes and arrived at the doctor's office on the outskirts of downtown just in time. The surrounding hills made for a beautiful view from the four-story building.

She walked through the courtyard toward the elevators. Dr.

Reyes' office was on the second floor. The doors parted and she walked in to the sound of Billy Joel on the Muzak system. Pressing the second-floor button, Katie could feel her palms growing clammy. There was a reason to feel anxious. Never in her life had she been to a therapist and was unsure of what to expect. *Maybe just a prescription for sleeping pills would do the trick.* She was beginning to second-guess her decision.

Inside, she expected to see a receptionist, but there was none. In fact, the lobby looked more like a living room than a doctor's office. Two doors at the back that presumably led to Dr. Reyes' office were marked "entrance" and another marked "exit." There was even a television mounted on a wall broadcasting a news channel. Her nerves began to calm in the homey environment, and she assumed that was the intention of the design. A moment later, Dr. Reyes opened the door labeled "entrance."

"Hi, Katie, come on in." Her pleasant tone further relieved Katie's tension.

"Take a seat." Dr. Reyes motioned to the small two-seater couch that was kitty-corner to a chair where she took her seat.

Hands still slightly clammy, she avoided greeting the doctor with a handshake. Instead, she nodded and sat down on the couch, eagerly anticipating the first question.

"So Katie, you mentioned you've been having difficulty sleeping through the night."

There it was, the first question. "Yeah, I guess. This dream I keep having has been disrupting my sleep. Not every night, but enough so that it's starting to annoy me a little. Not to mention my fiancé." That was a slight understatement.

"I see. So you're engaged?"

Katie smiled. "Yes, recently, just this week as a matter of fact."

"Oh, congratulations. And you've been with him for a while?"

"Yes, about seven years. We met in college and moved in together after graduation. He has actually just passed the bar exam."

"Sounds like life is going well for you, except for the occasional sleepless night. Have you been overly stressed at work?"

"No, not really. No more than usual, I'd say. This has been going on for more than a few months now. I guess it's been about three, actually." Katie watched as Dr. Reyes took notes. She tried to peer over the edge of the notepad to catch a glimpse at what she'd written, but couldn't quite see.

"Anything happen around that time you think might have brought about these dreams? Any work issues or home issues you were worried about?"

Katie focused on what had been going on three months ago, but couldn't think of anything that would cause so much stress as to bring on the dreams. "Not really. I mean, my friend asked me to be her maid of honor, and I suppose that could have added some pressure. Although, I didn't really feel like it had."

"And you're close with this friend?" Dr. Reyes asked.

"She's my best friend. We grew up together and went off to college together. She moved back home—well, near home—after that."

"So you don't think her getting married caused any stress for you? Especially since she asked you to be her maid of honor?"

"I hadn't really thought of it that way, I guess. I thought of it more as a privilege, not an obligation." Katie was trying to figure out where the doctor was going with this line of questioning. She knew none of this had anything to do with Sam. "Dr. Reyes. I have to say that I don't think I can attribute one particular event as to why I'm having these dreams. I'm so frustrated and confused that I don't know where to turn. I just don't want to experience this any longer. It's become so real and vivid that sometimes I'm afraid to even fall asleep."

"Okay then, let's talk about this dream. Can you tell me what it's about?"

Katie went on to describe the nightmarish dream and its frequent occurrence. When she was finished, Dr. Reyes started writing more notes. The room was silent, save for the second hand on a clock, ticking away the very expensive hour she was allotted. She began to wonder if any of this was worth it. *Just give me some sleeping pills.*

A moment later, Dr. Reyes looked away from her notepad. "Katie, you inquired on the phone about hypnotherapy."

Was this a question or a statement? She wasn't sure but took a stab at an answer anyway. "Yes. I asked about hypnosis for relaxation."

"I have used hypnotherapy in the past, on occasion. But the majority of treatments were for smokers and people who had certain fears, like flying, for instance. They were successful, and I think maybe, based on what you've told me today, that a similar treatment might work for you. Now, I can just prescribe you some sleeping pills."

Had she read Katie's mind?

"And maybe over time, whatever is preventing you from a good night's rest will pass. Or we can try a relaxation technique. My hope is that we will be able to free your mind of whatever stressful thoughts might be bringing out the recurring dream.

"Just know that sometimes our bodies are trying to tell us something. Whether we are uncomfortable in a situation at work or at home or whatever it might be. Our subconscious mind can create strange and unusual images based on a conglomerate of ideas and emotions."

"I'd like to try the hypnosis, Dr. Reyes. Whatever this is, I want to get to the bottom of it so that I can focus on my future." This seemed a better way to go than the pills and she hoped it would be the right decision.

"Okay then. Let's get you in here again, say next week, at the same time, if that works and we'll get started."

Katie stood up and felt confident this course of treatment would be the solution. "Thank you, Dr. Reyes. You've been very helpful. I'll see you next week."

"Goodnight, Katie."

THE FUNDRAISER KATIE had been organizing for the past few weeks had finally arrived. The "Hope for Children" charity event sponsored by the foundation was the last one of the season. Katie enjoyed her work raising funds but was ready to get back to researching cases and working with the attorneys. They gave her purpose, although, without funds, there would be no cases on which to assist.

Only days after her initial visit with Dr. Reyes, and tonight Katie was beginning to feel confident this would all blow over very soon.

Spencer led her into the ballroom. The theme was primary colors and the room was filled with hand-drawn pictures that children from all over the country made for the event.

"This is the last one for a while, Spencer, so you'd better enjoy the open bar."

"Yes, ma'am; I'll be back with a red wine for the lady."

Katie spotted her boss, Richard, and headed toward him. She admired him very much and appreciated the opportunities he had given her. "Hi, Richard, you look very handsome."

"Well, thank you, Katie. That's a lovely gown you're wearing. And where is your handsome—fiancé, now, I hear?"

"You are not misinformed. We are engaged. He asked me a couple of weeks ago after he passed the bar."

"That is wonderful news. So he's officially an attorney now. Has he received any offers yet? You know, I could put in a good word for him with Mr. Johnston. I hear they're looking for fresh talent."

"That would be fantastic, Richard, thanks for the offer. Although, he is still hoping for a position with the firm that he's at now. He's been there on a two-year internship."

"Well, they'd be fools not to hire him. You let me know if you'd like me to make that call, Katie. I mean it."

Spencer approached the two of them with drinks in hand. "Good evening, Richard, how are you?"

"Doing well, Spencer, thank you. I hear you've passed the bar and asked our lovely Ms. Reid to marry you?"

"I did and fortunately for me, she said 'yes.'"

"Congratulations. Well, I'd better make the rounds. We don't want our supporters to feel neglected. You both have a wonderful night if I don't see you before you go."

Katie took the glass of wine from Spencer. "Thanks, honey. Richard said he'd put in a good word for you with one of the partners from the firm we use if you don't get an offer from Schwartz."

"Wow, that's generous of him. Hopefully, I'll know by next week. I waited almost five months for my exam results and now I've got to wait for a job offer. Can't I just practice law?"

"I know it's frustrating. It'll work out, I promise." Katie leaned in for a quick kiss.

"Your appointment is Thursday, right? Did you want me to take you? Will you be able to drive?"

Katie glanced around to be sure no one overheard their conversation. No one at work knew about it nor did she want them to. "We can talk about it later, too many ears around here. Let's just eat dinner then try to bug out of here, okay?"

"Sure, but I thought you liked these things?"

"I do, but I guess I'm just not really in the mood for it tonight." Katie surveyed the room in search of their table when a glint of light caught her eye. A woman whom she did not know stood near the bar and it came from her. The woman turned slightly and there it was again, a reflection of one of the chandeliers. It appeared, at that distance, to be bouncing off the pendant necklace that rested low on her chest. Delicate, but with a design in which light seemed to dance around it. Katie thought it strange that something so ordinary had captured her attention. She glanced down at Spencer, who had taken a seat and was trying to get her to do the same. Dinner was being served.

~

It wasn't until Thursday arrived that Katie realized how quickly time had flown by now that she was busy planning her own wedding.

She hadn't been troubled by the dream for the past few days and felt well-rested. She wondered if maybe this phase was passing and thought about canceling her appointment with Dr. Reyes. But what harm could it do? It was intended to relieve her mind of stress. *Who couldn't use that?*

"Hey, honey." The call connected from the car as Katie was pulling out of the parking lot of her office. "I just wanted to let you know that I'm leaving for the doctor. Why don't I give you a call when it's over so you know I'm all right?"

Spencer was silent on the other end for a moment. "Are you sure? Because I don't mind going with you. I'd really like to be there for you."

"I know you would. But honestly, it'll be fine. I'll call you on my way home. Love you."

On arrival at the doctor's office, her nerves were much calmer this time around, since she felt more prepared for the session. Katie waited in the lobby, or living room, depending upon how one viewed it, of the office for Dr. Reyes. The "exit" door slowly opened and a gentleman, probably in his sixties, quietly walked out. He gave a quick nod as he stepped out of the main door. Dr. Reyes soon peeked out.

"Katie, are you ready?"

Walking into the office, she felt unafraid and uninhibited. She read somewhere that hypnotherapy was most effective on patients who didn't have any preconceived reservations about the process. She supposed an open mind was a better recipient to suggestions.

"Why don't you go ahead and lie down, Katie? You'll feel a little more relaxed." Dr. Reyes took the seat across from her.

"First, I'd just like to explain what we're going to do. I'll start by counting backward from ten and when I get to one, you'll be completely relaxed. From there, I'll be making some suggestions to assist with further relaxation. After the treatment is complete, I'll count back to ten and you'll feel refreshed and relaxed, okay? Any questions?"

Katie shook her head.

"Let's get started. Go ahead and close your eyes. Now I'm going to count backward from ten. I want you to think about a place that makes you feel happy and peaceful."

Dr. Reyes began her countdown. Katie could hear the numbers with clarity, but with each one, the doctor's voice seemed to grow distant until she reached the number one. Katie felt like that moment just before falling asleep, like her body was sinking into her bed. Images of the beach filled her mind. It was her favorite place.

"Where are you, Katie?" Dr. Reyes asked.

"At the beach."

"Are you comfortable?"

"Yes. It's warm and sunny and I'm on my favorite towel."

"Sounds wonderful. Now, I want you to take a deep breath and exhale."

The sound of Dr. Reyes' voice seemed to become even more distant. Katie felt the warmth of the sun penetrate her skin as it began to tingle. Her mind opened to the doctor's suggestions and her body sank deeper and deeper. Soon, Dr. Reyes' voice became muffled and barely audible, as if her words were fading to a whisper until finally they were gone.

Katie searched for the doctor on the beach, but could only see wave after wave breaking against the shore. Time seemed nonexistent, but it felt as though only moments passed when the towel beneath her dissolved into the sand and then the sand turned to mud. Everything around her was transforming and imbued Katie with that familiar sense of terror once again. Massive trees erupted from the water and the ocean vanished, replaced by a dense forest. Her own body morphed as her limbs were no longer her own, but appeared like those of a young child.

Behind her in the distance came a horrific, quaking mass lumbering toward her. *No, not again.* The events happening around her felt very real, more real than even the most terrifying dream she had experienced so far. She ran as quickly as she could through the forest, away from the giant, and screamed for help, but no help was coming. A loud clap sounded in her right ear. Muffled sounds soon became clear again. It was Dr. Reyes telling her to wake up.

Her eyes opened and she quickly scanned the room. She had to be sure it was gone.

"You're safe, Katie," Dr. Reyes said.

She rose from the couch and began to cry. "What happened?"

"I don't know. You were there, and we were talking, and then you were—gone. I think we may be dealing with something a little deeper here."

KATIE WAS STILL VISIBLY SHAKEN when Spencer arrived home. She had been sitting in the dark with only the television casting a dim glow in the apartment when he flipped on the lights. She squinted at the sudden brightness.

"Katie, are you all right?" He moved to the sofa and sat down, gently placing his hand on her thigh.

Her eyes were red and swollen, drained of tears. Spencer's face transformed, filling with distress at the sight of her up close. "What's wrong? Did something happen in therapy?" He reached out to comfort her, but she was stiff and did not move toward him.

"What the hell is wrong with me, Spencer?" She tried hard not to start crying again. "Dr. Reyes wants me to come back for another session next week. It was so strange, different from any other time before, more...real, I guess. I don't know. The doctor said I didn't behave the way most of her patients under hypnosis behaved."

"What does that mean?" Spencer's voice took on a confusing, almost defensive tone.

"I don't know. What should have been a simple relaxation exercise turned into this horrible vision that was terrifying. I can't explain it any better than that. It was so much more than a dream."

"I'm not sure I understand. You're going to go through this hypnosis thing again and what, continue to relive the nightmare? Wasn't this supposed to just be a way to help you sleep?"

He was upset, Katie could see it, but then there was reason to be. "She just wants to get to the bottom of whatever this is and honestly, so do I. You have no idea what this feels like. I'm exhausted but afraid to sleep. It's affecting me in ways I haven't told anyone, not even you. I need to know what's going on, whether it's stress or fear of the future or whatever it is."

"Fear of the future? Is that what has brought all this on?" Spencer pulled his hand from hers and lowered his gaze.

"You know this started long before we got engaged. This has nothing to do with you or us."

Spencer closed his eyes. "I just want you to be okay. I want things to be normal. We're supposed to be planning our wedding and this thing seems to be taking over. I'm sorry, Katie. I don't mean to sound like a jerk."

"No, you don't. Believe me, I want this to go away more than you know. And I'm trying. I think Dr. Reyes will help me figure all this out. Then we can get on with our lives, our future."

"Okay. We'll handle it together." Spencer kissed her. "You haven't forgotten about Saturday, right? We're meeting with the wedding planner."

Katie had forgotten but didn't dare say as much. This was his way of diverting from the fear he felt. "Of course not."

HER RARE AND peaceful sleep was disrupted by the vibration of Spencer's cell phone, bouncing off of his nightstand. Katie glanced at her clock, blinking until it came into focus. A dull light that seeped through the curtains suggested it was early. When the clock was clearer, its amber numbers glowed 6:00. Was it a weekday? No, it was Saturday. Who in their right mind would be calling him at this time on a Saturday morning?

Spencer began mumbling into his phone, not realizing she had already been awakened. A restful sleep was interrupted by the sound of Spencer's boss calling him to work on a Saturday. Never mind that they were supposed to meet with the wedding planner. Katie lay on her side, facing away from him. She closed her eyes and pretended to be asleep. The bed shifted as he sat up. His footsteps were soft and Katie knew he was trying hard not to wake her. A moment later, the sound of the running shower told her he would be going to work. She rolled over onto her back and stared at the ceiling. "Guess I'll be meeting the wedding planner on my own."

Katie was making coffee when Spencer walked into the kitchen.

"I thought you were asleep?" He wrapped his arm around her waist.

"I was, but I heard the shower. So, you're going into the office?" She continued scooping the coffee into the filter.

"Looks like it. I did some research on this case and now it's finally been scheduled to go to trial and they want me on the team. It's kind of a big deal."

"What does this mean? You've been offered an associate's position?"

"Not officially, but I'd say this is a good start. I guess this would be considered more of an administrative position, but my fingers are crossed."

His excitement was obvious and it made her feel guilty for being irritated about him going to work. "I'm glad for you, sweetie. It is a big deal. And don't worry, I'll handle the wedding plans. I just wish Sam was here to help me."

"Why don't you call one of the other girls?"

"Maybe." She smiled and went back to making the coffee.

KATIE ARRIVED at the offices of The Big Day, Wedding & Event Planners. The lobby was filled with color boards showcasing a variety of themes, photos of couples, and beautiful flower arrangements. They were the most popular event planners in town, according to Jennifer at work.

Katie sat in the chair across from Megan, the head wedding planner. Her office, heavy with the smell of potpourri and parchment paper, was too frilly for Katie's taste. This was supposed to be an exciting day, but she was having difficulty enjoying the moment, partly because she was alone and partly due to the distraction of unwelcome dreams. She found herself thinking about her next session with Dr. Reyes, and what it might bring.

"Is that all right with you, Katie?"

"I'm sorry, what was that?" She hadn't realized the woman was deep in conversation.

"I was asking you about the shade of green on your invitations." Megan paused for a moment. "Is everything okay?"

"Yes. I'm sorry. I've just been so busy at work and now with Spencer getting called in today...well, I guess I just don't feel like a bride right now."

"I understand. It's daunting, the work that goes into planning a wedding, but that's why I'm here. Listen, why don't we reschedule for another time, maybe next week? Then you and Spencer can both be here." Megan began closing up the enormous book of invitation samples. "You've got plenty of time."

"I appreciate that. I'm sorry for wasting your time." Katie stood up to leave.

"Not at all; I've got plenty to do before my next appointment. I'll see you next week." She flipped through her schedule. "How does Thursday evening look for you?"

"Actually, I have something that night." Katie remembered that was her appointment with Dr. Reyes. "Could we push it to next weekend?"

"Of course. I have an opening next Sunday afternoon. I'll put you down for 2:00?"

"That would be great. Thank you so much."

THE SUN HAD ALREADY BEGUN its slow descent into the horizon when Katie arrived home after a short visit to the beach to clear her mind. She looked at the clock on the shelf, wedged between an ever-growing collection of law books. Spencer would be home soon and she looked forward to seeing him. His presence in her life was treasured and she would not see their life together suffer the same fate as her parents. They would be happy, raising their children in a house in the suburbs. She had always hoped for this life and now here was her chance to experience it. Nothing would change her desire for that future.

The handle of the front door jiggled. Katie closed the refrigerator door and looked toward the sound. Spencer entered and wore a smile on his face not seen since agreeing to marry him and it was the first thing she noticed. He held a bottle of champagne along with a beautiful bouquet of spring flowers.

"Wow! What's with the champagne and flowers?" She walked over to greet him.

"Well, first of all, the flowers are for you as an apology for missing our appointment today, and the champagne is for us to celebrate."

Katie waited with anticipation for him to continue.

"I was asked to officially join the team on the case. I've been offered an associate's position."

"That's fantastic! I'm so happy for you!"

"For us," he began. "They were impressed by my research while I was interning and it's a chance for me to get in good with the partners."

"Absolutely it is. So should we get take out, or do you want to go out to eat?" She took the bottle and flowers from him. The small vase in the cabinet below the sink would do the trick. Katie filled it with water and arranged the flowers.

Spencer dropped to the couch. "Let's just stay in tonight. I don't mind running out for some Chinese if that's all right with you. Besides, I want to hear about the appointment. I'm excited to see what you chose for the invitations."

Katie cringed knowing she would have to tell him about rescheduling the appointment. "Well, actually, I got to Megan's office and we had just gotten started when something came up and she had to reschedule us. So, you didn't miss anything and we're going next Sunday."

"Oh, okay. I guess it turned out for the best, then. I didn't miss anything after all. What did you end up doing today?"

"I was going to head home after I left Megan's, but it was such a nice day that I decided to stop at the beach. I hung out there for a while and then came home not long before you got here." She continued trimming the ends of the flower stems and placed them in the vase.

"That sounds nice. I'm sure it felt good just to relax. You probably needed some time on your own."

He was right. It had been exactly what she needed. Their lives were going exactly as she had planned now that Spencer had been offered a job. These dreams, this little hiccup, would be resolved soon enough.

KATIE WAITED in the lobby and flipped through a fairly recent copy of *People*, its content still somewhat relevant. Not long after, Dr. Reyes poked her head out and motioned for her to enter.

"Hi, Katie. How are you doing?"

"I have to say, Dr. Reyes, I haven't slept this well in some time. I really believe the hypnosis worked. In fact, Spencer had to convince me to come here tonight."

"I'm thrilled you've had such positive results from our first session. But I think you'll benefit from a few more. Let's see how we do tonight. Go ahead and lie down on the couch and we'll get started."

Katie's familiarity with the process and the sound of Dr. Reyes' voice allowed her to relax and leave behind the apprehension she felt on arrival. She began feeling the same sinking sensation as the first time and felt herself drift into a place of her own choosing. As before, the doctor's voice grew distant as her body sank deeper into the sofa.

From the moment she entered the dreamlike state, something strange began to happen, something that felt familiar and frightening. Her mind took her to that dark place, cold and damp. She was afraid, crouching on the forest floor, behind a tree. The scarf tied around her neck was wet with tears. She remembered pulling it off her eyes so she could see to run from him.

"Katie, where are you? Are you safe?"

Katie shook her head. "I'm lost. I don't know how to get out of here. He's going to find me." Her voice was small and fragile. "Where's my mommy and daddy?"

"Where are you, Katie?" the doctor asked.

"I don't know. I just ran away from him. There are a lot of trees and it's dirty on the ground. My feet hurt, but I have to run before he finds me."

"Before who finds you?"

"The man who took me. He's looking for me and I have to go. Oh no, he's coming." Katie screamed; her arms flailed and her legs thrashed.

Dr. Reyes worked quickly to bring her back. "Katie, you're safe. Wake up now."

She could hear the doctor somewhere off in the distance telling her she was safe, but all around were branches brushing past her, scratching her as she ran. The sky began to transform along with the entire forest. Soon, she was back on the sofa and could hear Dr. Reyes clearly.

Katie opened her eyes and slowly sat upright. Tears streamed down her face. "Oh my God. Somebody took me when I was a kid."

"Calm down, Katie, that might be a bit of a leap. This could simply be a manifestation of some other stressor. I can't explain, though, why it is that when you reach that suggestible state where I would normally continue with the relaxation techniques, you drift off into these nightmares. It's like they're right there at the surface, waiting to be exposed."

"Do you think it's possible that something could have happened when I was young? Some traumatic event?"

"I suppose it's a possibility, but that is something you should discuss with your parents first. I don't think you should jump to any conclusions before speaking to them. At least then, you could rule it out and we could continue to look for the source of the stress that's bringing on these frightening dreams."

"It was more than a dream, Dr. Reyes. It has to be."

4

S**pencer sat on** the edge of their bed, listening as Katie retold the events that occurred at Dr. Reyes' office. "You think you may have been kidnapped as a child? Don't you think you'd remember something like that or at least that your parents would have said something to you?" Spencer appeared tense, almost as frightened as she had been.

"Look, I know this must sound crazy, but you don't know what it felt like inside that dream. I'm telling you, it was more like a memory. I don't know how else to describe it. When I woke up, I swear my arms were still stinging from the branches that scratched me."

"I'm sorry, Katie, but it does seem a little bit out there. What did the doctor say?"

"She said I should talk to my parents so I could 'rule it out' and continue with the treatments."

"So she's not entirely convinced something happened to you?"

"Well, no, but it would make sense. I've told you how miserable it was at home for me, but it wasn't always like that. We used to be happy; we used to have fun. I don't remember when all that changed, but it did. Why are you having such a hard time believing me? It's like I've been missing this piece in a puzzle my whole life and now finally I have it."

"You're convinced of this? That you were taken from your family, escaped, and no one ever told you and you didn't remember before now?"

He didn't believe her. The doctor didn't believe her, but she knew it was a fact. How could Spencer not stand by her now when she needed him the most?

Katie pushed herself off the bed feeling the anger well up inside her and began pacing the room. "Look, I don't know what I believe right now. I'm beyond freaked out. All I'm saying is that something bad may have happened to me when I was a kid and I'd like to find out the truth so I can move on with my life, with *our* life. For God's sake, Spencer, why can't you be with me on this?"

"Because it scares me, okay?" He pounded his fist on the mattress. "You think I want to know that someone might have hurt you a long time ago? Don't you see? I can't help you with this. I can't fix this for you." He took a deep breath and lowered his voice. "Katie, I just want you to be okay and for us to be okay. What good is it going to do if you try to start digging up something from the past? If this really happened, you didn't remember and no one told you probably for very good reasons. You need to let it go and move on."

"You don't get it. I need to find out what happened so I *can* move on." Katie walked toward the bedroom door, ready to end this discussion. "I'm going to book a flight home as soon as I can."

KATIE WASTED no time and was on a flight that evening. Worn out and exhausted from the journey, her argument with Spencer made the situation even more difficult. He wasn't happy with her decision to go home, but in the end, he did not try to stop her. Instead, he merely stood by and watched her pack a bag. There was nothing he could say that would alter her decision. She was going to go with or without his blessing.

Those last moments before leaving home were all Katie could think about until she noticed Sam waiting for her in baggage claim at the Eureka airport. Her welcoming smile and warm embrace were comforting and made Katie feel safe. She was back home, which to her meant back home with Sam.

"Come on, let's get you out of here." Sam helped her with her bags.

Katie didn't say much on the drive and was grateful her friend didn't push the issue. The weather was only slightly warmer than it had been on her last visit and maybe a little drier, but still cold by Katie's standards. She untied the sweater from her waist and pulled it on. "Hasn't warmed up much since I was here last month."

"Did you forget what it was like here in April? You have been gone too long, spent too much time in the SoCal sun," Sam replied.

It was early morning when they arrived at Sam's house. The tall oaks loomed over her home, casting odd-shaped shadows against the covered porch. Katie thought how lucky Sam was to have such a perfect little house in a perfect little neighborhood. It was similar to Sam's parents' home, where Katie had spent so much time.

"Come on in," Sam opened the front door. The scent of blooming flowers was everywhere. Sam took pride in her rose bushes that stood majestically along the front of the home and always had them freshly cut and in vases throughout the house.

"You know where the guest room is. I'll put some coffee on if you'd like."

"That'd be great, thanks. I'll go put my stuff down." Katie walked up the stairs through the hallway to her room. She hadn't expected to be back here so soon and certainly not for this reason. She would have to tell Sam everything.

Katie freshened up, threw on some clean clothes, and followed the scent of coffee toward the kitchen.

Sam held two mugs, placing one in front of Katie on the breakfast table. "So, are you ready to talk yet? I'm guessing you're not here to talk about your wedding plans?" Sam pulled out a chair and sat across from Katie, taking a sip of coffee.

Her mind raced as she tried to figure out the best place to start. "No, not exactly." She took a sip as well and began retelling all the events of the past several weeks.

Sam exhaled with some despair. "So, what do you think now? You think maybe someone really did take you when you were little? Why wouldn't your parents have told you?"

"I don't know, Sam. Maybe because I didn't remember anything, they decided not to tell me. I mean, I couldn't have been more than what five, maybe six?"

"I guess, but you need to sit down and talk to them. I know that's not easy for you, but you have to know what happened. It could have been anything and, maybe it just appeared as dreams of you trying to escape from someone. Did Dr. Reyes suggest that you could have been kidnapped, or did you?"

"I did. She said not to rush to conclusions." Katie wrapped her hands around the warm mug.

"Exactly. You can't just jump to conclusions like that. It could be anything that your subconscious is trying to deal with. The best thing you can do is speak to your parents. Whatever it is, I'm sure they can shed some light on the situation. After that, you can go back home to Spencer."

Katie's half-hearted smile wasn't going to convince anyone. "You're right. Thank you." She finished her coffee and a short while later, stood up to leave.

"Are you sure you don't want me to drive you to your folks' house? You're still welcome to take my car. Jarrod's going to be home all day, so it's not like we'll be without a vehicle."

"I appreciate that, Sam," Katie began. "I'll just borrow your car if that's all right. No point in you driving me and picking me up again."

"Sure. No problem."

"Thanks. I'd probably better get going. I told my mom I'd be there around lunchtime. Of course, she has probably laid out some huge spread just for the occasion. You know Deborah, ever the consummate host."

"All right, I'll walk you out." Sam opened the front door. "Here are the keys. No rush, whenever you're ready to come back."

Katie hugged Sam and gave her a peck on the cheek. I'll call you later and let you know how it went."

"It'll be okay," she whispered. "I'm sure everything will turn out fine."

A thin smile briefly appeared on Katie's lips as she turned away and walked out into the crisp spring air. The scent of roses lingered as she stepped off the porch. "Beautiful roses, Sam." She didn't turn around for a reply, only continued to the car.

THE DRIVE TO HER PARENTS' home, Katie's childhood home, wasn't long. Within about thirty minutes, she'd arrived and now was unsure of what to do next. She made no mention of the reason for her visit other than that she'd planned a trip to see Sam and decided to swing by.

Her father's car wasn't in the drive as she'd expected, although this was no surprise. He knew she was coming. Katie shut off the engine and sat in the car, waiting, staring at the house that used to be her home.

The vision of herself as a young girl, sitting on the front steps, playing with her favorite doll flashed before her. It was a warm summer evening and the sun was setting. Her dad pulled onto the circular drive, home from work and he stopped short of her bike that was in his way.

"Katie, how many times have I told you to keep your toys out of the drive?" he shouted.

She dropped her doll and ran over to pick up her bike. "Sorry, Daddy."

He grunted, pulled forward, and got out of the car. She stood in front of him, waiting for him to greet her, but he only patted her on the head and walked past her and into the house.

The memory was gone and it wasn't until she spotted her mother peeking out from behind the kitchen curtains that she knew she'd better go in.

A soft knock on the door and her mother was there to greet her. Their embrace felt awkward and forced, as it usually did.

"Come in, sweetheart. I've made lunch." Deborah guided her in and closed the door.

The table was set with flowers, beautiful stemware, and amazing food. Katie had to snicker a little, as this was exactly as she imagined. She politely sat down as Deborah began serving lunch.

"Do you need anything else, Katie?"

"No, Mom. Thank you. Can you please sit down? I'd like to talk."

"Certainly." Deborah pulled out a chair. "What is it, honey? I was a little surprised when you said you were coming. I thought you and Spencer were planning on visiting together. Is everything all right? Are you two having troubles? Did he break off the engagement?"

"No, Mom. Spencer and I are fine. I'm here about something else." Katie thought of the various ways to bring up the topic, but could not find an easy path. "For the past few months, I guess it's been, I've been having difficulty sleeping. To be more precise, I've been having nightmares."

Deborah furrowed her brow as she listened.

"At first, I just chalked it up to stress because I was being stretched a little thin helping Sam with her wedding from San Diego, work...you know." Of course, she quickly realized that her mother probably had no idea what that felt like.

"But then, they seemed to get worse—more intense. I started losing more sleep. So, Spencer and I talked about it and decided I would try hypnotherapy. People say it helps relieve stress, so I thought, what harm could it do?"

Deborah shifted in her seat and seemed to be hanging on Katie's every word.

"I started seeing Dr. Reyes, but the hypnotherapy began bringing these dreams I'd been having to life almost. If that makes any sense. They felt—real." She paused for a moment, allowing her mother to speak, but Deborah remained silent. "I'd like to ask you, Mom, if something happened to me when I was a child. If maybe those dreams are really memories, at least, to a degree."

Deborah brushed the crumbs from her placemat into her palm and onto the plate. She then proceeded to dab the corners of her mouth with her napkin and placed it neatly on the table. She continued to straighten and organize as if Katie had said nothing.

Irritated by her mother's lack of response, Katie raised her voice. "Mom! Can you please answer me?"

Her mother's gaze burned deeply into Katie's eyes. It was as if this was a moment that Deborah had sought to avoid for Katie's entire life and she was desperately trying to figure a way out. But Katie would not release her; she held onto that gaze as if her life depended on it.

Finally, it broke. Deborah cast her eyes down, pushed her chair back, stood up, and left the room.

Katie was stunned. She watched her mother walk out of the kitchen in disbelief. "What the hell is going on?" she said to an empty room and dropped her head into her hands.

A few moments later, she heard Deborah's footsteps and looked up. Her mother held an accordion file. There was no writing or markings of any kind on the folder. Deborah laid it down on the table.

They both stared at it. Katie's heart was racing at the unknown contents of this file.

"Mom, please tell me what's going on," Katie pleaded, her voice barely above a whisper. The passing seconds felt like hours until, finally, her mother spoke and began pulling out the contents of the folder.

"After your father opened his business in town when you were very young, we were so excited. The move from San Francisco was tough, but we knew this was the perfect place to bring up our little girl; such a beautiful and safe neighborhood."

Katie looked at the papers her mother placed on top of the folder, news clippings, typed papers, and photos. The first thing she spotted was a newspaper headline: *Missing Girl Found on Side of Hwy.* She reached for the article and pulled it toward her.

"Thank God that family stopped when they saw you. They were on their way to a camping trip in the Redwoods."

"That was me?" Katie's voice trembled. Her eyes rapidly scanned the newspaper clippings spread out before her as her mind tried to reconcile what she was seeing. *Missing girl! Local girl still missing; Community rallies around parents of missing girl.* Her throat tightened as she struggled for breath. Her stomach churned from the dizzying effect of the words she was reading.

"Yes. You were missing for three days and they found you." Deborah's voice was steady, but her eyes turned red and welled up with tears.

Somewhere in the back of Katie's mind, she didn't really believe something had happened to her, that there must be another explanation for the awful dreams, but there it was, in boldface type. "Did I wander off and get lost? What happened?"

"You were taken from us, Katie." At this, Deborah seemed to lose what little restraint she had on her emotions.

The words echoed in Katie's ears. Disoriented, she had to close her eyes to steady the thoughts and images. *This can't be happening.* "Why didn't you tell me? Why didn't I remember?"

Her mother's voice trembled and her clasped hands shook against the table. "When that family found you, they said you only knew your name, not how you ended up on the side of the road. But they knew who you were because it had been all over the news. They took you to the nearest police station and we were called straight away." Deborah reached out and squeezed Katie's hand. It was the first time in years her mother's touch felt so genuine. "The police said you were okay, but I couldn't be sure until I saw you. When your dad and I arrived at the station, there you were, dirty clothes and hair, some scrapes and bruises, but you were there and you were alive." Tears spilled down Deborah's cheeks. "We took you to the hospital to have them make sure you were all right. But you didn't seem to remember anything before they found you. You didn't know how you ended up in the woods. The doctors said that it looked as though you took a hit on the head and maybe that was the cause for your memory loss. Nobody knew for sure and since you couldn't remember anything, it was decided that it was in your best interest not to force the issue. We were so grateful God returned you home."

Katie sat motionless as her mother recounted the events and could only focus on the report from the Rio Dell Police Department. When she was finished, the only sound in the room came from the ticking of a small kitchen clock that sat perched on the windowsill.

Katie finally broke the silence. "Why didn't you tell me when I was old enough to understand?" This amounted to a betrayal in her mind. What sort of parents could keep this from their own child?

"It was just too difficult." Deborah released Katie's hand and lowered her head. "By that time, you were becoming withdrawn and we thought telling you would only make you pull away more. We all changed and we didn't know how to get back to normal. We should have gone to counseling, but your father wanted to pretend that none of it ever happened. He never wanted to talk about it, but I needed to. I had to bury it deep inside because he just couldn't bear it. It affected him in ways I couldn't comprehend. I tried to hold our family together and it was exhausting. My little girl wasn't the same and I felt helpless to do anything about it.

"Your dad worked more and more, you were home less and less, and so what was left for me to do? All I could do was offer my help to others. It was the only way I could handle it. If I couldn't help my own daughter—my own family—maybe I could help others."

Katie turned away, unable to look at the woman before her. "So, you and Dad decided just to leave well enough alone? Not to bother getting help for me, or us as a family? You want to know why I was never home?" She turned back now, ensuring Deborah caught every word. "Because Sam's parents treated me as if I *was* their daughter." Katie leaned back, shaking her head. "Did they know what happened to me?"

"No. They moved into the neighborhood when you were eight. We were a much smaller town back then and everyone who knew what happened knew not to talk about it. Everyone wanted to put the whole thing behind them as much as we did. So much negative attention was brought to the community. It was painful for everyone."

"I can't listen to any more of this." Katie's chair scraped hard along the wood floor as she stood up.

"Katie wait, sweetheart, please! Your father will be home from golf soon and we can sit down and talk as a family. Please don't leave."

Katie swung around toward her mother. "Why isn't he here now, Mom? Didn't you tell him I was coming home? He decided to schedule a golf game rather than see me? Don't pretend Dad gives a shit." Katie stormed out of the front door.

Deborah ran to catch her daughter. "Katie, please come back. You don't know what this has been like for your dad."

She was already in the car and slammed the door shut. Quickly speeding out of the driveway, Katie had no idea where to go. The knuckles on her hands turned white from the grip of the steering wheel, working to keep from swerving off the road. How could this be happening? Everything she thought she knew about her life was a lie. Everyone around her had lied to her for so many years. The only people she could trust were Sam and her parents. They had always been there for her.

Katie had driven all the way through town before realizing she had to tell Sam. The grocery store up the street would do and so she pulled into the parking lot, slammed the gearshift into park, and cut the engine. Her head fell against her hands and she began to sob, quietly at first, until finally everything came pouring out of her. Why didn't they try to get her help? There were too many questions that still needed answers.

Katie grabbed her cell phone, called Sam, and proceeded to tell her what happened.

"Just stay there, Kate, I'm coming to get you. You shouldn't be driving right now."

"No, please don't. I just need to calm down and I'll be all right."

"You just found out something terrible, Katie. You're not going to be all right for a while. Now please, let me come and at least sit with you until you figure out what you want to do."

"Okay, Sam. I'll wait here."

Katie stared out of the driver's side window at the tall pine trees. She imagined the six-year-old version of herself standing along the roadway, scared and alone. How had she ended up there and why couldn't she remember? The last dream she had at Dr. Reyes' office was of her running through the woods, away from him, away from the giant. Katie had no recollection of anything after that.

It wasn't long before Sam pulled up and got in the passenger seat next to Katie. She hugged her so tightly that Katie went limp in her arms, buried her head, and cried.

"It's okay. You have every right to be angry and you just need to let it out." Sam stroked her hair as Katie tried to regain her composure.

She took a deep breath and sat back up, wiping her eyes with her shirt sleeve. "Can you believe this, Sam? What the hell were they thinking not telling me something like this? What kind of parents would do that?"

"I'm sure they thought they were protecting you. Can you imagine what it must have been like for them not knowing if you were dead or alive for three days? My God, I couldn't imagine that and I don't even have kids. They must have thought the best way to keep you safe was for you not to have to relive it. I don't know. Things were different then. It was probably a lot easier to keep something like that quiet so you would never have to know."

"Until now." Katie took a tissue from the box on the dashboard and dabbed her eyes. "I don't know why this is happening to me now. Why I even started having those dreams."

"Can you think of anything that might have triggered them?"

"Dr. Reyes thought that it was just my mind's way of coping with stress." Katie stopped short, her eyes widening.

"What? What is it?"

"Oh my God." She raised her hand to her mouth.

"Katie, what is it?" Sam prodded.

"A few months ago, I was watching a news story about a little girl who had been abducted while she was playing in the woods behind her home. I think she must have been like eight or nine, maybe. The family lived in Eureka, I think it was. Everyone was searching for her, police, volunteers, but no one had been able to find her. I don't think they've found her yet."

"We hear about those kinds of stories all the time. Why would that one have triggered the nightmares?"

"They showed a picture of the little girl on TV and Spencer commented about how much she looked like me. And I looked into the eyes of that girl, her little school picture, and I saw it too. It hadn't occurred to me until just now, but I think that was around the time they started."

Katie's cell phone rang, startling both of them. It was her mom. She looked to Sam for confirmation.

"You should answer that."

With trepidation, she picked up her phone. "Yes."

"Katie, honey, your dad is here and he'd like you to come back so we can all talk about this. Will you please come back?"

She pulled the phone away from her ear and covered it with her hand. "My dad's there now and they want me to come back to talk."

"You should go. You all need to start to heal and get past this."

Katie put the phone back up to her ear. "Okay. I'll be there soon." She ended the call and looked at Sam, not entirely sure she should go back.

"It's the best thing for you, Kate. Just get everything out in the open."

"You're right. I'll give you a call when I'm heading back to your house."

"No rush. This is obviously far more important. I'll see you later tonight." Sam began to get out of the car.

"Sam?"

She turned toward Katie.

"Thank you."

"You're my best friend, Kate." Sam closed the passenger door and smiled.

THE FRONT DOOR stood open when Katie arrived back at her parents' home. She accepted the invitation to enter and stepped inside. After a moment's hesitation, she continued into the kitchen. Both Deborah and Katie's father, John, sat at the table with the folder and all its contents laid out before them. Katie noticed clippings of articles about other missing children.

"Katie, would you please sit down?" John asked. "I'm sorry I wasn't here earlier today. Your mother and I had no idea you had been having trouble with any of this and so this took us quite by surprise. Your mom called me in hysterics after you left and I came home right away."

"I certainly didn't intend to make you call your golf game short, Dad." Katie immediately regretted the comment.

"You are understandably upset and have every right to be, but before you lash out any further, I'd like to tell you about what happened when you went missing." John closed his eyes seemingly to prepare himself. "That summer, there had been stories of missing children around northern California on the news. Of course, this was long before all that internet stuff, so mostly only the Eureka and

Sacramento news covered it. However, the local communities stepped up and started searching for the children.

"Three had gone missing in a three-month span, all within about 100 miles of each other. The police had very few leads on the case. The children were between the ages of five and eight. Two had been taken while they were walking home from school. The youngest, five, was taken from his bed in the middle of the night.

"We honestly hadn't thought much more about it because the abductions were happening pretty far away from us here. But that all changed the day we got the call from your school." John swallowed hard and struggled to find the words to continue.

"The last time the teachers saw you, you were playing on the swings. When it was time to go in, they couldn't find you. Back then, there weren't iron gates and security cameras around schools like there are today, especially in our small town. It was very easy to slip in and out, unnoticed. The best the police could figure was that he was parked up the road, came walking down toward the playground, and somehow convinced you to walk over to him. You were only six, for God's sake." John cleared his throat and wiped his eyes with the back of his hand.

"The police did what they could and tracked down every lead they had, which weren't many. They assumed the cases were linked, but could never find any hard evidence. If they were linked, you were the only one to survive. The other children were never found."

This was too much, too hard to understand. Katie trembled in her chair, chilled to the bone, her entire body felt faint. The look in her parents' eyes, full of regret and pain. Shock had begun to set in.

"About a year later, up in Portland, there was another similar case," John continued. "The police up there contacted our Rio Dell police and asked for help, but they couldn't connect the dots. That was the last we heard of any of this. You never said anything about any bad dreams or had any recollection of the abduction.

"Your mom and I tried to move on and give you a normal life. But as you got older, you pulled away from us for reasons we... obviously...

tried to ignore." He looked at his wife. "We worried every single time you left the house until you went off to college, so much so that I couldn't stand it. It was everything I could do to hold myself together."

John quickly wiped away the tears again. "I know I wasn't the best father. I pulled away just as much as you did. Your mother and I should never have kept this secret from you. Maybe if we'd just gotten it out in the open." He took Deborah's hand and looked her in the eyes. "If we'd just told you sooner, we'd have been able to get through it."

Katie quietly rose from her chair, walked to her father, and wrapped her arms around his big round shoulders. It all became clear to her—his drinking, her mother's need to help others. Their family had been torn apart by this and, unfortunately, she had suffered the most.

"I love you, Dad, and I'm sorry. I'm sorry this happened." She fell into his lap, holding him like she had never held him before.

"None of this is your fault, Katie. Don't you ever think that. I should have been there to protect you. That was my only job, protecting you and your mom." He squeezed her, no longer able to stop his tears. "I wanted so badly to kill the son of a bitch who took my little girl."

Katie sat up and tried to pull herself together. "Wasn't I able to at least give some sort of description of him? Couldn't I have helped at all?"

"Honey, you were six years old," Deborah started. "When they found you, you were scared and exhausted. You didn't remember anything except that you had been in that forest. They found a scarf tied around your neck and figured whoever it was must have kept you blindfolded anyway. I was so grateful to have you back I didn't care. I just wanted you home with me, so I wouldn't let them prod you after that."

"The scarf," she whispered.

"What do we do now, sweetheart?" Deborah asked.

"I don't know, Mom. I just don't know."

"I think you should stay here with us tonight," John said. "Will you do that?"

Katie nodded. "I'll call Sam. I've got her car." She would have to call Spencer and check in with him too. She hadn't spoken to him since arriving early this morning. Katie would not tell him about any of this, though. Not on the phone.

Soon, Katie found herself lying in the same bed she had slept in for most of her childhood, unable to settle the racing thoughts. Her mother promised to help her get through this and would do whatever it took to heal their relationship. John couldn't find the words to comfort his daughter and Katie knew it would take time for him to forgive himself. It would take time for her to forgive them both.

As she continued to stare into the darkened room, a single thought played in her mind on a loop. Who was her abductor and was this person still out there?

Arriving home from the airport, Spencer grabbed Katie's bag from the trunk and walked up the steps behind her to their apartment.

"I'm going to go freshen up a little before we eat if that's all right?" Katie said.

"Take as much time as you need, babe. I'll keep this warm in the oven." He walked into the kitchen with the Chinese take-out they'd stopped for on the drive home.

Katie tossed her bag onto the bed and unzipped it; the clothes inside still smelled of her parents' house. She held one of her shirts to her face and breathed in deeply, immersing herself in the home in which she had grown up. Her entire world had been turned upside down and she had no idea what to do. But it suddenly occurred to Katie that her life choices had all been based on this one event that she never even remembered. Why else would she have chosen to work for the Advocacy Group? Would she have stayed in Eureka, like Sam, if this had never happened? It all started to fit together like pieces of a puzzle, only this was her life. This was a life altered by something so horrific that her mind buried it deep in order to keep her sanity.

Katie threw on a t-shirt and shorts and rejoined Spencer, who had dinner set out on the table.

"Listen, I can see that you're not ready to tell me what happened, but you have to know that I'm here for you. Just don't shut me out, okay?" He pulled the chair out for her.

Katie placed her hand on his face. "You're always there for me, I know that."

Her entire body felt trapped in the remains of this terrible secret. She pushed around the food on her plate, listening to Spencer talk, none of his words sinking in.

"I suppose we can focus on happier things in our life now, right?"

It was an awkward thing for him to say, but he didn't know the truth and she couldn't fault him for that. "Things can get back to normal now," she said. "I'm sure of it."

5

Katie covered her ears to block out the loud music coming from above her. The vibrations filtered down through the walls, shaking the metal cot where he forced her to stay. The music was always loud when it grew dark. She stared at the peanut butter and jelly sandwich and apple juice that had been placed on the table next to her. Her stomach ached from hunger and her mouth was so dry, her lips started to crack. But she wouldn't eat or drink; she wouldn't give in to him. Some ethereal force must have given her this kind of strength. Her short years on this planet would not have given her the required life experience to display such resolve. She was too frightened to sleep and the music made sure she couldn't anyway. The same song replayed in her head long after the music stopped.

Katie flew out of her bed, startled awake. She was no longer on the cot; it was her bed, the one she shared with Spencer. Her head swung back and forth, eyes consuming everything around her. She had to be sure it was her own room again. Feeling confident that it had been a dream, she dropped down on the side chair and the fear gave way to dread. Would the dreams ever stop?

Light peeked in through the bottom of her bedroom door. It hadn't occurred to her that Spencer wasn't there in bed with her. It was 12:30 and she was surprised he hadn't come to bed yet. Maybe now was the time to tell him. They could not continue like this.

Katie opened the door and walked down the hall to the den. Spencer was sitting at the desk, his face distorted by the glow of the computer and the shadow the desk light had cast. He looked up, seeing her tiny frame which looked even smaller beneath the oversized t-shirt she wore to bed. At his glance, she burst into tears.

Spencer immediately pushed up from his chair and walked to her, wrapping his arms around her. "Please, let me help you, Katie."

"I just didn't know how to tell you. You're so good for not forcing me to talk about it, but I know I have to share this with you. It's going to and already has affected our lives. You have a right to know."

"Let me get you some tea and we can sit down." He led her to the living room.

"I'm sorry. I know you're working on your case. I shouldn't be taking up your time with my problems."

"What? Why would you say such a thing? Your problems are my problems too. My eyes are burning from reading pages and pages of depositions and I need a break anyway."

Katie realized how lucky she was to have Spencer in her life. But how would he react to this news?

She curled up on the couch while he brought her a cup of hot tea. He sat down next to her and waited.

With a deep breath, she began. "When I was six, I was abducted from my school playground. My parents said that after three days, I was found on the side of the highway by a passing car. I had no recollection of anything except that I had been in the woods."

Spencer's face became solemn and looked as though he'd just been told his best friend died.

Katie reached for his hand to comfort him. "The doctors apparently told my parents that since I didn't remember the traumatic event, it was probably best not to tell me."

"Oh my God, how could they..." He trailed off for a moment, searching for an explanation. "Okay, maybe I could understand them not telling a six-year-old, but what about when you were older? For God's sake, didn't they think it would come out eventually?"

"I don't know, honey. I guess they were just happy to have me back and pretending it never happened allowed them to move on. But what they didn't realize, of course, was that it would come to light now. I'm sure they must have thought it would never surface. Now that it has, they've come clean. They showed me the police files, the pictures. I guess there were other missing kids, but they didn't know if any of it was connected."

Katie, who hadn't had a chance to comprehend the situation fully, was now trying to help Spencer cope with the news.

He kept rubbing his forehead as if trying to figure out quantum physics. "I can't believe this happened to you, Katie. My God, you don't remember anything?"

"I wish I did. I don't even know if what happened in my dreams was what *actually* happened. It may have been a combination of random images I've seen over the years. I don't know."

"So, now that you know, what do we do? Are these dreams going to stop?"

"I don't think so, at least, they haven't yet. I woke up from another one when I came to see you. Only this one was different. I was somewhere else, like a basement or storage room or something, I'm not sure. It's like my mind keeps showing me these images to help my memory. Maybe it's possible that if I continue with the therapy, I'll be able to remember." Katie had a sudden revelation. "What if I could remember enough to see his face? They never caught him. I'm assuming it's a 'him,' but I really don't even know that much."

"What are you saying? You want to keep putting yourself through this therapy and be forced to remember something horrible and terrifying? Why?"

She didn't know why for sure, but it was going to eat away at her if she couldn't figure it out. "What if I can help find this person? Three other children didn't make it home. What if there were more?"

She stood up and started pacing the room. "I don't know, Spencer. I just feel like there's this hole in me now. This was something that obviously shaped who I am today. Wouldn't you want answers?"

"Yes, of course I would."

"I don't know what to do right now, I just knew that I had to tell you. God, it feels like this whole thing is a dream."

"Come sit back down and finish your tea."

Spencer sat close to her on the couch, neither saying anything more.

KATIE AROSE early that Monday morning, having no intention of going into work. Although she had been able to get some rest after the long talk last night, her mind still burned with a desire to discover more information about her and the others' abductions.

She intended to call in sick, not a usual occurrence and she doubted it would raise any suspicions. Only two people at work knew she was flying home over the weekend, but they didn't know why.

With that detail worked out, she had to figure out what to tell Spencer. He wouldn't object to her plans, but she was afraid it would cause him to worry.

He was still asleep next to her, so she carefully pulled herself out of bed. Maybe some research on the internet before he woke up would be okay. Based on what she could find in the next hour before Spencer's alarm went off, that would determine her story.

Late August of 1989, that was when it happened, August 27th, to be precise. She searched for the *Times-Standard*, the major northern California coast newspaper. Would they have anything online from more than twenty years ago? That was well before the age of the internet and online media, but it was the only place she had to start.

The coffee machine finished its brew cycle and began to beep. Katie peered around her laptop screen to see if her bedroom door had opened. The smell of coffee filled their small apartment and she wondered if it would wake Spencer.

Katie poured herself a cup, confident he was still asleep and she began her research. A cursory glance at the landing page of the online newspaper revealed a section called "Archives." She held out hope that something might be found there.

No, nothing there; those stories only went back two years. Police records, maybe? No, they wouldn't be online. She considered the public library. Surely the Eureka Main Library would have an online site. Katie typed the name into the search engine. Yes, they had a website.

Scrolling down the page, she found a section that covered the *Times-Standard* articles from 1989-2005. *There must be something here.*

Katie typed in the word "kidnappings" in the index. Several articles popped up, and one was from August 13, 1989. It was about the five-year-old boy who had been taken from his bed in the night. She continued to scroll down the list of other articles. *Missing Girl Found on Hwy 101.*

"That's the one," Katie whispered. The only problem was that these articles could only be accessed on microfilm at the library; the website just showed a list of available content, which left her feeling frustrated. "Damn."

A few moments later, Spencer shuffled down the hall. "What are you doing up so early? Did you sleep all right?"

"Yes. I woke up a while ago and couldn't go back to sleep. There's coffee if you want some."

He continued into the kitchen. Katie quickly closed the lid of her laptop. "You've got a pretty busy day today, right?" she asked as he made his way to join her at the table.

"I'll be sorting through pages of depositions so, busy, yes, but not exactly exciting. What about you?"

"I was actually kind of thinking I'd take the day off. Maybe try to get in to see Dr. Reyes."

"Oh. Okay. I guess I thought you'd just keep your Thursday appointments for a while until...well, until you felt better."

"Spencer, I know you want me to feel better. And, so do I, but I think it's going to take some time. I hope you can understand that."

"Of course, I do. I just don't want to see you get hung up on thinking you can find this person. It's been more than twenty years and the police haven't found anyone and I'm not sure you'll be able to."

"So, you're okay with me continuing with my therapy, for a while, but I'm just supposed to let it go after that?" Something clicked inside her that triggered a defensive response.

"That's not what I mean, Katie, you know that."

"I'm not sure I do, actually. Seems to me that you think I'll go to a few more sessions, get all the memories out, and be able to just let them go."

"Come on, babe. I'm not trying to start a fight. Look, we're getting married this winter. I thought maybe you'd like to focus on that. Focus on us getting a house, and starting a life together. I don't know. Those things were important to you before all this dream stuff."

"You're right, all that is important to me. I just need some time to process what's happened. For Christ's sake, I just found out that I was abducted. I need to get my head around this. I need answers."

Spencer leaned in and kissed Katie gently on the lips. "That's what scares me."

KATIE ARRIVED at the library in downtown San Diego. Other libraries had archives from newspapers and the *Times-Standard* couldn't have been the only one to publish the story.

She approached the information desk. "Excuse me, but do you

happen to have newspaper articles on microfilm from August of 1989?"

"Well, that would depend on the newspaper." The kid on the other side of the desk couldn't have been older than about 20. Katie wondered if he was a student, working part-time at the library.

"I'm specifically looking for articles from the *Times-Standard* in Eureka."

The student clicked away on his keyboard, she assumed, searching for the requested information.

"Yes, here it is. MF10, entries 1-15. You'll need to go to the second floor, across from videos and CDs." He handed her a scrap of paper with the reference numbers. "Enter these numbers and you'll find what you're looking for."

"Thank you. Thank you very much." Katie walked up the stairs to the second floor. The last time she had been in a library was when she was about twelve. It still looked the same, maybe not as big as she remembered, but still filled with rows and rows of books. The difference now was seeing little stations that had e-readers for use.

The microfilm station was small but sophisticated. Katie sat down and proceeded to enter the reference numbers. She hoped that what she would find would give her more insight as to what happened.

The first article to appear was one about the missing eight-year-old girl, near Arcata. Katie began to read. *"Eight-year-old Ashley Davies went missing on Tuesday afternoon. She was last seen by her classmates, walking home from school. Her mother said she never arrived. Police and volunteers have launched a massive search for the little girl, but so far have found no clues."*

Katie's heart dropped as she continued to read. Although she had not known this girl, there was a connection to her. Maybe she was grasping at straws, trying to connect dots that were not there. But the fact remained that this little girl never made it back home to her parents. Katie was the lucky one.

After scrolling through several more articles, she came across a second article about a missing child in McKinleyville, farther north of Arcata. This one was a red-haired girl, seven years old, named Madison. They showed a school picture of the girl, big eyes, face full of freckles, and a beautiful, toothless smile. Madison was riding her bike around the park near her home. The summer sky turned to dusk, but Madison didn't make it home, per her parents' instruction.

How times had changed. Now, even in small towns, young kids today probably wouldn't be at a park on their own.

At last, she came across the article her mother had shown her. *Missing Girl Found on Side of Hwy 101.*

She read the article, searching for any possible connection between her and the other victims. The one thing that set her apart from the other children was the fact that she was the only brunette. Maybe there really was no connection. The kids were all abducted from random places, boys and girls, nothing particularly similar about them. What could she possibly discover that the police wouldn't already have? They were trained for that sort of thing. Her training was in social sciences, not forensic sciences, though she wished it had been now.

The only thing she had discovered was that she should be grateful to have survived. Spencer was right; she would need to move on with her life. But Katie needed closure and the only way to get that would be to finish the therapy, and get it all out in the open. Maybe then, she would truly be able to move on.

Katie logged out of the machine and went back to the main floor of the library. As she passed the information desk, the student was still there.

"Did you find what you were looking for, ma'am?"

"Yes, I think so, thank you."

THE DAY HAD PROVEN to be disappointing and Katie felt that she was no closer to getting to the truth. Her research at the library revealed little more than she already knew. Still, there was more to learn, but she had no idea how to go about it.

At the dinner table, the topic of conversation revolved around everything but Katie's whereabouts for the day. She had the feeling that Spencer was just biding his time, waiting for her to give up and accept what had happened.

Katie wanted to give him the time he needed, but she'd seen a side in him he'd never shown before. He was afraid for her and afraid for their future. That fear, however, could prove to be more detrimental than facing the unknown.

Spencer kissed her goodnight as they lay in bed together. When he turned to sleep, with his back to her, Katie sensed he was slipping away. She raised her hand to caress his shoulder, letting him know that she was still there. An all too brief moment found him returning the gesture, resting his hand on top of hers until it slipped away.

Upon waking in the morning after an abrupt alarm sounded, Katie realized that if therapy didn't reveal any more answers, then she would have to talk to the experts, the ones who dealt with investigating these types of crimes.

Her work at the Advocacy Group provided many avenues to different divisions within the organization. One such avenue was the Victim's Assistance Department. Cases were assigned to that division in circumstances where Child Protective Services had been involved. It was there to assist the victims and act as a liaison between the police and the community. Katie had never worked with anyone directly in that department, but word often traveled around when they received extreme abuse cases. Sometimes, in cases where a child had disappeared, the advocates would speak with the victim's relatives, teachers, etc. They often worked alongside the detectives who were assigned to investigate.

This was where Katie needed to be, assigned to just such a case. Her credentials in that area were weak and she doubted an assignment like that would be given to her, but if she could convince Richard, maybe she could assist in some way.

KATIE WALKED into her office and several people asked how she was feeling. It had slipped her mind that she'd called in sick yesterday.

"Hi, Katie. Welcome back," Jennifer began. "Glad to see you're feeling better. Don't worry, you didn't miss much."

"Good to know. Thanks, Jen." Katie put her purse down and turned on her computer. "Have you seen Richard yet this morning?"

"No, not yet, but I've been in the kitchen getting coffee." Jennifer swirled the spoon in her cup and flashed her kind smile. If one were to look up the girl next door in the dictionary, a picture of Jennifer would be there, shoulder-length blonde hair, fair skin, and big round eyes. About as wholesome as one could be.

"I'll go have a look in his office."

"Is everything all right?"

"Yeah, yeah, everything's fine. I just wanted to ask him about working on a case for the Victim's Assistance program."

"Oh, well that would be in a different department, wouldn't it?" Jennifer continued with her sometimes annoying line of questioning.

"I've been thinking about venturing into some different areas. You know, broaden my horizons a little."

Jennifer creased her brow, seemingly unconvinced of Katie's motives, but finally decided to drop the topic.

Richard had always been a reasonable boss and rarely said no to Katie's requests. However, this would be the first time she'd ask to work in another department, albeit, only temporarily.

He was modest and kind, exactly the type of person one would expect to hold a middle management position in an organization that advocated for children, though he had no children of his own.

"Knock, knock." Katie leaned in the open doorway of Richard's office.

"Good morning, Katie. Welcome back. Feeling better today?"

A slight twinge of guilt passed through her as she smiled in return. "Yes, thank you. I was wondering if you had a minute. I'd like to ask you something."

"Sure, come on in. Close the door, if you need to."

"No, it's nothing like that." She took her seat opposite Richard's desk. "I'd like to see if there is any chance I might be assigned to a case in the Victim's Assistance program. I was interested in possibly doing some work for them."

"I see. Does that mean you don't want to work for me anymore?"

"No, of course not; it would only be temporary. I'd like to gain some experience in other areas and get involved with the community on a more direct basis, rather than the research work and fundraising. It seems interesting." Katie thought her answer was a little vague, even bordering on suspicious.

"Okay, well, I'd have to call down there to see what they've got and if they need any help."

Katie felt his eyes prying her for some deeper insight, instead, she remained casual, not wanting to divulge her true reasons.

"So it would just be the one case?" Richard asked.

"Yes. I'd like to gain as much experience here as I can. I'm not really sure where I'd like to eventually end up, but I definitely want to stay with the Advocacy Group, and adding a few extra responsibilities to my resume might be a good idea."

"All right then; I'll give Susan down there a buzz and see what they can do for you."

Katie was relieved he agreed so quickly. Of course, it would ultimately be up to that department, but this was the first step. "Thank you so much, Richard. I really appreciate it."

"You're welcome, but how am I supposed to fill your shoes if they need you for a month or more?"

This was something that hadn't really occurred to Katie. "I can handle most of my duties, but maybe I could talk to Jennifer to see if she could help with a few things."

"Okay. If Susan can use you, you'll still have to stay afloat on this end, whether that means having Jennifer help out is up to you and her."

"Thanks again, Richard. You have no idea how much I appreciate the opportunity."

"Don't get too excited. I haven't asked her yet."

Katie feared she might be taking on too much, but with Jennifer on her side, it would work. She would owe her big, but it would work.

By mid-day, Katie received an e-mail from Richard. He'd sent her Susan's response to the request.

"We would be grateful for Ms. Reid's assistance on the Isabelle Thompson case. There are several moving parts to this one and we are short-staffed. The work will be difficult, given the subject matter, but if you feel she is capable of handling herself then I would welcome her addition to the staff."

Above this was a reply from Richard to Katie.

"They've agreed, Katie. Good luck and I would like to sit down with you and Jennifer in the morning to figure out our workload."

Katie was excited and terrified. If nothing else, she had just been given an opportunity to help with something that mattered. But in the end, what mattered to her was learning everything she could about investigations, and working with the police department would be a good start.

KATIE WIPED her hands on the dish towel and tossed it onto the counter. The meal was prepared and she'd hoped she was too. "Spencer, dinner's ready."

"Smells great. What's the special occasion?" He emerged from the den.

It was no secret she was not the cook of the house and takeout seemed to be a better fit for their busy schedules anyway, but tonight would require an explanation of her new work assignment. Dinner was intended to soften the blow.

Katie brought out the plates of somewhat questionable-looking pasta and salad. Her repertoire of meals amounted to only a handful of items and even then it would be hit or miss.

With the bottle of red wine already on the table, she poured Spencer a glass. "I was assigned to work on a case with the Victim's Assistance program today."

"Really? Were you moved to another department?"

"Not permanently, this is just a one-time thing. They're understaffed and need some help."

"That's a little outside your wheelhouse, isn't it? You generally stick to the admin side of things."

Katie poured her wine and quickly took a sip as she prepared for the barrage of questions. "Yes, I do, but this is the Isabelle Thompson case and I thought that maybe I could help, so I volunteered."

"That's the girl who went missing, what, like a couple of weeks ago? The Advocacy Group is working on that one?"

"The Victim's Assistance program is, yes. They're working with San Diego PD since it involves community coordination. You know, talking to the kids at her school, the neighbors, that sort of thing. Jen is going to help with my regular duties, but I'm going to continue to keep as much of my responsibilities as I can in addition to assisting with the case. It's an incredible opportunity, Spencer."

"It doesn't sound like you're going to have much spare time." He appeared deflated by this unexpected news.

"I haven't forgotten about our wedding. It's not for eight more months. I think we have time. Your long hours don't seem to be a problem and mine won't be either. Look, you asked me to move on and that's exactly what I'm trying to do. Don't you see that?"

"Yes. I guess I just thought you'd move on in a different direction. Most women want to do all the wedding planning."

In the seven years she'd known him, his impression of what women wanted never seemed to have sounded so 1950s, but that was exactly how he sounded now. Her frustration grew, but Katie remained calm and continued to try to persuade him. He had to see how important this was to her, and by default, how important his support would be. "Well, most women planning a wedding probably didn't just find out they had been abducted as a child." She paused and took a deep, calming breath. "It's only been a few days since I found out my entire life has been a lie. I'm asking for your support here." Katie pushed on. "Please understand that I do want to marry you and I do want to plan this wedding. But you have to let me do what I need to do to move on. We've agreed to continue the therapy and this is just another extension of my therapy. I need you to see that."

His expression softened. "Okay, you're right, Katie. I'm sorry. I'm trying to get through this as well and I should be more supportive. If you can handle working on a case in addition to everything else, then I have no right to question it."

"Thank you, Spencer. This has changed me, who I thought I was, and who I want to be, but it hasn't changed how much I love you."

6

A brief team meeting between Katie and Jennifer began as they sat in Richard's office, reviewing the workload while Katie assisted on the Thompson case. After the meeting, the women returned to their cubicles and Katie began gathering a few of her belongings. The move downstairs would take place in the coming hours.

"Why the sudden interest in victim assistance cases?" Jennifer leaned on the cubicle wall, waiting for a reply.

"I guess I just want to be a little more hands-on, you know? Get involved in directly helping a victim. We do so much paperwork and fundraising and I know all that matters, but I want to see a more direct impact. I want to make a difference."

For the first time, Katie felt her response was genuine, that she'd actually been able to identify a clear reason. It might not have been the entire reason, but it certainly was part of it and was enough to make Jennifer understand.

"Well, good luck, Katie, and I mean that. I know it's going to be a little more hectic around here, but honestly, it's nothing I can't handle."

"I know that, Jen. Believe me, I won't forget what you're doing. It means more to me than you could know."

An email came across and Katie turned to her computer. "I'll catch up with you before I head down." On opening the email, she discovered it was a meeting request from Susan, her new temporary boss. Katie was asked to attend a meeting scheduled by the District Attorney's office today at 1 o'clock.

Not only would this be her official introduction to Susan, but it would also be her introduction to the Thompson case.

Katie placed her few personal items into a small box and headed to meet her new boss. With the box propped against her waist, Katie stood in front of Susan's office. "Is there any place you'd like me to sit?"

"Katie, welcome. Come on, I've got a place already set up for you." Susan moved around her desk to shake the hand of her newest assistant.

It was a pleasant surprise to find that she would be given an office. This wasn't exactly a promotion and she certainly hadn't been given a raise. Since the department was shorthanded, she assumed space must be plentiful and this was close to Susan's office, which was probably the real reason for the upgrade.

Susan handed over a flash drive. "The meeting starts in an hour. Why don't you have a look at the correspondence files, then meet me in the conference room? I'd like you to sit in on this one and meet everyone. You'll be taking minutes as well."

"Okay. Thank you." She took the flash drive and loaded it up on her computer.

An hour later, Katie was the first one to arrive in the conference room. Everyone involved with the Thompson case would be there, from the police detectives to the District Attorney's office, and the supervisor in charge of the case for the Advocacy Group. It was their second meeting and was the first one in which Katie would be involved.

Her nerves were on edge as she sat waiting patiently, pen and paper in hand.

The second to arrive was Detective Marshall Avery of the San Diego Police Department. He introduced himself and extended his hand to Katie. It appeared weathered beyond what she assumed his years to be. His face was lined, more from stress, she thought, than from age.

"Katie Reid. Nice to meet you," she said.

"Are you with the courts?" the detective asked.

"No, I work for the Advocacy Group. I'm going to be assisting Susan with any help she might need."

"Great. Welcome aboard, Katie."

Soon after, the others arrived and the meeting began. Katie was more than a little intimidated but soon began to feel at ease as she learned more about the team. Her supervisor, Susan, acted as the liaison for the DA and Police. She was responsible for working with the child psychologist and helping Detective Avery with gathering background information on the neighborhood, teachers, and so on.

The DA's office rep was Eric Jennings, who seemed less interested in the case than in ensuring his office maintained its appearance.

The Thompson case was a difficult one. As the conversations went on, Katie learned that Isabelle had a history of hospital visits, thanks to her mother. Child Protective Services had been called in several times, but Isabelle was never taken away. Two weeks ago, she went missing. The mother appeared on television, begging for her return, proclaiming her innocence. Search parties were formed, but the eight-year-old girl had not yet been found.

The Victim's Assistance Department was appointed by the DA's office to help the police in the case. A child advocate was often appointed in these cases to accompany the police on school visits. It wasn't uncommon to have discussions with classmates and teachers. The advocate's job was to ensure the safety and well-being of any other children who might need to be questioned.

At the end of the meeting, Katie understood why Susan warned that this would be a difficult case. It had become clear that Isabelle was abused, but it was as of yet unclear if her mother was involved in the girl's disappearance.

It would be Katie's job to review statements and write summaries to submit to Susan. It was a minor role, but enough to give her access to Detective Avery. He would know how to help her find the answers she sought.

"Detective Avery," she called, following him into the parking lot.

He turned around. "Yes, Katie?"

"Have you ever worked on an unsolved case?"

"You mean, like a cold case?"

"I think so, yes."

"No. I don't usually get assigned cold cases. They're a sort of special division in the department. My job involves active cases. Why do you ask?"

The two continued to walk toward the detective's car.

"I was just curious. If I wanted to know something about a case that was opened some twenty-odd years ago, where would I go?"

"I would suggest contacting the police department where the case would have been filed. I'm not sure it would have a cold case division. I suppose that depends on the size of the department. But they would at least have someone who was likely familiar with the case and could possibly help. I can tell you that they would probably not discuss anything with you unless you had pertinent information." Detective Avery paused, appearing to consider her questions. "Is there something you'd like to add?"

Katie wasn't about to tell him the real reason. Who knew if it would cause a problem with her work here? Defense lawyers could dig up anything and if they thought someone who had been abducted as a child worked on this case, they might try to call some sort of prejudice and have the case dismissed.

"I was thinking about getting more involved in forensics, maybe going back to school."

"That's great." Detective Avery opened his car door. "Good luck, I hope it works out for you. In the meantime, glad to have you on our team."

He drove off, leaving Katie standing alone in the parking lot. She was a little disappointed at his abrupt departure but figured there would be more opportunities.

"It's getting late and I've got more depositions early tomorrow morning. You don't mind if I head off to bed?" Spencer pushed up from the couch, stretching his back.

"Not at all, you go on. I'm going to stay up and catch up on some paperwork for Richard."

"Okay, but don't stay up too late." A perfunctory kiss followed and he shuffled toward the bedroom.

It was already ten o'clock and she didn't know how long she'd last, but she wanted to try to get a few things done before going to bed. Keeping up with her other responsibilities was part of the bargain. It wasn't fair to ask Jennifer to take on too much, especially since she wasn't getting paid for her extra efforts.

After finishing her budget updates for Richard, Katie loaded the files from the flash drive Susan had given her. She opened the Child Protective Services files and began reading the history of Isabelle Thompson.

The social workers had been out half a dozen times to check in on Isabelle; each time the report indicated the need for a follow-up. There was no visible evidence of any injuries, but she appeared pallid and thin. The other children in the house, her siblings, never suggested any mistreatment to the social workers. When Isabelle went missing on the morning of April 10th, it wasn't until the mother came home from work that she reported Isabelle's disappearance, although she had received a message on her cell phone from the school indicating the child had not shown up. It remained unclear as to why the mother hadn't acted earlier upon hearing the school's message.

The police and protective services arrived at the Thompson home shortly after the mother's call. The report indicated that the other children were questioned separately, but nothing arose of any material significance. It was also noted that the mother, claiming to have been at work, could not explain the late hour at which she called 911. It was 8 p.m., two hours after her shift was over.

It was becoming clear that Susan's cautioning was warranted. Based on the information in these files, anyone would feel a little unnerved at the possibility of who was responsible for Isabelle's disappearance.

"Katie, are you coming to bed?" Spencer rubbed his eyes as they adjusted to the light in the living room.

She looked up at the wall clock; it was nearly 1 a.m. "Oh, I had no idea it was so late." She closed the lid of her laptop and rose from the couch. "Yes. I'm coming."

THE SAN DIEGO police station was thick with the frenetic pace of officers, civilian staff, and what she assumed were detainees when Katie arrived the next morning. She had expected to find only a few cops here and there, exchanging whimsical gibes with one another, but then remembered that this wasn't a movie.

Susan sent her to the station to have Detective Avery sign off on some requisitions for the Thompson case.

"Excuse me," Katie said to the officer behind the front desk. "I'm looking for Detective Avery. I have a 10:00 appointment with him."

"Can I get your name, please?"

"It's Katie Reid, from the Advocacy Group, regarding the Thompson case."

The officer raised the phone receiver and pressed a few buttons. "Detective Avery, there's a Miss Katie Reid here to see you. She says she has an appointment."

Katie watched as the officer nodded and put down the phone.

"You can go on back. Andrews, can you show this young lady where Detective Avery's office is?" he asked the officer sitting at a desk in what appeared to be a sort of bullpen area.

"Sure. Come on back with me, miss."

Katie followed Officer Andrews through the maze of hallways. They passed a holding room, the break room, and finally arrived at Detective Avery's office.

"Thank you, officer."

Andrews nodded, made a brief gesture of acknowledgment to Detective Avery, and then disappeared.

"Come in, Katie, and have a seat. I understand you have a few things for me to sign?"

"Good morning, Detective Avery. Yes, I have a couple of things for you."

"Please, call me Marshall." He motioned her to sit.

Katie pulled out a manila envelope from her carrier bag and handed it to him. "Here you go, Detective, I mean, Marshall." She watched as he read through the paperwork. He was older than she was, by at least ten years, she guessed. His light brown hair was longer than that of the other officers', not long, but not crew cut either, more styled. He wore street clothes, a blue polo that was sharply pressed, and khaki pants with a perfect crease down the middle of each leg. It was late April in San Diego, and rarely did men dress in suits, with the possible exception of lawyers.

She noticed his brow furrow with every signature as if he objected in some way. Katie was just the messenger, so she was not privy to the contents of the requisitions. The detective picked up the newly signed papers, straightened them on his desk, and slid them back into the envelope. When he handed it back to her, Katie finally got a full view of his face. Up until that point, he had only briefly made eye contact with her when he introduced himself. Even as they stood in the parking lot yesterday, he was fumbling with his keys as he spoke.

His olive skin stood in stark contrast to his light hair and bright green eyes. They were so perfectly green, she wondered if they were contacts. Although he didn't seem the type of man to wear colored contacts. No, that had to be his God-given color, beautiful in its shade and tired in its appearance.

"Detective—I'm sorry—Marshall, can I ask how long you've been a police officer?"

Marshall's eyes narrowed at the question. "Seventeen years."

"So, you must have been what, about twenty then?"

A hint of a smile crossed his face. "Yes, that's right. I joined the force when I was twenty. That's very perceptive of you."

"I guess you could say I'm pretty good at reading people. Did you start as a beat cop, I think they call it?"

"Sounds like you watch a lot of cop shows on TV, but yes, most of us start on the streets."

Katie felt at ease with the detective and wanted to inquire further about unsolved cases. "I suppose I do watch a few." She paused briefly. "I was wondering if you knew anything about when a case goes from active to unsolved and then is filed away. I was curious as to how long it would take and what the criteria would be for a case to be considered cold."

"That's a good question. Typically, a cold case is a murder or other felony that has no statute of limitations. Disappearances or cases where a suspect has yet to be identified could be considered cold cases as well. That just means new evidence could present itself, like DNA. Now that we have this technology, it's not uncommon for police to re-open a cold case if other forensic or DNA evidence becomes available.

"A case would probably turn cold if all leads had been exhausted and no new evidence came into play. The length of time would be determined by the officers in charge of the investigation. They would know the most about it and be able to make that call."

Katie was engrossed in the detective's every word, so much so that she hadn't realized it was her turn to speak.

"Katie?"

"Oh, yes, thank you, Detective Avery. You've been a tremendous help." She gathered her things and made her way to the door.

"Aren't you forgetting something?" He held out the manila folder.

"Thank you," she said, slightly embarrassed.

"Have a good day and tell Susan 'hello' for me."

"Of course, and thank you again." She quickly made for the exit.

"Do you have the signatures?" Susan lowered her reading glasses and raised her head above the computer screen, catching sight of Katie as she walked in.

"Yes. Here they are." She handed her the envelope.

"Great. Thank you. I'd like you to make a few calls to the school for me. Here are the people I need you to contact." Susan handed over about a dozen business cards. "There've been some students having a difficult time and they'd like us to arrange for the counselor to come down again. Could you coordinate that for me, please?"

"I'll get started on it now."

THE COORDINATION EFFORT managed to take up much of the rest of her day. By the time she was finished, she had just enough time to touch base with Jennifer, then she headed for home.

It was nice that the days were getting just a little bit longer. Katie enjoyed watching the sunset on her drive home, instead of it already being dark by the time she left the office. It had a calming effect on her.

She opened the door to her apartment to find Spencer already home. He was rarely home before 8 p.m. and here it was only 7:00.

"Hi there. I didn't expect you to be home so early. I guess we can sit down for a nice home-cooked meal tonight then?"

"So, I'll be doing the cooking?" He greeted her with a kiss.

"Haha, very funny; but hey, if you're volunteering?"

Spencer walked into the kitchen and opened the refrigerator. "How was your day?"

"It was good. I'm really enjoying this work. How about you?" She followed him into the kitchen and grabbed a large pot. "How about pasta?" It was her go-to meal.

"Sure. That sounds good." He took some meat out of the freezer and stuck it in the microwave. "It was busy today, but since I had gone in early, I was able to wrap things up a little earlier than usual."

"So you got your depositions?" Katie filled the pot with water and set it on the gas stove.

"Yep. It was tedious, but we got what we needed. Oh, before I forget, I've rescheduled us to review the invitation proofs tomorrow night, instead of Sunday, if that's okay?"

"Yeah, of course; that should be fine." Katie actually felt a little excited about seeing how the invitations turned out. Megan, the wedding planner, had sent some samples the other day via e-mail. She forwarded the message to Spencer and left it up to him to make the final decision.

Spencer brought two large plates of pasta to the table while Katie took the bread out of the oven.

"Let me get that for you," he said, taking the breadbasket from her. "You feel like opening a bottle?"

"Sure. You don't have to ask me twice." Katie was beginning to feel that things were getting back to normal between the two of them.

They sat down to a pleasant meal where the conversation flowed as freely as the wine.

"That was wonderful, Katie. But I thought you were hungry. You hardly touched your plate."

"Are you kidding me? Did you see how much you piled on? You'd have thought I was eating for two, which I'm not, so don't freak out. Besides, I'm supposed to be picking out a dress soon, if you'll recall. But I enjoyed dinner too, thank you."

"It was nice to be cooking together, you know. It's been a while."

Katie reached for Spencer's hand. "I know. You know what else would be nice?" She placed her napkin on the table and rose from her chair. "How about I go run us a hot bath?"

Spencer raised an eyebrow. "Should I bring the wine?"

"Meet me in the tub in ten minutes, and yes, bring the wine." Katie winked as she sauntered into the bedroom.

A SMALL PACKAGE waited on Katie's desk when she arrived at work this morning. She picked it up and searched for a name on it. In the top corner was an SDPD stamp.

Inside the brown paper wrapping was a book, a textbook on researching cold cases. When she opened the cover, a note fell out.

"This might help you with whatever it is you're working on." It was signed, Marshall Avery.

Apparently, she wasn't the only one who could read people. She opened up her e-mail and began drafting a message to him.

"Thank you so much for the resource book. I guess I wasn't very good at hiding my agenda. I'll return it once I have finished reading it. I'm sure it will be a great tool to aid in my research. Thanks again, Katie."

She walked into the kitchen for a cup of coffee and on her return, Detective Avery had already sent a reply.

"No problem, Katie. If you need anything or I can be of assistance,

outside of the Thompson case, please don't hesitate to let me know. I am happy to help and enjoy sharing what I've learned over the years. Have a good day, Marshall."

The day seemed to have flown at break-neck speed. When Katie finally had a chance to look at her watch, it was almost five o'clock. She hadn't forgotten about the appointment at the printers but still had some time to finish a few things before heading out.

"Katie," Jennifer called in on the speaker. "Don't forget you have to leave on time tonight."

"Thank you for reminding me!"

Just as Katie was packing up for the day, Spencer sent her a text message. *"You're still planning on being there at 6:00, right?"*

"Of course! Wouldn't miss it. C U soon," she replied and headed out the door.

Traffic was proving to be troublesome, but Katie managed to find an alternate route and made it to the printer's right at 6:00, as promised. In fact, she was the first to arrive, although Spencer wasn't far behind. She spotted his car pull into the parking lot as she walked to the entrance of the building.

"Oh good, you made it on time," she said.

"Yes, well, I did have a longer commute. Shall we go in?" He opened the door, allowing Katie to walk in as he followed closely behind.

"Hi there," Katie greeted the receptionist. I'm Katie and this is my fiancé, Spencer. We're here to view our invitation proofs."

"Hello. I'll call back to Maggie and she'll get them for you," the receptionist replied.

The two of them sat down, waiting for the lady with the proofs. There were samples of several beautiful invitations in a book that sat on the lobby table. Katie began flipping through them to kill time.

The words were almost all the same. *"Bobby and Suzy, together with their parents, request the honor of your presence."* Or *"Please join Bobby and Suzy as they exchange vows in front of their friends and family."* This one had to be Katie's favorite and only wished she had thought of it first. *"After several years, Bobby has finally asked Suzy for her hand in marriage. Please join....."* Katie chuckled as she showed it to Spencer.

"Are you trying to say something?"

She continued to look through the book, wondering about married life. What would happen after the wedding, when they were expected to live a normal life? She wasn't even sure what normal was. Her parents certainly weren't shining examples of a happy marriage. Of course, now she understood why, but the fact remained, unexpected things, dreadful and painful things happen during the course of a marriage. How would she get through it when she was put to the test? Spencer's parents remained happily married and so, of course, he seemed to have no reservations at all. But Katie was afraid—afraid of failing.

"Katie, Spencer?"

They both glanced up to see a woman holding a brown box.

"Why don't you two come back with me and we'll get started."

Spencer led Katie toward the back office where Maggie was headed. She opened the box and pulled out the proofs.

"Oh my gosh, these look beautiful." Katie pulled one closer to get a better look.

"Spencer James Harris and Katherine Grace Reid
Together with their parents
Request the honor of your presence..."

"They look amazing," Spencer said.

Katie had chosen ivory and sage for the colors and she was thrilled with the result. "Yes, these will do, Maggie. Thank you."

"Okay then. We'll just need the remainder of the balance in order to go to print. It should take about two weeks."

Katie was beginning to feel reassured about the wedding. Seeing the invitations made it real for the first time. She loved Spencer and was happy.

Friday morning had arrived and Katie reminded Spencer of her appointment with Dr. Reyes after work. It was supposed to be date night, but Spencer insisted she keep her appointment.

On her way into work, she remembered the book from Detective Avery. She reached over onto the passenger seat, where her laptop bag rested. In the front pocket was the book, *Researching the Cold Case: An Investigative Guide.*

The thick textbook must have weighed a couple of pounds. She glanced briefly at the cover and then set it beside the bag. It would make for interesting reading over lunch later today.

The office was quiet when she arrived, which was fairly typical for a Friday. Many of the employees had flexible schedules and Fridays and Mondays tended to be slow. Katie put her bag on the lateral file cabinet behind her desk and then switched on her computer. Before she could sit down, her intercom buzzed in.

"Katie?"

"Yes?"

"Can you come to my office?"

It was Susan. It must be important because she would have sent an e-mail otherwise.

"Of course; I'll be right in." Katie grabbed a notebook and pen and joined Susan in her office.

"Good morning. I know you just got here and probably haven't even gotten your coffee yet, but I've been on the phone with Detective Avery and the DA's office." Susan started clicking on her computer, appearing to look for something.

Katie's interest was piqued as she waited for Susan to continue.

"Ah. Here it is." Susan began reading from the screen. "*The department has just received an anonymous tip regarding Isabelle Thompson. We will make every effort to exhaust this lead. As our resources will be stretched, we are asking everyone involved with the case to continue their due diligence and assist in any way as may be required by the department. We thank you in advance for your continued support.*

"This e-mail was from Detective Avery. I don't know what new information they've received, but we will continue to move things forward on our end. Now, if the detective needs help with any of the data we've collected so far, I want you to be at his beck and call. Are you good with that?"

Katie was ecstatic. This was exactly what she wanted, to be more involved and work more closely with the detective. This was her opportunity to learn from him.

"Of course, yes. I'm more than happy to step in and help where I can."

"Will this be a problem with Richard? It will likely mean less time in his department."

"I'll talk with him about it this morning. I'm sure it will be fine."

Katie wasn't sure at all. In fact, she suspected it might be a problem. Jennifer could only handle so much.

"Great. I'll let the detective know he can count on us. In the meantime, continue with compiling the week's reports for submittal. They're due by the end of today."

"I will. Thank you, Susan." Katie returned to her office. She would have to let Richard know what was going on. That would be the tough part. She began to draft an e-mail, then thought better of it. This would require a conversation in person. Katie buzzed his office. "Richard, do you have a minute?"

"I have a feeling I may already know what's coming, but yes. Come on up."

Katie wondered if Susan had given him a heads-up on the issue. She quietly knocked on Richard's partially opened office door.

"Come in, Kate."

He rarely called her "Kate." This was not going to be easy. She approached the chair opposite his desk.

Richard sat patiently with his hands folded.

"I just spoke with Susan regarding the Thompson case," Katie began.

"Yes. I heard. Have you come to resign your position in my department?" His cool tone brought the room temperature down a few degrees.

"No, of course not; that's not my intention at all, Richard. I was just hoping that we might be able to get a short-term replacement for me. Just until the case is over."

"You realize that could be a year from now? Did you not see this coming? They've been short-handed for so long, I'm not surprised they've asked you to take on a bigger role. Look, Katie, I can't say I wouldn't be disappointed, but I think we may need to find a permanent replacement for you."

Katie opened her mouth, but Richard stopped her.

"I can see how much this new position means to you. I haven't seen that look in quite a while, working for me."

She glanced down, feeling guilty at his remarks.

"You're the type of person who enjoys a challenge and I respect that, very much in fact. You've done a lot of good for me here in this department, but you need more and I'm afraid I don't have much more to give. Your options here are limited. It was bound to happen sooner or later. I guess I was just hoping it would be a little bit later than this." Richard paused and took a deep breath. "If you can tie up any loose ends with Jennifer early next week, I'll start looking for your replacement. I think she'll be able to handle the workload for a while and I'll make sure she's rewarded for her extra efforts. So, go on now. No need to get sentimental. You're only down on the second floor, after all. And, if you don't mind, I'll have a word with Jennifer about all this."

Katie smiled at Richard. "Thank you so much. It has been an absolute pleasure working for you. You've taught me so much."

"All right, all right; like I said, no need to get all mushy on me. Just go back to work and I'll catch up with you on Monday. So, if I don't see you, have a good weekend."

Katie nodded and took her leave. She wondered how Spencer would react to the news. She supposed as long as it didn't interfere with their wedding, he would probably be on board. For now, she needed to get back to work. Her reports had to be finished on time, not to mention she didn't want to be late for her appointment with Dr. Reyes.

The day continued with no urgent calls from Detective Avery, which was slightly disappointing. She did, however, manage to submit her weekly reports a half an hour early and now it was time to pack up and head out for the day. One last check of her e-mail; there was nothing important, so she shut her computer down.

Looking at her watch, she noticed it was already 5:15 and she would need to hurry to make 6:00. Friday traffic was less than pleasant. The highways were usually jam-packed with weekend tourists heading to the beach. The opposite was generally true of San Diego residents heading for Las Vegas for the weekend. So, either direction would be a nightmare.

"Ah, you made it," the doctor said as Katie walked into the lobby. Her receptionist was already gone. It was ten past six.

"I'm so sorry, Dr. Reyes. Traffic was terrible."

"No problem. You're my last appointment of the day. Come on back." The doctor waved Katie in and pointed to the reclining chair. "Have a seat."

Katie wasn't sure how productive this was going to be. Her mind was still on the Thompson case, but she knew this nightmare wasn't over yet.

Dr. Reyes began with her relaxation techniques. "Now, go ahead and lie back, Katie. We'll get started with the breathing. Slow, deep breaths in through the nose and out through the mouth."

Katie closed her eyes and began breathing.

Dr. Reyes reclined the chair so Katie would be lying almost flat.

"We're going to start where we usually start and that is at a good place for you in your mind; a place that makes you happy and content. From there, I'll start my countdown and you'll feel yourself sinking farther and farther into the chair and becoming more and more relaxed."

Katie was already beginning to feel calm and relaxed. Dr. Reyes began her countdown.

"I'm going to start my countdown. Ten, nine, eight, seven, six...."

Katie's body felt heavier and heavier as the numbers got smaller. Dr. Reyes' voice began drifting off into the distance. The image Katie conjured in her mind was of the garden at the beautiful hotel she and Spencer had visited for Sam's wedding. Soon, Dr. Reyes' voice disappeared and Katie was alone in the garden. She wore a flowing yellow spring dress that brushed gently against her calves as she walked along the path. The roses were in full bloom and she stopped to smell each one. As she continued down the stone path, the smell of roses began to fade, replaced by another, familiar scent. It was the very faint, lightly perfumed scent of a tree. Katie knew right away what kind of tree. A redwood.

The scent became stronger as she was transported to a cold, dark, and damp place. Her blindfold was tight around her head. He shoved her into the darkness. She stumbled, then managed to get up when the door closed. Extending her hand, she felt around for the cot. Katie knew this place. He kept her down here most of the time, only letting her out to use the restroom. The tight scarf was beginning to make her head ache, so her tiny fingers made their way to the back where they worked on loosening the knot. Pulling and tugging, she managed to slip her fingers between her head and the scarf, edging it down to her neck. He lowered it around her neck whenever she went inside the bathroom, but down here, in the dark, well, that was a blindfold in and of itself.

A sliver of light penetrated the cracks in the cellar door and cast a dim glow onto the ground. It was barely enough by which to see. Katie made her way to the cot and sat down. She no longer cried for her mother, knowing she wasn't coming. Katie began quietly singing a song she'd learned in school just a few days before. Swaying back and forth, knees tucked up to her chest, Katie sang. Her voice was dry and hoarse. The small cup sitting on a crate next to the cot was empty. Her daily allowance of water was exhausted.

As Katie hummed, she heard a thud on the floor above. It shook the floor and rattled the walls. It wasn't until that moment Katie spotted a twinkle out of the corner of her eye. This small shiny object sat on a shelf on the other side of the room. She stood up and tiptoed toward it and reached for the object that now lay against her small hand. It was a necklace with a heart pendant on the end.

Footsteps could be heard again and Katie quickly ran back to her cot. She sat quietly, waiting for him to come back down the stairs. He didn't leave her for very long.

A voice in the distance became louder.

"Katie, I'm counting back up again... six, seven, eight, nine, ten. Katie?"

She could hear the doctor, but could not respond.

"Katie? You should be back with me now. Can you hear me?" Dr. Reyes grabbed her arm. "Wake up, Kate."

The touch finally brought her back to the present. She opened her eyes and saw a slightly panicked Dr. Reyes leaning over her.

"I'm okay, I'm awake."

Dr. Reyes sighed with relief. "You had me a little concerned. Do you remember the room you were in?"

"Only a little; it seemed too much like a dream. The other memories seemed to come back with a vengeance, but I felt like I was hovering over myself, watching myself as a little girl. Why was this time so different?"

"I can only speculate that your emotions were detached from that moment. It may have been your mind's way of protecting you and separating yourself from the situation. I believe it was probably for your own good."

"It was very strange. I don't know if I really learned anything more." Katie rested her head back on the chair. "I don't know, doc, maybe you were right; you and Spencer both. If my subconscious could recall my abductor's face or reveal any physical characteristics, it would have done so by now. That was just so surreal, whereas the other sessions felt like they'd happened yesterday."

"Some memories are buried too deep, Katie. Those are the ones that aren't meant to come to light."

7

———

Saturday morning, Katie sat on the balcony of the apartment and raised a steaming cup of coffee to her lips while she read the book given to her by Detective Avery. It was filled with several case studies and information on tracking down cold homicides, disappearances, and serial murders.

She was taken aback by the sheer volume of information; software programs that tracked credit card use, national crime databases, and of course, DNA evidence. And that was only in the first couple of chapters. While daunting to read, Katie remained completely fascinated. So much so, that she hadn't noticed Spencer in the kitchen, banging coffee mugs together, still half-asleep. She heard his footsteps approach from behind.

"Good morning." Her eyes never left the book's page.

He grunted and sat down next to her. "How long have you been up?"

"I don't know. I lost track of time." She paused to find the clock. "Oh wow, it's ten? I can't believe you slept in so late."

"Well, I didn't get in until midnight. The team was given some last-minute evidence by the prosecution. We were supposed to be beyond the discovery period, but they keep handing things over whenever they damn well feel like it." Spencer glanced at her book as he sipped on his coffee. "What's that you're reading?"

"Oh, this was lent to me by the detective working on the Thompson case. I had expressed some interest in learning more about the field and he shared this with me. Since I'm going to be working for Susan from now on, I thought I'd better get a feel for this stuff."

Spencer squinted and reached for the cover of the book. *"Cold Case Research.* I didn't realize you were working on a cold case. I thought the Thompson case was an ongoing investigation."

"It is. Detective Avery had this on his bookshelf when I went to the station the other day. I glanced at the back cover while I was waiting for him to sign some documents and he said I could borrow it if I was interested." That little lie had come all too easy for her.

Spencer looked out over the balcony. The breeze was teetering on the edge of feeling warm, but the sky was still overcast. Their "ocean view" apartment revealed just a sliver of blue water between several buildings that were far off in the distance.

Nevertheless, Katie watched as Spencer looked on. She knew what he was thinking, but didn't say as much. He was getting tired of the whole thing. She believed he wished it hadn't happened even more than she had. But there would be no going back now. Katie found something she was truly passionate about in her new job. And if in the course of her employment, she might discover the truth about her past, she wasn't about to let Spencer or anyone sway her otherwise.

Spencer placed his mug on the table. "You know what? I think we could use some downtime. Why don't we catch a movie and maybe go for a walk on the beach? It's beautiful out today and I could use a break."

"Absolutely. I'd love that." Katie gave him a peck on the cheek. "I'll go jump in the shower."

～

THE OVER-CROWDED PACIFIC BEACH wasn't surprising. It was spring break for the schools, after all. That didn't matter to Katie, though. They had enjoyed a movie and a long lunch, followed by a few drinks at the Green Flash, a local favorite. The sun would be setting soon and it had been far too long since the two of them watched the sunset over the ocean. Spencer was right, a break was indeed what they both needed.

Now, Katie held her flip-flops in her hand as they walked along the shore, digging her toes in the wet sand. The water was still cold as it washed over her feet along the way.

The noticeable silence was broken when Spencer cut his foot on a large shell that was shattered and protruded only slightly from the sand.

"Oh no, are you okay? Let's go sit down and take a look at that."

Spencer put his arm around Katie's neck and hobbled as they walked toward the wall along the boardwalk.

"I'm okay. Just let me look." He pushed her hand away and began feeling around for any remaining shards of broken shell lodged in his skin.

"Do you want me to get a Band-Aid?"

"No, I'll be fine. It's not that bad." His tone softened at her concern.

The silence lingered once again until Spencer finally came out with it. He was never quiet for long and Katie sensed he wanted to get something off his chest.

"Do you still want to get married, Katie?"

"What? Of course I do. Why would you say something like that?"

"I just feel like I'm losing you." His eyes did not hold onto her gaze, only the ocean's mesmerizing shifts.

"You're not losing me, Spencer, I swear it. It's just that I'm not the same person I was a couple of months ago. You expect me to just go on with my life as if nothing ever happened."

"I don't, Katie. I really don't. I guess the thing that gets to me is that I can't help you. I can't make it go away. I mean, here you are doing a different job, one that seems, quite frankly, a little dangerous. You're reading up on cold cases. What am I supposed to do? We're getting married in a few months and it's like I have to constantly remind you of that fact."

Katie took his hand. "You don't have to remind me we're getting married. I want nothing more than to marry you. But I'll admit, this thing has thrown a wrench into the works. I know I haven't been focused. I'm still having the dreams and I don't sleep well. My sessions with Dr. Reyes aren't progressing as I had hoped and the one ray of sunshine I see is that I'm really excited about my work."

"The one ray of sunshine?"

"You know what I mean." Katie turned away toward the setting sun. "It's beautiful, isn't it?"

"Yes, it is. Katie, what are we going to do?" His desperation could not be ignored.

"You're going to let me resolve this in my own way and in my own time. The wedding will take care of itself. We have a great planner and when she needs us to make decisions, I'll make sure I take the time to do so. I won't let you down. We are getting married and things will get back to normal. We will get through this."

"I hope so." Spencer stood up to test the pain in his foot. "Come on. I can walk now. Let's go enjoy this sunset." He reached for Katie's hand.

She gladly offered it.

Fifty unread emails awaited Katie when she arrived for work on Monday morning. What did people do all weekend, send useless emails? But there was one that stood out. It was from Detective Avery. He was confirming that Katie would be available to come along and interview the surrounding neighbors of the Thompson home.

Farther down was an email from Susan. She needed to see Katie as soon as she got in.

"Good morning, Susan. You wanted to see me?"

"Good morning. Yes. Please come in and have a seat."

Katie sat down, impatiently waiting for her to begin.

"I got a call from Detective Avery early this morning. Based on the leads he received late last week, he has asked that you accompany him on interviews in Isabelle's neighborhood. They've already spoken with many of these people, but whatever new information he's gotten his hands on, requires further inquiries. He didn't go into much more detail than that. I expect he'll fill you in when you meet him at the station at 9:00."

Katie leaped out of her seat. "Okay. I'll get my things and head out in a few minutes."

"You've got a little time, Kate. Relax. And, don't worry, you won't be asking any questions. You're just there to take notes."

"Thank you, Susan." Katie struggled not to break out into a sprint back to her office. She immediately sent a reply to the detective indicating confirmation of her arrival.

THE DRIVE WAS LONGER than expected but then it was still rush hour. The only solace was that it allowed Katie to find calm from her eagerness, feeling as though she was at a crossroads in her life and this event would carry her on her chosen path.

On arrival at the station, Katie sat in the row of chairs across from the front desk, waiting for Detective Avery. Next to her sat what appeared to be a homeless man and a woman, or rather, girl who looked like she'd been in a fight. Katie felt outside of her comfort zone. Her privileged life rarely exposed her to criminals and it would take some getting used to.

"Kate? Are you ready to go?" The detective appeared from around the corner.

"Yes." She rose from her chair and quick-stepped to catch up with him.

He walked almost as fast as he spoke and was obviously in a hurry. "Okay," he began. "We've talked to most of these people already, but we're going to make another visit."

Katie reached a near-jogging pace to keep up while listening intently.

"I have to warn you, we will be interviewing Level 2 and Level 3 sex offenders. These are the most likely to re-offend. Level 2 offenders often abuse the trust of their victims and are in a position of power, or have committed long-term abuse. Level 3 are generally more violent and have more predatory characteristics. They seek out their victims."

The idea reared its head that perhaps Katie had ventured far outside her wheelhouse.

"Kate, you okay?"

She nodded.

They arrived at his car and he opened the passenger door for her. "Listen, I know this is new for you and you're probably freaking out a little, but don't. I'll be doing the questioning and we won't be going inside the homes. I just need you to take down the responses. These people are used to it. Every time we get a case like this, we have to question the sex offenders in the area."

"It sounds like they're still dangerous. How can they live in normal neighborhoods and communities? Shouldn't they all live together somewhere else?"

"Well, I suppose most people would prefer that and the law can dictate, to an extent, where someone can live, if they're a serial offender. However, most can still choose where to call home." He shut her door and walked around to the driver's side.

Once inside, he turned the engine. "Besides, they've already paid for their crimes. We just have to hope the treatment programs and rehab worked so we can keep these communities safe."

They pulled out onto the street and Katie attempted a discreet glance at the detective wanting to ask more questions, but figured it might make her appear amateurish.

"What is it?" His eyes maintained contact with the road ahead.

"I was just wondering what's come to light that the police need to question these people again."

"We have a hotline for anonymous tips and so far, we have received about 300. Now, several of those tips aren't valid, but we have to exhaust the ones we think might be legitimate. On Friday morning, we received a tip that a neighbor spotted a small, white, older model Chevy pickup parked on the street the day Isabelle went missing. They said it had been there at that same time for the previous two days."

"Why did this person wait so long to call it in? She's been missing for more than two weeks."

"Hard to say; maybe they didn't think it was relevant or had forgotten about it altogether. Who knows. People sometimes don't like to get involved. Anyway, we cross-referenced everyone within a five-mile radius of Isabelle's house who owns a similar type of vehicle. We found six; two are registered sex offenders, and the other four are within the search radius. These are the people we're going to talk to today. We had to go through the proper channels and are trying to get search warrants for the vehicles now. I'm hoping to narrow that down by the responses we get today. It's not the strongest lead, but it's something."

"But there are still volunteers and police out there looking for her, right?"

"Oh yeah, like I said, we're following up on every lead we can. The problem, Kate, is that there is a very small window of opportunity to find a missing child unharmed. Generally, it's only about three hours. A very high percentage of children won't be recovered alive after that. Not to mention the fact that it can sometimes take a parent a few hours to realize their child is missing in the first place. There goes the window."

"So, do you believe Isabelle is still alive, Detective?"

"We're going to exhaust every lead and continue our search to find out."

They pulled alongside the front of an apartment complex. Detective Avery verified the address on the building with his paperwork. "Okay, this is it. When we get to the door, I want you to fall behind me, got it?"

"Yes." She inhaled a deep breath, feeling anxious and excited at the same time.

"Let's go." Avery hopped out of the car and Katie followed closely behind as they approached the door of the ground-floor apartment. He didn't tell her who they would be interviewing first. She had her pen and paper at the ready.

The door opened just a fraction at the knock.

"Mr. Lopez, I'm Detective Avery from the San Diego Police Department. Can I ask you a few questions about Isabelle Thompson?"

"I already talked to you people. I told you I don't know anything about that missing girl."

"I understand, Mr. Lopez, and we thank you for your help. But we just have a couple more for you if that's all right?"

The man was silent but opened his door a little more.

"Thank you, sir. This is Kate Reid; she's just here to take some notes for me."

The man grunted in her direction.

"Do you own a white Chevy pickup, Mr. Lopez?" Detective Avery continued.

"Yeah. What about it? Has it been stolen?"

"No, sir. A white Chevy truck was spotted on San Miguel Drive the day Isabelle went missing. The witness said it had been parked there at the same time for a few days."

"It wasn't mine. I use it for work every day."

"And where do you work, Mr. Lopez?"

"Not that I have to answer your questions, but just so you know

I'm cooperating, I work at the JBS body shop on Estrella. That's pretty far from San Miguel Drive, Detective."

"Yes, it is, Mr. Lopez. I don't mean to imply you are a suspect. We're just trying to narrow down our search. We just want to get Isabelle home to her parents. I'm sure you can understand that."

The man's face softened. "I understand. I'm a father. I'm sorry I couldn't be of more help."

"You've been a great help and we thank you for your time. Good day, sir." Detective Avery turned back toward Katie. "Let's go."

Katie waited until they got in the car before speaking. "Wow. That's it? You just take his word for it? He seemed pretty ticked off by the questioning."

"Wouldn't you be? Someone coming to your door and implying you are somehow involved in the disappearance of a child? We have to make them feel like we aren't accusing them of anything. We don't accuse unless we have evidence. That's what we're looking for today. And as far as 'taking his word for it,' I can tell you that I've been doing this long enough to tell when someone is hiding something. That man was no more guilty of taking Isabelle than you or me."

"I'm sorry, Detective Avery. I didn't mean to imply..."

"Don't worry about it, Kate. I'm not easily offended. This is your first go around and, understandably, you'd have questions."

The more people they spoke with, the more at ease Katie felt. Detective Avery handled each of them with respect and kindness. It became obvious that the more comfortable they felt, the more willing they were to answer his questions. Still, they weren't any closer to finding the owner of the truck parked on Isabelle's street that day.

"Listen, let's go grab a bite for lunch. It's already 1:00 and I'm sure you must be starving. After that, we only have two more people to question."

"That sounds good. I am hungry," Katie replied.

"There's a great food truck that stops at G Street. We aren't too far from there and they have the best barbeque pulled pork anywhere in town."

DETECTIVE AVERY LEFT the truck holding two baskets and approached the table where Katie sat. "I'll be right back with the drinks."

She looked at the gooey sandwich with barbeque sauce oozing out of the bun. It was piled high with pork.

He set the drinks down and climbed over the bench to sit. "What are you waiting for? Dig in."

With hesitation, she picked up the enormous sandwich and proceeded to take a bite. The thing wouldn't even fit in her mouth, so she was only able to pick off some of the meat.

"It's good, right?" Detective Avery wiped the sauce off the corner of his mouth. "So, what do you think of the book I left for you? Have you had a chance to get into it yet?"

"A little bit, yeah; I took a look at it on Saturday morning and it's really fascinating. Unfortunately, I've got a million things going on right now, so I didn't get to read too far into it, but I'm hoping to this week."

"So, you married, Kate?" The observant detective easily spotted her engagement ring.

"Engaged, due to be married at the end of the year."

"Congratulations. That must be one of the million things you've got going on."

"Yes, part of it." She returned a pleasant smile.

"And the rest of it? You mentioned going back to school or something and studying forensics?"

Katie felt guilty for lying to him at their first meeting. After watching him question people all morning, she spotted the same look in his eyes when he asked her about this. He was looking for something she might be concealing.

Lying wasn't her strong suit and she cast her eyes downward in search of an answer he would buy. "Yeah. I was thinking about it. I'm not sure yet. With the wedding and all, I've been pretty busy."

"Uh-huh. You know, I thought it was interesting that you requested to join this case. Didn't you work in what--fundraising or something—for the Advocacy Group before?"

She began to consider that he might not be buying it after all. "Yes, I did some research too, but I was looking to make a difference and find something more rewarding."

"After you asked me for help the other day, I went back through my collection and found that book. Then I thought, cold cases are an interesting and very specialized unit, not a common subject for someone wanting to study forensics."

Katie's pulse began to rise as the lie began to crumble. It wouldn't take much to run her name through a database. Although she had been a minor, her parents would have been on record for filing the missing persons' report, not to mention the local media stories. She wasn't ready to tell anyone else about what happened to her. Certainly not someone she'd only met a few weeks ago.

"Well, anyway, I hope the book helps. Don't hesitate to ask me anything. I'm not an expert in that area, but I can point you in the right direction. I'll help where I can, Kate." He washed down the rest of his food with a final drink. "You ready to get out of here? We still have a couple of people to talk to, then I'll let you be on your way." Detective Avery gathered the baskets, tossed the trash away, and returned the baskets to the truck. The shade from the trees lined the sidewalk on his return and his face was obscured in shadow.

She watched his approach carefully. He walked with such confidence. The man was proving to be a very fascinating individual. It was as though he could look right through a person and see their true intentions. Something she'd have to keep an eye on the more closely they worked.

The two drove off to speak to the next person on the list. Katie had been unable to decide and Detective Avery was unwilling to reveal which of the leads had been the sex offenders. She assumed that it would be obvious, but so far, she had been wrong about many things today.

Approaching the door, Detective Avery cautiously glanced into the front window. The curtains were pulled back slightly, which only allowed him to see a small section of the living room. He knocked on the screen door. "San Diego Police. I'd like to ask you a few questions, Mr. Johansen."

They stood there for a few moments, with no reply. He knocked again. "Mr. Johansen, this is Detective Avery from the San Diego Police Department, can I speak with you, sir?" He looked back at Katie and nodded as if to say, everything's fine.

Had she appeared nervous?

Just as they were about to leave, the door opened. A man, appearing to be in his mid to late twenties stood in a t-shirt and denim shorts and looked like a surfer. He was clean-shaven with short, high-lighted hair. The screen door remained closed as Detective Avery began questioning the man.

He behaved differently, more guarded than the others. But surely, he was not one of them, not this handsome, albeit thin, man around the same age as she was. Maybe his behavior was just reactive as if he was used to the police coming to his door.

"Sir, can you tell me if you were in the vicinity of San Miguel Drive on April 10th?"

"No, I was at work, like I am every day. What is this about, Detective...?"

"Avery. Were you in possession of your vehicle on that day? The white Chevy pickup?"

"No, sir; I let a friend borrow it a few weeks ago. Dumbass let it get jacked a few days later."

"Stolen? And has it since been recovered?"

"Hell no, I've had to bum rides for the past two weeks. You find it, you let me know, detective."

"Of course. Thank you, Mr. Johansen. I appreciate your time. By the way, is there any way to reach your friend who borrowed the truck? I'd like to ask him some questions."

"Good luck trying to find him. He lets my ride get stolen, then skips out on the 200 bucks he owes me."

"Does this friend have a name?"

"Hernandez. Steven Hernandez."

"Thank you, Mr. Johansen." Detective Avery motioned Katie to follow as they walked back to his car.

Katie got back into the passenger seat. Detective Avery said nothing more. He started the car and pulled away. It wasn't for several more minutes that he began to speak.

"Michael Johansen said his truck was stolen a few weeks ago. That would have been somewhere around the 12th or 13th, a few days after Isabelle disappeared."

"Right." She waited for further explanation.

"The witness said the truck had been there at that same time for at least two days. This guy's friend is nowhere to be found, no truck to be found, either. I never said why I was there. I only asked whether he was around San Miguel on the 10th."

"Okay, I'm not sure I follow you exactly." Katie was good at figuring things out, but this was well beyond her reach. She didn't think like a detective; she couldn't even tell whether this man was one of the offenders.

"This investigation has been all over the news, but we usually leave details out, in this case, where the victim lives. As far as the general public knows, Isabelle was taken on her way to school; they don't know she lived on San Miguel. The neighbors do, of course, but certainly Johansen, who lives several blocks away, wouldn't know that unless he knew her. So, she disappeared on the 10th. Doesn't it seem a little strange that Johansen said his 'friend' had borrowed his truck and a few days later it was stolen? The timing of his story seems a little too suspicious. Nope, I've got a bad feeling about this one. It won't be hard to find out where he works, since he's registered. And he never reported the truck stolen because it would have come up on the search."

"He's registered?" she asked.

"He's a Level 2 sex offender. We know everything about him. It's getting late in the day, I can handle the last one. I'll go ahead and take you back to the station. You'll need time to draft the reports from the interviews."

Katie's eagerness to learn from the detective ended with her exposing an apprehensive and naïve girl who had no business entering a world of which she knew nothing. He must have seen as much. It occurred to her that if she continued on this path to finding her captor, it would likely be someone far worse than Michael Johansen. This wasn't a game; this was real and she would be dealing with a very real and very dangerous individual.

It was still light when she arrived back at the apartment that evening, signaling that spring was nearing its end and summer was coming. Spencer would be home late as his team prepared for trial. Such was the life to which she would grow accustomed. However, this gift horse would provide her an opportunity to continue perusing the cold case textbook Detective Avery lent her.

Continuing where she left off, Katie read about something called NamUs, the National Missing and Unidentified Persons System. This system was available to the general public in addition to coroners, medical examiners, and law enforcement. Three separate databases could be searched: The Missing Persons database, in which anyone could enter information about a missing person, but it had to be verified by NamUs first; then, there was the Unidentified Persons database, which could also be searched by anyone and contained data on bodies that have not been identified. Finally, the Unclaimed Persons database, for people who had been identified, but no next of kin had been found.

She began to think of the possibilities. Could the other children, whose disappearance the police suspected had been connected with hers, be included in one of these databases? Was it likely though?

Given the fact that the reports had been filed on each victim long ago and if a body was discovered, the local police would easily be able to identify it, unless, of course, identification was impossible. The thought sent a chill through her.

Katie didn't know if anything that happened in her dreams actually occurred or not, save for the escape, but the thought of what could have happened to those other poor kids who didn't escape, well, it was too much to think about.

The focus had to be on how this information could help her. Was it possible to dig up any information that would give cause to the Rio Dell police department to reopen the investigation? Was this what she really wanted, especially after today?

Katie set the book down and walked into the kitchen to pour herself a glass of wine. With her wheels spinning, she thought perhaps she did have something. Now that she could recall at least some details, albeit uncertain of what happened and what didn't. Would that be enough to reopen the case?

What do I have, really? Some random memories about being chased in the woods? That I had a scarf tied around my eyes and I was kept in a dark room? Frustration grew at the seemingly wasted time spent on her hypnotherapy. Nothing of any significance had been uncovered in recent days.

It was at that moment that the evidence presented itself to her. *Oh my God, the necklace. The missing girl from Arcata wore a necklace in her school picture. I remember now. It was a heart pendant; something as ordinary as a little girl's heart pendant necklace in a school picture. It was the same one I saw in the dark room during my last session. And the necklace I saw on that woman at the fundraiser. God, my mind has been trying to show me this whole time. How could I have not seen it before? What was it about the necklace? Does this connect our two cases?*

8

Katie vacillated back and forth for the next few days as she tried to figure out how to handle this newly exposed information. This would be a giant step in getting the case reopened and that would have dramatic consequences on her relationship. Spencer would not be supportive of her flying home and digging up more of her past. And would it be possible to continue to be productive on the Thompson case while her mind was occupied with her own abduction?

As she sat in the conference in preparation for the weekly meeting, maybe the time had come to ask someone who was detached from the situation, someone who could offer realistic advice as to whether she had enough to warrant a new investigation. She trusted Detective Avery and he was who she needed to consult, even if it meant sacrificing the responsibilities of her new position.

"Good morning, Kate. Nice to see you again."

"Good morning, Detective Avery."

"It's Marshall, remember?"

"Of course, Marshall; can I get you some coffee?" Katie walked to the credenza at the back of the conference room where a coffee bar had been set out for the meeting. "I'm getting one for myself if you'd like one."

"Sure, that'd be great. Black, one sugar, please."

Katie carried two cups and handed one to Marshall. Just as she was about to take her seat again, Susan arrived, followed by the assistant district attorney.

"Good morning, everyone. Why don't we get started?" Susan opened the meeting and began going through the agenda.

The assistant DA knew the case was heading toward a dead end, with one exception, Detective Avery's lead on Johansen. "Detective Avery, I understand you and your team have been working diligently on the Johansen lead. According to Captain Hearn, you are still exploring this lead?"

"That's right. We haven't ruled him out just yet."

"And from your standpoint, Susan, your team is assisting the detective with documenting neighbor interviews? We need to be sure we are letting the public know that the Victim Assistance Coordinating Council is out there to help anyone who feels they might have any information on Isabelle's location."

"Yes, we are at the detective's beck and call and are assisting in any way possible. The public coordinating effort has helped ease the tensions between the community and the Thompson mother. As I'm sure you are aware, the media has swayed the public point of view in such a manner as to condemn the mother, justifiably so or not," Susan replied.

Detective Avery jumped in. "We haven't ruled out the mother yet, either. She remains an investigative lead along with the others."

"We'd like more than just leads at this point, Detective. I've got the mayor and the city manager breathing down my neck about the negative press. With tourist season kicking into high gear, they've made it clear they do not want this blemish on the city," The assistant DA replied.

"No, we would not want the disappearance of this eight-year-old child to become a blemish on the city and detract tourists." Detective

Avery's agitation was becoming apparent to everyone around the table. "You just let me do my job and I'll let you do yours, agreed?"

"Gentlemen, please," Susan interrupted. "This is not helping us find Isabelle or the person who took her. If we could please just continue with the meeting?"

Another hour had passed and it had been decided that the plan was to pull back unless Detective Avery's team came up with something very soon. Katie cringed at the possibility of never knowing what happened to Isabelle Thompson. She would be just another missing child.

After the meeting ended and everyone left, she and Marshall were the only two in the room.

"So Kate, you wanted to talk to me?" He still appeared frustrated.

"Yes. Do you think we could run out for a coffee or something? I don't really want to talk here."

"Sure. Let's go. I need some air anyway."

The coffee shop around the corner from the office was emptying as the morning rush ended. They sat down at a table in the corner.

"Can I get you a coffee this time?" Marshall asked.

"Yes, thanks. Cream and two sugars please." Katie couldn't be gone for too long without going unnoticed, so she had to make this quick.

Marshall set the cups on the table and sat down. "Okay, so what's this about?" He leaned over on his elbows, his full attention seemingly directed toward her.

"It's a long story, actually, so I'll just give you the abridged version," Katie started. "When I was six, I was abducted. My family and I lived in Rio Dell outside of Eureka. After three days, I was discovered by a family heading north for a Labor Day camping trip. I was found alongside Highway 101, at the edge of the woods. I had no memory of any of this when my parents picked me up at the police station in Trinidad; that's where the family took me. I was able to tell them my name and that was all they needed. Pretty much everyone knew who I was because I guess it was all over the news in Humboldt

County. There had been other abductions in northern California earlier that summer, but I was the only missing girl to have been found.

"But I guess I should preface this by saying that my parents never told me about any of it. Because I had no memory of the incident, they didn't, or rather, my mother, didn't see the need to subject me to any further trauma. The doctors told her that I might never remember what happened and she was just fine with that." Katie noticed Marshall's expression had remained unchanged as she revealed this life-altering event. He had to be the most even-tempered man she'd ever come across. Either that, or he'd heard much worse in his time.

"Well, like I said, it's a long story, but a few months ago, some of these memories began to surface, mostly through my dreams. It took a while, but about a month or so ago, I confronted my parents and they told me everything. My mother still had the newspaper clippings."

Marshall paused and eyed her closely. "I can't imagine what that must have done to you, Kate."

"Well, it hasn't been easy. But I feel as though I need to know who took me and what happened. That's the reason I asked you about cold cases. That's also the reason why I wanted to work in this department. I had hoped to learn something from you that might help me find a resolution."

He glanced down at his cup, swirling around what remained of his coffee. "Before you go any further, I have to tell you something." He caught her gaze this time. "There's a reason why I gave you that book and there's a reason why I asked Susan to send you along with me on the Thompson investigation."

Katie was growing concerned about what was coming next, although she suspected she knew what it was.

"After our first meeting, I was curious why someone with a degree in Social Sciences wanted to learn about cold cases. So I ran your name and found the file on your abduction case. Please. Don't be upset with me. I just wanted to help. That's why I sent you the book. That's all I wanted to do, was just to give you a leg up. And I figured if you wanted any more help, you'd come to me. I promise you, I didn't pry any more than that."

Katie remained silent as she processed this distressing news that her secret was no longer a secret and that it had been without her consent.

"Then, when we got the lead on the white truck, I thought asking you along would help you see the real world of investigating. I could see where you were headed with the cold case questions. I wanted you to know that it's not like what you see on TV. Cases aren't solved in an hour; sometimes they aren't solved at all. I'm sure you can see that now with Isabelle. Look, I know you're probably pissed off and I'm sorry. I should have said something the other day in the car. But I thought you'd tell me if and when you wanted to."

Finally, she was ready to speak. "You're right; I am pissed. I guess I understand to a point, but you should have just asked me."

Marshall nodded, swirling the stir stick in his coffee.

For the first time, she saw a vulnerability in him that he had so far been able to keep well hidden. "The reason I wanted to talk with you today was because I think I might have enough evidence to reopen the case. But I'm not sure if I should." She proceeded to tell him how she came about the information regarding the necklace and how she had seen it in one of her therapy sessions.

"I don't know, Kate. You were under hypnosis and had a repressed memory surface about being locked in a dark room and that you saw the same necklace the other victim wore in a picture. It's tough to say. They'll probably want to interview you and request your doctor's notes on the sessions. They're going to want to verify that at least some of the memories you had surface correlate in some way with what they already know of the case. But I suppose it's not unheard of to open a case based on a victim's recollections, however they were brought forth."

"So you think I should go back and talk to the police in Rio Dell?"

His comments were encouraging and she felt a small glimmer of hope igniting.

"That's up to you, Kate. You could be opening up Pandora's Box and you won't be able to close it again. Are you sure you're ready to relive what happened? Not to mention that it could take you away from your job here, and didn't you say you were getting married soon?"

"In seven months."

"Just be aware, that once it's open, it's open." Marshall threw back his final swig.

"You're right. Thank you." Katie walked to the garbage and tossed her cup. "You ready to go?"

Marshall got out of his chair and followed her toward the door. "So what are you going to do?"

"I have no idea."

KATIE POKED AT HER DINNER, not really eating as Spencer sat across from her. She had spent the day trying to figure out what to do and wasn't the least bit hungry.

"You okay, Katie?"

She looked at him and set her fork down. "I think I need to go back home. I want to talk to the police about reopening my case."

"What? What are you talking about? Why?"

She knew this would be a shock for him, having said nothing of the fact that she'd remembered the necklace or talked with the detective. Katie took a deep breath. "I know this isn't what you wanted. I know you thought I'd just get better and forget about all this. But I can't, Spencer. I really need your support right now. I'm scared to death."

"Then why put yourself through this? Are you even sure they'll reopen it? They'll need some kind of new evidence. Do you *have* new evidence, Katie?" He was starting to sound like a lawyer.

"As a matter of fact, I believe I do. Look, I don't want this to turn into a fight. I just need you to have my back. I don't know what's going to happen, but I know if you're with me, then I'll be okay."

He was quiet and stared at his plate of food for longer than she'd expected. She didn't know if he was about to break off the engagement or if he would stand behind her.

He finally looked up at her with glossy eyes. "Okay. I don't think this is the right thing to do, but I will support you. I always have, Katie. I just hope you know what you're doing."

Saturday afternoon was the soonest she could catch a flight to the Eureka/Arcata airport. She would have to fly into Sacramento and then into Arcata. But there was no time to waste. Katie needed to be sure to get back home by Sunday night.

"Spencer, I'm leaving."

He came out of the bedroom with a bag over his shoulder. "Not without me, you're not."

Katie's eyes swelled with tears. "You're coming with me? Oh, honey. Thank you so much. You have no idea how much this means to me."

"I know I was an ass last night. But I got to thinking and if this is what you need to do, then I'll be damned if I let you do it alone."

She wrapped her arms around him in relief. Any fear she had about her decision to come forward had all but disappeared. "I love you."

"I love you too, Katie, I swear I do. Come on now, we don't want to miss the flight."

The afternoon turned to evening when they arrived in Eureka. Rio Dell was south of the airport by about forty miles. Katie didn't tell her parents they were coming home because she knew they wouldn't want her to have the case reopened. It would be painful for them, probably more so than for her. She, after all, didn't have much memory of it.

They checked in at the hotel and arrived at their fifth-floor room. The old building left an odor in the room that mixed with the already muggy air. There were only a few hotels in Rio Dell and this one was probably the nicest.

"Do you want to do this now? There may not be anyone there who can help," Spencer said. "It's a small town."

"I know, but I'd like to try. I can at least find out who to speak with."

"All right, let's go and see what happens."

"Wait." Katie unzipped her bag and pulled out a manila envelope. "I'll need this."

"What's in there?"

"Press clippings from my abduction, some research I did back home, and contact information for Dr. Reyes."

"I haven't even seen that stuff," Spencer said.

"I know. I should have shared this with you, but I was afraid you wouldn't approve."

"Whether I approve or not doesn't matter. We don't keep secrets from each other, okay?"

Katie nodded as she picked up her purse.

THE POLICE STATION was considerably smaller than the San Diego station. Almost no one was in there other than a few officers typing away at their desks.

"Can I help you two?" One of the officers asked.

"Yes. Hi. I'm Katie Reid and this is my fiancé, Spencer Harris."

"Good evening. What can I do for you two folks on this lovely Saturday night?"

Katie pulled out her envelope and set it down on the raised front desk. She opened it up and pulled out the newspaper clippings about her abduction. The article on top read, *"Missing Girl Found on Side of Hwy 101."* She pointed to the headline. "This was me and I was wondering if anyone here might be familiar with this case?"

The officer looked at her and then to another officer sitting at his desk. He motioned his colleague to take a look.

"You're Katie Reid?" the second officer asked.

"Yes, sir."

"Ms. Reid, I'm Sergeant Reynolds. I know your parents."

"Hello Sergeant Reynolds, nice to meet you." Katie shook his hand.

"Would the two of you like to come back with me and have a seat?"

"Yes, thank you," Katie replied.

Sergeant Reynolds led them to a small room at the back of the station, next to a couple of empty holding cells. Inside was an old metal desk surrounded by folding chairs. A small round table with chairs in the corner was opposite the desk. The linoleum floor was well-worn and covered in black scuff marks; the place looked like it was in desperate need of updating.

"Please, sit down." The sergeant motioned to the chairs. Upon taking his seat, he reached out. "Can I see that?"

"Yes, of course," Katie replied.

"You know, I just saw your folks recently, actually. Your mother was handling a police charity event earlier this year; very nice people."

"Thank you. She does a lot of good work for the community, always has. So, sergeant, are you familiar with my case?" Katie wasn't up for small talk. It had already been a long day and she was anxious to discuss reopening her file.

"I'm familiar with it in the sense that we haven't had many child abduction cases here in our small town in the last 30 or so years, so when something like that happens, it's not easily forgotten. And yours was rare in that you returned home."

"Do you know who worked on my case originally? Does he still work for the department?"

"Yes, Chief Wilson was the lead detective in charge of your case at the time."

"Is he here? May I speak with him?"

"It's Saturday night, Ms. Reid. I'm afraid the chief is at home. What is it that you're inquiring about? I'm sure you didn't come all this way just to show us some old newspaper clippings."

"No, sergeant, I didn't. I came here because I believe I might have some information that would give cause to reopen my case."

The sergeant sat back in his chair and looked at Katie with great interest. "I see. Can you tell me what that might be?"

Katie looked at Spencer for reassurance. He nodded his permission. "Well, I don't know how much you know of my case, but I was only six and had no memory of the event. My parents swept it under the rug and had a difficult time coming to terms with what happened; they still do. But the reason I'm here is that over the past few months, I've been recalling small, random memories, mostly dreams that I couldn't make any sense of. I thought it was stress-related. And so it wasn't until I saw a therapist that more memories began to surface during my treatment and I was able to start connecting the dots. When I confronted my parents with this, they finally broke their silence and filled me in on the missing pieces."

"Let me get this straight. You had dreams, or what you thought were memories that a doctor helped you to uncover? And your parents then told you the truth?"

Katie could see Sergeant Reynolds was trying to figure out if all this was legitimate. It came to her as no surprise; repressed memories had often been discredited and for good reason. But this was different. If not for her parents' revelations, she would have believed the same. "I understand your skepticism, but the nightmares happened. I don't know how much of it was real, but I was kidnapped."

"I don't doubt the memories are real, Ms. Reid. Your case is well documented. What I doubt is what evidence you have to warrant reopening the investigation. Did you see your abductor in any of the dreams? Could you point him out if I showed you pictures?"

Katie resigned, feeling she was fighting a losing battle. "No. I don't know what the person looked like. I haven't been able to recollect that memory if there ever was one."

"So how can we reopen this case, Ms. Reid? What can you tell me that we don't already know?"

She squeezed Spencer's hand. "I have reason to believe that my case is related to the Arcata girl who went missing earlier that summer."

Sergeant Reynolds leaned over the desk. "Well, now you've got my interest. But before we go any further, I'm going to have to get the chief involved." He glanced at his watch. "How long are you in town for?"

"I'd like to head back tomorrow if I can."

"Well, you may be in for the long haul, if this checks out, Ms. Reid. But why don't we do this, it's getting late, the two of you look like you've had a long day, and I'm not too keen on dragging the chief down here tonight. He doesn't usually come in on the weekends, but I think I can convince him to hear you out. Can you two come back down here in the morning, say, around 9:00? I'll get the chief in and we'll go from there."

"Yes, sir. Thank you. We would be happy to come back in the morning."

"All right, then; I'll show you both out."

Sergeant Reynolds walked them back to the front of the station. "You go on and relax this evening. I'm sure it's been a busy day for you. Say 'hi' to your parents."

AFTER A RESTFUL NIGHT, Katie was ready to face the chief. She was prepared for whatever might happen, whether he decided to reopen her case or not. If not, she knew she was on her own and would continue without the help of the police. But the question remained as to whether Spencer would follow down that same path. He was there for her for the time being.

At the station, the same officer from yesterday was posted at the front desk.

"Good morning, Ms. Reid and Mr. Harris, was it?"

"Yes," Spencer said. "Good morning. We're here to see Chief Wilson."

"If you'll have a seat, I'll call the chief down."

Katie and Spencer sat down in the lobby chairs and he took her hand to calm her.

A man who appeared to be in his mid to late fifties approached them from around the corner. His salt and pepper hair, mostly salt, was on the verge of being a comb-over, trying to disguise the fact that it was slightly receding. He had a medium build and stood probably 5 feet 10. Katie found him to be fairly handsome, for an older gentleman.

"Katie Reid?" the chief asked.

"Yes, I'm Katie and this is my fiancé, Spencer."

"It's very nice to see you again, Ms. Reid."

Katie rose to meet the chief's extended hand.

"I don't believe I've seen you since you were about sixteen. I'm sure you don't remember that. It was only briefly when your mother was organizing an event for the lodge. Anyway, I understand you're here on a different matter?"

"Yes sir, I am."

"Please, call me 'Chief.' Everyone else does. Why don't you two follow me back to my office?"

They sat down in the chief's office. Katie struggled to get comfortable in her chair. The seat cushion was worn and the metal arms were bowed out too far for her to rest on.

"Sorry about the accommodations around here. We're a small town with an even smaller budget. We try to make do without asking the taxpayers to fork out more money for things like comfortable chairs."

"It's fine, sir. I don't mean to make a fuss. I was just trying to get my files out." Katie rifled around for the envelope.

"Of course, that's why we're here, isn't it? Sergeant Reynolds filled me in on your meeting yesterday. First of all, I want to say how sorry I am that you've had the misfortune of recalling some of the events of your abduction. I was in charge of your case. I had just been transferred a month before from Sacramento PD. After learning of the other abduction cases around Eureka, I wanted to be involved and there happened to be an opening here. I thought I could help, but it proved to be a highly complex case, as I'm sure you're now aware."

"Yes. I am now," Katie replied.

"Believe me, Ms. Reid. I worked day and night on your case. We thought for sure there was a connection to the other missing children, but we just couldn't get any solid evidence. The other kids, well, they weren't as lucky as you. When the family dropped you off in Trinidad, your parents were very protective of you, as you'd expect. I tried to press them on the importance of having the doctors work with you to help you recall what happened. Our only chance at making any real connection to the other cases was finding out what you knew. But I don't blame them, not one bit. If it were my kid, I would have done the same thing. So, we did what we could to find the man who abducted you. DNA testing was fairly new back then and CODIS, our DNA database system, wasn't around until the mid-1990s. We didn't have much to go on back in those days. Search parties scoured the area near where you were found. We tracked footprints, but it was a well-traversed area of the park and many of the prints were untraceable." The chief paused and looked Katie directly in the eyes. "I'm sorry, Katie. You probably don't want to hear how I failed to capture the man who took you."

"Chief, I'm sure you did everything you could. I'm not here to lay blame or imply you didn't do the best job possible with the resources that you had. I'm here to find him. I want to reopen this case."

So far, he seemed receptive, and she was grateful for that. It was a good sign, but would he remain so after the mention of the necklace? It wasn't DNA evidence, it wasn't much, but it was all she had.

"Okay, well, let's start by you telling me what you've got. Sergeant Reynolds mentioned something about you and the Arcata girl?" the chief said.

"I know it isn't much and may not even be useful at all," Katie started, already doubting her confidence.

"Before you dismiss it, just give it to me straight."

"Well, back home, I've been doing some research of my own. Since my parents told me that I wasn't crazy and that my dreams were in fact memories of the abduction, I wanted to find out more."

Chief Wilson nodded, casting occasional glances at Spencer.

"I looked up the other three missing children cases. I was able to pull up pictures of the kids who were taken. Now, it didn't occur to me right away, but about a week ago, I had another one of my therapy sessions."

"Hypnosis, right?" the chief asked.

"Yes; hypnotherapy was used to relieve what I believed at first to be stress. Anyway, I recalled being in a dark room, like a basement or something similar. I was blindfolded, but I removed it when I was alone. Across the room, I saw light reflecting off an object. When I walked over to see what it was, I found a heart-shaped pendant necklace. I was brought back out of the hypnotic state and didn't realize the significance of the necklace at the time. In fact, it wasn't until several days later when I was reading a book on cold cases that it hit me. The school picture I saw of the girl from Arcata showed her wearing a heart-shaped pendant necklace."

No one spoke and the chief only stared out his office window in silence. Katie and Spencer exchanged looks, uncertain of how he would respond.

Finally, he spoke. "Mr. Harris, you're an attorney, is that correct?"

"Yes sir, I am."

"Would you consider what Katie has told me here to be admissible in court?"

"Repressed memories are generally not admissible as evidence in court unless other physical evidence or other testimonies were concurrent. The difference here, I believe, is that her abduction was an active case. She escaped and was discovered by the side of the highway. That much is fact. What Katie is aiming to do here is discover, through her recalled memories, any new evidence that is relevant to solving the case. If she can establish a connection to the other cases, that may be enough to reopen the investigation. Whether or not it will result in the capture of her abductor remains to be seen. But the fact of the matter is, she is the only known surviving victim and if the victim can remember details not previously known, I'd say that would make for legitimate evidence."

The chief, once again, sat in silence. Katie's pulse raced as she waited for him to continue.

"Katie, did your parents tell you anything more about the abduction?" the chief asked.

"I'm sorry, but I'm not sure what you mean?"

"Let me sit on this for a few days." He leaned back in his chair. "If I decide to reopen the case, it will take an extensive amount of resources I'm not sure this department can afford. Not to mention, what it would do to the families of the other victims, if, in fact, we were able to determine a connection. We'd have to keep it local to start until we could find out more. No media, no tweeting, or Facebooking or anything like that from either of you, is that clear?"

"Of course. I'm not looking for anyone to find out about this," Katie replied.

"Well, just so you're prepared, if we open this thing up and it involves those other kids, the media will be all over you, your parents, Spencer, everyone. You will be under intense scrutiny and so will your therapist. I suggest you go see your parents, tell them what you're considering, if you haven't already, and ask them to tell you everything they know and I mean everything. You need to know what you'll be getting yourself into."

The chief stood, hiking up his trousers. "Leave your contact information with the officer at the front desk. I'll be in touch once I've had a chance to get my head around this."

Spencer helped Katie out of her chair and they followed the chief back to the lobby.

Chief Wilson turned back to Katie. "I would love nothing more than to find the person responsible for taking you from your family, please know that. But this has to be done by the book and I need to make sure we can handle everything that will be hurled in our direction."

"Thank you, Chief. I sincerely appreciate what you're doing for me."

"It won't be just for you, Katie; it'll be for all the victims and for me."

Spencer and Katie walked through the parking lot and returned to their car. They were both quiet, stunned by the sudden reality of the situation.

"Am I doing the right thing, Spencer?" Katie's eyes welled with tears.

Spencer reached over the console and took her hand. "I had no idea the impact this has had on you, Katie. I've been in denial all this time and I'm so sorry. Hearing the chief go on about your case and everything they put into it has just put it all in perspective for me. But I think we need to see your parents before you decide to move forward. Something the chief alluded to makes me think they might not have told you the whole story."

"Okay, you're right." Katie wiped the tears that had spilled onto her cheeks. "Let's go see them."

THE GRAVEL DRIVE CRUNCHED beneath the tires of their rental car as they pulled up to her parents' home.

"We'll have to push our flight back and catch one later tonight," Katie said.

"That's fine. This is more important. We'll make it back in time for work tomorrow, even if we have to catch a red-eye. Let's get this over with." Spencer yanked the keys from the ignition and stepped out of the car. He hadn't been to Katie's family home in probably three years.

Katie could see he was nervous. She had made certain that he hadn't gotten to know them very well. How stupid all of that was, she thought, and how regrettable to have lost so much time trying to distance herself from them. If only they'd told her years before, when she was old enough to have understood, maybe their relationship wouldn't be so strained. But what more could they have glossed over? What else could they be hiding?

Deborah opened the door. "Oh my word, what are the two of you doing here? What a wonderful surprise. Please, come in. Your father's in his study. I'll go get him."

Spencer and Katie sat down on the couch in the family room when Deborah and John entered. Spencer immediately stood up, wiped his hand on his jeans, and shook John's hand. "Nice to see you again, sir; it's been a long time."

"Yes, it has, son." John went in for the fatherly hug and Spencer responded in kind. "So, what brings you two into town?"

"Mom, Dad, I need to talk to you about something. Can you both sit down?"

An unsettling tension seemed to hover in the air.

"Can I get anyone a coffee or tea?" Deborah asked.

"No thanks, Mom. We're fine."

Deborah placed her hands on her lap as she sat perched on the edge of the side chair.

"Okay well, I'll start." Katie was barely able to disguise the anxiety in her tone. "We flew in yesterday evening to speak with the police."

"Oh?" Deborah interjected.

"Mom, please, just let me get this out." Katie took a breath and continued. "We wanted to talk to them about reopening my case." She squeezed Spencer's hand tightly in anticipation of their reply.

John's face lost all expression and turned white, while Deborah clasped her hand over her mouth.

"I told you about seeing a therapist to help me with some of the memories I've been recalling and was, of course, the reason why I was here to see you last month. Well, something new and possibly significant was discovered in one of my sessions. We don't know if it's important yet, that's what we're waiting for the chief to decide. But, in the process of discussing this with him, he asked that we speak to you both first. He wanted to be sure that I was aware of everything before we went any further. Can you explain what he might have been referring to?"

"Other than the fact that we took you to the hospital after we got you from the station because of injuries, what else is there to know?" John's back was stick straight, appearing as though he was hiding something.

Deborah turned to her husband, her face, pale, drained of all blood. She looked back at Katie. "You want to know what happened at the hospital?"

"If you think it's important, then yes."

"Deborah," John pleaded.

"She has the right to know. I don't want to keep secrets anymore. This has done enough damage to our family."

John closed his eyes tightly as Deborah continued. "Kate, honey, we took you to Trinidad Hospital. It was near their police station, where the family brought you. You were covered in bruises and had a huge knot on your head. They assumed you had fallen and hit a rock or a tree stump. Your bare feet were dirty and bloody. The first thing the doctors did was to take you to x-ray and make sure that lump was nothing more serious. Then they examined your external bruises and that's when they asked you your name. Luckily, you remembered that much." Deborah swallowed hard. "When I saw my little girl, bruised and bloody, well I'm sure you can imagine it wasn't easy. Your father wanted to squeeze you so tight, but he couldn't. We didn't know the extent of your injuries. We were just so grateful that you were alive. The doctors got us up to speed on the tests they'd run to that point. That's when we knew you couldn't remember what had happened. Then, they suggested we allow them to check you for assault."

"Sexual assault?" Katie asked. Spencer tensed up at the suggestion. This was just as hard on him, she could see that now.

"Yes, honey," John replied. "You see, the problem was that at the time, we didn't know for sure if you had been abducted or just wandered off the school grounds and got lost. We believed it was the former, but if that was the case, we needed to know if you had been abused while you were held captive. And it would give us a definitive answer as to what had happened."

Deborah continued on behalf of her husband. "We allowed them to examine you while I was in the room." She reached over to hold John's hand. "It was too much for your father, so he waited in the hall." Her lips began to quiver and her voice cracked. "They examined you while I held your hand and stroked your hair. You were so quiet; you didn't cry. You just looked at me while I sang your favorite song." Deborah could no longer hold back her tears.

Katie knew what her mother would say next, but couldn't bear to listen to the words. A lump rose in her throat as she realized the true horror of what happened to her. And then that sadness turned to anger. She looked toward Spencer. He knew and she could see it in his eyes. Not only had this monster taken her from her family, but he had taken *her*.

Deborah closed her eyes, forcing the tears to stream down her cheeks. Katie cried and moved to embrace her mother.

"That's what Chief Wilson wanted you to know," Spencer said quietly.

"I just couldn't tell you before, Katie. It was already so much for you to take in, I couldn't add on to it. I had no idea you wanted to pursue this. I just thought you wanted to understand why you were having those dreams. I thought you had already been through enough."

Katie grabbed a tissue from the side table. "It's okay, Mom. I understand; I do. I don't think I would have wanted to know otherwise. But now that I do, I can decide if I'm ready to be exposed to everything this man did to me. I suppose I was lucky enough not to remember it, but now I'll have to relive it if I want justice."

"Katie, it's getting late. Should I call and change the flight?" Spencer didn't seem to want to interrupt, but the question had to be asked.

"Oh no, please don't go; not yet," Deborah started. "You both could use a good home-cooked meal. Let me make something for you. I'd like you to stay and talk for a while."

"Okay, Mom. We can stay for a while longer. Spencer, will you call the airline and get us on the late flight?"

"Of course."

Deborah made dinner while Katie and Spencer talked with her father. She felt numb at this latest news. But somehow, she had suspected this was the case. It was only by the grace of God she had no memory of the assault. Still, this latest blow didn't sway her from wanting to pursue him. In fact, it only served to provide her with greater determination.

As they sat at dinner, the conversation was about anything else but what had just been revealed. Katie felt herself begin to harden; any trace of innocence of the ways of the world that remained had been wiped away. The idealistic girl that Spencer had fallen in love with was gone.

9

Three hours of sleep after the long red-eye flight back home, the alarm clock sounded. 6 a.m. Katie wasn't the only one to mourn the early hour. Spencer seemed to suffer from exhaustion as well, groaning as he struggled to find consciousness.

So much had been brought to light in the past twenty-four hours and Katie had yet to process it fully. Now, Monday morning had arrived and they would be forced to see to their respective jobs.

A quick coffee and pastry to go and Katie was out the door. On her way to the office, she knew none of what they'd discussed with Chief Wilson could be shared. Although there was one person in whom she'd hoped to confide. Detective Avery could offer guidance, but how much to disclose to him remained to be seen. Katie felt guarded now as if she'd been violated simply by the revelation of what the monster had done so long ago.

She slipped into the office, carefully avoiding conversation with any of her colleagues. Her desk was clean, organized in a manner verging on compulsive. She turned toward the window and pulled open the blinds, allowing the light to bathe the room in its warm radiance. It was only the sound of her ringing cell phone that forced her to turn away from the comforting glow. "Good morning, Marshall. How are you?"

"Great thanks. Listen, there was a development on the Thompson case over the weekend. You remember meeting Johansen?" The detective's note of urgency came through loud and clear.

"Of course, how could I forget?"

"The team found his truck and got a warrant to search his house. Just about everything in the guy's place has been transferred to the warehouse for entry into the system. I was thinking you might like to come with me and take a look at the truck and some of the other evidence."

A sudden rush of excitement replaced her earlier apprehension at what the day would bring. "Did you clear this with Susan? I'd love to go, but not without her approval."

"She said anything we needed, we could count on you guys to help us out with. I need help processing the paperwork on all this evidence. Now, do you want in or not?"

"Yes, definitely. I'll let her know and I can meet you down at the station in thirty minutes."

"Great, see you then."

The request was unusual. Katie had no experience in this type of work, but what she wouldn't give to see an investigation in action. She'd have to spin it carefully.

"Susan?" Katie peeked into her office.

"Good morning. What can I do for you?"

"I just got a call from Detective Avery. I guess some new evidence came in over the weekend and he was asking if I could come down to the station to catalog it. He says they're shorthanded and could use some administrative help."

"I wonder why he didn't call me first." Susan seemed mildly offended by the circumvention. "That should be fine. This case is our top priority, so whatever we can do to help. All right, I'll see you later on today, then?"

"I'm sure I'll be finished by this afternoon, but please let me know if you need me sooner."

"No, that's fine, Katie. Go on. I'll let the detective know I gave you authorization."

Katie was more than pleased and quickly disappeared back to her office to gather her things. The day was unfolding better than expected.

DETECTIVE AVERY ARRIVED in the lobby of the station where Katie waited patiently. "Kate, glad to see you. Follow me; we've got a lot of work to do today."

She followed Marshall back to a large storage area that held boxes and boxes of what she assumed to be evidence. "Oh my God, is this all from Johansen's house?"

"No, no. This is where we keep evidence for several pending cases. See the labels on these boxes? They have different file numbers. The ones we're looking at today are over here." He continued down through the warehouse, where she spotted the white truck and several other items laid out on a table in bags, labeled Case No. 13-619030.

"Is Johansen under arrest?" Katie asked.

"Yes ma'am, he is. After you left on Friday, I checked with the Sex Offender Tracking Division. They notify local authorities when an offender has registered a change of address or other pertinent information. He was no longer required to be under the supervision of a parole officer, but he is and will always be required to notify the Division of any change that occurs, employment, residence, anything. Mr. Johansen did not inform the division of his change in address and, in his case, because he was convicted of felony sex abuse, not notifying the department is also a felony. That gave me and the Department of Justice the right to arrest him."

Katie was reeling at Marshall's enthusiastic pace. This was the break he had been looking for. "But why didn't this come up during the initial interview?"

"That's a very good question. At the time, we had no idea someone knew there had been a white truck parked on Isabelle's street for two days. No one came forward until the call on the hotline last week. When our officers conducted their initial five-mile sweep of the area, Johansen was questioned. It wasn't known that he was a sex offender because that address, according to the Tracking Division, wasn't registered to him. The officer who spoke with him asked if he was Mr. Hollinger, who was previously at that address. Of course, Johansen agreed. Where he screwed up was that he changed his address with DMV to get his car tags. It wasn't until we ran a DMV check that his name came up as one of the six people who had that type of vehicle. DMV also alerted us to the fact that he was a registered offender. They keep that information as well. They're supposed to send monthly updates of any changes to the Tracking Division. It just so happened that the report hadn't yet been sent. You'd be surprised how often we lose track of registered offenders. It's not a perfect system, that's for sure."

"Was there any evidence in his house that might have belonged to Isabelle then?" Katie asked as she tried to keep up with him.

"We don't know yet. That's where you come in. I need your help cataloging the evidence in these bags. We have civilian staff who assist in this type of admin work, but they're completely swamped right now. Forensics is already running prints and DNA, but there could be something else here that might lead us to Isabelle. Time is of the essence."

"Okay, I'm ready. Just show me where to start." The excitement about a break in the case was rubbing off on Katie. She wanted to find Isabelle, now more than ever.

Marshall proceeded to guide her through the process. "You are only to enter the numbers onto the forms. Do not handle anything inside the bags, understand? I need to get back and check on the lab. If you have any questions, just ask Officer Reilly."

"Got it."

Officer Reilly was the man in charge of everything that came into and out of that warehouse. He, along with a few others, appeared to have their hands full but had been instructed to monitor her progress closely.

"Great. I'll check in with you later. This will be extremely helpful in expediting our review of the evidence, Kate. Thank you."

Katie worked diligently throughout the morning. Her hands were cramping as she wrote everything down on the forms. This information would then be entered into their database. She thought they could have skipped a step and just entered it directly into the computer. Maybe she'd make the suggestion to Marshall later, but right now, she would do as directed and was glad to have been given the chance to help.

So far, she hadn't found anything particularly interesting. Most of these items were random things that could be found around most people's homes. Receipts, utility bills, a few DVDs. Then she came across a radio-controlled car, not a sophisticated replica like some hobbyists keep. No, this was a child's toy. Katie was repulsed by the idea that he might have used this toy possibly to lure a young child and wondered how he would have convinced Isabelle to go with him. In her mind, she had already condemned Johansen. It would prove difficult to stay impartial on a case like this. Marshall must have figured as much.

No sooner had his name crossed her mind did he arrive back at the warehouse.

"How's it going?" He examined the table, nodding in approval. "Looks like you've made good progress. Why don't we get some food in you?"

They walked outside, leaving the police station, and headed toward a taco stand around the corner.

"These guys make *the* best tacos anywhere."

"You don't take much time to eat do you?" Katie asked. She was beginning to get a glimpse into the life of a cop.

"What do you mean? You want to go to a restaurant or something? I like restaurants."

Katie laughed. "No, no, this is fine, really. I'm starving and there's too much to do anyway to sit around in a restaurant."

"Well geez, now you're making me feel bad, like I'm some kind of slave driver."

"Not at all, Marshall. In fact, I want to thank you for letting me help you with this case. I can't tell you what it means to me. You've already taught me a lot."

They sat down on a bench opposite the stand.

"Wow, these are good tacos," Katie said.

"See? I told you." He smiled, pausing for a moment to take another mouthful. "Listen, Kate. I really do appreciate all your hard work. You have a knack for this sort of thing. Maybe someday I'll convince you to come over to my side of the fence."

"I appreciate the vote of confidence, but I've got some pretty major things going on in my life right now. I honestly have no idea what direction I'll be headed."

"So you decided to pursue reopening the investigation?" Marshall seemed to turn serious.

Katie had wanted to tell him, but he'd been consumed with Johansen and she just didn't know how to bring it up, but it seemed he had just opened the door for her. "I flew home over the weekend and talked to the Chief of Police in Rio Dell. He was the detective on my case. I asked him to consider reopening the investigation based on what we discussed last week, you know, the necklace?"

"And is he going to?"

"He's looking into it. Says it will take up a lot of his resources and he needs to be sure what I've given him is enough."

"That makes sense. Are you sure that's what you want?"

"Yes, I'm sure." Revealing the reason behind her assurance wasn't an option. No one could know what happened to her, what he had done to her. Katie didn't want pity. "My main concern is of the impact this will have on my fiancé and my family, and everyone else who will get caught up in it too."

"You want to find him, don't you?"

Here was someone who understood her. Someone who knew what it meant, this need for justice. "He ruined my family, my parents' lives."

"You think he ruined you too, don't you?"

"He did, Marshall. I'm not sure I would be okay with knowing he'll never have to pay for what he did."

"A lot of people have to learn to be *okay* with the terrible things that have happened to them. Too many bad people get away with their crimes, but you can't prosper in life if you're living out some sort of vendetta. Listen, I understand what you're going through. Believe me, I've worked with enough victims to be able to empathize. We catch the ones we can and try to help the ones whose offenders go unpunished. Ultimately, it will be up to you to decide how you'll best be able to move forward."

"Thank you, Marshall. I suppose we ought to be getting back now. I think I still have a few hundred items to log."

"I'll give you a hand. I've done everything I could do today, it's up to forensics now. The important thing is that Johansen is off the streets. You know, I can help with the other stuff too, Kate. Just ask, got it?"

Her thin smile conveyed her appreciation but she knew this was on her now.

Detective Avery had to pull a few strings but managed to get Susan to agree to let Katie continue her work at the station for the remainder of the week. The sheer volume of evidence required close attention to detail and this was exactly up Katie's alley. And this work helped her keep her mind off the fact that she still hadn't heard from Chief Wilson about reopening her case.

They weren't any closer to charging Johansen with kidnapping either. Forensics hadn't finished analyzing the fingerprints, fiber samples, or sweeping the truck. Marshall was right; cases were never so neatly packaged that they could be solved in as short amount of time as the crime shows on TV were.

At the end of the week, all the evidence had been processed. Boxes and boxes of items were stacked in a corner of the warehouse, ready to be filed away on the shelves that ran along the walls and down the center of the storage facility.

"You're interested in learning about this stuff? Come on, let's take a walk down these aisles and I'll show you what we deal with," Marshall said.

Katie followed him as he led her down a row filled with boxes similar to the ones she had just cataloged.

"You see this one?" Marshall pointed to a box that appeared to have yellowed with age. "Case number 04-245195, a homicide from 2004, unsolved. These boxes will sit here until the case is closed because there is no statute of limitations on murder. Now, if you've got a good investigating officer, he'll ensure the destruction of evidence once a case has reached its statute, like a burglary. Here in California, kidnapping, arson, and even embezzlement have no statute either, which is why our storage rooms are bursting at the seams."

They continued down toward the back of the warehouse. Katie was fascinated by the inner workings of the department and willingly listened.

"DNA evidence is something altogether different; it's handled very carefully and kept indefinitely or at least until the convicted inmate has exhausted all appeals and then sometimes even after that. You see why the Rio Dell chief is carefully considering his options right now as it relates to your case? He's right to be concerned about resources. It would take an officer years to identify and clear out old evidence. You're asking him to go back and pull case files that God knows where they ended up, if they are even legible at this point, and to reopen an investigation based on some dreams or memories you had."

Katie began to reconsider whether or not Detective Avery was really her advocate. He was certainly doing his best to discourage her at the moment. "Don't you think it's worth some time and money to capture a murderer?" Her defenses were high and she realized that probably came out a little harsher than she had intended.

"I'm only trying to point out the complexity of the situation, Kate. You need to be fully aware of what you're asking of the chief and yourself. You dig into this further and you could risk everything you've worked for. Trust me on this, I know how obsessions begin and how they usually end."

His reality check hit her hard and she had no further line of defense.

"Looks like you can go back to your office on Monday. I'm sure you're tired of being stuck in this place anyway." Marshall seemed to sense her growing antipathy and changed the subject.

"Actually, I have really learned a lot this week and I appreciate you giving me a chance to see how things work on this side. I mean that. And, well, I get your meaning, too."

Marshall brushed it off and put his arm around her shoulder in a big brother sort of way. "So, are you ready to come work for me, then?"

Katie couldn't tell if he was serious or not, but after everything she had learned this week, admittedly, the idea was intriguing. "Sure; you just need to convince Susan to let me go. They've been short-handed for so long, I'm not sure she's going to give up the help willingly."

"You never know. How about we go and grab a drink? I think we've earned it."

"Okay, why not?" Katie reached for her cell phone. "I just need to let Spencer know I'll be home late. I'm sure he's busy working on his case anyway. He's due to go to trial next week." When she looked at her phone, there had been three missed calls and two messages. Two were from Spencer and one was from area code 707. "That's a call from back home. It must be from Chief Wilson."

They both stopped in their tracks while Katie listened to the message.

"Katie, this is Chief Wilson with Rio Dell PD. I'm sorry it's taken me so long to get back to you, but I had to get several people involved with the issue we discussed last week, including the Humboldt District Attorney's office. After reviewing your case files and the information I received from you, it has been decided that there is not enough for us to go on and we cannot reopen the investigation. I am truly sorry, Katie, but if you need anything from me, I am glad to help out where I can. And, if at any time you can provide further details into the case, please let me know and we will re-evaluate your request. Goodbye, Ms. Reid, and I wish you the best of luck."

Katie felt completely deflated; her heart sank at the news.

"What is it?" Marshall asked.

Her voice trembled as she struggled to keep it together. "They're not going to reopen the investigation."

"Did he say why?"

She looked up at him. "They said I didn't have enough for them to go on."

"I am sorry, Kate. Listen, I'm sure you'd like to go home and discuss this with your fiancé. I'll buy you a beer another time."

"No." She continued walking. "I could use one now. I can't handle talking to Spencer about it now because, to be honest, he'll be more than happy they're going to let this thing go, but I need some time to process it. I'll send him a text and tell him about it later tonight."

"Okay. I'll take you down to Paddy's. It's as good a place as any to forget your troubles."

~

PADDY'S WAS a hole-in-the-wall Irish pub that many on the police force frequented. It was near the station; quick and easy to get to.

"I'll have a bourbon and whatever the lady wants." Marshall gestured to Katie.

"Make that two, please," she replied.

The bartender grabbed the bottle and placed two shot glasses in front of them.

"I didn't realize you were a bourbon-drinking kind of girl, Kate."

"I am tonight." She downed her shot without hesitation.

Marshall appeared more than a little surprised by this. "Okay, well, maybe you should reel it in a little and tell me what happened with the police chief. What exactly did he say? Why the no-go on the investigation?"

"The DA said they didn't have enough new evidence to open it back up."

"So, they didn't think they could link the cases based on that necklace you saw in your dream?" Marshall threw back his shot and motioned to the bartender for two more.

"It wasn't a dream. It happened. I remembered it." Katie closed her eyes, knowing she was jumping down his throat for no reason. He wasn't the enemy here. "I'm sorry. It wasn't much, I know, but I thought it might be enough." Katie paused as the bartender placed another shot in front of them. "It was the same necklace I had seen in a picture of a victim from another kidnapping. She was from Arcata and disappeared around the same time as I did."

"Yeah, I'm familiar with the other cases. I, um, saw them mentioned in your file."

She figured he already knew and didn't fault him for it. "It's okay. I know you were trying to help. Anyway, I told the chief that maybe that was enough to establish a link between the cases and they could open it up based on that."

"I'm sure you don't want to hear this, but I think the chief was right. The problem with that, Kate, is that you saw the necklace first and then recalled a memory in which the necklace appeared."

Marshall swallowed the second shot and continued. "That's a tough one. If you had remembered it first and then saw the same one on the little girl, you might have had something, albeit still pretty thin, in terms of real evidence to link the two. It would be all too easy for anyone to discredit that because of the fact it was in a memory recalled some twenty years later. I can see why the DA doesn't really want to open that can of worms."

Katie was disheartened by the way he laid out the facts. It wasn't right and it wasn't fair. She was the victim here. "What do I have to do then?" The desperation in her voice was too difficult to hide. "You have no idea how many nights I've had these horrible dreams, remembering what happened. I wish to God that I hadn't remembered any of it. I just want to get back to my old self. That's what Spencer wants too; I know it. He wants to marry the sweet girl he met in college; the idealistic one who takes everything at face value. This person you see in front of you now? He doesn't want her. She's broken."

"Kate, come on. I'm sure he doesn't see you that way. Give the guy a break. He probably feels helpless about the whole thing. I know I would."

Katie didn't usually drink hard liquor, but she was grateful that the shots had begun to calm her nerves.

"Look, when this investigation is over, I'll do some digging around without getting deep enough to be noticed. I have a few contacts here and there," Marshall said.

Katie's eyes lit up at the idea that he was on her side once again.

"Just think about what I said earlier. You can't change what happened and you'll have to come to terms with it if you want to be happy in your life with Spencer."

Marshall's contradictory advice only served to confuse her even more. He offered help but then suggested just moving on. She didn't know what to believe or why he seemed conflicted about the situation himself.

"It sounds like you speak from experience," Katie replied.

"Maybe I do." He tossed back yet another shot.

On her arrival home, a sober Katie opened the door of her apartment and inside Spencer waited.

"How was your day?" His words came without his eyes ever leaving the television screen.

Katie leaned over the couch to kiss him, his irritation with her was impossible to ignore.

"You taste like whiskey. That isn't usually your kind of drink."

"Yeah, well, it was a whiskey kind of day." She dropped her purse on the kitchen counter.

"I could tell by your text. You and Detective Avery have a nice time?"

A not-so-vague accusation to be sure and in her present state of mind, she considered it unacceptable. "Really? Do you think something is going on between us?"

"No, I don't. I'm sorry. I'm just not used to abrupt text messages saying you'll see me later without any explanation."

"Spencer. I'm the one who's sorry." Katie joined him on the couch. "As I was about to leave for the day, I checked my phone and saw a message from Chief Wilson. He told me they decided not to reopen the case. And then I figured you'd be working late and Marshall asked if he could buy me a beer because I helped him out all week." Defeated, Katie continued. "I guess I figured I could use a drink after hearing Wilson's message."

"Katie, I had no idea." Spencer embraced her and she relaxed in his arms. "So, what does that mean for us?"

She knew what he wanted to hear, but didn't want to be coerced into saying it. "I don't know," she pulled away from the embrace. "It means things will go along as usual, I suppose. Isn't that what you wanted? Good ol' fun-loving Katie, eager to marry her lawyer-boyfriend?"

"Look, I know you're upset right now, so why don't we just calm down."

"Come on, Spencer. Don't pretend this isn't exactly how you wanted it to play out. You wanted the whole thing to disappear so the number one priority in my life would be to plan our perfect little wedding."

"Kate, don't do this."

"Do what? Be honest?" She walked into the kitchen and grabbed a bottle of wine.

"Feel like another drink, do you?" Spencer asked. If he wasn't trying to pick a fight before, he most certainly was now.

"As a matter of fact, I do. I didn't think that would be a problem for you. Not like, say, your other problems. Imagine, having a girl-friend who found out she had been held captive and violated when she was just a child." She poured herself a generous glass of wine. "You know this case I've been working on? Well, they think they know who did it, a pedophile. The guy lived five blocks down from the victim and had already been in prison for assaulting other children. The sad thing about this case? They can't prove it yet. They can't find the girl and they have no physical evidence. He's under arrest for something as minor as not registering a change of address because he's a sex offender. If they don't find her, or can't get the proof they need, he'll serve some time for the registration offense and then go scot-free. Scot-free, just like the bastard who took me and probably killed those other kids too."

"Okay, Katie, that's enough." Spencer took the wine from her and grabbed hold of her again, this time, she couldn't wrangle out of his grip.

She finally let go. Everything that had been building up inside her spilled over, the anger she felt toward her parents for lying, anger with the man who took her, and now anger at the police who won't help her find him. The weight of her entire body was in Spencer's arms now and he wasn't letting go.

∼

Katie woke up Saturday morning with a dry mouth and a pounding head. She and Spencer had been up most of the night talking about everything. It was exactly what they both needed.

Today, she would refocus her energies on the positive things in her life. Detective Avery was right; she would have to decide to live her life or become paralyzed by the events of her past.

"Good morning, sweetie." Spencer rolled over to find Katie sitting at the edge of their bed, gulping down water and some aspirin. "You feeling all right?"

"Yeah, just a little headache." She didn't want to tell him her head felt like it was about to explode. It must have been the bourbon.

Katie slogged into the living room and turned on the TV. The news rambled on in the background while she made the coffee. It wasn't until she heard the words, "Isabelle Thompson" that she rushed back in and stood in front of the screen.

"Police arrived just after dawn this morning at the Miramar landfill after a worker notified his supervisor that he had spotted human remains just before his earthmoving equipment was to begin working the area. The unidentified body is thought to be that of missing eight-year-old, Isabelle Thompson. The little girl disappeared last month after she failed to arrive at school on the morning of April 10th. Her mother has not yet been cleared in the investigation, however, she and the other family members maintain her innocence in the disappearance of Isabelle. Community volunteers and police have been scouring the surrounding neighborhoods for any clues as to her whereabouts. There is an ongoing investigation of a suspect already in custody on another charge, but police are reluctant to release any further details pending positive identification."

Katie listened, hoping for more on the story, but that was all, a three-minute blip for this little girl who had been taken and was now presumed dead.

Spencer walked into the room. "What are you doing?" he asked as she stood motionless.

"They found her."

"They found who?"

"Isabelle. They found her in a landfill. It was just on the news."

"Oh my God. I'm so sorry, honey." He put his arm around her. "That poor little girl. They're sure it's her?"

"Not yet. They haven't identified the remains."

"Well, maybe it's not."

"Spencer, it's her. I know it is. The police know it is, they just won't say anything until they know for sure."

"Oh babe, that's why I was so concerned about you working on this type of case. Unfortunately, this is how they usually turn out. You have to be able to stay emotionally detached or it will eat you alive."

Katie stepped away from him and headed toward their bedroom.

"Where are you going?"

"I need to go for a walk or something. I just need to be alone for a while."

"Katie, please. I know this is devastating for you, but you can't let it get to you. You've been through enough and don't need to carry this burden as well. Let's go somewhere together. Somewhere that will take your mind off of it. Maybe we can go cake tasting or something. We haven't picked out our cake yet."

She whipped around, looking at him as if he had just lost his mind. "Cake tasting? A little girl, whose case I've been working on, has just been found dead and you want to go cake tasting?"

"Jesus! Yes, Okay? I want us to do something normal, something that doesn't involve thinking about child molesters and murderers. You think I don't get enough of that in my own work? For God's sake, I want us to have fun and be happy, you know, like we talked about last night? Have you forgotten about everything we discussed?"

"No, I haven't. I just need an hour to myself, please. Just to clear my head, okay? I know I can't let this stuff get to me like this, I just need to figure out a way to handle it and right now, being alone for a while will help. Then, when I get back, we can go and do whatever you want, I swear."

He said nothing more, just gave her a nod, and continued into the kitchen.

This was not how she expected the day to begin. It was as if nothing they said last night made any difference at all.

She threw on sweatpants and a t-shirt, grabbed her keys and phone, and headed toward the front door. "I'll be back in a little while." Katie left without waiting for a response.

Their apartment was a few blocks from a park and that was where she was headed. On arrival, the workers at the park were preparing for the Memorial Day celebrations. With everything that had been happening, she hadn't realized the parade was tomorrow.

A bench under the shade tree seemed the perfect spot. She watched the children play on the playground. They were innocent and beautiful and she just couldn't stomach the thought that Isabelle was in that landfill. She wanted to call Marshall. Of course, he was probably one of the first ones to go out there. It was his case, after all, and he was bound to be knee-deep in it right now.

The sun began poking through the morning mist. The park soon filled with parents setting up for their children's birthday parties and the smell of barbeque floated by, making Katie's mouth water. How long had she been here? It must be nearing lunchtime.

The shock of this latest development in Isabelle's case was beginning to sink in. It was time to bring the girl's murderer to justice and she would continue her work with Marshall as long as he needed her. However, making amends with Spencer was what she needed to do now.

When she returned to the apartment, he was exactly where she left him. Katie sat beside him and held his hand. "So, you feel like picking out our cake?"

Spencer's weary smile gave her pause. She'd not seen him look at her in that manner before.

"I'm exhausted, Katie," he began. "I feel like an insensitive ass when I say anything to you about our wedding like I should be ashamed of myself for speaking of such things when you're going through something I can't even hope to comprehend. Now, you're working with the police on missing persons cases? Since when did that stuff even interest you?" He rubbed his forehead. "I don't know what's happening here, but it scares the hell out of me. I'm afraid to help you, afraid not to help you. Christ, I don't know which way is up anymore."

She'd already felt terrible for lashing out at him earlier. Clearly, he'd been hurt by it. "I know you don't and it's my fault. I'm so damned confused myself, I don't know what direction I'm headed either. I wanted to work with the police so I could learn about investigations, leads...that sort of stuff. I thought that maybe it would help me find him. Spencer, I wish I could make you understand what this feels like for me. I'm just so frustrated by my own lack of understanding. But please, just hang in there with me a little while longer; I promise, this won't last forever. I will resolve it somehow."

"Let's figure this out together then, okay? I mean it." Spencer replied.

"Okay."

KATIE SAT QUIETLY at her desk, the long weekend having passed by while she remained uncertain of the future, unsure of what to do next. Now, there were no messages from Marshall, no emails; nothing to indicate that he needed her help in any way.

Her office line buzzed and Susan's voice emerged. "Katie, can you come to my office, please?"

"I'll be right there." A moment later, she stood outside Susan's door. "Good morning. You wanted to see me?"

"Well, I'm not sure how good it is, but come on in and take a seat. I'm sure you heard the news over the weekend."

Katie nodded.

"We'll need to turn over all the files and notes you've taken on the Thompson case. The police and the DA are going to need everything we've got. From what I gather, forensics on the body should be completed tomorrow and they'll have a positive identity. Once they have that, we're going to help Isabelle's school provide counseling services through our Crisis Center. I'll let you coordinate those efforts. In the meantime, let's go ahead and copy the files to flash drives. They'll want paper copies as well."

Katie, believing she was being dismissed, stood up to leave.

"One more thing, Katie; you were working pretty closely with Detective Avery on this. There's no shame in talking to someone if you need to. It's never easy when it ends this way, but the first time is always the toughest."

"Thank you, Susan. I'll keep it in mind."

The next few hours were spent compiling the data, copying emails, and gathering various other correspondences. The unsettled feeling, as though she was already burying Isabelle, wouldn't go away.

"Hi, Kate."

She glanced up from her computer screen to find Detective Avery standing in her doorway.

"Marshall? Please, come in."

"It's been all over the news, so I'm sure you heard." His question elicited merely a nod of acknowledgment. "We've been able to positively identify her. It's Isabelle. We won't release it to the press until tomorrow after we've had a chance to talk to the family."

Katie swallowed hard, not wanting her weakness to show through. It was what everyone suspected, but knowing for certain made it all the more difficult.

"The only good thing about this is that we'll be able to get DNA evidence from the body. Forensics hasn't had much luck with Johansen's home or vehicle. Some tests are still pending, but DNA will put an end to any question of his culpability."

"How much time will he serve?" she asked.

"Hopefully, it'll be the death penalty." He turned to leave.

"Marshall, wait. Will you help me find him? I–I just can't let it go; not after this." She didn't elaborate any further, knowing he would understand her meaning.

"It won't be easy, Kate. We have virtually nothing to go on but your memory."

"I understand, but I have to at least try. I know if Chief Wilson can help, even if it's off the record, he will. He's a lot like you, I think, determined to find the truth."

"I'll do what I can." Detective Avery walked away.

10

It **had been** two weeks since she'd asked Marshall to help with her case. He had access to databases, like CODIS and the National DNA database system. They were meeting for lunch today so he could fill Katie in on his progress. This wasn't official police business, in fact, he had no authority whatsoever to work on a cold case in Humboldt County. They both knew what was at stake if it got out that he was involved. Nevertheless, Marshall kept his promise to help Katie and she knew he wouldn't let her down.

She arrived at the restaurant and found Marshall already seated. It would be the first time they'd be served a meal that wasn't contained in a red basket where they sat on a street bench or concrete step.

He waved her over. There was no exchange of pleasantries as she sat down at the table; she wondered if that was a good thing or not.

"I don't know how much you know about CODIS," Marshall began, straight to the point, "but it doesn't just keep DNA profiles on convicted felons. When a missing person is reported, the relatives can provide their DNA to cross-reference in the event unidentified remains are found. The system runs periodic checks to compare the profiles. The same goes for crime scene DNA evidence. It's entered into CODIS and cross-referenced with the profiles of known felons to find matches."

The waiter politely interrupted them by setting down two glasses of water. "Are you two ready to order?" he asked.

Marshall seemed very abrupt today and she wondered if he was under pressure on the Johansen case. "I'll have the club sandwich and salad, please."

Marshall opened up the menu again and pointed to the jalapeño burger and fries. "I'll have that, thanks."

"Thank you and I'll be back shortly with your meals."

Marshall watched the waiter leave. "As I was saying, unfortunately, DNA evidence wasn't widely used until the mid-90s, which doesn't help us out much in your case. But what I was hoping to accomplish was determining if any unidentified remains had been entered into the system from within a hundred miles of the vicinity of your case and the other kidnappings."

"And was there a match?"

"There were some unidentified remains entered from the Eureka area, so I had to confirm the age of those remains. We know we're looking for young kids here, so if they were from an adult, we'd know that wasn't going to work for us. Eureka is obviously a larger city than Rio Dell, so there were quite a few missing persons in the National Database. So far, I haven't found any that would match the ages of the children who disappeared around the same time you were abducted."

"So, we don't have anything more to go on, now?"

"Not necessarily, Kate. Are you still going to that doctor for the hypnotherapy?"

"No. I stopped going a couple of weeks ago. I just didn't see that I was making any progress. It was getting to the point that reliving the events, as much as I knew of them anyway, was getting to be too much for me."

"And what about your dreams? Are you still having them?"

"Sometimes, but they're usually the same now. I'm running through the forest and he's chasing me. I have to admit, they're not as bad as they were, but yeah, I have them on occasion."

The waiter approached, once again, only this time with their food. He seemed to know better than to ask any more questions. "Enjoy your meal," he said, quickly leaving.

"What if we went back to where you were found?" Marshall continued. "Have you ever been back there?"

"No, I don't think so. I suppose it's hard to say because I didn't know about all this when I was growing up, but I imagine my parents wouldn't take me back there." Katie began stabbing her fork at the salad.

"No, probably not. How do you feel about revisiting the place? Do you think you could handle it?"

She set her fork down and considered the proposition while watching Marshall tear into his burger. She hadn't seen him so agitated before and wanted to question it, but thought it might only irritate him more. Something was going on and he didn't want her to know about it.

"What are you hoping we'll get out of it?" Katie asked.

"I'm not sure, exactly. Maybe I'm getting way off base here, but what if going back helped you to remember more? It's not unheard of, having victims revisit the scene to help them recall the events of the crime."

The thought of having to go there, to see it in real life, terrified Katie. But what if it was the only way to get answers? So far, they'd been hitting nothing but brick walls. This was either going to die on the vine, or she would have to take more drastic measures.

"You won't be alone. I'll be there with you."

It was a comforting offer, knowing she wouldn't be alone, and helped confirm her decision. "I don't know exactly where I was found. I'd have to contact Chief Wilson."

"I just don't know what else I can do, Kate. No hits on CODIS, no hits on NamUs; I'm running out of options here unless you want to stop. We don't have to go any further. You can take solace in the fact that you did what you could."

"No, I can't. I haven't done all I can do. We need to go there. I'll contact the chief. He offered to help if I needed it."

"Okay, then." This decision seemed to improve his mood a little. "I've got to get back to the station. I'm meeting with the DA later on the Johansen case. We think we've got what we need to prosecute. Let me know what you find out." He opened his wallet, pulled out a couple of twenties, and dropped them on the table. "Sorry to eat and run, but I'm slammed right now. Catch up with you later?"

She nodded and he was gone. Now it would be up to her to take the next step.

KATIE ARRIVED BACK at the office and closed her door to call the chief. "Chief Wilson, this is Katie Reid. I was wondering if it would be possible to take a look at my case file?"

"You know I don't have much, Katie. If I did, we could have pursued your request. What is it that you're looking for?"

"I'd like to know the location of where they found me."

"Okay. Can I ask why? Our officers, including me, searched that area with a fine tooth comb."

He seemed to be on the defensive. She still needed him and couldn't risk pushing him away. "I'm not implying there might still be evidence and I'm certain your officers did a good job. My thoughts were that if I revisited the area, maybe I might remember more details."

"I can see you're not going to give up on this and I admire you for that. But I'm concerned that you might only bring further pain to yourself and your family."

"I appreciate that concern, Chief, I really do. If I can uncover anything of relevance, believe me, you'll be the first person I turn to."

"Well, I guess there's not much I can do to sway you otherwise.

Okay. I'll have to get the file from archive and send something over to you. You got an email address?"

"Katherine dot Reid at agi dot com." Her work email was probably the safest as it wasn't one that Spencer had access to. *No secrets, Katie.*

ON THE DRIVE HOME, Katie ran through her mind about how she was going to tell Spencer about this. They'd been getting along pretty well this past week or so and any talk of her case had been practically nonexistent since the day they found Isabelle. He wasn't likely to be accepting of her heading up north with Detective Avery to the place where the nightmares took her.

Would he feel better if he went along? Either way, he wouldn't be happy about it. The thought had crossed her mind not to tell him at all. Maybe that would be best for everyone, or maybe just best for her.

Spencer could never really understand why she needed to do this; why she had to know the truth. But lying about this would change their relationship forever. She had promised him and now was considering breaking that promise.

What if, in the end, she went there and discovered nothing? Remembered nothing? Then all the arguments over it would have only served to put further strain on their relationship.

She gripped the steering wheel with white knuckles and let out a scream, filled with all the anxiety, guilt, and pain that sat like a rock in the pit of her stomach.

No, she thought. Until there was something solid, there was no point in getting him involved anymore. He had enough on his plate and she had scarcely considered that up until now.

Upon arrival, Katie pulled into the parking lot and walked up the steps to the front door of their apartment. It was opened just a crack and when Katie pushed it further, a beautiful candlelight dinner sparkled in the darkened room.

"Wow! What's this all about?"

"I just thought a little celebration was in order for achieving my first win in court. Well, technically, it was a team win, but I played a significant role."

"Oh my God, Spencer, congratulations!" She had been so wrapped up in her own work that she'd forgotten about his trial. He wasn't part of the defense team but was on the team that researched and drafted the court papers. "That is wonderful and definitely cause for celebration!" Katie was relieved by this welcomed turn of events. This reaffirmed her decision to withhold her intentions. She would not tell him about her plans, not now, when he was so happy. "So, tell me all about it!"

Spencer pulled a chair out for her as she sat down at the table. Almost immediately, he began retelling the events of his day and looked happier than she'd seen him in a very long time. The candle-light cast a soft glow on his face and he appeared young, almost as young as when they first met. His deep brown eyes sparkled with enthusiasm and he wore a smile that made her heart stop. Maybe it was just the boyish excitement that radiated from him, but she could have sworn he looked like a teenager.

"Look at me, I've been talking for twenty minutes straight and haven't even asked how your day was."

"It was fine. I went with Susan today on a new case. The police were questioning a child who had been abused and it's required for victim advocates and CPS to monitor the questioning. It's a way to protect the kids from any undue duress. But the cops were really careful not to scare the kid in any way. They're trained for that."

Spencer reached across the table and held her hand. "I'm really glad I can share this with you. You've had to put up with me studying to pass the bar and working long hours, and now I can finally see the fruits of my labor. It means a lot to me that you stuck it out, Katie."

She knew he was referring to their recent troubles as well. "What else would I do? I love you."

ARRIVING at work after little sleep from last night's celebrations, Katie eagerly checked her email and there it was. The chief had sent the location of where she'd been found. Immediately retrieving her phone, she called Marshall to give him the news. "I just got an email from Chief Wilson. He gave me the location."

"Great. When are we leaving?" Marshall asked.

"I was thinking maybe we could leave Friday after work and then get up early on Saturday to drive out there."

"I think that'll work. Spencer's okay with it?"

"Yeah, he's fine. He wanted to go, but his firm just won a big case and he's going to have a lot of paperwork to finish up." The silence on the other end made Katie think Marshall might be suspicious of her comment. The excuse was weak, but she glossed over it. "So, I'll check on the flights and get back to you?"

"Okay. I'll talk to you later."

"Hey, Marshall... Are you sure you can do this with me? I know you've been slammed with the investigation. I just don't want you to feel obligated, you know?"

"I don't and yes, I can do this. It's a day or two out of my life. I think I can manage it. Besides, I said I would help you and this was my idea, remember? It's what I want to do. Goodbye, Kate."

Her next call would be to Sam. She was going to have to ask her best friend to lie.

"Katie, think about what you're doing here," Sam replied.

"I *have* thought about it. It's all I think about anymore, Sam. I just need to do everything in my power to find the truth."

"I understand that Katie, I do, but lying to Spencer? This is not the way to handle it and you know it. Look, I'll cover for you if he calls because I love you and you're the nearest thing I have to a sister. But I'm terrified you're getting in over your head. I don't know this Detective Avery and you don't either."

"I trust him, Sam. He's the only one who understands what this means to me. He doesn't have an agenda. You'd like him; he's a good man and a great cop. If anyone can help me, it's him."

"That's not true. I understand and I'm sure Spencer would too if he knew. You're not giving him a chance."

"I did in the beginning and I know he tried his best to step up and accept what happened, but ever since the chief said he wouldn't reopen my case, Spencer's expected me to drop the whole thing. And, as far as he knows, I have."

"I don't like this, Kate. I don't want you to get hurt."

"I won't. We're just going up there to see if it jogs my memory at all. Chances are that it won't. The therapy stopped working, so it's really just a shot in the dark that this will. Then we'll come home and that'll be it. That'll be the end of it."

"And what if you remember more than you want to?"

"Then I'll deal with it in my own way." Katie knew she'd swayed her by the silence on the other end.

"Fine. You better call me when you get into town. Do you want me to go with you to the redwoods, you know, as a precaution?"

"Precaution? No, I'll be fine. Like I said, I'm not going to hold my breath that anything will come of this, but I won't know for sure until I get there. Detective Avery will be with me. He won't let anything happen. I just need you to call me if Spencer contacts you. I doubt he will. He'll try my cell first anyway. Look, it's one day, then I'll be back home."

"All right. You call me when it's over too, got it? If I don't hear from you by the end of the day on Saturday, I'm coming to find you."

Sam was genuinely concerned and Katie didn't want to dismiss that. This was her best friend and she was asking something above and beyond anything she'd asked of her before. "Okay, okay. I've got to go. I'll call you Friday night when we get in."

"You make sure Officer Friendly keeps his hands off of you, too."

"Please. That's the last thing I have to worry about. The guy thinks of me like I'm his little sister. I'll talk to you later, Sam. Bye."

11

THE REDWOOD VIOLET

K atie stood in line at airport security, keeping an eye out for Marshall. She hadn't heard from him since his text at lunch confirming he would arrive around 5:30, giving them plenty of time before the flight that was scheduled to leave at 7:00.

She glanced at her watch, 5:45, and no sign of him. Just as she approached the front of the line and was taking off her shoes, she heard an incoming text message. *"Look behind you."* Katie looked back and saw Marshall waving his hand in the air. He was at the back of the line. She smiled, relieved that he had shown up. The man standing behind Katie pointed toward the TSA guard, who was asking her to step forward.

After getting through security, she waited for Marshall at the gate. Their flight was about to board when he finally made it through.

"Took you long enough," Katie said.

"Yeah, I know; I got held up at the station."

"Flight 2389 to Sacramento is now boarding."

"Looks like I made it right on time." Marshall grinned.

It was going to be a long commute. Probably 10:00 before they would arrive in Trinidad. It was just south of there, along Highway 101, where she had been found.

Katie sat in the window seat, watching the ground fall farther and farther away as the plane climbed higher. Flying hadn't gotten any easier for her, though it had become more frequent as of late.

"Can I ask what you told Spencer about this weekend? I gathered you weren't completely honest with him," Marshall said.

"I've already gotten enough grief from my friend Sam about this; I don't need to hear it from you too."

"Sorry. I was just asking. It's none of my business."

"No, I'm sorry. I shouldn't snap at you like that. You're the one who's helping me. It's just that I knew he wouldn't want me to do this, so I told him I was visiting Sam for the weekend, and that she was going to help me shop for a wedding dress."

Marshall groaned.

"Yeah, I know. It was a shitty thing to do. But this has put a huge strain on our relationship and I just didn't want to make matters worse. In the end, he would have grudgingly supported this, but honestly, I just didn't want to fight about it anymore."

"Lying always makes things worse, Kate, no matter what the reason behind it. If it was me, I'd want to know. It doesn't sound like you've given him enough credit. I can't imagine what this must feel like for him, watching the love of his life go through what you're going through and not be able to do anything about it. I'd want to be involved every step of the way," Marshall replied.

"Well, I'm not sure he would feel that way. He's a good man, but I don't think he expected such a test to our relationship. It has been hard for both of us."

"Let's just hope we can end this thing for you, Kate. You both deserve to get on with your lives and be happy."

"Doesn't everyone?"

Katie was right on the money. It was ten o'clock when they checked in at the hotel, well more like a motel, really. Trinidad wasn't exactly known for its five-star accommodations, but it was just for one night.

"Here's your room key, Ms. Reid. And this one's yours, Mr. Avery. You two have a pleasant night."

They were both exhausted and headed straight to their rooms. The single-level motel sprawled out into a U-shape and in the center was a pool. It was a little hard to see in the dark, but Katie thought it looked a little worse for wear. The idea of stepping into it was the least appealing part of the journey so far.

"I've got to go this way," Katie said, turning left at the end of the corridor.

"I'm over here, I think. I'll catch up with you in the morning. You'll be all right to get to your room?"

"I think I can handle it." She grinned. "Good night, Marshall, and thank you for everything."

"Good night."

It was a bright morning and the two of them were already on the road. There was no time to waste.

"I think we're getting close, Kate. Chief Wilson said you were found near milepost 620, just north of Westhaven." Marshall pointed to a turnout just beyond the mile marker as he drove the rental car.

She had traveled this road before but had never known of its significance. Katie grew chilled the closer they got.

Marshall pulled off the side of the road. "Are you sure you're ready for this?"

The forest looked beautiful and peaceful as she stared into it, not at all like the distorted trees and sky and rocks her dreams portrayed. Still, this didn't seem real. Her memory of the event was still so vague, so surreal that finally being here didn't feel anything like she had expected.

Upon stepping out of the car, her shoe left an imprint in the damp earth. She expected a flood of memories to wash over her, but there was nothing. In front of her was a metal guardrail, which she stepped over with ease, out ahead of Marshall. He was a few steps behind and she could hear twigs snapping with each step he took until he finally stood next to her.

Katie gazed out among the giant redwoods. The scent of the forest triggered a brief flash of something she hadn't recalled before, the flowers, particularly the violets. The beautiful yellow flowers spread across the forest floor. It hardly looked like a place that held such deep, dark memories.

"Where would you like to start, Kate?"

"I don't know. Let's just go for a walk."

They started into the woods in silence. The only sounds came from the animals that called this place home. The enormous trees were surrounded by flowers and shrubs. Katie was amazed by how much was able to grow in their shadow. Her dreams made the forest appear much more ominous. The jagged rocks sliced through her feet and the dead branches littered on the ground, black, as if they'd been burned in a fire. It looked beautiful now. The birds chirped and butterflies flew around her legs. "I don't know what I'm supposed to do here. It just looks like a forest. I couldn't tell you if this was the place or not." Katie threw her hands to her hips.

"I've got the map of the search area the chief emailed you. This should help point us in the right direction."

Katie glanced at the grainy image. "My God, they searched everywhere, didn't they?"

"It looks like it. They would have used dogs to pick up scents and probably analyzed the shoeprints as well. It's a very remote location to have held you captive. I don't see homes anywhere near here, nor did I on the drive up. Didn't you say you thought you were being kept in a cellar or something?"

"I think so; I'm not sure. It could have been a basement or a storage area. I just remember that it was cold. My feet were cold when they touched the concrete floor."

"It may have been in his home. He may have lived nearby, but I'm sure they would have checked out the locals. But then, you could have run for miles to get here. Can you remember anything else?"

Katie lowered herself to the ground, resting against a tree. She closed her eyes and imagined the dreams—running, falling, screaming, but still, there was nothing new, nothing that gave her any clue as to the identity of the man. She dropped her head into her hands. "What am I doing here? I don't remember anything except for the nightmares. Why am I trying so hard to remember something so terrible?"

"So we can catch the bastard," Marshall replied. "You and I aren't all that different, you know. I knew that the moment I met you." He sat down next to her. "Look, Kate, I can't imagine what this must be like for you, but I do know how much you want to be able to unlock your past. I got to be honest with you, what your parents did, keeping this from you. Well, let's just say they made it much more difficult for you. Maybe if you had known earlier, you could have come to terms with it. But having found out because of some nightmares, seeking help from a therapist; I don't know. I think this could have all been avoided, but nonetheless, here you are today. You want justice for yourself and all the other kids who were taken from their families, including Isabelle. Just do what you can here, and if you get something, great. If not, maybe this will be the final step in your acceptance of what happened. But that doesn't mean you have to stop helping to find the other sons of bitches out there. In the short time I've known you, I've watched you blossom like these flowers." He pulled a yellow flower from its stem. "What did you say this was? A violet?"

"A Redwood Violet," Katie replied.

"That's what you are. You're able to bloom in the darkness and shadows, just like this flower. Like I said before, I'll find a place for you in the department if you want. It isn't easy, this line of work, but you can help others and yourself. Believe me, I know a little something about that."

"I appreciate that, Marshall. Thank you." Katie forced herself up off the ground. "Come on, let's keep going. I'm not ready to give up just yet."

"I didn't think you were."

They continued on the path, studying the map Chief Wilson sent over. They must have searched a two-mile radius. Everything looked the same. Tree after tree, passing a few empty trails along the way, spotting a few blackened twigs that sparked a momentary flash of recognition, but quickly faded.

"I'm sorry, Marshall. There's nothing here. We've been walking around for two hours and I just can't remember anything more."

"That's okay. I have a feeling, now that we've had a good look around that you probably weren't here for too long. I suspect you were being held somewhere nearby, but we'd have to dig pretty deep and see where the chief's investigation left off. You want to get out of here?"

"Yeah, I'm done. I'd like to see the chief before we head back to the airport if you don't mind going out of our way a little."

"Not at all; we've got plenty of time."

Neither one said anything more during the forty-minute drive to Rio Dell.

This was the end, she thought. No more leads, no more memories. It was over. What a waste of energy. Marshall was right; she should put her time to better use and go to work with him. It wouldn't be as a detective, of course. She didn't have the background. But inside the department, there were plenty of opportunities for her to work alongside him.

"Here we are." Marshall pulled into the parking lot and cut the engine.

She wiped a stray tear from her cheek and hoped he hadn't seen, but he must have because he quickly looked away.

Marshall stepped out of the car and waited for Katie. When they entered the station, Chief Wilson was at the front desk. He was expecting them.

"Well, how'd it go?" He directed his question to Katie.

"I'm sorry we troubled you, Chief. It didn't help."

"I'm sorry to hear that, Katie. I wish there was more I could do for you, but as you know, my hands are tied."

"I understand, Chief. Sorry to have taken up so much of your time with this already. I just wanted to stop by and say thank you for everything you've done for me."

"If it's all right with you, Katie, I'd like to have a quick word with Detective Avery."

Katie looked at Marshall, suspicious of the Chief's intentions. "Yeah, I guess so. I'll wait in the car."

After several minutes, Detective Avery emerged from the station and headed toward her. She watched him approach, his face revealed nothing of the conversation. When he got in, she expected him to tell her what the chief had wanted, but he said nothing, only started the engine and pulled away.

"You mind telling me what that was all about?" Katie soon realized he wasn't going to divulge anything voluntarily.

Marshall stared at the road in silence, but Katie wasn't about to let this go. Her eyes were burning a hole in the side of his head.

Finally, he spoke. "He thinks I wasted your time and that you have been through enough."

"I see. Did you tell him that I wanted to come back here? That I wanted to try my damnedest to see if any of it would jog my memory?"

"Kate, he doesn't want us to continue down this path out of fear we might find something he missed."

"What do you mean? I don't think he missed anything. I just wanted to go where they found me. Get some answers."

"I know, and I know what it means to you to get answers. But I can see that it eats away at him, just like it does me when I want to solve a case, but it just doesn't work out how you plan. He told me how difficult your investigation was. The other children involved. He believed the disappearances were linked, but just couldn't get the proof. He spent so much time and resources his department didn't have that eventually, after the media died off, his captain said that was enough, but he didn't stop. It took its toll on his marriage, but he continued. It wasn't until your mother told him she didn't want to continue to relive it every time he had a hunch that he finally stopped. The chief really wanted to believe you had something when you told him about the necklace, but then the DA shot him down. There's not much you can do about that."

Katie watched the trees pass by in a blur as they drove down the highway. "So, what do we do now? Do I just go home and go on about my business?"

"Yes, that's exactly what you do, Kate. Go on about your business of helping other victims' families find answers. Keep them from going through what you and your family went through. Get married. Live your life."

"I just don't know if I can do that, Marshall. I don't know if I'll ever sleep without the nightmares."

"I believe they will pass, eventually. You even said they were coming less frequently. Maybe continuing with your therapy will help."

"Maybe."

It was late Saturday night when Katie arrived back home, weary from the journey, both physically and emotionally.

She forced a smile as Spencer greeted her. "Welcome home, babe. How was the dress hunting? Did you find one you liked? I'm surprised you decided not to stay until Sunday."

Katie realized she couldn't continue the lie. She would have to accept whatever consequences would come, but she wouldn't lie to him any longer. He deserved better than that. "Do you think we could sit down and talk for a minute?"

Appearing concerned, Spencer sat down on the sofa. "What's going on?"

She squeezed his hand and steadied her tone. "I went home, but not for the reason I told you. I went back to the place where they found me. I had hoped that maybe, if I was actually standing there, I would be able to remember something, but nothing came to me."

What had initially been his concern was now turning to anger. This was it, the moment she dreaded, but she had brought it on all by herself.

"You lied to me?" Spencer released her hand and began pacing the room, breathing shallow, quick breaths. "Why would you lie to me? Didn't we just have a long conversation about this? I thought you were ready to move on. Katie, have I not been there for you through all of this and you repay me by lying?"

"I'm sorry, Spencer. I knew you'd be upset. I know how much you want to get past this."

"I thought you did too!"

"I do, I swear. That's why I went. I had to see for myself if there was anything there. Anything at all I could remember. Detective Avery said it can help sometimes, going back to the scene. It can help victims remember things."

"Detective Avery? Was he there with you? Are you fucking kidding me?"

"Yes. He was helping me. I didn't want to go alone." She thought it best to leave out the fact that it had been his idea in the first place and that she'd secretly been working with him for the past few weeks.

"And so you thought it best to lie to your fiancé, go out of town with another man, and have him help you? Jesus. I knew something was going on. How could I be so stupid?"

What response had she expected? If she lied about her intentions, why was it so unbelievable that she might lie about her relationship with Marshall? Still, she thought he knew her better than that.

"Spencer, I've told you before, nothing is going on with him. What kind of woman do you think I am? I would never cheat on you."

"Well, certainly not the kind of woman to go flitting about with another man on the pretense that he was helping you."

"He *was* helping me! God, I knew you wouldn't understand. That's why I wasn't even going to tell you at all."

"So why are you telling me now?"

"Because I don't want our marriage to be built on lies. I've had enough lies to last me a lifetime. Everyone in my family has lied to me my entire life."

He started to laugh. "Our marriage? You think we're still going to have a marriage?" Spencer stormed off into the bedroom.

After several minutes, it became apparent he wasn't coming back out. She walked softly down the hallway and into their room. He was packing a suitcase.

"What are you doing?" Her heart fell into her stomach.

"I can't deal with this anymore, Katie. I thought I knew you, but clearly, I don't. It scares the hell out of me how easy it was for you to lie like that."

"Easy? You think any of this has been easy for me?" She stood next to him now and placed her hand on top of his suitcase. "Stop, okay? Please stop."

"You've turned into someone I no longer recognize. I caught a glimpse of who you used to be when we talked a few weeks ago, but now I can see that it was just a fleeting glimpse. You've become obsessed with this. You changed your job... you lied to me." He turned away and looked at the picture on his nightstand. "You see this? This is what we used to be. Happy. I saw this coming. I supported you as much as I could, but it just wasn't enough, was it?"

"I know this has been hard on you. Please don't give up on us. I will get through this. I just had to do this one last thing; one last try to figure out what happened to me. Can't you understand that?"

"Katie, I don't believe this was the last thing. I don't believe you'll stop until you find what you're looking for." He pushed her hand away from his bag. "I just don't think I can hang around until that happens because it may *never* happen. I don't want to live out my life with someone who is always searching for something, no matter what the cost to others." Spencer zipped up the bag and threw it over his shoulder.

Katie's eyes swelled with tears. There was nothing more she could do to make him stay. "I'm sorry I did this to you...to us. I wish to God none of this ever happened."

"So do I. Goodbye, Katie. I hope you find the answers you need and that it will bring you some peace."

She watched him walk away. Life as she had known it for the past seven years was over.

12

In the light of the morning, Katie reached for her cell to call in sick for work. Her eyes were red and swollen, having found no comfort in her tears during the long hours of the night. She had no one to call, not even Sam; especially not Sam. Wasn't she the one who warned her that this would happen? Detective Avery, too, but Katie didn't listen. He warned her not to take this too far. But at least he understood why she had to continue, even if he knew it would come to this.

The wedding would have to be called off. Whose side would their friends choose? Spencer would surely not reveal the reason for the breakup; he was a good man and he would not put Katie in that position. But what did any of that matter now? She lost the man she loved and was no closer to finding the man who stole her from a loving family, which was forever changed.

It was too exhausting to think about. Katie lay down on the couch and finally drifted off to sleep.

The late morning sun was shining through the front window when Katie's phone rang, waking her from the deep sleep that always comes after the pain. She looked at her phone; it was Marshall.

Speaking to him right now was the last thing she wanted. No one needed to tell her she brought this on herself; she was already quite confident of that fact. But what if he had news? Curiosity got the best of her and she answered.

"Katie? I tried your office but didn't get an answer. Are you in today?"

"No. I wasn't feeling well and decided to stay home."

He was going to see through that.

"Oh. I'm sorry to bother you. I just wanted to let you know before you heard it on the news that we got the evidence we needed on Isabelle's case. DNA came back and matched Johansen. He's going to go to jail, Kate. I can only hope after the jury sees what we've got, they'll send him to death row."

Katie was silent on the other end.

"Did you hear me, Kate? We got him. And you had a hand in that."

"Yeah, I heard you. That is very good news. I hope he gets what he deserves."

"Is everything all right? You don't sound like your usual self."

"I'm fine, Marshall. I've just had a rough night."

"The dreams again?"

"No." She paused, hoping he would continue, but he had a way of creating awkward silences that forced a person to speak. "Spencer left last night. Left for good, I'm pretty sure."

"Oh man, I'm so sorry, Kate."

"It was my fault. I told him the truth about our trip and he lost it. Then, I watched him give up and walk away; can't blame him though. I probably would have done the same thing if he went off with a woman and lied to me about it."

"Does he think something is going on between us? I can talk to him."

Katie interrupted. "No, no, he doesn't, not anymore. He just got tired of dealing with me and this situation, everything really. So, the wedding's off."

"Is there anything I can do to help?"

There was one thing he could do. One thing that could help her come to terms with why she'd just destroyed her relationship. "I'd like to come down to the station when you bring Johansen in to formally charge him."

"You sure about that, Kate? We've got hard evidence on him now, so it's only a matter of determining what happened to Isabelle. It won't be easy to listen to what he's got to say."

"I know, but I have to see for myself the kind of monster he really is. I have to know why he did it."

"You can come down, but don't expect Johansen to suddenly be remorseful or to beg for forgiveness. That's not what they do. They take pleasure in the details of their crimes, especially when they know we've got them. They wear it like a badge of honor."

"I'm prepared, Marshall. Please, I need to see this."

KATIE ARRIVED at the station and she was escorted by two officers to the viewing room. She expected to see a two-way mirror, like in the movies, but there was a table with a monitor on it. The closed-circuit camera showed an adjacent room. In that room, sitting handcuffed to the table, was the monster. He couldn't have been more than twenty-seven, maybe twenty-eight. His defense attorney, no doubt court-appointed, sat next to him.

This was not the same man who answered the door several weeks ago when she and Detective Avery had first met Mr. Johansen. Sullen and pale, he appeared to have lost weight, so much so that his skeletal frame poked through his thin jailhouse uniform.

Detective Avery entered the interrogation room and glanced up at the camera. Katie thought he was looking directly at her. Although he hadn't seen her beforehand, he knew she was there.

"I'm sure the camera's already on, detective," Johansen said.

"Just checking if the little red light is flashing. We're planning on uploading this to YouTube." Detective Avery smiled.

Johansen unveiled a sly, unnerving grin in return.

"Detective, I'm Mr. Johansen's attorney, Jim Bernard." The man rose to shake hands.

Marshall quickly dispensed with the pleasantries and immediately jumped in. "So when did you graduate from molestation to murder?" Avery asked as he pulled the folding chair out and sat across from Johansen.

"Don't answer that." The lawyer turned from his client. "Detective Avery, are we to expect this sort of behavior from you right at the start?"

"You flatter me, Detective. What makes you think I'm a murderer?" It seemed Johansen wanted to bite at the carrot Marshall had dangled.

"We found Isabelle in the dump where you left her. You know, someone like you, I would have thought, would have taken better care to dispose of the body."

Johansen's eyes flickered vaguely at the revelation that Isabelle's body had been found and he shot a glance to the lawyer. He'd been in jail since his arrest for the registration offense and presumably hadn't heard they found her. Johansen suddenly stared up at the camera.

Katie gasped, taking a step back.

One of the officers held her shoulders. "It's okay, Miss Reid. He can't see you."

"Thank you. I'm okay." She wasn't. At that moment, she saw something terrifying in his eyes. She had seen that look before, a brutality that flashed before her in an instant.

"We'd like to discuss a plea deal, Detective." Just as Mr. Bernard began retrieving the papers from his briefcase, Johansen opened his mouth.

"She was so pretty with her brown hair blowing in the wind and her tan skin," He started. "I saw her riding her bike one afternoon when I got home from work."

"Yes, she was a very pretty little girl," Avery replied.

Johansen glared at him as if he'd just been roused from a pleasant dream.

"You must have had your eye on her for quite a while," Avery said.

"Don't say anything more, Mr. Johansen." The lawyer seemed to grow more incensed by the minute at the back and forth between the two men.

"I guess so. I had only seen her once more on my street when I decided to follow her home one day. I just watched as she rode up onto her driveway. Saw her brothers and sisters come out and play. Her mom didn't seem to be around, though. Boy, is she a piece of work."

Katie saw the disgusted look on Marshall's face. *The pot calling the kettle black*, she thought.

"Shut the hell up, Michael," Bernard continued.

"But she stopped coming down my street and I missed her. She was only five blocks away. I parked along her street and watched her ride her bike to school. Sometimes she rode alone, sometimes with friends." His face tempered slightly as he turned to Detective Avery. "I swear I just wanted to make sure she got to school okay. No one else seemed to give a shit about her. It wasn't until that boy started riding along."

He revealed himself once again as the monster Katie thought him to be.

"That boy." Johansen shook his head. "She liked him. I could see it in her face. She was gonna end up turning into a whore just like all the others, just like her mother. She was gonna let that boy touch her."

"She was eight," Avery said, growing even more exasperated.

"For God's sake." Bernard shook his head. Any hope of a deal for his client had just evaporated.

Johansen looked at him, smiling again. "Those whores start early, detective."

Katie watched as Marshall tried to keep from losing control.

"So you decided to kill her? Because you wanted to keep her from becoming a whore?"

"I tried to protect her." Johansen appeared agitated. "I wasn't gonna hurt her. Tell him, Jim, I wasn't gonna hurt her."

"How did you convince Isabelle to get in your truck?" Avery asked.

"Well, that's the genius that is me, detective. Puppies. All little girls like puppies, don't they? One morning, before she was supposed to leave for school, I waited outside the truck a few houses down. I saw her riding down the street; she was alone, which was a good thing because it would've put a damper on my plans."

"I think we're done here, Detective Avery." The lawyer started packing up his files.

"So, anyway, I started calling out for my poor lost puppy. I named him Max; admittedly, not very original. Young Isabelle came riding up toward me on her bike. I was standing on the sidewalk and blocked her way so she had no choice but to stop. I asked her if she'd seen my lost puppy. She asked what Max looked like and I said I had a picture of him in my truck. I swung open the passenger door hard enough to knock her off her bike. She was on the ground, so I grabbed her, put my hand over her mouth, and shoved her in the truck."

Katie clutched her chest and closed her eyes. She was shocked by the ease with which he had been able to speak about such a thing.

"Would you like to leave, Miss Reid?" one of the officers asked.

"No," she whispered.

"Where I really messed up was in forgetting that damned backpack. It was hanging on one of the handlebars and I didn't have enough time to grab it. Didn't want to be seen, you know, had to be quick."

"Got it," Avery interrupted. "What did you do with her after that?"

"I'm warning you, Mr. Johansen. You need to stop talking right now." Bernard was already on his feet.

"Luckily, I had some prescription pain meds and I just fed 'em to her to keep her quiet. It wasn't easy. She put up a fight sometimes." Johansen chuckled.

"Did you assault her?" Avery pressed on, ignoring the pleas of the lawyer.

Johansen was quiet. He glanced again at the camera. Katie could swear he knew she was watching.

"We're gonna find out sooner or later, so you might as well come out with it."

"I'll tell you that I treated her better than any man would ever do. I guess the pills weren't enough, though, because, after a while, she got a little too feisty. You see, I had to punish her that day you and little Miss Priss came along, knocking on my door. I could hear her rattling around in that closet when I was talking to the two of you. I was surprised you didn't hear anything, detective. There she was, right under your nose. Of course, that first officer who came round... well, he was just an idiot, thinking I was the old man who I rented the place from. But, after that close call, I had no choice."

Detective Avery launched out of his chair and grabbed Johansen by the collar of his uniform, pulling him as close as he could. "She was still alive? You fucker, you're gonna get the needle for this."

"That's assuming they start executing again here in this beautiful state of California, detective."

Avery swung at Johansen, striking his jaw so hard the bone could be heard breaking under the weight of the blow.

"Son of a bitch!" One of the officers ran out of the backroom and into the interrogation room, pulling Avery off Johansen.

Bernard pressed down on Johansen's shoulders to keep him in his chair.

He touched his jaw and looked at the blood on his fingers. "I hope everyone saw that!" he muttered at the camera. "You see that, Mr. Lawyer?"

Detective Avery stormed out of the room and Katie ran out after him. She found him in the hallway, bracing himself against the wall, out of breath.

He looked up at her. "She was there, Kate. God damn it! She was there!"

"There's no way you could have known that, Marshall." Katie reached for his arm.

He pulled away. "It's my God damn job to know!" Marshall turned his back and walked away.

Just as Katie was about to follow him, the officer who pulled Avery off Johansen appeared around the corner. "Just leave him, Miss Reid. He needs time to cool off."

EVERY DETAIL that occurred at the station today replayed in Katie's mind as she drove through traffic and made her way home. Detective Avery left without a single word and she was forced to deal with this on her own. She couldn't blame him though; he'd warned her it would be difficult and she clearly underestimated his advice. He was having a hard enough time coming to terms with it. How naïve she had been to believe in her ability to handle the situation. The line she crossed was well beyond her periphery now and there was no turning back. There was no Spencer to come home to; no one to comfort her at all.

Alone in her apartment, she looked around to find no sign that Spencer had ever even lived there. He must have come back earlier in the day to take his belongings. None of that seemed to matter just now. Isabelle was gone, just like the others, and Katie was face to face with the psycho who took her. Was she prepared to come that close to her own would-be killer?

Time lost all meaning until darkness began creeping down the walls of the living room. It was at that moment she heard a pounding on the door. She uncurled her body from the couch and peered out the front window to find Marshall on the landing. She opened the door.

"Jesus, Kate! Where the hell have you been? I've been calling your cell phone all afternoon." Marshall walked in without an invitation. "Where are the lights around here?" He ran his hand along the walls to find a switch until eventually, there was light. "Are you okay?" He guided her back to the couch. "I'm sorry I left you earlier today. I can't imagine what that must have been like for you. That's why I was hesitant for you to be there at all."

"She was there, Marshall." Her own realization of this fact hit her hard. The hoarse sound coming from her was a culmination of dehydration and exhaustion. She had no idea how long she'd been sitting on that couch, but thirst summoned her.

"Let me get you some water." Marshall went into the kitchen and returned with a glass of tap water.

Katie grasped it with both hands and drank nearly all of it at once. She placed it on the coffee table and turned to Marshall. "Where did you go today?"

"I'm sorry. I had to get out of there. I wasn't expecting that and I should have handled it better."

"How could you possibly have handled it any differently? Just knowing that she was there....God, I wanted to throw up."

"I know. It's all right." Marshall placed his hand on her knee to calm her. "The important thing is that we caught him. That's what you have to keep telling yourself. We did the best we could to find Isabelle."

"Is that what you really believe?"

"That's what I have to believe. It's the only way."

Katie stared into his bright green eyes. She saw compassion and tenderness, no trace of the anger from earlier remained. His ability to transform himself in that manner amazed her. She was mesmerized by this man who had shown her so much, taught her how to redirect her pain, and put it to a more useful purpose. And now she felt something she hadn't experienced before in his presence. Almost instinctively, she leaned into him. Closing her eyes, she let her lips gently touch his.

He pulled away. "Kate, please... don't. Not like this."

Suddenly aware of her mistake, she sat upright, embarrassed by his rejection.

"With everything that's happened to you today—your breakup— this isn't you right now. Damn, I shouldn't have let you see him today. I don't know what I was thinking." Marshall took to his feet. "I'd better go now. I just came here to make sure you were all right. I was nervous when you didn't answer your phone."

"Fine, just go," she whispered, waving him off and turning away from him completely. There was no sound, except for his breaths that came quickly as a result of his raised pulse. She could feel him standing next to her but refused to acknowledge him. A moment later, his footsteps trailed away as he opened the door. He stood there again in silence and then the door closed. He was gone.

In the late hours of the night, Katie's restless mind refused to surrender to sleep. The thought of calling Marshall occurred to her more than once, but seeking his comfort was not the answer. These demons were hers and hers alone, though she suspected he would be dealing with demons of his own tonight.

She got out of bed and walked to her medicine cabinet in search of a drug that would quiet Isabelle's screams, which echoed in her head. Two samples of Valium that Dr. Reyes gave her for the bad nights lay on the shelf next to the aspirin. Although some nights had gotten so severe she wished she had taken them, the fear of squelching any new memory that might be recalled was enough to keep the pills at bay. But not tonight; tonight she wanted to think of nothing, remember nothing, and feel nothing. Katie threw both pills in her mouth and swallowed them down.

She didn't know how long her alarm had been sounding, but she must have hit the snooze button a few times before full consciousness finally returned. Katie's head ached as she tried to focus on the time. It was 7:30 and she was going to be late for work. Her body would not cooperate as she struggled to make it to the shower. It would have to be a cold one to jolt her back to life.

Having had virtually nothing to eat or drink all day yesterday, Katie felt the full wrath of a Valium hangover. She had no idea of the dosage she consumed, which was a stupid idea now, in the light of day. Although the desired effect had been achieved, her recollection of anything beyond standing in front of her medicine cabinet was completely wiped away.

Wrapped in a towel and slightly more alert, Katie walked into the living room and turned on the news. *"Prime suspect in the Isabelle Thompson case, Michael Johansen, has been charged with the murder of the missing eight-year-old girl. Police say DNA evidence was found on the girl's body and in his home. His arrest comes after weeks of searching for Isabelle and days after finding her in the Miramar landfill."*

That was it; Johansen had been charged and it was all over, except for the trial. Katie turned off the television and finished getting ready for work.

She grabbed her purse and her cell phone and headed out the door. Glancing at her phone on the way down the steps, she noticed several missed calls from Marshall. It occurred to her that he had tried to get hold of her before finally coming over late yesterday evening. She felt so foolish about her behavior and hoped he would be able to forgive her. It would take some time to cope with the snow-ball of events over the past few days, but she needed him. He was a good friend.

It wasn't until Katie arrived at work, that she sat down to check her cell phone voicemail. Several were from Marshall, but there was one very much unexpected call from Chief Wilson. As Katie listened to the message, she grew pale and froze in her seat.

Susan walked past her office and doubled back, noticing the look on Katie's face. "Hey, are you all right, Katie? Still feeling sick?"

Her questions hardly registered a response. "Katie? Are you feeling okay?" Susan took her by the shoulder, shaking her from her trance. "Oh my God, you're cold as ice. I think you should go back home. You're not well and you shouldn't be here. Should I call Spencer and have him pick you up?"

Katie's eyes blinked a few times as she managed a reply. "No, I'm sorry, Susan. I guess I'm still not well. I think I will go back home and get some rest."

"That's a good idea. You sure I can't call someone to come get you?"

"No, I'll be all right. I just had a little dizzy spell, but I'm okay now. I can manage to get home."

"Okay, well don't rush to come back here until you're better. I mean it."

"Thank you, Susan. I appreciate that." Katie hadn't even put her bag away and she was grabbing it once again to leave. Only she wasn't going home. She was going to see Marshall.

"I need to see Detective Avery, if he's available please," she asked the officer at the front desk.

"He's in his office, Katie. Go ahead on back."

"Thank you." Katie rushed back to find Marshall hunched over several open files, filling out paperwork.

"Marshall?"

"Kate? What are you doing here?"

"I tried to call you first, but I had to see you."

"Sorry, I was probably still in with the captain. What's going on? If this is about last night, please..."

"No. It's not." She took her phone from her purse and placed it on his desk. "There's a message on there from Chief Wilson."

"Why don't you have a seat and calm down? You seem really upset."

"Please, Marshall... just listen to the message." She pressed a few buttons and the message played back on speaker.

"Katie, this is Chief Wilson from the Rio Dell Police Department. I'd like you to give me a call at your earliest convenience. We need to talk about a recent development in the case you inquired about several weeks ago. Miss Reid, this is urgent and a returned call would be greatly appreciated."

Marshall looked at Katie. "What does he want? When did this call come in?"

"I don't know. I think he called yesterday, but I wasn't answering my phone. I only saw the message this morning when I got to work. I came straight here. Marshall, I'm terrified to call him back. Do you think they're going to reopen the case?"

"I don't know. You need to call him back now."

She snatched up her phone and began dialing.

"Put it on speaker," Marshall said.

"Rio Dell Police Department, how may I help you?"

"Good morning. My name is Katie Reid. I'm returning Chief Wilson's call."

"Oh, yes, Miss Reid. I'll put you straight through."

They waited impatiently, even though the chief picked up in less than ten seconds.

"Miss Reid, this is Chief Wilson. Thank you for calling me back."

"Of course. Your message sounded urgent. I've got you on speaker and I'm here with Detective Marshall Avery. What can I do for you?"

"Katie, if you don't mind, I'd like to speak with you in private, please."

"If it's all the same to you, Chief, I'd like Detective Avery to be involved. He's helped me a great deal with my situation."

"Fair enough. We received an anonymous letter yesterday with your name on it. It was addressed to our station but was sent to your attention. First of all, I would like to apologize in that I'd much rather discuss this with you in person, but I understand that would be difficult. It seems as though the local media caught wind of our discussions and my discussions with the Humboldt County DA's office regarding reopening the investigation. As a result, the *Times-Standard* ran an article in the local news section about the cold case and the impact it had on the community. You were not directly named, but the article stated that a victim might have information that could lead to the reopening of the file. That article would have been posted online as well as in print, there for anyone to see. I was not informed of the article, nor was the DA. The journalist cited an anonymous source."

She looked to Marshall. He appeared just as shocked as she was. "Well, considering I escaped, it sure as hell wouldn't be hard to find out my name. They only have to look at the old papers," Katie replied. Her knees were growing weak and she had to sit down fast. A corner of Marshall's desk would have to suffice.

"Not necessarily. When you were found, it was only reported that you had no recollection of what had happened. No one knew of any possible connection with the other missing children or that we were profiling the likes of a serial killer. However, because of this media attention, it has brought about a more concerning matter and the one to which I called so urgently. Katie, the letter was from him."

Terror swept through her as she, once again, looked to Marshall for help.

"Wait a minute. Are you sure about that, Chief?" Marshall asked.

"I'm quite sure, detective. Not only did I spend years hunting this man down, studying his profile, but in the letter, he mentions details that only those of us who worked on the case would know about. And he asked about Katie by name."

"Oh my God."

"It's all right, Kate," Marshall said, "Chief, what did he say about her and was there any indication he knows Kate's whereabouts?"

"He asked how his 'little Katie' was doing. Apart from that, there was no further mention of her. He's taunting us, detective, challenging us to find his other victims, to find him."

"Other victims?" Marshall asked.

"Yes. Although it was never concluded that the three other missing children on the north coast were tied to Katie's case, we always suspected it as you and I discussed. I can only assume he is referring to those children."

"But there could be more?"

"I suppose so, yes, detective. There could be more. Serial killers don't stay quiet for long. It's entirely possible there have been other victims in more recent years. It's possible he never stopped."

"So, what now, Chief?" Marshall asked.

"We don't have any more to go on except for this letter. The DA wants us to keep it quiet, but to follow up on any evidence that might have been left on the envelope. Not that I expect he would have left any. He's evaded capture for this long; my guess is that he has an understanding of new technology. Other than that, we need to wait and see if he contacts us again, or you, for that matter, Katie."

"Do you think he will try to contact me?"

"Right now, there's no indication of that. He wouldn't know where you live. But, Detective Avery, I suggest you help Miss Reid stay vigilant and keep me informed of any new information you might receive. I don't see any reason for you to panic, Katie. We will stay on top of this, making sure you're protected. That being said, I believe this is directed more at me than at you."

"I'm just the only one who survived." Katie disagreed with the chief. She believed her former abductor was after her. She was the one who had been digging around, insisting the case be re-opened.

"Thank you, Chief. Please keep us informed if you get anything more and we'll do the same on our end," Marshall said.

"Thank you, and Katie, I won't let anything happen to you, not again."

The line disconnected and Marshall turned off the speaker. "We need to think about setting up patrols around your home."

"Wait, wait. Look, I know you want to watch out for me, but how are you going to explain a request for patrol? We have no case here and the chief wants us to keep it quiet until they have more information."

Marshall didn't like the feeling of being helpless any more than she did, but they had nothing to go on.

"We don't know who we're looking for." Katie stared off into the distance, realizing she was sounding more like Marshall every day. "What's that saying? Be careful what you wish for?" she began. "For the past several months, I've wanted nothing more than to find out who this son of a bitch was; this man who had destroyed so many lives. And now . . . now that I know he's really still out there, I'm terrified. I guess this whole time I thought maybe he was already dead."

Marshall hoisted up from his chair. "You know what? There's something we haven't tried yet." He started to pace the room, seemingly processing his latest idea. "I don't know if the chief has considered this or not."

"What is it?" Her anticipation was palpable.

"He said something that struck me. He said serial killers don't stay quiet for long. He's right about that. When I asked if there could be other victims, I originally considered other victims from the time frame of your case, but we tried that already, looking for a connection to the other twenty-year-old cases. But what if he never stopped? How many kidnappings are similar to yours, Kate? How many kids along the north coast, Oregon, Washington, anywhere along the Pacific Northwest, have been abducted over the past fifteen, twenty years? What if we can connect some of them? Any of them? Some may still be unsolved and there could be enough similarities that might link them to yours."

"Don't you think that possibility would have been explored already? My dad mentioned that the last time the chief contacted them was when a similar case in Portland turned up. It was a year or so after I came home."

"Not necessarily. The cases could have spread out over several years in several different jurisdictions. Unless there were striking similarities, a link might have been overlooked. And without the cooperation from your parents or the parents of the other missing children, the chief wouldn't have had much to go on. But that was before new forensics data became available. We started down this path before, but I was so wrapped up in the Thompson case that I overlooked current cases. Not to mention the fact that up until now, there was no indication the man was even alive." Marshall continued to pace the room.

Katie was becoming dizzy by his frantic movement.

"Look, I'm not saying any of the guys in charge of these cases weren't diligent. I know how hard they work. I'm just saying that unless there was information in CODIS that would trigger a connection, it was probably never considered to span decades. You're the only evidence that this guy ever existed, Kate, except for the letter we have now. And now that you remember at least some details, I believe we *have* something."

"So where do we start?" she asked.

Marshall finally sat back down. "We start by searching missing persons' records. We profile children, around the ages of 5 to 8, since we believe this was his target age range, and we broaden our search to include not just northern California, but all the way up the coast. It's hard to say if he would have been in these areas, but the Portland connection is a good place to start. I'll need to contact my friend at the Eureka PD. I can poke around a little without giving away the farm."

Katie started to think about her parents, and how this would affect them. She hadn't thought to involve them any further. Was it possible he would find them? "Oh my God. What about my parents? Do you think he knows where they live? What if they're not safe?"

Marshall walked around his desk, sitting on the edge in front of Katie. "One thing I think the chief was right about was the fact that we shouldn't panic. He believes that the letter was an attempt to get at him, not you, and not your parents. Now, I'm not entirely convinced of that. I think this psycho is playing games with us right now. However, as far as your parents are concerned, I think I'd like to get the chief to step up patrols around the area. I don't believe it's likely he would go after them. He likes kids, remember? But I think we ought to err on the side of caution. When I read your file, it was obvious that Chief Wilson fought long and hard in trying to find him. I know what that feels like; not to catch them in the end. The chief doesn't want you to overreact or draw any further media attention. This guy's looking for attention, wanting to stroke his ego. I don't know why it's taken him so long, but he's probably been monitoring the internet for some time, waiting. And finding that article was probably what pushed him over the fence. If he is looking to get caught, you'd better believe I'll be the one to do it."

He got back on his feet and looked at Katie. She saw his determination and drew strength from it. For so long, she'd been feeling like she had no control over her life. Ever since the nightmares started, her entire world began unraveling. Anger grew not only toward Spencer because he couldn't understand her need for answers but also toward her parents for covering up her abduction for so many years. Not Marshall; he knew. They were very much alike in ways that were only now becoming apparent. It was as if he brought her out of this place she'd been hiding. She was afraid, but her will was growing stronger.

"I know this is a lot for you to take in. Why don't you go home? You're supposed to be out sick today anyway. I can get started on the search and fill you in as I get more details."

"No. I want to stay. This is what I'm supposed to do. I see that, now. It's taken me a long time finally to see who I am. I won't shrink away from it any longer. This is about *me* now."

It was getting late in the day and Detective Avery had pulled several files that fit the criteria. There was nothing that stood out;

nothing that would indicate any similarities with Katie's case, except one.

"That's her." Katie pointed at the screen.

"Who?"

"This girl. I remember seeing her on the news and thinking how similar we looked. Her long brown hair, stick straight, a little on the gangly side, those big, bucktooth front teeth. She reminded me of what I looked like when I was a kid. I remembered thinking how sad it was that she was missing and how many times I had gone around on my bike in my neighborhood without a care, not even considering the evil that was in this world. That was when I started having the nightmares. For a long time, it hadn't even occurred to me that she was the catalyst. Spencer was studying for his bar exam; we had a lot going on and I thought I was just stressed out. God, that seems so long ago, but it wasn't."

"If this is too much, Kate . . ." Marshall said.

"No, it isn't. My point was that she looked very much like me. Do you think that could be something?"

"I don't know. We need to see the file. This one happened up in McCloud. Certainly the vicinity we're looking at. It'll take me a day or two to make contact and get the case file. I'll have to come up with some reasonable explanation. I think that's enough for today, anyway."

"I agree with you on that one. I'm feeling a little burned out." Katie stretched her arms, letting out a small yawn.

"If it's all right with you, I 'd like to just follow you home tonight and check out your place, just to be on the safe side."

"That's not necessary, Marshall."

"Just humor an old man, okay?"

"Old?" Katie started laughing. "You don't look a day over forty-five." She knew very well how old he was, only thirty-seven, but she took pleasure in giving him grief about it.

"Hey, thanks for the ego boost." Marshall led her out of the station, which was still bustling for 7 p.m. on a Tuesday. San Diego was a big city with big problems and Katie knew hers was only one of many.

~

Upon arrival at Katie's apartment, Marshall followed her upstairs. "Let me go in first, okay?"

"Really, you don't have to do this. Weren't you the one who told me not to worry?"

"Yeah, well. I'd rather be safe than sorry if it's all the same to you."

"See? It's still locked." After Katie unlocked the door, he pushed it open.

He held a hand up to quiet her and walked in. The summer sun was only just beginning to set as the season got into full swing, and her apartment was filled with its dusky light when they arrived.

"All right, you can come in. Everything seems to be in order."

"Thank you. Do you want to stay for some dinner?"

"No. I've got a lot to catch up on. We're handing over the rest of the files to the DA on the Thompson case. I'm going to head back to the station and wrap that up."

"I'm sorry for taking you away from your real job. You don't have to do this, you know. I can coordinate with Chief Wilson."

"I want to help, Kate. If we get enough solid evidence to reopen this thing, the captain will be happy to take the credit anyway." Marshall started to leave. "You'll be okay?"

"I'll be fine. Goodnight, Marshall, thank you."

"Goodnight. I'll talk to you tomorrow."

Marshall was walking out the door when Spencer appeared on the landing in front of him.

"Spencer?" His unexpected presence startled Katie.

Marshall glanced at her, appearing confused, but waited for reassurance that it was still okay to leave.

"Hi, Katie."

There was no reason for the awkwardness that followed, but it was there, nonetheless, and everyone seemed affected. Katie felt as though she was staring at two different chapters in her life. Before the dreams and after.

"Kate, you okay?" Marshall asked.

"Yeah, of course. I'll talk to you later."

Marshall continued on his way, extending a polite nod to Spencer.

"Did I interrupt something?"

"No. What are you doing here?" They hadn't spoken since last Saturday night and he'd already cleared out his things. She was angry with herself, more than anything, but was projecting it onto him.

"Can I come in?"

Katie stepped aside and let him in.

"I heard they charged the guy who killed Isabelle Thompson and I just wanted to make sure you were okay. Is that why Detective Avery was here?"

A loaded question, if there ever was one. Katie was surprised he still believed something was going on between the two of them. "No. Why are you here?" she asked again, trying unsuccessfully not to sound defensive.

"I left a few of my law books in the office and I wanted to pick them up if that's all right."

"Sure, yeah, feel free." She sat down at the dining table as Spencer collected his books. Feeling awkward and hurt, she didn't really know what to say and only watched him walk around the apartment as if he was a stranger.

He placed the books on the table and sat down next to her, taking hold of her hand. "I miss you, Katie."

"I miss you too." The sincerity in those words was very real.

"How have the dreams been over the past few days? I mean, I figured you'd be under a lot of stress with everything that's been going on."

"I haven't been losing too much sleep, thankfully, but I appreciate you asking." That probably didn't come out right, judging by the look on his face. "Where are you staying?" Changing the topic would allow her to avoid having to tell him about the letter, the existence of which she wasn't sure whether or not to reveal to him, but it hung heavy in her mind.

"With Kevin. I'll probably start looking for a place soon, maybe after the firm removes my temporary status. I'm sure he doesn't want me hanging around too long. And after the team won this last case, it's looking pretty good that I'll get my permanent salary and benefits."

"I'm sure you won't have any problems there. You're very good at what you do."

"Thanks. Of course, I thought I'd be looking for a house with you, not another apartment." Spencer gripped her hand more firmly. "Please Katie, can we just get back to where we were?"

"I don't think I can be who you want me to be anymore. Too much has happened." She still vacillated about the letter. It would only serve to prove his point that she should have just let it go. Now there was the possibility that she could be in real danger.

"It isn't too late. We can still move on," he pleaded.

"That's the problem, Spencer. You want me to move on and I can't. I'm a different person. How can I not be? I know you want to protect me and that's why you want me to let it go, but I can't and I won't. Especially after what happened to Isabelle. I saw the look in that monster's eyes. He took pleasure in her pain. I can't let *him* get away with that."

Spencer sat back in the chair and dropped his shoulders. "I'm afraid something will happen to you, Katie."

"Something already has. That's what you refuse to see."

He cast his eyes away from her.

"Look at me, Spencer."

With reluctance, he did as she asked and returned her gaze.

"I was kidnapped. I was raped. By all rights, I should be dead. It's only by the grace of God that I don't remember the worst of it."

"We can get you counseling to help you deal with it. Why do think you can find this man and catch him when the police haven't been able to for more than twenty years?"

"Because I have to." That was it. She knew it was really over; his face revealed as much. The resolve she felt frightened the hell out of her. It must have terrified Spencer.

He stood up and kissed her on the forehead. "Goodbye, Katie. I'll never stop loving you, no matter what." He retrieved the books from the table and approached the door. It seemed as though he was waiting just another millisecond, maybe hoping she'd reconsider. The door then opened a moment later and Spencer Harris walked out of Katie's life, for good this time.

13

_____

The **missing girl** from McCloud was a dead end. Summer was over as nearly three months had passed with no new information from the chief or their research. Marshall continued with his new case involving the abduction of a five-year-old boy from La Jolla. The high-profile investigation brought with it a lot of media attention. The family was wealthy and had hired private detectives to work in conjunction with the SDPD. This made life difficult for Detective Avery.

Katie was with the Department now—only in a civilian role—but it was a start and she had transferred a couple of weeks ago at Marshall's recommendation. She had to pass an exam, but she was now part of the department that collected and analyzed crime scene evidence. It also allowed her an opportunity to continue working with Marshall and gave him a chance to take her under his wing.

However, progress on her search was at a standstill and was growing colder by the minute. She felt like they had lost the momentum they had at the discovery of the letter to the chief. There was nothing left for them to do, so she buried herself in her work.

"Kate? You ready to head out? I want you to come with me to the

Whittaker house. We're gonna meet with Callahan and the parents. They want updates."

Callahan was the private detective. He seemed to be more interested in the media than in solving the case, but Detective Avery was asked by his captain to stay on the guy's good side. He didn't want any bad press for the department.

Katie grabbed her file and notebook and walked into Marshall's office. As they were about to leave, his phone rang.

"Detective Avery," he answered. "Yeah, Dave, how are ya?" Marshall glanced at Katie.

She had no idea who Dave was but felt a little concerned about the look he gave her.

"Okay, yeah. I'd appreciate that, Dave; thanks very much. Get back to me when you know more. Okay, bye." He returned his cell to his pocket. "That was Dave Landon from the Eureka P.D. He's the guy I asked to look into Jennifer Chase's file?"

"Yeah, of course; did they find her? Is she alive?" Katie never stopped thinking about that little girl who reminded her so much of herself. Even though they believed it was a dead end, her heart leaped at the possibility that they might have found her alive.

"They don't know, Kate. Landon called to tell me that they found a sweater a few miles from the girl's house. It was the one she wore the day she was abducted."

"They know it was hers?" Excitement turned to dread. Finding articles of clothing was never a good thing if one expected the victim to be alive. She'd been around Detective Avery enough to know that much by now.

"The parents confirmed it. He called to tell me they're going to run forensics and let me know the results. It'll take a few days."

"Then they'll enter it in CODIS to find a match, right?"

"You're getting the hang of this stuff, Kate. Yeah, they'll cross-reference to see if anything comes up. Don't hold your breath, though. This girl might look like you, but that doesn't mean whoever took her is the same person who took you. Right now, I'm just looking for some sort of connection; anything that we can run on."

Katie tried to hide her disappointment and made a valiant attempt, but she could see he wasn't buying it.

"I know this has been a long road that hasn't led us very far, but we have to remain diligent. You know what they don't do in the cop shows? They don't show you that it can take months and years to solve a case. It's not glamorous and only occasionally is it exciting. Mostly, it's long hours, sifting through mountains of profiles, interviews, evidence. You know that. You caught a glimpse of that helping me with Johansen. But we will get there in the end. I'm not giving up and I know you won't either. Let's just sit tight for a few days and see what Landon comes up with."

Katie wondered how he did it; how he stayed so positive. In the face of all the evil that surrounded his daily life, how could he manage that sort of clarity? She supposed that was what made him such a good detective. However, it also made her wonder about his personal life. They never spoke about it much and in the time they'd known each other, she had never seen him with a woman. He never mentioned if he had a girlfriend. Only now did Katie realize how selfish she must seem to him. He knew everything about her and she knew virtually nothing about him.

"You're right. I'm sorry; it's not at all like TV. If it was, you'd be dressed in an Armani suit and driving an SUV."

"Hey, you gotta problem with my polo shirt and khakis? And I happen to like my Camaro, thank you very much. I had to wait a long time to get my pick of a car like that. That drug dealer didn't want to give it up. Grab your stuff; we've got to go meet Mr. Private Detective."

Marshall and Katie walked down the front steps of the palatial Whittaker estate, which overlooked the ocean. The meeting lasted more than an hour and several news stations' vans were still parked out on the lawn. This sort of crime didn't discriminate. Here was one of the wealthiest families in southern California and they couldn't protect their child any more than the parents of the McCloud girl could.

"So what was the point of that meeting?" Katie asked.

"You got me. I think it just gave Callahan an excuse to get in front of the cameras again. I wonder when he'll realize this case isn't about him; it's about that little boy."

"Those poor parents. Did you see the mother? She looked like she hadn't slept in days." Katie said. "I don't know how she manages to keep it together."

"She's doing what she has to do to get her kid back." Marshall checked the time on his watch. "I'm thinking it's getting too late to head back to the station. You wanna go and grab a beer?"

"Sure, why not."

It had been a long time since they'd done anything social together. After Isabelle's case went to trial, Detective Avery had to prepare to be called to the stand. Katie had helped him to ensure that the *i*'s were dotted and the *t*'s were crossed. All of this left little time to work on finding *him*, but Marshall did what he could and it was proving to be more of a challenge than he expected. Neither of them had given up, not yet anyway. So, she was glad for an opportunity to go and hang out with him and not think about it for a while.

They arrived at the sports bar near the courthouse. It seemed that was where most of the cops hung out when they were waiting for their cases to be heard in court. Katie was still very new to the scene and only recognized a few of the guys they bumped into as they looked for a table. It was slow, but then again, it was a Wednesday afternoon and probably a little too early for a beer, but in this line of work, you take a break when you can. She'd put in a lot of late nights working on Marshall's cases. They both had.

"Can I ask you something?" Katie asked, sipping on her light beer.

"Shoot."

"In the time we've known each other, you've never mentioned a girlfriend or wife or anything. Do you have either one of those things?"

"Why? You want to ask me out or something?"

Katie smiled and a flush of pink filled her cheeks. "Be serious. You never talk about your personal life. You've read my file; you know everything there is to know about me and yet I know nothing about you. Have you ever been engaged, married, or lived with a woman?"

"Yes, no, and yes." He finished off his beer and motioned the bartender for another.

"Care to elaborate?" she asked.

"Not exactly, but I'm guessing you'd like me to."

"Marshall, I'm being serious here."

"Okay, so I was engaged once when I was about your age actually, so I guess it's been about eight years or so. I met her in college. We moved in together after we graduated and then I went into the police academy. She wasn't happy with my decision. She thought it would be too dangerous, being a cop."

"Doesn't seem an unreasonable assumption," Katie said.

"No, not unreasonable. After I made it onto the force, she supported me. It was hard, but she kept herself busy with her work and I was busy with mine. She never really asked me about the job. I think she was afraid to know." He had already started on his second beer now.

This was probably the most uncomfortable Katie had ever seen him. His voice sounded tense and uneven.

"A few years passed; she was getting anxious to get married and I loved her and wanted her to be happy, so we got engaged. By that time, I had been made a detective. My hours grew longer and my patience grew shorter. Not a good combination." He took another swig. "You know, it's funny; I actually see a lot of myself in you.

We've gone down completely different paths in life and yet here we both are, looking for the same thing."

"I guess you're right. So, what happened? Did you two just grow apart?"

"No, nothing like that. I was working on a sexual assault case. That's what I used to do before I moved to missing persons. We'd been working a case and followed up on a lead from an anonymous tip. We showed up at the suspect's house. The place smelled like a damn meth lab." Marshall looked away, appearing hesitant, but after a moment, he continued. "Long story, short, the guy had a knife on him and he took a swing at my leg after I got him to the ground. He just missed my femoral artery. It was the first and so far, God willing, the only injury I ever sustained on the job. But it freaked her out. She insisted I quit and of course, I couldn't do that. So, that was it. We were done."

Marshall hid his emotions exceptionally well, but not this time. Katie saw a glimpse similar to the look Spencer had given her on their last encounter. A hint of regret.

"You loved her," she said.

"Yeah, well, that and three dollars will get you a cup of coffee. It's not like this job accommodates a healthy relationship anyway. I'm always working; I hang out with the dregs of society. Present company excluded, of course. These are not appealing things to most women."

"I assume you have a family? You don't talk about them either."

"What is this? Are you planning on writing a book? Maybe you should be a detective."

"Maybe I should."

"Maybe you should." His green eyes pierced through her protective exterior with a fervent look that took her by surprise.

"I can't imagine where I'd be if you hadn't come into my life, Marshall. I tried so hard to be the person Spencer wanted me to be. Then you gave me that book. You saw right through me. I don't know how, but you did."

"I know what it means to need to find answers. I see so much of myself in you, it scares me sometimes."

"What answers are you still looking for, Marshall?"

He grinned and shook his head. "See? You're just like me." He took the last mouthful of beer. "Well, I suppose you'd like to get home. I don't have anything for you tomorrow, so that'll give you time to catch up on your paperwork. I assume we'll hear back from Landon by Friday or Monday. Either way, I'll let you know." Marshall threw a couple of tens on the bar. "I'll drop you back off at the station to get your car."

THE EAGERLY ANTICIPATED call came in on Monday morning. Marshall's contact at the Eureka PD had the forensics results on Jennifer Chase's file. Katie believed the little girl from McCloud who looked so much like her as a kid had to get some sort of justice. And, if it just so happened that maybe they might get a suspect as a result, all the better.

Her drive to work stretched into an eternity. Why was it that when one was in a hurry, delays hurled themselves from every direction? Her expectations grew dangerously high. Marshall already warned her not to get her hopes up. This was a shot in the dark that any connection at all could be established. The missing girl was similar in appearance and age and she had disappeared in a similar fashion and location. But the difference was that their cases were twenty-three years apart. Katie was pinning her hopes on a very slim chance.

If the suspect had DNA entered into CODIS for any previous conviction and that was cross-referenced for a match with Jennifer's clothing, they would have an identity. They would then have to hope that the suspect was at least in his late forties to be connected to her. It was rare for a serial killer to be younger than twenty, although it was not impossible. There were so many variables and she struggled to maintain focus.

Katie rushed into Marshall's office. His face revealed nothing, but that was no surprise. He was a master at poker face; it was part of the job.

"Sorry I'm late. Traffic was pretty bad."

"No problem, Kate. Have a seat." Marshall turned his computer monitor so she could see it. He opened up an email from Detective Landon. There were several files attached to the email. Marshall opened the file labeled "Labs."

"Have you already seen this?" she asked.

"Yes."

His refusal to offer further details was a cause for concern, but still, Katie waited patiently as the file loaded on the computer screen.

"Okay, what we're looking at is the summary from forensics. They were able to pull a good sample of DNA off the victim's sweater. The results were cross-matched in CODIS, but nothing came up, no match." Marshall was now looking Katie squarely in the eyes, ensuring she'd heard him correctly. "There was no match, Kate. I'm sorry."

Her breath became labored as she struggled to keep her emotions intact. "So that's it? No match means we don't have a suspect? There's no place else to look?"

"We don't have a suspect. But what this does mean is that they've entered the information into CODIS, so if another sample is cross-referenced down the road and a match is found, they'll be able to connect the cases. That's a good thing."

"That's a good thing, but not for me."

"It was a long shot, Kate. You knew that going in."

"I did. I guess I just thought I had some sort of connection with her. All the dreams and the memories, everything that I've been through in the past six months boiled down to seeing this little girl on the news. I know it was a long shot, but I was banking on it."

"Kate, the important thing here is that you're helping other victims now. That is the purpose of your having survived something so unimaginably horrible. I did say that this would be a long row to hoe. He showed his hand by sending that letter to the chief. He's not done. I promise you that. We just have to be patient." Marshall tried to comfort her, but she resisted.

Katie walked out, her anger consuming her beyond the point of consolation. Marshall might have thought the two of them were alike, but she hadn't anywhere near his level of patience. Of course, she had been the victim, not him.

IN THE DAYS THAT FOLLOWED, Katie's nightmares returned with a vengeance, but they were now about Isabelle Thompson, Jennifer Chase, and the others whom she could not save. She was losing her sense of self, the one thing of which she had always maintained control until she had discovered the truth of her past.

Marshall hadn't called her; she expected as much and knew it was his way of giving her time to deal with this latest blow. However, she discovered later on in the week that he had taken the liberty of contacting Sam, a fact that Sam revealed during their conversation.

"Do you want me to come see you? I can be on the next plane," Sam said.

"No. I'll be fine. I just need to get my head around this. I know Marshall's right; I just don't know if I can sit back and wait."

"But there's nothing else for you to do, Katie. Maybe you should go back to Dr. Reyes and continue with the counseling, especially since the nightmares have been so bad."

"I don't know if it'll do any good. I feel like I've lost everything."

"You will get through this, Kate. You're stronger than you think. I can't say I'm not a little relieved you're taking a step back from pursuing the man who tried to kill you. It's not something I can even hope to understand because it wasn't me who went through what you did. I just want you to be safe."

"I know, Sam. Thank you. It's getting late; I've got a lot of work to do in the morning, so I'm going to call it a night. I'm glad you phoned, although I wish Marshall hadn't worried you."

"He was concerned. You know, I'm glad you have a friend like him down there for you. I wish it could be me, but there's a reason certain people come into our lives. He is supposed to be there for you now. I believe that very much."

"Listen, you know I love you and I'll be okay. I plan on coming to see you around the holidays. I'm going to stay with my parents. It's been a long time since I've been home for Christmas. Goodnight, Sam."

Dusk was giving way to dark when Katie opened the door to her apartment. The fall nights were getting cold now, even by San Diego standards. She tossed her coat on the back of the dining chair. The mail had been strewn across the table along with her bag and keys. Sifting through the barrage of junk mail, Katie spotted an envelope with no return address. The child-like handwriting sent a bolt of adrenaline through her as she read the name. She slowly pulled the letter toward her in order to be sure she was reading it clearly. It was addressed to "Little Katie Reid."

Suddenly doubtful if she was alone, Katie surveyed the dimly lit room. Instinctively she twisted her body toward the front door, ensuring it had been relocked. Her index finger slid under the flap of the envelope, gently pulling it apart. *No, this can't be from him. It's not possible. He doesn't know where I live.* She carefully removed the paper tucked inside, unfolding the top, then the bottom.

"*Dear little Katie,*

I wonder how much you remember of the wonderful time we spent together those many years ago. Do you recall how much fun we had; just you and me? I do. I remember your shiny dark hair, so long and soft, and your sweet, tender lips. I knew you were frightened, that's why I tried to comfort you. It was a shame you left me, little Katie. I had such big plans for us.

Although I suppose now that you're engaged, for which congratulations are in order, you've made plans of your own. Tell me, Katie, does he make you feel the way I did? You were so young and unspoiled. Does he know he wasn't your first?"

She trembled as she read the words. Nothing her dreams had unearthed prepared her for the reality of his existence.

"Oh Katie, why did you start digging around the past? See, I knew that could be a problem down the road. Even when I read those articles saying you couldn't remember what happened, I always wondered if it'd ever come back to you, all those wonderful things we did together. I must admit though, I was a little surprised when I read that you met with Chief Wilson. He was only a detective then, but incompetent just the same. Of course, the press didn't name you, just calling you a 'victim,' but you and I both know you were the only one who got away.

I was angry at first, but then I found another to take your place, and then another. But, I digress. Let me just say this, you should have left the past alone, little Katie Reid."

The letter slipped from her hands and glided to the floor. She stood immobilized, frozen by the echo of his words swirling around her head. Once again, he had control over her, but she would not give in.

Katie snatched her cell phone from the dining table. "Marshall? Marshall, he sent me a letter."

"What? Who?"

She waited a moment for him to comprehend what she was saying.

"Oh my God, are you sure, Kate?"

"Yes." She was the calm one this time.

"How did he find you? I don't understand."

"My engagement announcement; he must have seen it. If he found the article in the *San Diego U-T*, it couldn't have been that hard to find me."

"I'm coming over right now."

Before she could respond, he hung up. It didn't matter; the important thing was that he was coming. She was angry, frightened, and about a million other emotions that coursed through her body.

It took nearly thirty minutes before Marshall arrived. Katie was still sitting in the dining room chair, staring at the letter.

He pounded on the door. "Kate? It's Marshall. Open the door."

She slowly rose from the chair and walked toward the door, calmly and quietly. Katie turned the handle and opened it.

He rushed in and grabbed her by the shoulders. "Are you okay?"

She only nodded.

Marshall saw the letter on the table. "I wonder if we can get prints. What did you do with the envelope, Kate?"

She pointed to the floor.

"Come here and sit down," he said. "This was mailed yesterday according to the postmark. It had to have come from here in California to arrive so quickly. How could he know where you live?"

"He found my engagement announcement and figured I must live in San Diego. How hard can it be to find someone's address? You can find just about anything on the Internet. He only had to search my name. Damn it, I had completely forgotten about it."

"You're right. Jesus, I wish you'd told me about the announcement."

"I'm sorry, Marshall. It slipped my mind. Do you think I wanted him to find me?"

"No, of course not. It's okay, Kate. You'll be safe, I'll make sure of that. I think we need to call Chief Wilson." Marshall glanced at his watch. "He's probably gone for the day, but I'm sure the station will patch me through to his cell."

Within moments, the line answered. "Chief, this is Detective Avery in San Diego. Fine sir, thank you. Chief, I'm here at the home of Kate Reid; she has just received a letter from her abductor. It seems as though he was able to find her location as a result of an engagement announcement that was published back in April of this year.

"Yes, sir. He made reference to the previous letter sent to your station. It is the same guy.... She's all right. I'm going to stay with her for now, but I think it's imperative we take a serious look at reopening the investigation. Although no direct threat was made, a vague warning was mentioned. I think he plans on contacting her again...."

"Thank you, sir. We will e-mail the letter to you now. Please let me know how you intend to proceed as soon as possible and we can coordinate with SDPD. He just crossed over into my jurisdiction now. .... Of course. I'll speak with you tomorrow. Goodnight, Chief." He turned to Katie. "He wants to show the letter to the DA. We still won't have much evidence, but we have enough to reopen your file, he believes. Any threat of harm to another individual, whether known or unknown to the victim, is enough to warrant an investigation. You may get what you want, after all, Kate."

"Did you read what he said about replacing me? There have been others, Marshall; we know that for a fact now. He's hurt others the way he hurt me, only they didn't escape."

"Yes, we can only hope he screwed up somewhere along the way and left an opening for us. I'm not entirely sure where we go from here, but we'll know more after we hear back from the chief. I'd like to stay here with you tonight, Kate; I can sleep on the couch. I don't feel right leaving you alone."

"Okay. I would appreciate it very much if you stayed here, thank you. Are you hungry? I can call for some pizza."

The perplexed look on his face seemed to require that she explain her need for food at such a time. "I've got to have some sort of distraction right now and food seems like a good idea."

"I'm fine. Don't worry about me."

"You still have to eat."

"Okay, okay. Get some pizza."

Katie ordered the food and they settled in for a long night of mindless television, though neither of them could think of much else except for what was to come.

The silence that followed as they stared at the TV wasn't awkward but was comforting because Katie knew she didn't have to say anything. Marshall had an understanding of her that very few had.

The quiet hours lingered on until she drifted off to sleep, curled up on the end of the couch. She roused only slightly when a blanket was placed over her.

"There's my little Katie." The voice traveled to her ears, but she could not see from whose mouth it came. The tightly bound scarf around her eyes made sure of that. *"You know, a lot of people are looking for you,"* the voice continued.

She screamed as loud as she could, but he only laughed. "Oh, Katie, you don't think anyone can hear you, do you? You're far away from everyone."

"I want to go home, please. I want my mommy." She felt a large hand brush the hair from her forehead.

"I know, honey, soon. You'll see your mommy soon. But first, I have lots of fun things planned for us. Do you like games, Katie?"

She nodded.

"Good. I have lots of games we can play together."

His weight lifted from the cot and she listened as his footsteps faded away. He was gone, for now. She pried the scarf down enough to catch a glimpse of her surroundings. The only thought she had was how upset her mother would be because she talked to the stranger. How many times did she tell her not to talk to strangers?

Katie was hungry and thirsty. She saw a cup of water on the small table next to the bed. There wasn't much in it, but it was enough for now.

The footsteps were back and she quickly pulled the scarf back over her eyes.

"You must be getting very hungry. You haven't eaten in nearly two days, little Katie. Remember what I told you? You do something for me

and I'll give you some food. That's how our little game works. I don't want you struggling with me again, like yesterday."

"But you were hurting me," she whispered.

"Mmmm, don't these pancakes smell good? I've got a big glass of milk for you too."

The pain in her stomach worsened with the scent of the food, so this time, when he placed his hand on her thigh, she didn't fight him.

"Please don't hurt me," she cried.

He slid her pants down around her ankles, then slowly felt his way up her thighs. Katie shook with fear as she squeezed her eyes shut behind the scarf. Terror ripped through her until she no longer had any control over her own body.

"You stupid little bitch!" he yelled and jumped off the cot.

That's when she felt it. She had soiled herself. Katie pulled down the scarf to see him hunched over in disgust, wiping his pants.

"Grab the lamp, Katie," a voice whispered as if coming from inside her head. She knew what to do as her body filled with strength far beyond that of a six-year-old. He rose just in time to see her swing the lamp. It struck him squarely on the side of his head. Blood poured from his temple as he stumbled back in pain.

Katie reeled from the blow, almost falling back onto the cot, her tiny body thrown off balance. He stumbled and now was her only chance. She could make it to the stairs before he regained his footing. She reached the bottom step and heard him lurching toward her. "Run," the voice in her head whispered again.

The door at the top of the stairs was stuck. He was only a few steps behind. She finally pulled it open with all the might she could muster.

"You think you can get away from me?" he bellowed, laboring toward the final step. "I'll find you, Katie. There's no place for you to go. There's no one around for miles."

It was so bright in the house; it must have been the morning sun. Katie looked left, then right, and spotted the front door. She had no shoes and no pants, but she ran as fast as she could.

He was almost on top of her now, barely making it out the door *ahead of him. Ahead of her were the woods. Looking behind her one last time, there he was. His bloodied face stared directly at her and he smiled. "I'll catch you, Katie. You can't get away from me."*

Katie sat, bolt-up on the couch. She was out of breath and sweat poured from her brow.

Marshall lurched toward her. "Are you okay? I'm sorry, I must have fallen asleep. Did you have another nightmare?"

Katie looked at him with renewed vitality, grasping what had just happened.

"Come on, Kate, talk to me. Are you okay?" he asked again.

"I saw his face."

Marshall's expression hardened instantly at her words. It occurred to both of them exactly what this meant.

Katie rose from the couch and stood in front of him, breathing heavily, not just from the adrenaline the nightmare forced her body to pump, but because of the certainty that nightmare had just laid at their feet. The emerging idea brought a fleeting hint of a smile to her face. There was no mistaking it this time; there would be no more dead ends.

"Marshall, we are going to find him."

14

THE GIRL WHO ESCAPED

This was the part that she dreaded the most: opening her apartment door first thing in the morning to get the paper. Would they be there again today; the three or four reporters who lingered outside her quiet building in hopes of getting a statement from the girl who escaped? Their appearance had almost become part of her daily routine. So much had happened since she came forward. Was it still September? Katie had to look at the front page just to be sure.

An unusual morning for this time of year; bright blue sky and air so still that as she looked out among the palm trees lining the street, not a single frond moved. A nice breeze could generally be counted on to drift in through the open windows of her apartment; the air having been cooled by the ocean only blocks away.

But in the past few weeks, Katie's life had been dramatically altered, leading her down a path she still feared, and so "unusual" had become the norm. No sign of the reporters yet, but it was still early. She stepped back inside and closed the door. The latch clicked and she cringed, wondering if it would stir Marshall. He was still asleep on the couch. He hadn't left her side since the sketch of her abductor went public.

After the night of the last dream, the one that changed everything, Marshall had accompanied Katie to the police station, where the composite artist had sketched out the face. She brought to life her worst nightmare and it was the first time others would see the monster who had been haunting her dreams for the better part of a year. His long, thin face, round eyes, and high forehead offered a good starting point, but the version she had in her mind was more than twenty years old. It was a distorted, scowling image of a man, angry that he had been bested by a child. But what about now as his youth had given way to middle age? Receding hair, skin leathered with age, waist expanded from years of excess. These were all things that needed to be considered. One thing was certain; she would recognize that scathing stare and twisted mouth if she got the chance to see him again.

Katie remembered everything now: the smell of smoke that lingered on his clothing, the taste of ashes on his mouth as he forced his lips onto hers. Her ability to recognize such things when she was a child hadn't existed and it was only now, as an adult, that she could put a name to those unmistakably pungent odors. Even the origin of the scar on the back of her calf had come back with a fierce, vivid recollection. The lit cigarette he pressed against her delicate skin, twisting and turning it until the flesh burned off because she dared struggle against him.

When the sketch artist finished his work, the drawing was scanned in and "aged" to reflect more accurately what he might look like now. Soon after, it was released to the media and he was everywhere. Her nightmare had become inescapable. Katie was overwhelmed by the attention. Everyone was fascinated by the girl who had no memory of her daring escape until now—especially Marc Aguilar. A reporter from Channel 9 News, he had been ever-present since the story broke.

Today would prove to be no different. By the time Marshall and

Katie left her apartment, they were prepared for another day of a game of survival against the media and a search that had been fettered by anonymous tips flooding the station. Each one took valuable man-hours to vet, but it had to be done.

As the two made their way into the police station, where Katie still had a job working evidence, Aguilar made his way to the front of the usual crowd of reporters until he was less than 50 feet from Katie.

"Ms. Reid! Ms. Reid!"

Marshall instinctively stretched his arm out across her midsection as if he would, at any moment, knock her down to protect her.

"Ms. Reid, Marc Aguilar, 9 Action News."

She knew exactly who he was and tried hard not to roll her eyes in front of the cameras, an action that, if spotted, might turn an influential audience against her. He'd been showing up at the station almost daily since the sketch went out.

"How can you be sure your memory is reliable?" Aguilar continued. "Isn't it possible that the rendering of the man who allegedly took you could resemble someone else; someone innocent of the abduction charges? Our minds do play tricks on us, Ms. Reid, don't they? This did happen more than twenty years ago."

Katie felt Marshall gently nudging her. It was his way of telling her not to fall into this guy's trap.

"Mr. Aguilar," she began. "I appreciate your concern, but I can only rely on the memories that have come back to me and this is the man that I saw, at least, how he might look today. This is the man who kept me locked away for days. The man who tied me up, beat me, and then raped me. A man who is still on the loose." A vision of the monster's bloodied face forced its way to the forefront of her mind; it was the final impression she had of him. "My memory hasn't yet betrayed me, Mr. Aguilar, since I have been able to recall certain details of my case that only law enforcement was made aware of at the time. I'm sorry if it's not enough for you, sir, but I don't believe you have any indication that this sketch is of an innocent man."

"My point exactly, Ms. Reid."

But before he could continue, the police captain appeared, launching himself in front of Katie. "I think that's enough for now, ladies and gentlemen. We'll issue further announcements as the case develops. Thank you."

Captain Ronald Hearn, the man in charge, ushered Katie through the large sliding glass doors and into the lobby of the station. Marshall wasn't far behind and could be heard mumbling obscenities under his breath.

"It's okay, Marshall, really," Katie said. "The guy's an ass. Every time I see his spray-tanned face and over-gelled hair, I change the channel. He's just trying to get me to slip up, I guess. Like he somehow thinks I made all this up, you know? Anyway, he's harmless; you know that."

"You're right." The heat that had risen beneath the collar of his polo shirt evaporated, returning his face to its normal shade. The air had become downright thick in the center of town, not at all helping an already tense situation.

One of the warmest months on record in San Diego, this was just another in the string of unusual events Katie had endured over these past weeks. Since going public, nothing had been as she had expected. Spencer had not made an appearance; something that surprised her, to a degree. She hadn't seen or heard from him since their last meeting when he came back to the apartment to get the rest of his things.

According to one of the few of their friends who had chosen her side, he was quickly becoming a rising star at the law firm and had been seen casually dating a few different women. The friend insisted it was nothing serious; not that Katie inquired as much. That chapter in her life was over and she was sure of it now that he hadn't so much as sent her an email asking how she was holding up. *You can't have it both ways, Katie.*

"We've got to go meet with forensics." Marshall led the way to the back of the station. "They've got the results back on the letter he sent you."

"Do you really think they've got anything?" she asked.

"I don't know. We have to hope he's going to screw up somewhere down the line before he hurts anyone else. Chief Wilson's coming down in a few days with the archived files and I want to be able to share the results with him. He's got the letter sent to him too. We'll be able to identify any similarities and hopefully find some kind of clue as to where we can find the son of a bitch."

Katie noticed how Marshall always referred to her abductor in such terms: son of a bitch, bastard, whatever term he felt conveyed his contempt for the man at that point in time. She was no different. But when she first approached Marshall and he got to know her situation, he seemed to focus on helping her deal with what had happened. Now, he took it all so personally, as if the man that hurt Katie had, by default, hurt him as well.

Captain Hearn had been insisting that Katie enter into protective custody since she first came forward, but that wasn't an option for her. Even Marshall was pushing for it; he wanted to protect her. But there had to be another solution. She'd been hiding from this for far too long already. Her agreement to let Marshall stay with her, at least in the interim, was more to placate the two of them than anything else. That was what she kept telling herself.

THE FORENSICS LAB had become a familiar place. Katie's work often revolved around it: collecting evidence from crime scenes, usually thefts, home invasions, and sometimes arsons, if robbery had been involved. She wasn't assigned any homicides. That required special training and years on the job. She had neither of those qualifications and, for now, that was just fine with her. This past year had brought about enough of a dramatic shift in her life and career. She was content with her work identifying low-life criminals. That was safe, as far as she was concerned. The same couldn't be said for what she was dealing with on a personal level.

"How are we coming along on the Reid letter?" Marshall asked the techie. That was what he called the guys in the white coats.

"I hate to be the bearer of bad news here, detective, but this guy left nothing behind. We've run it for prints, DNA, fibers; you name it. I can tell you how old the paper is and where it was likely purchased. It was watermarked."

"He used watermarked paper?" Marshall's rhetorical question was answered with a nod from the guy in the coat. Marshall turned to Katie. "It's not much, but we might be able to narrow down a location. What's going to be really interesting is to see if Chief Wilson's letter has the same watermark."

Turning back to the man, he continued. "So where do you think this paper came from?"

"Not one of the big box office supply stores. No, this came from a small stationery store. The type and quality of the paper and the watermark have been identified as having come from a mill in the Pacific Northwest. We believe it's the Green Mill Paper Company in Oregon City. Much of what they produce comes from recycled materials, which is what we're seeing here in the fibers of this sample." He held up the letter with a large tweezers-like instrument. "This is one of the watermarks they use. Although they mainly sell to publishers and newspapers, they have a loyal base of mom-and-pop stationery stores that have bought from them for generations. We tracked down their customer list and narrowed it down to five shops in Oregon. These locations were the ones that purchased this particular style of watermarked paper." He handed Marshall a list of names.

"Well, we thought he hadn't traveled far and this proves it. We need to get our guys out there and talk to these storeowners; see if they recognize the sketch. You mentioned you knew how old the paper was?"

"Right; yes." The techie seemed to have been distracted by Marshall's small but meaningful recognition of his handiwork. "I believe it's about three years old."

Marshall deflated, like an old birthday balloon from a party that had ended long ago. "Three years?" He closed his eyes and took a deep breath, appearing to fight off the despondency that was building inside of him. They had been hit with so many roadblocks up to now and here was another one.

"That doesn't necessarily mean he purchased the paper three years ago," the technician continued. "It could mean the store had it in stock for three years."

"Yeah, you're right. We need to go back and see if we can get the captain to sign off on sending a team to question the store owners. We'll have to run it by local PD, of course."

They had started out the door when Marshall stopped and turned back to the lab tech. "Thank you. Nice work."

A perfunctory smile crossed the technician's face as he continued with his work.

The halls were bustling as usual, but they walked in silence. Katie imagined her abductor; his eyes visually consuming what was likely a teenage girl behind the counter of a stationery shop. A girl who came face to face with a killer; completely unsuspecting of the customer in front of her who was purchasing a box of cream-colored, watermarked paper.

"Kate, you okay?" Marshall asked.

"Huh? Oh yeah, I'm fine. Looks like you were right. He might have slipped up. Something as simple as paper; seems too easy."

"Don't get your hopes up too high just yet. We have a lead; that's all we know right now. But yes, it's usually the small things."

"Marshall, do you think we should get the chief to send a patrol to my parents' house?" A sudden fear for their safety came over her. "I don't know how big this story is going to get, but I'm worried for them. And not just because of him. I can't stand the thought of the press harassing my parents. They went through enough the first time around."

"We could, but I don't believe that they're in any danger. So far, he hasn't shown any interest in anyone else but you and the chief, and we haven't heard from him in almost a month. I'm not saying we become complacent, but I don't want to rattle any cages by creating a presence around your family's neighborhood."

Katie was nauseated by the thought that her parents could get wrapped up in all this again. Although she'd already been warned it could very easily go that direction.

"Hey." Marshall stopped and turned her squarely in front of him. "They'll be okay, I promise."

He wasn't one for breaking promises, but even he couldn't control what she had unleashed.

As soon as they arrived back in the bullpen, Captain Hearn called them into his office. A veteran of the first Gulf War, Hearn had a reputation for a lack of tolerance for the media or anything that distracted his officers from doing their jobs. His military-style leadership meant he expected a level of dignity and honor from those under his charge. This included the utmost level of professionalism as the rule when dealing with the unruly press. But for whatever reason, he'd developed a soft spot for Katie and he handled them, for the most part, protecting Katie from the bulk of the onslaught. Maybe it was because he had a daughter; maybe it was because that was just what he did for one of his own.

"Have a seat. I need to talk to both of you."

The ensuing looks exchanged between Katie and Marshall signaled that this wasn't going to be good.

"Katie, I think you've been doing a great job since you came to work for us. But with everything that's going on, I just don't think it's a good idea for you to continue with your fieldwork." He immediately held up his hand, pre-empting any comments from either of them. "You need to understand that you have drawn a lot of attention since coming forward. Even before you both came to me with this, you'd been working on it without my knowledge. That's something that Detective Avery should have realized was going to be a problem with me." A stern look shot out in Marshall's direction.

"For whatever reason, this Channel 9 reporter seems to have it in for you, Katie. He's not going to go away and he will find out that you two were working on this case long before it became public. I have no doubt he's going to drag Chief Wilson, your parents, your friends, and everyone you've been in contact with over the past six months into this."

"I don't get why the hell this guy..." Marshall leaned forward on his chair, suggesting this was an important point he was about to make.

But Captain Hearn only held up his hand again. "It doesn't matter what his motives are, Avery. He's going to get his story. He's going to question your doctor too, Katie. Not to mention that we have no idea if, or when, the man we're after is going to make contact with you again. I can't risk it."

"Aguilar can't dispute what happened to me." Katie glossed over his last point.

"Of course not, but he can and will try to discredit how you came to identify your abductor." The captain seemed to be growing weary of the conversation. "And what happens when he learns this man might be connected with other cases? That we could be dealing with a serial killer? How much mercy do you think he'll show you or the other families who might be involved? Look, I don't give a shit about this guy. What matters is that you cannot continue to be exposed in the field and I'm pulling you out."

Katie stood up, looked Hearn in the eye, and tried to think of one reason why she shouldn't be pulled, but none came to her. He was right. The threat was real not only from the man who took her but from the media as well. "Fine; may I go now?" Almost immediately, she turned to leave, not waiting to be dismissed.

"There's one more thing, Katie," the captain started. "I strongly suggest we place you in protective custody."

She whipped back around and looked at Marshall in astonishment.

"Wait a minute; I thought we discussed this, captain?" Marshall asked.

They both knew that protective custody meant some crap shack in the middle of nowhere. No contact with anyone and no way she'd be able to continue to be involved in the investigation.

"She needs to stay low, Avery. This isn't some random kidnapping case for you two to solve. There's a possible killer out there, looking for her. We aren't going to take this lightly. You, of all people, should understand what's at risk here."

"Where are they going to send her?" Marshall asked.

Katie's irritation grew at his concession to this arrangement.

"I can't tell you that. There's a high probability that the FBI is going to get involved with this case. That happens and you can rest assured they're going to take her far away from here."

"Why would the FBI get involved?" Katie asked.

"Multiple jurisdictions, suspected serial killer; they'll get involved if there's evidence this asshole was involved in the other disappearances that happened the summer you were taken. They'll get their Behavioral Unit involved. We'll be pushed out to pasture."

"I'm assuming you must have some reason to think there's a connection, captain?" Katie asked.

"I've had some interesting discussions with Chief Wilson. We'll know more when we meet with him the day after tomorrow."

"Look, what if Kate stays with me, at my place, at least until we know more? She'll be safe there; you know that," Marshall said.

Relief passed through her at the thought that he was backing her; that she wouldn't be whisked away to some remote location, unable to contact anyone, especially Marshall. He'd been with her practically every day since the last nightmare; sleeping on her couch almost every night. Some nights, they'd stay at his apartment because it was closer to the station, but her place was bigger. She sometimes felt a little awkward at his place, like they were just a little too close. Although so much had happened since he rejected her kiss that night, she still felt embarrassed. He'd never said a word about it.

"I don't want her at her apartment anymore, Avery," the captain started. "He knows where she lives and I don't care if you're there or not. I'm not okay with that."

"Understood, Captain. She'll stay with me at my place until we figure out what we're doing with the FBI."

"From this point on, Katie, you're to stay close to Avery. Go back to your apartment and pack enough stuff to get you through a week or so. We'll have a better idea of what to do with you then. She's your responsibility, Avery. You understand that?"

"I wouldn't have it any other way."

Captain Hearn went back to his computer without saying another word; his actions were a clear sign they had been dismissed.

Marshall's office wasn't far, but it seemed like miles as they walked the halls together once again. She was either going to have to stay with him or be moved to a secure location, period. He opened his office door to let her in and, just for a moment, she noticed a hint of regret on his face.

"You're sure you're okay with this?" Katie asked.

His back turned to the door; he looked left down the hall, then right, stepped inside, and finally closed it. "We've been hanging out for the past month anyway. So, now it's official. Nothing changes." His matter-of-fact tone was off-putting, to say the least.

"Except I can't go back to my place anymore. I guess that's not so bad; a lot of memories there that I don't mind leaving behind." In a fleeting moment of nostalgia, her thoughts turned to Spencer and the safe and happy life they had shared. Sitting on their balcony, watching the sunsets, the Sunday mornings spent lazing around in bed till noon; these were things she was better off forgetting. That Katie was long gone now.

"Well, let's get a few things wrapped up here and we'll head out to get your stuff."

WAKING up in Marshall's small apartment on Day One left her feeling out of sorts, but now, Day Two left Katie feeling downright ambivalent. Now that her place was out of the question, where did she belong? She had become a transient; just another unexpected result of her new reality. What was worse was that Marshall had been burdened by her. Not that he would see it that way, but it was how she felt.

Her overnight bag and a larger suitcase had been stacked against the wall along the entryway. Katie rose from the pullout sofa and retrieved the bag. When she unzipped it, the scent of her apartment spilled out; its salty odor reminded her of the beach and brought a smile to her face. The toiletry bag was on top. Katie grabbed it and went into the bathroom. The apartment had only one, but with two doors; one that led to the hall and one that led to Marshall's bedroom. She quietly locked the door that led to Marshall's room, not wanting to wake him. He, of course, had offered up his room, but she refused.

She hadn't slept well, given the new living arrangements, and decided she couldn't lie in that bed any longer. The hour was still far too early. So early, in fact, that the streetlamps in front of the building were still burning.

Marshall's place was in the Gaslamp District of downtown San Diego, a highly coveted area because of its proximity to businesses, nightlife, and attractions. But for Marshall, it was just close to the station. She once asked him if he had purchased the apartment before or after he broke up with his fiancée. She wanted to know if they had shared a life there but phrased the question in such a way as to inquire only as a strictly financial curiosity. Katie was pretty confident he saw through the ruse. Nevertheless, he answered truthfully, as he always did with her. Yes, they had chosen the place together and shared it for a brief time until she left; well before the housing bubble when a cop could still afford such a place.

By the time she finished her shower, Marshall was sitting at the breakfast bar, drinking coffee and eating a slightly burned piece of toast, staring at a rather large textbook that laid out before him.

"You want some breakfast?" he asked, holding up the overcooked toast.

"No thanks. I'm fine. I'll just get myself some coffee." She already knew where everything was and grabbed a mug from the cabinet next to the sink.

"You okay about seeing Chief Wilson today?" he asked.

"Yeah; I just keep getting that same old feeling like we're running around in circles again."

"It's different this time, Kate. We have a lot more information than we did six weeks ago. I think it's a good idea for the chief to bring all the files down and officially reopen this case. Frankly, this should have happened months ago, but his hands were tied."

"Right." Katie sipped her coffee, resting her elbows on the breakfast bar opposite Marshall.

"What's that you're reading?" She leaned in.

"I'm just trying to get up to speed on ViCAP."

"Sorry, what's that?"

"It stands for Violent Criminal Apprehension Program. It's another nationwide database that the FBI operates in an effort to link cases together that show similar signatures. It's used to help identify serial killers."

Those words still sent a shiver down her back, no matter how many times she'd heard them. "Do we have any signatures? If he is linked to those other kids' disappearances and they haven't been found, what signatures are we looking for?"

"There are quite a few we already know. But I want to meet with the chief to see what else he discovered during his original investigation that he hasn't already shared. He always suspected there was a link, so I want to know why.

"Damn, we're going to be late." He glanced at his watch, took a final drink of coffee, and grabbed his keys.

She grabbed her bag and hurried to catch up, but he was already one foot out the door.

15

C hief **Robert Wilson**, from the Rio Dell PD, was already in the conference room; his files spread out across the table. Katie spotted Captain Hearn a few feet ahead and she and Marshall filed in behind him.

The conference room was large and well-appointed with the latest technology. Katie thought the chief might be envious of the sheer amount of money this police department had, given his lack of resources in his rural town. An enormous 75-inch flat-panel television hung on the wall and just below it, resting on a credenza, was a slim notebook computer. On the cherry-stained oval table sat another laptop and three speakerphones that looked as though holographic images might suddenly appear and hover above them. Economic downturn be damned; this department had money.

"Katie, it's very nice to see you again." The chief offered his hand.

"Nice to see you again, Chief; although I wish it were under different circumstances."

"Me too, Katie."

With the requisite pleasantries exchanged, Captain Hearn took the lead. "Thank you, Chief Wilson, for coming down to see us. I see you have the files we requested. Might we take a look?"

"The latest piece of evidence is this letter that I received a few months ago, back at my station in Rio Dell." Chief Wilson pulled out the letter, which had been sealed in an evidence bag. "I immediately informed Ms. Reid and Detective Avery that this came to me and advised them to take caution in any further inquiries into this investigation. All was quiet until last month when Ms. Reid received a similar letter at her home. I'd like to see that letter, Katie."

"Yes, we have that." Katie looked at Marshall, who had the case file and pulled out the sealed bag containing the letter. She glanced over at Captain Hearn, who was sifting through some of the documents the chief had brought with him. One of the items of particular concern was a photo of the girl from Portland. Captain Hearn began jotting down some notes.

"I think we should consider entering this case into ViCAP," Captain Hearn said, still taking notes.

"There are clearly some similarities between Katie's case and the others who went missing that same summer. If we can get the details down, we just might get a hit from another agency."

"I'm sorry; I don't know that much about ViCAP," Katie said.

"If another jurisdiction or agency entered similar signature marks from an ongoing investigation, or cases that have gone cold, then we might be able to match up some of those marks."

"I don't know, captain," the chief started. "I would doubt cases this old would have been entered into a system that most jurisdictions still aren't very familiar with. I've never used it myself, but its widespread use among local authorities is still fairly uncommon and, from what I understand, the FBI is slow to provide assistance in utilizing it effectively. You may just be wasting valuable man-hours here."

"I respectfully disagree, Chief," Marshall chimed in. "We need all the help we can get and it wouldn't take long to get the data entered. We aren't talking but maybe half a dozen markers to identify."

"Respectfully, Detective Avery." The chief's tone was quickly changing. "I've been doing this a long time and I know every detail about this case, and I'm telling you, you're wasting your time with ViCAP. We need to be focusing on leads from the hotline and, from what I understand, you've got some kind of lead on where this stationery was purchased. That's current and relevant information we need to be running on. Not spending hours sifting through this file, trying to figure out if our guy preferred to rape little girls or little boys or how he might have disposed of the bodies." The chief's eyes widened as he realized his callous choice of words. "Jeez, Katie; I'm sorry. I didn't mean to say..."

"No, it's fine. I'm wearing my big girl pants today. I can handle it." It wasn't fine. And when Marshall looked to her for assurance that it was, her eyes told a completely different story. Still, she held it together even as memories of her captor's hands touching her thighs flashed through her mind. Taking a deep breath, she refocused on the task at hand.

"We can discuss this another time, Chief, but I'm telling you, it is something this department will pursue," Captain Hearn replied.

The chief appeared to be agitated, which surprised Katie. She had only ever seen him as a calm, rational man.

"On another note, we'd like to discuss setting up patrols around Kate's family home. The constant presence of the media is a cause for concern and after discussing it with Captain Hearn, we are in agreement that we want to shield her family from it as much as we can, at least for the immediate future. Is that something your department can take care of, Chief?" Marshall asked.

In a slightly less inflammatory tone, Wilson replied, "That's something we can agree on, detective. I'll set it up immediately after we've finished here today. Katie, have your parents been informed of the situation?"

"I have spoken with them, yes. They are aware that the sketch has been made public. But to my knowledge, they haven't been approached by any media. Or anyone else, for that matter."

"Good. We'll be sure and keep it that way. It hasn't been made public that the suspect could be linked to other cases, but when it is, and it will be soon enough, the chief will need to step up patrols. If and when that time comes, we're going to have to talk to those other families," Captain Hearn said.

"That won't be easy, captain. I doubt they want to hear from me again." Wilson seemed hard-pressed to continue. "Not after I let them down every time I had a lead that didn't pan out. Most of those parents just want to let their kids rest in peace. They've come to terms with what happened."

"I'm not so sure about that," Katie said. "It's only a matter of time, like Captain Hearn said before we have enough solid evidence. I believe they'd very much like to close the book on the past. I've lived with what this has done to my own family. And I made it home."

"If it's all right with you, Chief, I'd like to have my team scan your files into our system for reference. I plan on sending a couple of guys up to Oregon City to follow up on the paper lead. They'll need to get up to speed on the case," Captain Hearn said.

"Listen, I don't know how much more help I can be here. I haven't been contacted by him since this letter he sent months ago. I gotta be honest with you; I don't know where to go from here."

"I'm surprised to hear you say that," Marshall started. "You put your soul into this case and now, forgive me if I'm wrong, but it seems you just want to give up. We *know* what he looks like now."

"You know what he looked like twenty years ago, detective. I'm sorry to say, but apart from this minor lead you've got on the paper, you don't have much else to go on."

Marshall pushed the sketch across the table toward the chief. "This is what we've got. It's been scanned in and adjusted by a software program that ages a person based on certain factors that we input. You can't sit there and tell me we've got nothing. What is it about this case that gives you pause?" Marshall's frustration had become obvious to everyone. "Can't deal with the fact that you let the child killer get away? Is that it? We're supposed to just give up because you did twenty years ago?"

"Detective Avery!" Katie said.

"It's all right. I doubt Detective Avery has ever been forced to deal with the fact that he didn't do his job; that he let a monster slip out from under him and then have it thrown back in his face twenty years later. You be sure and let me know what it feels like when your failures are thrust back in your direction. Then, maybe we can talk. My point is, detective, I've been down this road before. I'm just trying to save you the frustration that I've been dealing with for most of my career."

"I think we're forgetting one thing here," Katie interrupted. "This isn't about you or Detective Avery. This is about me and the other missing kids. I'd appreciate it if you both would put your egos aside and remember that." Katie stood up, shoving her chair hard and, as it rolled back and hit the wall, she stormed out. She was angry and had every right to be. Katie walked back to her desk with speed and purpose.

"Kate, hang on a minute," Marshall said, jogging to catch up with her. "I'm sorry. You're right. I don't know what's gotten into the chief. This is the first time I've seen him so defensive. It just caught me off guard, okay?"

"Neither one of you was there with me, sitting on that damn fold-out cot while I waited for that fucker to come down and put his hands on me. And now that I've come forward, put out this sketch of what I remember him to look like, you think he's done with me? Because I sure as hell don't. The letter will attest to that. So I've got to deal with you two pissing all around me; trying to prove that you're each a better cop than the other."

"I know." He shrugged. "I just thought he was on our side. That's all."

"He is on our side. He just doesn't want you or the FBI taking over and trying to prove he screwed up the first time around. You can't tell me you'd feel any different in his shoes."

"All right. I get it. I'll go back in there and make nice. Let him know he's in charge. For now."

"I need to talk to my parents. Tell them to get used to seeing patrols on their street. Thanks to me...again." Katie sat down at her desk. Since she was no longer allowed to conduct any fieldwork, she'd be entering the data that the rest of her team collected. It could be worse; they could have let her go altogether. Marshall, looking defeated, went back to the conference room to smooth things over.

She turned on her computer and opened her email. An urgent message from a sender she didn't recognize popped up. In the subject line were the words *I'll need my trinket back.*

"What?" she whispered, double-clicking her mouse to open the email. An image of the young girl from Arcata, Ashley Davies, stared back at her. The same picture she had first come across when all this started. *The necklace?* she wondered.

Her heart pounded against her chest as she looked around, wondering if she would find him staring at her from somewhere off in the corner. No one was paying any notice of her as they sat in their cubicles, clicking away on their keyboards. *First the letter to her apartment and now this? He knows where I work.* It had been almost a month since he sent the letter. Why now? Why here? She was scared and needed to find Marshall. Katie didn't want to risk anyone else looking at the email, so she texted him to come back as quickly as he could.

A minute later, she caught sight of him walking at a brisk pace toward her desk.

"What is it? What's wrong?" He kept his voice low enough so as not to raise suspicion.

"Look." She pointed to her computer screen at the photo. "It's him. He sent this. I don't understand what he means by wanting his trinket back, but this is the girl whose necklace I saw in my flashbacks, remember?" She took to calling them flashbacks now since they were no longer simply nightmares. They were a reality she had come to accept as a part of who she had been and they had shaped who she was now.

"I remember," Marshall stared at the screen. "How the hell did he get your email address? How does he know you work here?"

She shook her head. "He wants to find me." A deep breath helped to slow her pulse. "I just don't get why he's telling me he wants it. Wants what? That necklace? I don't have it. What the hell…" And then it came to her. "The necklace was on a stand on the other side of the room I was in. He took it from her."

"It was his prize," Marshall interrupted. "His signature."

"Damn. Was I wearing some sort of jewelry when he took me? I don't remember having a necklace on."

"Could it have been another piece of jewelry? A ring, earrings?"

"Not a ring, I wouldn't have had a ring at that age. Earrings? Maybe. I don't really remember when my ears were pierced. I'd have to ask my mom."

"Maybe he took a piece of jewelry—a trinket—from all his victims? Kate, do you remember seeing any other pieces besides the necklace?"

"No. We need to talk to the chief and take another look at the pictures from the other kids who went missing. Although the boy who had been taken from his bed—I doubt he had any jewelry on. That's not to say it couldn't have been some other trinket he found in the kid's room, I suppose. Maybe we'll find something there. If he had a habit of taking these shiny things, prizes or whatever, from his victims, he must want mine back; whatever it was. He apparently didn't keep it. Maybe he waited until they were dead before taking the souvenirs. A prize for all his hard work."

"We need to show this to Chief Wilson and the captain. He's getting too close, Kate. I think once they see this, they're going to insist you go someplace safe. I don't see how we're going to keep the FBI out of this now. He damn near just admitted to taking this girl. I don't *think* we're dealing with a serial killer; I *know* we are."

AFTER DEALING with the IT department, the chief, and Captain Hearn, Katie had had enough. She was glad to be back at Marshall's. The email rattled her hard, but she knew it could bring them one step closer to finding him. They were already working on tracing the email's origins. It seemed unlikely, given the history of the killer's methods, that he would have used a traceable IP address. Nevertheless, IT had their work cut out for them. Marshall was right about one thing: her abductor had just admitted to being the same man who killed Ashley Davies.

The apartment brightened in an instant as Marshall flipped on the lights in the living room. The dusky light outside filtered through shade-screened windows and cast a murky light. The conditions were a difficult adjustment to the already sore eyes of a person who'd been staring at the words of a killer on her computer screen for most of the afternoon.

It had been brought up, more than once today, that putting Katie into protective custody was the only option. The inevitability of the FBI's involvement was no longer in question and, in fact, Hearn made the call and an agent was already assigned. This new cog in an expanding wheel would be flying in tomorrow. He would help enter the case information into ViCAP and take point on coordinating between the multiple jurisdictions.

Katie dropped to the couch, exhausted and frightened. Maybe they were right; maybe she should be relinquished to the hands of the FBI, sent someplace far away where neither she nor her family would be in any danger. But she felt safe being with Marshall—conflicted about putting him in too much danger—but safe. He, of course, would not see it that way, but the fact remained.

Marshall joined Katie on the couch with two beers in hand. "Here, thought you might want to take the edge off."

"Thanks." It might take the edge off, but it would take a hell of a lot more than one beer to get her to sleep tonight.

"You defended the chief earlier today saying that I didn't know what it was like having to live with letting the bad guy get away."

"I'm sorry, Marshall. I was just upset."

"No, it's okay. But I want you to know something about me. Something I never, ever talk about."

He rarely talked about himself at all; in fact, Katie always felt he kept her at arm's length.

"You know I was born in Chicago, right?"

"Yeah." That much he shared only after she dragged it out of him one night because he'd had a few too many beers at the bar.

"We lived in the suburbs. Oak Park. My dad was an architect for a firm in the city. My mom stayed home with me and my little brother. We had a pretty great life there. We took vacations every summer and my parents seemed to be happy together. My brother and I always fought; no surprise since he was younger and wanted to hang out with me and my friends."

Marshall's eyes lit up as he talked about his family. An only child, she couldn't entirely relate, but it was the first time he'd ever spoken of them other than in passing.

"So my dad took the 'L' into the city every day. He was usually home by 6:30 and then we'd have a family dinner. My mom insisted on it and he complied with her wishes. Always. One night, when I was ten, my dad was late. Really late. It was almost 9:30 and my mom hadn't heard from him. She said he had to work late because of some project deadline, but that he was expected home no later than eight o'clock. This was well before cell phones, so she had no way of contacting him. He didn't wear a pager. That was the thing back then, right?"

Katie smiled at his reticent humor but remained silent. *Just let him talk.*

"It was about midnight when the cops showed up at the house. Me and my brother waited at the top of the stairs. Mom thought we were asleep, but we both heard the doorbell." Marshall took a swig from his beer; his eyes drifted far beyond the here and now.

Katie knew what was coming.

"The conductor found his body on the way back into the city. It was a late weeknight and the train was empty. The cops said he was robbed and then stabbed. Whoever did it got off at a random stop—they didn't know which one—and left him for dead. By the time the conductor found him, he'd bled out. No pulse."

The words reverberated in her head while she watched as Marshall's eyes glistened with tears. But he turned away and wiped them dry.

"They never found who did it?"

"No. They suspected it was a couple of kids, thugs, but no one saw anything. It just became another in a long line of unsolved murders in Chicago. So, my mom packed us kids up and moved here to live with my aunt. My mom, who, by the way, had never worked a day in her life, had to take a waitressing job while she went back to school to finish her college degree. She was hardly ever home. My dad had a small life insurance policy, but that ran out pretty quickly. I basically raised my little brother, who was only seven at the time. So much for my happy childhood."

"Is that why you became a cop?" Katie asked.

"I suppose it played a pretty big part. I wanted to catch the bad guys to try and make up for not finding the ones who killed my dad, at least at first. But after too many years on the job, I think I've learned how to accept what happened; accept that I couldn't fix it. So, I do know what it's like living with the cloud of failure over my head."

"Marshall, you can't possibly hold yourself accountable for what happened. You were just a kid."

"Maybe you should take your own advice. That's what I've been telling you practically every day since we met."

"I'm so sorry; I had no idea. You never talk to me about your family."

"I know. It's not easy for me to let people in. The last time I did, I got my heart stomped on pretty good." He moaned a little as he rose from the couch, his bones crackling along the way. "How about another beer? Feel like pizza tonight?"

And that was the end of it. He turned it off just like that. How selfish she felt. Insisting this was all about her and he knew nothing of what she'd gone through. It was a different situation, but he knew what loss felt like. What it felt like going through childhood with that emptiness.

Katie stood up and wiped her eyes so he wouldn't see how deeply saddened she was for him. He wasn't the type to accept pity. "Another beer would be great. And I could definitely go for some pizza." She joined him in the kitchen.

He handed her another beer and raised his own. "Here's to a couple of messed up kids."

16

The **airport baggage** claim teemed with weekend travelers. Midday on a Friday was the worst possible time to be at the San Diego airport. A man emerged from the crowd and Katie knew right away that he was FBI. With a shoulder bag draped over his front, he appeared to be fresh out of the training academy in Quantico. Military-style hair, high and tight, pressed white dress shirt, navy pants. Fit, but not overly muscular and he couldn't have been more than thirty-five.

"I bet that's him," Marshall said.

The man approached, seeming to immediately recognize the two of them. Katie wondered if he'd already run their profiles.

He offered his hand to Marshall first. "Special Agent Nicholas Scarborough, FBI, Behavioral Analysis Unit. You can call me Nick."

"Detective Marshal Avery, SDPD." They shook hands. "And this is Kate Reid."

His grip was firm, but not bone-crushing. At this point in Katie's life, she'd come to realize that there were those men who shook women's hands like a jellyfish, which she felt lacked respect, or those who shook with full-on, pain-causing hand compression, which meant they were trying to project their dominance. This was neither, and it was those rare men whom she respected most.

"Nice to meet you. Should we head back to the station?" Katie asked.

She relegated herself to the back seat so Marshall could get the agent up to speed. The FBI's involvement would mean some serious changes in the investigation and it wouldn't be long before she would know whose side Scarborough was really on; hers, or his own that followed a career-building path on which she was merely a stepping stone.

"We're getting some pushback from the original investigating officer, who now runs the Rio Dell Police Department. He has no interest in utilizing the ViCAP system," Marshall said.

"I'm not surprised. We get a lot of departments that just don't have the manpower to dedicate to entering old case files. With several cities going bankrupt and taking their public services down to bare-bones, I can understand it. But, without the participation of these jurisdictions, the system is virtually ineffective. I'll walk him through it today and see if we can get somewhere." The agent turned to Katie. "I'm sorry you have to go through this, Ms. Reid. I can't imagine how difficult this must be."

"I appreciate that, Agent Scarborough. So, what is the Behavioral Analysis Unit?"

"We handle cases involving child and adult victims; abductions, disappearances, homicides. I provide operational support to local law enforcement."

"I see. I don't know how much you are aware of, Agent Scarborough, but I've been working side by side with Detective Avery for months on this case, my case, and I don't intend to be pushed to the sidelines." She wanted to be sure to get that out of the way to avoid any confusion.

"Of course not, ma'am, and please, call me Nick."

She was beginning to like Nick already.

Reporters waited outside the station, as they had ever since Katie went public and there was Marc Aguilar, with his orange face and paper-white teeth at the head of the pack.

The three of them made a beeline to the entrance to avoid any questions.

"Ms. Reid, I understand the FBI is now involved in the investigation. Care to comment?" He shoved a microphone in her face, but Marshall reached around her and hustled her inside.

"How the hell does he know that?" she asked. "We only just found out ourselves."

"I don't know, Kate, but I can't say that Scarborough's appearance doesn't just scream FBI. Aguilar's probably talking to someone in the station. We need to get the captain to issue a statement that we can't comment on an ongoing investigation. Hopefully, that'll be enough to shut up whoever's flapping their gums here."

"Agent Scarborough, we've got a makeshift workstation for you set up in our small conference room. I hope that'll be okay for now."

"I'm sure it'll be fine. I'd just like to speak to Captain Hearn first. Is Chief Wilson still here?"

"Yes. He'll be here for a few more days," Marshall said.

"Good. I'll want to get a download from him too."

Katie was surprised at how quickly Hearn had the space set up for Agent Scarborough. They didn't mess around when the FBI got involved.

"I'll be at my desk if you need me," Katie said to Marshall. "I'm sure we'll catch up later, Nick. Thanks again."

Katie walked back to her desk; her files had piled up. Spending a lot of time with Marshall took its toll on her workload. The computer booted up and Katie opened her email, not realizing for a moment that she'd stopped breathing in anticipation of something terrible. But there were no surprises. When would he again make an appearance and catch her off her guard? If his goal was to frighten her, then he had accomplished that much.

She again thought about the trinkets—the prizes—and picked up her cell to call her mother while she slipped out the back and waited for an answer.

"Hello?"

"Mom, it's me." Katie listened as her mother flooded her ear with concerns as to why she hadn't been calling every day and how she tried her apartment but got no answer. For whatever reason, they rarely tried her on her cell. It was like the cell phone was some foreign technology that they just didn't understand. "I'm really sorry, Mom. I've been staying with Detective Avery as a precaution. Listen, I wanted to ask you something. Was I wearing any sort of jewelry on the day I went missing? Like earrings, a necklace, bracelet, anything?"

"Oh, honey, I don't remember. The only thing that I thought about was getting you back."

"It's okay, Mom, it's nothing, I was just..."

"Wait. Yes, as a matter of fact, you were wearing a pretty little silver bracelet your grandmother gave you for your birthday, the February before..." She trailed off.

No one around her seemed to complete a sentence that involved reminding Katie of her abduction; not even her mother.

"But, I honestly don't know if you were wearing it when we found you. Honey, I was so overwhelmed with relief, I didn't pay attention. But the thing is, I just don't remember seeing it at all after you came home. I can have your father bring down the boxes in the attic with all your things and see if it's in one of them."

"That would be great, Mom. It would be a big help, actually."

"Can I ask why?"

Katie couldn't mention the email; it would be too much for her. "I was just curious, that's all."

"Okay, then. When are you coming home? I don't like all these news stories showing his face. I want you home, safe."

Deborah wasn't completely off base. He seemed to know Katie's every move here, maybe staying back home wasn't a bad idea. "It's fine, Mom, really. I work in a police station; I don't think I could be much safer."

"Please, promise me you'll come home soon, okay?"

"I will. I promise. Send Dad my love and I'll do a better job at keeping in touch. Goodbye, Mom." Katie arrived back at her cubicle to find an agitated Marshall pacing around it.

"Where the hell have you been? Jesus, Kate, you can't just go wandering off without telling anyone."

This was a first. What cause did he have to be so on edge? "I just went out through the break room to call my mom."

He swatted the air as if to shoo away his concern. "Sorry. I've been working with Agent Scarborough on this ViCAP program. We think we have a match to the case in Portland. There are enough similarities to warrant a harder look, anyway."

"Well, that didn't take long."

"No, it didn't. Someone in Portland's been using the database and already had the case entered. So when we entered your case, the markers were there and we got a hit. Looks like the Portland PD has been utilizing the program for a while with a lot of success, according to Scarborough. Come on, I'd like you to see this. We need to call the chief in too."

"Has anyone seen him this morning?" Katie asked.

"He just showed up and is in Captain Hearn's office; probably complaining about me. You know he hasn't cared much for me since I took you up to the edge of the woods, where you were found. He told me then I was wasting your time."

"I know, I remember. It's a difficult situation, Marshall."

"Yeah, I get it."

They entered the makeshift FBI field office where Agent Scarborough was pulling some papers off the printer. Not far behind, Captain Hearn and Chief Wilson came into the room.

"I've printed off the identifying markers between your case and the Portland investigation of the missing girl from September 1990.

Her name was Angela Richards, eight years old." Agent Scarborough handed copies to everyone. "You'll see that the age of the victim is a match to the age Ms. Reid was at the time of her abduction, give or take a year or so. Going past the comparable appearances of each of them—dark hair, petite build—we get into even more important similarities. She was taken from her neighborhood in a rural community just outside of Portland, on her way home from school; very much like Katie. So, we're seeing his opportunistic nature. Many of these serial killers are driven by opportunity; very few are in fact, planned abductions.

"Her body was found about a year later in Forest Park, just west of downtown Portland. A hiker who had veered off the Wildwood Trail spotted some buried human remains, only slightly exposed above ground. It had been a particularly wet summer, so it was assumed the runoff from the rain washed away some of the material used to bury the body, exposing it just enough to be have been visible by passersby."

"We are somewhat familiar with this case, agent," Marshall started. "But to my knowledge, no DNA evidence was uncovered, since that technology was new at the time. And, not to be insensitive, but she's been in the ground a long time. Even if we could exhume her now, which I assume would be highly unlikely; none of her killer's DNA would still be present. How can we be sure there is a connection? None of the other presumed victims have ever been found."

"We aren't positive, detective, but if we can meet with the lead investigator for this case, or at least someone they've got working cold cases, we can take a look at the files for more information."

"I get that we need to establish a connection here, but aren't we well past this now? The guy is after me, right? You all think so and I agree. What good is this going to do us now? We know what he looks like and we need to find him. What about the lead on the stationery? Is anyone going to look at that? It's current, it's relevant, and I think we need to move forward with it." Controlling her frustration was becoming difficult and she began to fall in line with the chief's way of thinking. She was tired of this road they had been down far too many times. It was time for action, but no one else was seeing it that way. "And what about the hotline? Is anyone going to follow up on those leads?"

"I understand where you're coming from, Ms. Reid, I do. But believe me, we need to talk to the Portland PD. I'm not saying we can't continue exploring other avenues, but we cannot dismiss this. If we can find a pattern of behavior, we'll be one step closer, I promise you." Agent Scarborough scanned the room, seemingly looking for a general consensus among the rest of the team. "We do need to consider your safety, Ms. Reid, and I think the best way we can do that is by entering you into WitSec. Normally, this is reserved for witnesses who are about to testify or have testified in certain cases. But you've received threats to your life and, given the situation, you are technically a witness. I think we can justify this particular use of the program."

"No! Absolutely not! I am already under 24-hour surveillance from Detective Avery. I do not need to be shipped off somewhere where I'll have no idea what's going on. None of you would even be here if it weren't for the fact that I recovered my memory. I am a part of this, damn it!"

"Calm down, Kate." Marshall was the only person who could possibly get away with saying that right now. "She's right. She's the one who's been persistent and forced everyone's hand to reopen this investigation." He shot a disapproving glare at Wilson. "She is a part of this, whether you like it or not. Now, I can't say that I completely disagree with her needing more protection. I have been keeping her under my wing, but that's not to say that we shouldn't be monitoring her cell phone, her email, and anything else that may be a way for him to contact her. He's proven his ability to reach her time and again. We need to get on top of this before it's too late."

Before it's too late? That was the first time he'd ever expressed that he might actually be afraid for her. That the killer might find her and she wouldn't be able to get away again.

"I think Agent Scarborough is right about the Portland girl, Angela Richards. We can't dismiss that. But I believe Katie's involvement is still critical to this investigation," Captain Hearn replied.

Katie was surprised to have the captain's support. Hadn't he just said the day before he wanted her in protective custody? Had her words finally convinced him otherwise?

"Okay, Ms. Reid, you've gotten us this far." Scarborough seemed resigned. "I don't have any right to ask you not to see it through. But we will implement Detective Avery's suggestions. Our guys will tap your cell, trace your emails, and have a regular patrol set up around Avery's place. In the meantime, I think it's wise to get in touch with the cold case department at the Portland PD and move forward on this situation. Detective, I'll let you take the lead on that. I'm going to send some of my people up to Oregon City to follow up on the stationery stores. It's a start."

In an instant, Scarborough was on the phone, arranging for a team to be organized to go to Oregon City. With no clear direction, Katie assumed she'd been dismissed and continued back to her desk.

"I guess we'll finally get a team up to Oregon City. I think Hearn is happy he doesn't have to pay for it. You going to be all right?" Marshall accompanied her back.

"Yes. Thank you—for standing behind me. I just couldn't handle being shut away, not knowing what was going on. Not after everything we've done to get this far."

"I know. That was exactly the point. But be prepared because your privacy just went out the door. Every call you make on your cell, every email you send will be monitored. Does Sam know what's going on?"

"I talked to her a few weeks ago, before I came forward. She didn't want me to but understood why I had to do it. She's just afraid for me, that's all. I'll call her today before they get me wired up and let her know what's going on."

"I think that would be wise."

"When are we going to Portland to talk to those guys up there?"

"I doubt we'll go there. They'll send the lead detective down here, I'm sure. My guess is the guy will probably be here by tonight. I don't think Agent Scarborough wants to waste any more time and I couldn't agree more."

"It seemed like the chief was objecting a little less today. I don't think he said a word in there," Katie said.

"That's because he realized he needs to be on the right side of this deal or risk not being a part of it at all."

"I guess. I'm going to run out back and call Sam. Then I've got to sort through this backlog. I keep falling behind like this and Captain Hearn might just fire me."

"I doubt that. I'm going to head back into the conference room and talk to Scarborough, find out when our Portland guy's going come down. I'll catch up with you later."

Katie grabbed her phone and began dialing Sam as she walked toward the break room. It led out to a patio lined with lush greenery and clay pots filled with perennials in shades of red and yellow. It was quiet, save for the soothing buzz of a few bees in search of nectar. She inhaled the warm, but still damp air that had just a hint of salt in it. They were a few miles from any water, but still close enough to smell a trace of the sea. Sitting down on one of the stone benches, she listened to Sam's phone ringing on the other end. Voicemail.

Damn, she thought. "Hi, Sam, it's Katie. Just wanted to let you know that I'm fine and I'm staying over at Marshall's now, so you'll only be able to reach me on my cell. Oh, and after today, it's going to be monitored, so if you call me back and get my voicemail, just keep the language clean. Just kidding. I'll talk to you later, hon. Take care. Bye."

It had been too long since she'd spoken to Sam and Katie regretted not getting the chance to today. She could use a sounding board right about now.

THE APARTMENT WAS cold and dark, much the way it felt most of the time to Katie. Marshall's place was very modern and in stark contrast to her own. Concrete kitchen counters atop black cabinetry, slate-tiled floors, and Copenhagen-type furnishings. Katie much preferred her beachy décor with soft blue walls and bright white trim.

It was almost eight o'clock before they made it back to his place. He set the bag of take-out Chinese on the breakfast table and dished out their plates. Katie went to the front window and looked down at the street. "Aren't they supposed to be sending a car to patrol the area?"

"Don't worry, Kate. We've got plenty of eyes watching out for us. You forget we're in the Gaslamp. Lots of tourists and activity. I think we're pretty safe," Marshall said.

She released the curtain and sat back down. "Right."

"What's wrong?" he asked.

"I don't know. I'm still pretty freaked out by the email. I didn't mention this to you, but I asked my mom if I had been wearing any jewelry when I went missing."

"His treasures?" Marshall asked.

She grunted. "She thought I had on a bracelet my grandmother gave me for my birthday earlier that year. Apparently, I never took it off, but the problem is, she can't remember if I was wearing it when I came home."

"And you're wondering if he has it?"

"No. He said he wanted it back. Makes me think I was still wearing it when they found me."

"So, we figure he collects jewelry from his victims. That would explain the necklace you remembered seeing in the room."

"Yeah. I wonder how many of the kids he took were wearing some sort of jewelry."

"These are the things we need to be looking at. That's where I think that ViCAP program is going to help out a lot. You might have just found us a solid connection."

~

"Detective Avery, Ms. Reid, I'd like you to meet Detective Phil Larson from the Portland PD." Scarborough initiated the introductions.

The fact that it was Saturday morning and early at that, meant nothing to these very dedicated people. Katie wondered what their families must sacrifice on a daily basis for such devotion.

"Nice to meet you, Detective Larson," she said, extending her hand.

A simple nod and a firm handshake from Marshall were all the introductory niceties he generally ever granted anyone.

"Okay, let's get started." Agent Scarborough started up the laptop and triggered the monitor on the wall to come to life.

Katie looked at the picture of the missing girl from Portland, Angela Richards, as it came into focus on the big screen. It must have been the start of a slide show because another picture appeared a few seconds later of the girl's skeletal remains, partially exposed above the ground. The next image revealed the rotted flesh that remained on an otherwise severely decomposed body, the soil having been brushed away. These were obviously pictures of the original crime scene; a sight Katie had not expected to see. The next picture showed the girl's entire body lying in a shallow grave. The maggots left only patches of her young, fair skin; her wounds, still evident. Katie had to turn away from what she saw next.

The men all around her were speaking of this little girl as if she was something to be analyzed for evidence, describing her "lacerations" and "blunt force trauma." The stab wound to her lower abdomen. Katie couldn't listen to it anymore. Everything she feared was staring at her in the face and no one else seemed to be bothered by it. This poor girl was no longer a child, but an object to be debated with a casualness that repulsed her.

She launched from her seat and practically sprinted from the room, not wanting them to see her breakdown.

Katie made it to the patio and slumped down on the stone bench, nearly hyperventilating and drenched in tears. Never before had she seen such brutality and certainly not against a child. Even her job didn't expose her to such horrendous scenes. Sure, she had opportunities to look at crime scene photos, but given her past experiences, had little interest in the ones involving murders. Marshall seemed to be used to it, at least he was behaving as such.

"Kate?" Marshall appeared moments later, obviously having excused himself soon after her sudden departure. I'm sorry, I didn't think about..." He sat beside her and pulled her close.

She cried into his chest. His heart beat fast against her cheek and his breath felt warm on the top of her head. Marshall stroked her long, silky dark hair and let her cry.

Katie slowly breathed in the musky cologne that lingered on his shirt as she began to calm her anxiety. When her tears dried, she looked up at him, staring into his soulful green eyes. They were breathing each other's breath now. Their lips were so close, neither one dared to pull away this time. He pressed fervently against her mouth.

The kiss was the culmination of too many months of sharing a painful past and fearing an unknown future.

Marshall gently leaned back, but only a little. "I should have warned you about the photos and I'm sorry. Do you want to sit the rest of this out?"

"No. I'll be all right. I just need a minute to pull myself together. I'm sure everyone in there must think I'm a hopeless wreck."

"No one thinks that, Kate. Agent Scarborough apologized to me for not preparing you first. They all know what you've been through, including Detective Larson. They're just used to seeing this sort of stuff. They know how to handle it."

"But it was like they saw her as something to be studied, not the human being that she was."

"It has to be that way. They've got families, kids. They know not to take it home, or take it personally. It's just the way you've got to be in this line of work."

"I know. I just wasn't prepared and I'm sorry for running out like that."

"Don't be. You can rejoin us when you're ready." He squeezed her tightly, saying nothing of the kiss.

Her feelings for Marshall were difficult to define. She leaned on him for support, but did she really want it to turn into more? It was a complication that she was not prepared to face and certainly not when a killer was after her.

Katie opened the door to the conference room after regaining her composure. No one made a big deal about her disappearing act and only acknowledged her presence with a nod of approval and continued on.

"Ms. Reid, Detective Avery filled us in on your theory regarding the possible victims' wearing a piece of jewelry the unsub takes for his collection."

"Yes, Agent Scarborough." She figured as long as he was going to call her Ms. Reid, she'd take to calling him Agent Scarborough. "Based on the email we believe to be from my captor, he references the returning of the 'trinket' that I supposedly took from him, or rather, kept from him. If you'll recall from the files my therapist sent over, I mentioned seeing a necklace in one of my flashbacks. I believe it was the necklace of the girl from Arcata—Ashley. It was difficult to be sure. As Chief Wilson pointed out when the memory surfaced, I had seen a picture of her prior to the flashback and it could've just as easily been a memory of that first photo. But after receiving the email from him the other day, I questioned my mother if I had on any jewelry. A bracelet, she recalled but had no idea whether or not I wore it when I was found. Last we spoke, she was going to search for it."

"But we don't know if she has found anything yet?" Detective Larson asked.

"No."

"I would venture to say that this is a fairly significant discovery, Ms. Reid. If we can determine the other missing children were wearing something similar, well, I think that's a pretty good connection," Agent Scarborough continued. "We have enough right now to at least enter that marker into ViCAP and see if we get any more hits. We're also going to need to speak with the parents of the other suspected victims; ask them about any jewelry."

"You sure we want to get more people involved in this?" Chief Wilson asked, although his tone was much less confrontational than the other day.

"Respectfully, Chief, this guy's picture is being broadcast throughout most of California. It's only a matter of time before it hits the national news. If we suspect a wider involvement, we need to find out now before the media does."

"Detective Larson's right," Marshall said. "We need to stay in front of this."

"So we'll be talking to the families of the other three suspected victims? I'd like to be there when you do if that's okay. Knowing that I was able to get away and now I can possibly help them get closure, I think they'd be grateful."

The men looked around at each other in search of some form of agreement. Sometimes she hated being the outsider, feeling as though permission must be given by those in the brethren of law enforcement.

"Yes. You should be there," Marshall insisted.

17

The **he Eureka airport** terminal was quiet and gave Katie a moment to convince herself that her presence would be a good thing for the families. It wouldn't be easy talking to the parents of the other kids; the ones who didn't make it home. Two decades of making every attempt to lock away the pain in the dark recesses of their minds, only to have it haunt them in their dreams. She was no stranger to that condition. And would bringing the situation to the forefront cause them even more pain? *Yes*, she thought. But how much greater relief would bringing the monster to justice serve?

The files stated that two of the families had more than one child. She supposed the parents had no choice but to stay strong for them, but what of the Davies family, from Arcata? Ashley was an only child, so far as she knew. It was possible they'd had more since then; an attempt to fill a void that could never really be filled. Having known, firsthand, how this had shaped her and her own family, today would be no easy day. She survived and felt guilty for it.

"The patrol car is waiting for us in Arrivals. We'll head to the Arcata station, talk to those guys, and head out this afternoon. I'm sure they'll want one of their own to come along. We're getting an awful lot of cross-jurisdictional involvement here. Someone's going to need to take point. I don't want the families overwhelmed with a bunch of badges showing up at their doors," Detective Larson said. "Agent Scarborough, I'll defer to the FBI to take the lead. Have your people contacted the families yet?"

"Yes. It seems as though they'd been expecting a call from us. The news of Ms. Reid's case has spread. I'm just grateful we'll be talking to the families before the media gets to them."

The Arcata police station wasn't far. Agent Scarborough formed his core team and they were on their way. Fortunately, this still involved Katie.

"You're sure you want to do this? You don't have to," Marshall said as they jumped into the patrol car.

"I owe it to them."

The first stop was to the Davies' house, about forty-five minutes outside Eureka, on the outskirts of Arcata. Katie took in the familiar scenery along the drive. She hadn't been back home since traveling to the place in the woods where she'd been found, in hopes of stirring up more memories. That was the beginning of the end of her relationship with Spencer and the catalyst that had led her to this very point in time.

Agent Scarborough knocked on the door. Standing next to him were Marshall, Katie, and Chief Wilson. Detective Larson and Detective Wright, from Arcata PD, stood in the background. It was decided that they would go in only if the family was comfortable, and needed to be there as a show of local PD support.

"Mr. and Mrs. Davies?" The couple standing in the doorway appeared to be in their late fifties. The mother, slightly plump, but well dressed with short brown hair, tipped her head and opened the screen door. The father stood behind his wife as everyone filed in, his eyes followed Katie's every step.

"Sorry for the full house, Mr. and Mrs. Davies. I'd like to introduce everyone here." Scarborough proceeded with quick introductions as they moved from the foyer into the front room.

Katie could feel Mr. Davies' stare, which brought her nerves on edge.

"Please, sit down." Mrs. Davies gestured toward the flowery printed sofa. The room was very warm. Not many people this far north had air conditioning. Most of the time, it wasn't warranted, and certainly not this late in September. But today was hot and the humidity made the air sticky. A fan, the old box-shaped kind with the plastic handle on top, sat in the opposite corner of the room, stirring the warm air and bringing only mild relief.

The men waited for Katie and Mrs. Davies to sit down before finding a seat. On the coffee table were cookies, crackers and cheese, and a pitcher of iced tea, surrounded by clear plastic cups. Mrs. Davies took her time pouring everyone a drink. It seemed like no one wanted to discuss why they were all there, least of all, her.

It was Mr. Davies who took the lead. "I imagine if my Ashley were still alive, she'd look very much like you, Ms. Reid."

A rush of heat filled her cheeks and Katie immediately took a sip of tea for distraction. Her mind drew a blank from any of the things she had planned to say during the course of the flight. She glanced at Marshall, who picked up on the hint.

"Mr. and Mrs. Davies, we very much appreciate you agreeing to see us today. It's my understanding you both are aware of why we're here?"

The parents said nothing, only nodding in response. The father continued to steal glances at Katie.

"Thank you for inviting us into your home. I'll get right to the point as I don't want to waste any more of your time," Scarborough jumped in. "We have some fairly strong evidence that your child's disappearance may have been committed by the same person who took Ms. Reid in the summer of 1989."

"You poor girl," Mrs. Davies uttered.

Katie recognized the look in her eyes. It was the same heartbroken look her mother had when she first confronted her about the kidnapping.

Scarborough went on to explain. "I know you both have been through the wringer already, so I will keep this as brief as I can. Ms. Reid, after no memory of her disappearance, has recently been able to recall most of her time with her captor. In these 'flashbacks,' she remembered a heart-shaped pendant necklace we now believe was the same one your Ashley wore when she was taken."

Mrs. Davies gasped. "She always wore that necklace. It was a gift from her father on her sixth birthday. She always played with my nice jewelry." Mrs. Davies took her husband's hand. "He didn't want her to break any of my expensive pieces, so he bought her that necklace. She never took it off. I tried to keep her from wearing it to bed, but it was a constant battle that I eventually gave up. Are you sure it's the same one?"

"Unfortunately, there's no way to be entirely sure. We are relying on Kate's memories, which, so far, Mrs. Davies, have proven to be reliable," Marshall said.

Even from the beginning, he believed her; believed *in* her. Katie pressed her lips together, revealing a small but grateful smile at his confidence.

"Much of what we know about this individual, we've learned from Kate. I would say that the necklace is as good a lead as we have had to date."

Katie wondered for a moment why he hadn't mentioned the email about him wanting his trinket back. That seemed to be a more definitive connection. "Mrs. Davies," Katie jumped in.

"Please call me Patricia," she replied.

"Patricia, I can't tell you how sorry I am about what happened to your daughter. If only I could have remembered everything long ago, it might have been easier to find him and stop him from taking any more children. I can only hope that speaking with you today and getting your blessing on continuing the search for this monster will bring you both some closure. I know it will bring me closure too. We wanted to talk with you first, but there's a good possibility the other children who were taken that same summer are a part of this too. We intend to speak with them as well. Out of respect for your family and in honor of Ashley, we will do our best to limit your involvement, but you must be aware of the possibilities of the media attention this will bring when it fully comes to light." Katie was surprised by the clarity with which she was able to speak. Her mind cleared a path for her to make her point to these parents with a determination she thought she was beginning to lose.

Everyone's eyes were fixated on her, hanging on her every word. In that moment, she was transformed. But it was the look in Patricia's eyes that came from a longing for closure that she might finally bury her daughter, which completed Katie's transformation.

Mr. Davies looked at his wife, saying nothing, but knowing exactly what she wanted. It was something that came from years of suffering through the pain together, never letting it tear what remained of their family apart. "Ms. Reid, my wife and I will cooperate in any way we can and we can handle the attention. God knows we've been through it before."

"Mr. and Mrs. Davies, we can't thank you enough for allowing us to continue with your help. We won't take up any more of your time," Marshall said.

Scarborough was the first to rise. Taking his lead, everyone else followed suit. Mr. Davies opened the front door and offered his hand in parting. Nothing else needed to be said.

Two DAYS of reliving her own kidnapping through the eyes of the other parents left an exhausted Katie grateful to be back in San Diego. It seemed that the heat spell had finally passed, bringing the typically pleasant Southern California weather back to its rightful place.

Katie regretted not having the time to see her parents while traveling nearby, but they were on the FBI's schedule now and there was a job to be done. She had managed a call to check-in. Deborah only mildly complained about the patrols set up every few hours around their house. She said it was scaring off the neighbors from attending their weekly bunko games. Deborah had a way of glossing over certain realities she couldn't face.

It was midday and still early enough to go back to the station and brief Captain Hearn. Agent Scarborough was slowly taking the lead role in the investigation. Marshall seemed to be taking it well enough, respecting the FBI's authority over the case. He didn't have much say on the matter one way or another. It was looking more and more like a serial murder case spanning at least two states. He knew where the jurisdictional lines were drawn.

"I think we need to continue working our way through what we know of each of the victims' missing items. The killer seemed to have a proclivity for collecting these small, shiny things. That's the best indication of a pattern we have," Captain Hearn said.

Katie coined the term for lack of a better description of the killer's collection, given the fact that the boy, whose parents still maintained a small part of their home as a shrine to their son, said he kept a silver toy train engine on his dresser. He was the only victim to have been taken from his home. They'd never been able to find that toy.

Captain Hearn seemed pleased by their progress. "Avery, if Scarborough needs your assistance entering this new data, then that needs to be your priority."

After the briefing, Marshall assisted Scarborough, as directed. Katie was right on the money with her assumptions and the remaining families confirmed as much. The Portland girl, Angela, had been wearing a charm bracelet when she disappeared. It was noted in the Portland PD case file that she was not wearing it when they found her body, but that detail was never entered into ViCAP; a seemingly insignificant oversight, until now.

"You ready to get out of here?" Marshall leaned on her cubicle wall. It was already dark and neither of them had eaten since the plane.

"Yes, I am." She was more than ready to get back to Marshall's place. It wasn't home, but it was the closest she was going to get to it and better than the crappy hotels she'd been staying in for the past few nights. What about all the wasteful government spending she'd heard so much about? That must not have applied to the FBI's budget when footing the bill for this trip.

THE COOL EVENING breeze drifted in through the open windows of Marshall's apartment, although it did bring with it a mild scent of car exhaust from the streets below.

The soothing drone of the television soon quieted her racing thoughts and the couch she curled up on felt comfortable and safe. She was wound tight and could feel it in her stomach; like someone had a vice grip on her gut and was squeezing it with tremendous strength. She hadn't even noticed when Marshall sat down beside her, holding out a bottle of beer. The much-needed beverage signaled the end of a long few days. "Thanks."

"Agent Scarborough said his team is still up in Oregon City, checking out the customer lists at the stores. So far, no one recognizes the sketch, but they're searching their records for sales of that bond paper."

"Do you think that's a viable lead or are we grasping at straws here?" Katie asked.

"Nothing is insignificant; not in this case. Remember, it's the little things that bring down the worst criminals. We don't want to overlook anything right now. Besides, just because we've established a connection, it doesn't bring us any closer to finding him. It only allows us to find any additional victims that could be in the system that we hadn't thought were connected. It establishes a pattern of behavior that will work to our advantage. But our goal is to find him, and that still plays an important part."

"I can't talk about this anymore tonight; I'm sorry. I just need some time to process everything that's happened these past few days."

"Understood," Marshall replied.

He had an on/off switch that Katie hadn't acquired as of yet. It amazed her still.

They sat side by side, the television flashing meaningless images, but offered a welcomed distraction. Katie could feel the movement of Marshall's body every time he changed seating positions on the couch; resting one leg on the other, then changing again. He seemed anxious. She suspected it was because this was the first time in days that they'd been truly alone. While traveling, they stayed in separate hotel rooms, a patrolman stationed outside her door at all times, as Marshall had insisted.

It was the first time they had been alone since the kiss; the one he hadn't once mentioned.

Katie missed the ease with which they used to talk. They could talk about anything. But lately, and especially since the kiss, things have been different. He told her once before when fear consumed her enough to try to seek comfort from him, that it couldn't happen that way. He wouldn't take advantage of her like that. Did he feel he let her down this time when he gave in to her impulse?

Katie inhaled deeply, preparing to broach the topic, when her cell phone rang. "That's probably Sam returning my call from a few days ago." She stood up with obvious haste; a sense of relief that her topic would have to wait, and grabbed her phone from the kitchen counter.

"Hello?"

There was silence on the other end.

"Hello?" she asked again.

A look of concern crossed Marshall's face as he turned to her.

"Little Katie."

She knew those words; she knew that voice from a very long time ago. Her hand froze, unable to drop the phone that was now infected with the evil that sounded from it. She met Marshall's eyes with a wild look of terror, her body trembled as she waited for what would come next. It was the first time she'd heard him speak since her escape. Different from her dreams, but no doubt it was the same man.

Her mouth opened, about to reply, but instead gasped to fill her lungs with the air that had unexpectedly escaped. Marshall immediately leaped out of his seat and rushed to her side. The sight of her was enough for him to know what was happening. He motioned her to stay on the line, to get him talking. Her phone was being monitored. This was her chance.

"You have me all wrong in your little sketch, Katie. I saw it on the news. I'm much more handsome than that. Don't you remember?"

Marshall was trying to get her to respond.

"How did you get my number?" It was the only thing she could think of and regretted it immediately. He wouldn't be stupid enough to talk for long and that was the best she could do?

"What about my keepsake; my little trinket? Will you be returning it to me? I'm only missing the one. Yours. Don't make me find a replacement, little Katie."

And that was it; he was gone. Katie's knees collapsed from under her. Marshall reached out to grab her before she fell to the ground.

"You're okay, you're okay. Just sit down." He kicked the dining chair out from under the table and sat her down.

"Son of a bitch!" Marshall yanked his phone from his pocket and called Agent Scarborough. "He just made contact with Kate. He's got her number. Find out where the call came from!" he barked at the agent. "I'll meet you at the station in twenty." Marshall lifted her off the chair carefully. "I'm sorry, Kate, but we need to go now. We have to find out where he is. Can you walk?"

The most she could manage was a slow blink of her eyes as acknowledgment. *Come on, shake out of it.*

Was this it? Were they about to find him? Without a word, she followed Marshall out the door.

SEVERAL PEOPLE SWARMED the SDPD conference room by the time they arrived. Technicians from their station, the FBI, Captain Hearn; they were all there, buzzing around, scrambling to track down where the call came from.

Katie saw maps on nearly every computer screen; large, colorful circles overlapping one another on not only the city, but throughout northern California and up the coast.

"What is all this?" Katie asked. She spotted Agent Scarborough heading toward them.

"As you know, after the unsub emailed you, we had your cell phone monitored," he began. "The way we do that, in order to determine the location of a call, is through a device known as 'Stingray.' It's essentially a fake cell tower that tricks a phone into connecting to it. We can monitor calls and narrow down a cell phone's location."

"It's controversial, to say the least, because it can also pick up calls from anyone in the immediate area," Marshall said.

"Yes, but it is invaluable in tracking down the people we want to find. The other noise that comes through is discarded," Scarborough continued.

Katie couldn't have cared less about this and impatiently waited for one of them to make a point.

"But what this means is that we are able to locate the unsub, most of the time. The only problem is when the mobile phone is being utilized in a more remote or rural area." Scarborough pointed to one of the monitors. "There are far fewer cell towers in remote locations, which makes it much more difficult to pinpoint exactly where a call came from. This is the problem we're having now."

"So what do we know at this moment?" Marshall asked.

"We know the call came from somewhere northeast of Eureka. We can't get any closer than about a fifty-mile radius."

"Jeez, we were just there!" Katie prayed this would be the end of it, that they would be able to find him now.

"I'm sorry, Katie. I know that's not what you wanted to hear," Agent Scarborough said.

"But what about the email? Don't we know where that came from yet?" she asked.

"The IP address came from a server located at the public library in Eureka. He used one of their computers to log on and send the email. The address is no longer valid."

How many times had she been down this road? Dead end after dead end. Was he going to taunt her the rest of her life, or would he eventually track her down and kill her while the FBI and police used their hi-tech devices that didn't seem to be telling them a damn thing.

She wanted to storm out of there, find that damned Marc Aguilar, and broadcast to the world that if that son of a bitch wanted her, to come and get her. She wanted to scream at the top of her lungs, release the fear and the anger that had been building over these past several months. He was controlling her again, just like he did when he locked her in that basement. It had to stop. She would have to draw him out.

"I want to hold a press conference and direct it to him. I know he'll be listening. Tell him that I'm right here. Come and get me!" She shouted those final words.

Everyone in the room turned to look at her, but she didn't care anymore.

"Kate, I know you're frustrated," Marshall began. "But this is your life we're talking about. He's getting too close and I think it's time we consider getting you out of here."

"What?" Her anger was spilling over onto the person she trusted most. Was he turning against her?

"I think we need to reconsider protective custody." Marshall looked at Agent Scarborough as he spoke.

Katie could see by their exchange that they agreed. No, she would not let this happen, not now. "Absolutely not, Marshall! I am in this and I'm not going anywhere. The only reason we've gotten as far as we have is that he's been contacting me. Look, we know he's in northern California, just based on the call and the email. We may not know exactly where, but why the hell can't we send some people up there to find him? Go to the library; see if anyone recognizes him. Why the hell is this so hard for you to figure out?"

Marshall reached for her shoulder. "Kate, I can only do so much to protect you. We will obviously follow the leads we have and, trust me: he's going to screw up enough for us to find him. I promise you that. His arrogance will get him caught. But I can't be worried about ensuring your safety. The FBI will send you somewhere safe until we find him."

"So, I'm expected to stay there for how long? A month? A year? How long will it take for you to catch him, Marshall?" She stepped back and watched his hand slip from her shoulder. Her anger was lashing through him like a whip; deep and stinging with every sylla-ble. She could see it in his face.

She turned away, not wanting to see what her words were doing to him. "I'm not going to be hidden away, Marshall." Her tone calmed as she scanned the room again. This time, everyone looked away and went back to their assigned tasks. "You need me to draw him out and that's exactly what I intend to do."

The resolve in her gaze was enough for both Agent Scarborough and Marshall to concede. They almost simultaneously gave a single nod in her direction. The agent went back to his computer monitors and jotted down the coordinates that flashed on the screen.

"This is where we'll go first." Scarborough held up his tablet. "If we go now, we'll be there by first light."

Neither of them said anything further. Direction had been given. They would be going back to Eureka tonight and the team would scour the 50-mile radius from the cell signal.

BACK AT MARSHALL'S PLACE, Katie packed a few things for the flight. They were to fly out on the red-eye, which gave her only a couple of hours before they had to leave for the airport again. The two hadn't spoken more than a few words since returning to his apartment.

Guilt was setting in and she didn't know how to approach him for an apology. She was wrong to lash out that way. Marshall had been the only one so far to ensure her continued involvement in the case. He knew what it meant to her, so it took her by surprise when he was the first to suggest that she go into custody.

"I'm sorry, Marshall. I forgot myself for a minute and I had no right to say those things to you, especially in front of Agent Scarborough."

"It's all right, Kate. I understand what this is doing to you."

"No, it's really not all right. You're trying to protect me and all I give you is grief. I just want this to be over. I feel like my life is on hold, like he's taking more of it away from me."

"I get that. I do." He walked toward the couch where she was pulling items from one suitcase and putting them into another.

"I feel like a transient. I'm just moving from one place to another; unsettled and uncertain of where I'm supposed to go next."

Marshall reached for her hand as she grabbed a shirt from the big suitcase. He held the shirt with her. "Hey, you've been through more than anyone I know. You've changed your entire life, your career, everything to find this man. I had no right to ask you to stop now."

She stared into his eyes, which looked grey instead of green in the dim light of the apartment. It was late and she was tired—of everything. But it was then that she realized her feelings for him were real and wondered if they were one-sided. Too much had happened today to worry about it now.

Katie dropped her gaze. "I know you're trying to protect me, but please know that I have to find him. I can't sit back while you, the whole of the FBI, and all the other police departments track him down. It's me he wants and you know he won't leave me alone—not now."

THEY WERE BACK in Eureka after having been there not even a full twenty-four hours before. Nobody knew where the killer had called from, but Scarborough was about to meet the field techs who could get them as close as possible to where they suspected his location to be.

No one slept on the plane and it was now seven o'clock in the morning. The team arrived at a local FBI field office in Eureka, where they had much greater access to equipment that would provide the specifics they needed. Though unrelated to the Behavioral Analysis Unit, Scarborough seemed to be familiar with some of the other agents working there and quickly gave them a download of their purpose.

"Avery, Katie, come on over here. I'd like you to meet someone."

Within earshot of Scarborough's words, the two headed in his direction.

"Special Agent Rick Vance; he's in charge of this satellite office of DITU. Sorry, the Data Intercept Technology Unit, for those of you who aren't familiar with the many acronyms of the FBI."

"Nice to meet you, Agent Vance," Katie replied.

"Detective Avery, SDPD. Nice to meet you."

Scarborough continued. "These guys utilize a system called NarusInsight. It's basically a surveillance program that collects mass amounts of data. They can search emails, internet traffic, key search words; just about anything. It's installed directly into the internet service provider's infrastructure and the data it collects is stored externally for deciphering by technicians. They also utilize Stingray on a much broader basis."

Katie was beginning to realize there was no such thing as privacy anymore. But that held little weight right now, given the fact that this technology could very well lead them to the killer. "So, you're saying they can find him with the use of these systems?" Katie could only handle so much of the FBI's vernacular and wanted to get down to brass tacks.

"I'm saying we can get a hell of a lot closer with their help," Scarborough replied. "Look, I'm sure you must be exhausted. Why don't you two go get checked into a hotel, get some rest, and I'll be in touch later on this afternoon. I'm going to need to work with these guys for a while before we know anything further."

It was midday when Marshall's cell phone rang. Neither of them had gotten much more than about an hour or two of sleep. It was late in the week and the hotel they checked into was one of the few with rooms available. It seemed there was some big convention in town and the place was teeming with medical professionals making a lot of noise.

"Gotta be Scarborough. He said he'd call after they had a chance to analyze the data." Into the phone, he continued, "Detective Avery here." Marshall held the phone to his ear and soon began breathing hard, his chest heaving in and out, but still saying nothing.

No, not again, she thought.

He put his phone down, never taking his eyes off Katie. "That was Wilson. He just got a call from Jarrod Hansen. Sam didn't come home from work yesterday."

18

I t was six o'clock the next morning before they arrived back in Arcata. Scarborough didn't want to leave Eureka until he gathered as much information as possible from the surveillance team. And in the end, they determined the call came from the area around Arcata. It seemed they would have ended up there one way or another.

Katie could hardly remember anything that had happened since Marshall uttered those words yesterday afternoon. She remembered rushing back to the FBI's field office to meet with Scarborough, where Marshall went on to explain how the chief was notified of the disappearance.

Jarrod, Sam's husband, called the department when she hadn't arrived home from work the day before. Wasn't that the day the killer called? Katie couldn't remember; her head was still swarming. Sam, where was Sam? When was it that she tried calling her? Last week? Sam didn't answer; it went to voicemail. Katie should have known then something was wrong. Sam always called back right away, especially with everything that had been happening.

"Kate, come on."

Marshall led her to the rental car, where she sat quietly, staring through the passenger window at the sun's early rays that sliced right through the Redwoods. They were heading straight for Rio Dell. Scarborough's team followed behind as they drove to the rural police station for a visit with Chief Wilson. They hadn't talked with him since he returned home after the initial Portland meeting.

The skies eventually gave way to the flourishing light as dawn broke through. Katie had lost all track of time and couldn't remember what day it was. The others were moving at a frantic pace, but she had lost all purpose. With no one else in the car, she finally broke down. "She's gone, Marshall, and it's my fault. I did this. He's trying to get to me through Sam."

"Stop it, Kate. We don't know that."

There was no use in debating. She knew the truth. He had her, or he had already killed her, and nothing Marshall could say would change that. Katie turned away again and stared out the window through watery eyes, not bothering to try to convince him further of what she already knew.

It was the chief's pitiful look that pushed the knife in deeper. "Katie, I'm so sorry," he said, arms outstretched as he intercepted the team in the parking lot of the station. She hardly had a chance to get out of the car before he wrapped his burly arms around her, an uncomfortable and unexpected response that caught her off guard. Thus far, she had only been greeted with uncomfortable glances from the rest of the team. No one seemed quite sure how to handle this situation.

"Did they find her?" she asked, dismissing his gesture of kindness.

"No," Wilson replied. "I think it would be a good idea if you stayed with your parents tonight. I'm stepping up patrols and posting one of my men there."

"Do they know?"

"I thought you'd prefer to speak to them. We don't know anything yet, Katie."

"I can take her there, Chief."

She recognized the young officer from her last visit when Spencer was still with her. That seemed like a lifetime ago.

"If it's all the same to you, Chief, I'd prefer to drive her there myself, check things out, and have a word with your man on site," Marshall said.

He always took the lead where her safety was concerned, but right now, nothing, not even Marshall's gallant gesture, meant anything to her.

"I'll be fine with Officer Miller. You need to stay here with Agent Scarborough and I'd like to spend some time with my family."

On her way out, Marshall brushed his hand along her arm. She turned to face him. He wanted to say something—she could see it in his eyes—but he only looked at her, presumably searching for comforting words, but none came.

She saw something else too, something that went much deeper. Katie turned back once she stepped outside to see if he was still watching. He was.

Deborah stood on the front porch when she and Officer Miller arrived. He led her into the house and proceeded to search the rooms, ensuring everything was secure.

It was John, Katie's father, who seemed genuinely grateful to the officer for bringing her home. "Thank you, Officer Miller." He patted the young man's shoulder as he escorted him out.

"You're welcome, sir. We're stepping up patrols, so don't be alarmed if you notice a bigger presence out here."

"We understand and thank you again."

"Sir, ma'am, Ms. Reid." He gripped the rim of his hat and lightly tipped it.

No sooner had John closed the door, than Deborah rushed to embrace her daughter.

Katie fell limp in her mother's arms and released the emotions that had been pent up all night. "Sam's missing. They can't find her. What if she's dead?"

"They'll find her," Deborah stroked her hair just as she did when Katie was a child.

"Come on, you two. Let's go sit down and gather our strength. I'll get some coffee. I'm sure you're exhausted."

Katie couldn't recall a single instance where her father actually offered to do something instead of her mother. Things were so very different now—now that she knew everything. This was what it would have been like had none of this ever happened. And Sam would still be here.

The three of them sat in the family room and watched the news. Deborah set out a basket of pastries she'd picked up from the local bakery yesterday. And they drank their coffee and ate breakfast, not mentioning the possibility that Sam had been murdered. Her story wasn't even on the news yet.

Katie kept her cell phone in the front pocket of her button-down shirt, which was tied at the waist. The weather was much cooler today and she was glad for the long sleeves. It seemed the Indian summer had finally passed over much of California, bringing only the smallest sense of normality back into her world.

Completely unaware of the countless hours they'd all spent watching the news, the same stories being repeated on a loop, she was already beginning to feel the warmth of the noonday sun radiating from the family room window. They just sat there, waiting for news of Sam, when none came.

A hard knock on the door quickly brought everyone out of their dazes. John leaped out of his chair and made a beeline for the front door.

The footsteps in the distance meant John was not returning to the room alone. Katie immediately turned around and saw Marshall standing in the arched opening that led to the family room. Her father was close behind.

She shot up from the side chair and ran toward him.

One look and she knew immediately. Her head shook hard, trying to rid herself of the impossible realization of what she knew to be true. *She's dead, she's dead.* The words swirled at a dizzying pace through her mind. She continued to stare at Marshall for some sign that this was all just a misunderstanding. Her eyes grew red and pooled with tears at his continued silence. "No—please, Marshall, no."

Deborah grabbed Katie and pulled her close.

Katie howled an excruciating moan and couldn't keep her feet beneath her. The heart that beat so strongly in her chest was shattering into a million pieces. She wrapped her arms around her mother as cries echoed through the house.

Deborah led Katie back to the sofa, where she remained glued to her mother's side.

"I'm going to get her some water," Marshall said to John. But he did not return for several minutes.

When he reappeared, Katie was sitting up, wiping her eyes with tissue. He handed her the glass of water. "Kate, Sam's husband and parents are at the hospital. Do you want me to take you down there?"

Her body still trembled and she struggled to reply with any confidence. "Yes," she said in a whisper.

KATIE WALKED into the restroom at the hospital to check her face. The bloodshot eyes and tear-stained cheeks were all that remained of the earlier version of smudged eyeliner and running mascara. She splashed water on her face and held a paper towel against her skin to dry it. Katie couldn't help but stare in the mirror at this woman who she hardly recognized. She was about to see her best friend lying on a cold metal slab. *Stop, stop...* she squeezed her eyes tight to halt the stem of tears that tried to force their way down again.

A knock on the bathroom door startled her. "Kate, are you coming out?"

"Yes." She cleared her raspy throat. "Give me a minute." Marshall was waiting and it was time to face the reality of the nightmare she had brought to life. Opening the door, she saw Marshall standing only steps away. He moved forward to offer a hand, but she refused it. They walked in silence to the morgue.

The double doors could only be opened from the inside and Marshall pressed the button to be allowed entry. They quietly, slowly opened to bring into full view the room's living occupants: Sam's mother, Molly, who was at her husband's side, her father, staring at his little girl, and Jarrod, a widower after less than a year of marriage.

Shallow breaths were all she could manage, which left Katie lightheaded. Her heart pounded in her throat as she looked at the grief-stricken loved ones who surrounded Sam's body. It was too much; she felt sick to her stomach. What had she done to the woman who was like a sister to her?

Marshall's grip helped to steady her. "It's okay," he whispered. *The hell it was.*

Before she could take another step, Jarrod launched in her direction. "How could you do this? How could you get her involved in your fucked up little world? We were doing fine. We were happy and now she's dead! My wife's dead and it's your fault!"

Jarrod raised his hand, but Marshall grabbed it before it could land on its intended target.

"I'm sorry, I'm sorry, I'm sorry." Katie sobbed uncontrollably and was shocked by his reaction. Her words were barely audible between the gasps for breath.

Molly released her husband's embrace and took slow, deliberate steps toward Katie.

She'd been more of a mother to her growing up than her own had been and Katie's eyes begged for this woman's forgiveness. Molly opened her arms and pulled her close.

"This isn't your fault. You are not to blame. Sam loved you just as if you were a part of this family. We all love you, Katie. You can't control the actions of a madman. This is not your fault." She repeated those final words over and over until Katie slowed her tears and quieted her quivering body.

The medical examiner approached Marshall, who was still keeping hold of Jarrod. "Have you read the report, detective?"

Jarrod yanked his arm from Marshall's grip and went back to stand by his wife.

"I'd like to discuss this after the family leaves."

"Of course." The doctor walked back to her desk. Sam was shrouded in white sheets in an effort to conceal the violent wounds that covered her body. Katie hadn't yet been told how she died, but when she finally approached her, daring to stand next to Jarrod, Katie saw that her face was bloated and heavy bruising was visible around her neck. *My God, he strangled her.*

She wept over her discreetly so as not to make the situation any more tense and painful than it already was. Jarrod's anger was understandable and she did not hold it against him. He was a husband grieving for his dead wife.

Finally, it was Sam's father who gathered what remained of his family and said it was time to leave. "We will see her again, but not today. This is not how I want to remember my Sammy."

Katie watched as the three people, whom she would probably never see again after the funeral, left the room without saying another word to her.

"I need to talk to the M.E. Are you okay to stay here or would you rather leave?" Marshall asked.

"I'll stay."

"We'll need to perform an autopsy to confirm." The medical examiner began pulling back the sheets that covered Sam's body. "But the suspected cause of death is strangulation and secondary are the multiple stab wounds to the chest and upper abdomen. We will also need to determine if she died of asphyxiation prior to or during the attack in addition to determining if sexual assault took place. Right now, there is evidence of bruising along the upper thigh and groin areas. The family has given their consent to conduct the examination."

Katie looked away as the examiner pointed out the various horrific markings that had killed her best friend. She couldn't help but envision Sam screaming and crying as he repeatedly stabbed her, only to be silenced by hands clutching around her neck. Finally, she threw her hands over her face and desperately tried to block out the images.

"Stop, Kate. Come on, now." Marshall pulled her hands away from her face. "Look at me. Focus on me."

The doctor continued to examine Sam with unaffected determination.

Marshall began to take deep breaths. "Come on, you can do this. Take a deep breath."

She followed his lead, calming herself with each breath. "I'm sorry, Marshall. She's my best friend."

"Don't speak; just deep breaths." They breathed together, slowly and calmly, her eyes never leaving his. "I need to stay here and talk to Dr. Patel. I'll walk you to the lounge first so you can get a coffee, maybe something to eat and to sit down. Agent Scarborough is waiting outside and we need to discuss things with the doctor that I don't think you'll want to hear. Okay?"

But she'd heard enough already. The matter-of-fact tone with which the examiner spoke reverberated in her mind. Having no desire to suffer anymore today, Katie agreed. The thought of listening to them analyze and study Sam's body the way they did with Angela Richards made the bile want to rise in her.

The lounge offered little in the way of comfort. Burgundy chairs with chrome arms, placed side-by-side, an outdated TV mounted to the wall by a swivel stand, and the gurgling of the water cooler that was nearing empty. But Marshall brought her a coffee and a bag of chips from the vending machine. "Sorry, this was all they had."

"Thanks, but I'm not hungry."

He handed her the coffee and placed the chips on the table

beside her. "I'll be back in a few minutes, okay?" Marshall laid his hands gently against her cheeks and kissed her forehead.

Katie was alone. The daylight was turning to dusk. She had no sense of time, save for the dimming light shining through the plastic vertical blinds on the windows. It must have been nearly five o'clock. A calendar hung on the nurses' station wall. It was Wednesday evening in this small town hospital in Arcata; a hospital that usually took care of kids' broken bones or ear infections, maybe an injury in a fender bender or two. Murder wasn't something to which they were accustomed.

She stared at the ground until a pair of feet came into view. Katie raised her head, scanning the long, thin legs clothed in blue jeans and the hands shoved into the jean pockets up to their knuckles. It was Jarrod.

"Can I sit down?" he asked.

A sympathetic smile appeared just for a moment as she obliged, moving her purse from the seat next to her.

He took Katie's hand and pressed it firmly between both of his. "I was way out of line back there and I'm so sorry. I've never raised a hand to any woman; you have to believe me."

"My God, Jarrod. The last thing you should be is sorry. You were right. None of us would be here right now if I hadn't dug all this up."

"Sam told me about what happened when you were a kid; how all those crazy dreams or visions or whatever came back to you. How could you have known any of this would happen?"

"I called her a few days ago, you know, but I got her voicemail. She always calls me back; I should have known something wasn't right."

"She left for work on Tuesday morning, just as she always did," Jarrod began. "We said goodbye and I went back inside the house to work. There was nothing out of the ordinary. Believe me, I've run through every word she said to me over and over in my mind. It was just like any other day, Katie."

He was trying hard to keep it together; she could feel it in his tight grip, like he was holding onto her for dear life. "Sam loves you—loved you very much, Jarrod. She was happy with you."

"Do they know it was him—the man who took you—who did this?"

"I don't think they know anything for sure, but they're assuming it was. With the threats and the media attention..."

"What threats?"

"Threats to me, Jarrod. Not to anyone but me." She couldn't bring herself to tell him of the only real threat that mattered; the threat that he would find a replacement for her and it seemed he had. Everyone who saw that email, who knew of the phone call, was well aware of the threat. They might not have enough to be sure it was him, but Katie knew it was.

"Everything okay here?" Marshall headed toward the two of them.

"We're fine." Katie looked at Jarrod; her compassionate smile seemed to put him further at ease.

"Listen, Jarrod, I hate to even ask this, but was Sam wearing her wedding ring when she left for work on Tuesday?" Marshall asked.

"I guess she was; she wore it every day. Why?"

"It's not on her ring finger. We just wanted to be sure it wasn't sent somewhere to be cleaned or sized or anything."

"No. No, she never took it off. Ever. Are you implying my wife took it off for another reason?"

"Absolutely not. I mean to infer no such thing. We were just wondering where it was."

"If she wasn't wearing it, then I don't know," Jarrod replied.

"All right. I'm sure it will turn up in her things somewhere. If you find it, please let us know." Marshall turned to Kate. "I think we should get you back home now."

She stood up, her hand still bonded with Jarrod's. "Are you going to be okay tonight? Are you staying with your family?"

"Sam was my family." He stopped short. "No, I'm staying with Sam's parents at their house tonight. My mom and dad are flying in tomorrow from back east. They'll help with the arrangements. I'll keep in touch."

She leaned in to kiss his cheek. "Goodnight, Jarrod."

MARSHALL HADN'T SAID much since they left the hospital. It was likely that he just didn't know what to say anymore. Katie was grateful, though, for having the time with Jarrod, even if it did little to unburden her mind. She would always blame herself for what had happened to Sam. Just the thought of it made her want to erupt into tears again.

She wanted to talk to Sam, to see her again, beautiful and happy, just as she was on her wedding day. Katie's mind was relentless in its constant retelling of every detail of their friendship. Apparitions of Sam churned through her head; years of laughter, tears, giggling about boys.

A few of those sample pills Dr. Reyes had given her once would be a godsend right now. Valium would quiet the memories. Katie understood now, at least to an extent, why her father turned to alcohol in the years after her abduction. Right now, she would do just about anything to make the pain go away.

It wasn't until Katie heard the car treading over the gravel driveway at her parents' house that she jolted back from the depths of her mind's eye.

Marshall drove slowly until he reached the top of the circular drive and finally stopped. It was pitch black outside except for the single light that burned under the porch and the moths swarmed around it. The stars were veiled by the black, thunderous clouds that were about to spill over and drench the Earth at any moment. The smell of the imminent rain was calming. She hadn't seen any rain in months.

"Come on, let's get you inside before the rain pummels us." Marshall draped Katie's sweater around her shoulders.

Her mother was standing on the porch, holding the screen door open for them. "Looks like there's going to be a big storm tonight. Can I get you two anything?"

"No thank you, Mrs. Reid," Marshall replied.

One minor thought had escaped Katie today, insignificant by comparison, but nonetheless, just now dawning on her. This was the first time Marshall had met her parents in person. They'd spoken on the phone before but had never actually met.

"I'm fine, Mom, thanks."

"Your father's gone to bed, honey. It's been a long day and he just couldn't hold out."

"I understand. I know it's late." Before she even sat down, Katie turned on the television, flicking around for any news about Sam, almost dismissing her mother. If the news wasn't out yet, it would be soon, especially once they found out she was Katie's best friend. It wouldn't take long to make the connection.

"Detective Avery, will you be staying with us tonight?" Deborah followed him into the family room.

He looked to Katie for an answer.

"Of course he is, Mom. The weather's getting bad and I don't want him to drive back to the hotel."

Scarborough and his team had set up shop at the Victorian. There weren't many places in Rio Dell, so they went to Fortuna, the next town over. This part of Northern California had lots of small towns and communities. It was nice to visit, but not much fun as a teenager looking to get into trouble as she and Sam often had.

"Okay then. I'll get some blankets and a pillow. I'm afraid you'll have to sleep on the couch. The guest room is piled high with boxes of Katie's things."

"That'll be fine, Mrs. Reid. Thank you."

"Please, call me Deborah." She went upstairs, only to reappear minutes later, arms full of bedding.

"Just set it down here, Mom. I'll make it up for him when he's ready."

"Okay, honey." Deborah gave Katie a kiss, the kind mothers give when their kids have scraped knees or bruised elbows.

"Goodnight, Mom. I love you."

"I love you too, sweetheart. Try and get some rest."

Rest? She had hardly slept in days and the words were soon lost as Katie caught sight of headlights passing by the window. "Patrol?" She looked at Marshall.

"Yeah. Looks like the second shift is just getting started."

How did I get here? She wanted to go outside and scream at the top of her lungs as the heavy drops began to fall from the sky. But her body ached, her head ached and, worst of all, her heart ached. "I can't do this anymore, Marshall." Her voice was jagged, fracturing her words. This was not the first time she'd said as much, but this time, the words came with a certainty she hadn't expressed before.

"Are you telling me you're ready to go with the FBI?" He laid a blanket across her legs, which were covered with only a lightweight cotton skirt.

"Protective custody? Like witness protection?"

"Yes, something like that."

"But doesn't that mean I have to change my name? Start my life over? I don't want to do that."

"Well, I think this is a little different, and it wouldn't be forever; just until we find him. Once he's caught, he'll be put away for life, maybe even get the death penalty, all things being what they are here in this state. Then you can get on with your life."

"But that would mean I wouldn't see you, or my parents, or anyone I know."

"No, you wouldn't, not in the short term."

That wasn't the solution she was looking for, but what choice was there?

"They could assign you a protection detail, but that's pretty much what I am. Although if it were the FBI, you'd probably have more people assigned than just me."

"I'm so scared, Marshall. I don't know what to do."

"You and your family are safe here; that much I know. Let's talk to Scarborough tomorrow and see what your options are." He situated himself next to her on the couch, resting his arm on the back cushion until he lowered it behind her neck and gently pulled her closer. A moment later, he leaned in, parting his lips just enough to let her know what was about to happen.

He was going to kiss her. For the first time, it wouldn't be the other way around. Katie inched forward to meet his lips. They were warm and soft with no hesitation behind them.

His movements were slow and measured, his embrace grew firmer with each breath he drew. She felt the heat rise between them, surrounding her with enough warmth that she no longer needed the blanket.

He gently laid her down on the couch. The weight of his body pressed against hers. She melded into him.

"We should stop," he whispered.

"I don't want to stop."

Their lips almost touched again; he stopped and slowly took to his feet.

Katie's eyes flickered with the imminent fear of rejection. But instead, he extended his hand, wanting her to take hold of it. He lifted her off the couch with ease and grace, as if she'd floated up.

"We should go upstairs to your room."

The house was old with stairs that creaked at each step. The rain and occasional thunder seemed to drown them out, but Katie didn't worry about waking her parents; she didn't worry about what they might think. Her only thoughts were of him. Being with him was the only thing she wanted, the only thing she had wanted for a long time, but never truly realized just how much until now.

She was certain he was trying to convince himself that this wasn't the right time, as he had expressed before. But after today, everything has changed and it will never be the same again. Neither one of them would ever be the same.

THE STORM PASSED and a few rays of light broke through the remaining clouds and into Katie's old bedroom. Her eyes strained to open, but she rubbed the sleep from them and clearer vision came to her. She glanced around the room. At first, she'd forgotten where she was. Was it Marshall's place, her apartment? No, she was back home, in the same bed she'd slept in for most of her teenage years. It was the same bed she now recalled having shared with Marshall the night before, but he was no longer there.

She caressed the pillow that remained formed to the shape of his head. Had he even been there the entire night? There must have been a reason why he was absent from her now. Maybe he didn't want her parents to know he'd slept with her. In the light of day, that probably was the best thing.

She stepped out of bed and reached for her robe. The clock showed 7:30. It felt much later. And it didn't take long for her thoughts to drift back to Sam. No sooner had the memory been put to rest for the night, than it rushed back in a deluge. This nightmare was far from over.

Katie descended the stairs to the sound of several voices drifting up to meet her. She slowed her pace in order to listen before anyone caught sight of her. Peering around the banister, she saw Marshall, Agent Scarborough, Chief Wilson, and her parents.

I can't go down there now, she thought, and trotted back up before anyone noticed her.

The house was still buzzing with activity when Katie attempted to make an appearance again. This time, at least she was dressed.

"Katie, you're up," Deborah said. "How are you feeling? We didn't want to wake you."

"I'm okay, Mom. What's everyone doing here?" She stood at the bottom of the steps; the last one to the party.

It was Marshall who finally took his eyes off whatever it was he was studying with Agent Scarborough to see Katie. Scarborough hardly took any notice. "Good morning, Kate. We thought it best not to disturb you. Did you sleep well?" The manner in which he viewed her was markedly different from the day before.

Last night did happen. "Yes, thank you. What's going on?"

Marshall looked at Deborah as if asking permission to speak. She acknowledged his unspoken request; all the while, Katie witnessed the odd exchange. "Kate, the news is out about Sam. We're doing damage control now. Chief Wilson is preparing a statement and we'll be holding a press conference at 10:30 this morning."

"Oh God—I can't." She recoiled, clutching her stomach.

"It's okay. No one expects you to talk to the media. There's no need for it. The chief just needs to convey that we are handling it and we're pursuing any and all leads to find the suspect," Marshall continued.

"So, you're not telling them that we already know who murdered Sam?" They all knew damn well who did it.

"We don't know anything for sure yet, but we aren't going to let the media draw their own conclusions either. There is no way we're going to tell them that he's been in contact with you. We can't; it'll jeopardize everything we've been working toward. And we don't have forensics back yet, so there is absolutely nothing tying Sam's murder to your case."

"Right. It's just that she was my best friend and this was his sick way of getting to me." She pulled back, regretting how that sounded. They were doing this to protect her and the investigation; not to try to diminish what happened. "I'm sorry. I know you're doing what's best here. I guess the last thing we need is the media feeding into his plan; to get them thinking that no one in this town is safe if they come in contact with me in any way."

"Right now, all we know is that Sam was the victim of a random act of violence and until we know more, that's all we'll be sharing at this conference. That's why Chief Wilson is going to run the show. No one needs to know of the FBI's involvement. She was found within the town limits, so it's expected that he would be heading up the investigation."

"Yeah. I get it. When are we going to know more? What does forensics have right now?" Katie asked. By this time, she was already hovering over Marshall and Scarborough, trying to figure out what they were reading.

"Agent Scarborough has set up shop at the vacant warehouse where her car was found."

"They found her car? When?" Katie asked.

"Jarrod said she was headed to meet a client in Fortuna. Somewhere between Rohnerville and Fortuna is where she went missing. We found several calls on her cell from the client when she didn't show up. She'd left her phone in the car. That was around 10 a.m. Her office called her cell around 1:00 and then several calls from Jarrod showed up between 6:00 and 10:00 p.m. That's when he called Chief Wilson." Marshall motioned to the chief.

"But you didn't get the call until the following afternoon," Katie replied.

"I wasn't aware of the connection between you and Samantha, at least, not at first. I knew of her but didn't know her new last name, so when Jarrod put the missing persons call in, I treated it like any other case. When I sent out my officer along the route she would have taken and he found her car at that warehouse off the highway, he called it in. He also found her cell phone and searched for her recent calls. Your name came up on the list," Wilson said.

"I called her a few days ago, maybe a week; I don't know."

"As soon as he realized, Chief called me," Marshall replied.

"But they don't have anything yet?" Katie said.

"No, nothing yet. Once this conference is over, I'm going to run out there with Scarborough and take a look. I want you to stay here. There'll be an officer stationed out front and a patrol running every hour. You'll be safe here."

A part of her wanted to object, insisting that she be involved. But how could she be? It would be too much for her to see Sam's car. Had there been a struggle? Was there blood everywhere, or did he wait until he took her someplace else to murder her best friend? She couldn't handle it and knew better than to try. "Okay. I'll stay here."

It was clear Marshall had expected pushback from her on this, but he said nothing more and continued with Agent Scarborough.

THE CLOCK on the wall ticked away. Katie glanced up at it every few minutes, waiting for 10:30 to arrive. The house was empty now except for her and her parents. With only a few minutes left before the conference was to start, Katie turned on the television. The TV station, which broadcast from Eureka, cut into its normal game show program to a podium set up in front of the Rio Dell police station. A crowd had gathered. Not just the media, but people who lived in the town. Everyone from Rio Dell knew Sam had grown up there. They also knew of her friendship with Katie. How were they going to convince these people that Katie's abductor had nothing to do with Sam's death?

Chief Wilson emerged from the lobby doors and stepped up to the podium. Marshall wasn't there, nor was Agent Scarborough. She supposed a detective from San Diego would have no business being there unless they suspected a connection. The media would surely pounce on that.

She listened as the chief began to describe Sam. How she was the victim of a horrendous crime and how they would find the one responsible.

"Rio Dell is a quiet and safe town. We will continue to make it so and this random act of violence should not deter people from going about their daily lives."

But before he could finish, a reporter emerged, his mic dividing the herd right through the middle.

"Son of a bitch!" Katie yelled.

Her parents were in the room with her and were startled by her outburst.

"Is everything all right, Katie?" John asked.

"I can't believe it! It's that reporter from Channel 9 in San Diego. What the hell is he doing there?"

"Chief Wilson, isn't it true that Samantha Hansen, formerly Fields, was a long-time friend of Katie Reid, whom you are assisting in another investigation with which she's involved?"

And there it was. He had obviously done his research and was going to share it with the world.

"I'm sorry. And you are?" the chief asked.

"Marc Aguilar, Channel 9 News, San Diego. I believe you were in San Diego a week ago, working with the local PD on the Katie Reid case?"

"As of right now, Mr. Aguilar, these are two separate investigations, so if you'd like to let me finish..."

"Two separate investigations? Samantha Hansen was Ms. Reid's closest friend. Don't you find it the least bit suspicious that only weeks after Ms. Reid came forward with a description of her alleged abductor from more than twenty years ago, Samantha Hansen would be found, the victim of a 'random act of violence?'"

Katie thought she saw him using air quotes on that last statement.

"Mr. Aguilar, if you'd like to inquire further, or if you have any information pertaining to the Reid case, I'd be happy to discuss it with you after this conference. In the meantime, I'd like to inform the people of Rio Dell that we are doing everything we can to find out what happened to Mrs. Hansen and you should all please respect the privacy of the family and let them grieve in peace. That's all I have for now. Thank you." The chief began to make his way back inside to throngs of reporters shouting questions at him about Katie. He only continued and ignored their demands.

A resounding feeling of loss and defeat overcame Katie as she fell to the couch. This was all spiraling out of control. She looked at her parents and wondered if they would be next.

"I'm so sorry, sweetheart. This must all be so difficult for you. You have no idea how much I wish I could make it go away," Deborah said.

As she so often had in the past, Deborah tried to find words to soothe her daughter, but none could mitigate the situation. It wouldn't be long before the media would swoop down on the Reid house, knowing Katie was there. Her presence had now become all too obvious; the officer out front and a regular patrol trolling the neighborhood. These were not common sights in this small town.

The media was going to give her abductor, Sam's killer, all the press he could ever want. It was the opportunity he must have been waiting for; broadcasting Katie's every move, the location of her family. It would all be out in the open. *Serial killers are opportunistic.* There would be no safe place for any of them now.

Pandora's Box had just been opened and no matter how hard she tried, Katie would not be able to close it. It was too late to turn back and it would ultimately be up to her to find him. There had to be a way to draw him out, something would have to give away his position or some evidence he left behind. She would not let him get away with murder again.

There would be time to mourn Sam's death properly. But now, the best way for her to honor Sam was to find her killer.

19

"**I need you** to take me to the station, please," Katie said to the officer standing guard outside the house.

"Ma'am, I'm not supposed to leave here, but I can call the station and see if they can send someone to pick you up."

"Thank you; I'd appreciate that."

Katie paced back and forth, peering through the front room curtains, waiting for a car to arrive.

"Honey, why don't you sit down until they send someone?"

"I can't. I just feel so useless right now. There has to be something I can do. That news conference was awful. It won't be long before they all come here, Mom. I think I need to find another place to stay. Maybe a hotel; I don't know."

"She's probably right, Deb," John said. "I want her here as much as you do, but we need to think of everyone's safety. If she's at a hotel, there'll be plenty of officers stationed there to protect her. At least she'll be able to keep a lower profile. With Sam's parents living nearby, you know as well as I do the media will be coming."

"I can't bring more pain to Sam's family. I've done enough

already. At least if I'm not here, they'll be less inclined to hang around."

"Okay, fine. I'm not entirely convinced, but if the both of you think it's best, then I'll go along." Deborah's frustrations usually took the form of a large, heavy meal; which was exactly what she had in mind right now for her unexpected law enforcement guests. Her sudden disappearance into the kitchen was a sure sign.

Another half-hour passed before a patrol car finally showed up to pick up Katie. "I'll let you know where I'm at, okay? I promise." A quick kiss goodbye to each of them and she was out the door.

THE OFFICER PULLED into the parking lot around the back of the station. A few reporters still lingered at the front and he didn't want to toss fresh meat their way by showing up with Katie. He ushered her in through the back door and, as they entered, Katie noticed Chief Wilson in his office with the door closed. He caught sight of her through the window and instantly hung up his phone, heading to meet her in the hall.

He yanked the door so hard, the metal blinds rattled and crashed against the small window insert. "Katie, what are you doing here?"

"Where's Marshall? I need to talk to him."

"He's at the warehouse with Scarborough and his team."

"Why aren't you there?" she asked him.

"I've been keeping the media under control. We've been flooded with calls since the conference ended. It's been a damn madhouse around here. Avery and the others slipped out about an hour ago. They think forensics has found something on the car."

"Can I go down there?" she asked.

Chief Wilson glanced at the officer, an obvious unspoken exchange between the two, and the officer walked away, leaving the two of them alone.

"Katie, why don't you come in so we can talk?"

She followed him into his office as he closed the door behind her. "Katie, the FBI is pushing pretty hard for you to go into protective custody. Detective Avery's been doing everything he can to convince them otherwise, but with what's happened with Sam, they're not likely to give into him again." Wilson lumbered toward his chair and lowered himself down. He was not an overweight man but moved as though burdened by a heavy load. "We're all very concerned about your safety and the safety of your family, Katie. Avery won't admit it, but he's probably the most concerned. He blames himself for what happened to Sam. You know that, right? After the killer contacted you back in San Diego, he knew this was going downhill in a hurry. He was losing control of the situation, but didn't want to admit it."

"This isn't his fault. Are you trying to turn me against him or something?"

"No, of course not, why would you say something like that?"

"I've dropped all this at your front doorstep and, at first, I thought you wanted to help, but it just doesn't feel that way anymore, Chief. And now, you want me just to go away quietly and let you all handle this?"

"I don't understand where this is coming from, Katie. I've done nothing but try to help you."

"You've made it seem that way, but now I think you're trying to shove this under the rug. You even told Marshall you thought he was wasting my time, putting me through unnecessary pain. How do you explain your being so defensive with the FBI back in San Diego?" She placed her hands on his desk and leaned in, ensuring her final point would be clear. "I think you've wanted this all just to go away. Well, it can't now, not with what's happened to my best friend. Whatever happened with my case the first time isn't going to happen again. He won't get away, I promise you. No one blames you for whatever happened twenty years ago."

"Jesus, Katie. You have no idea what you've done." His plea was barely audible under his breath.

She stepped away, taken aback by his hushed comment. It was

clear to her now, by his furrowed brow and worried eyes, that he was afraid. "What are you not telling me, Chief?"

"You want to go to the warehouse?" This time, his resolute manner returned as he ignored her question. "Then go. Miller can take you. See if you can convince them not to send you away."

This was not the same man that she'd first come to for help. Something had changed in Wilson, something that left her unnerved.

THE ABANDONED WAREHOUSE SOON CAME into view as Officer Miller approached the parking lot. Windows were broken; the ones that remained were covered in soot. Rust stains ran down the corners where the flashing had fallen away. The exterior appeared grey with thick dust settled against its surface, while areas around the openings were blackened. The neglected building must have stood vacant for some time.

She remembered this place now. There had been a fire here. She couldn't have been more than fifteen when it happened. It used to be a feed manufacturer until the fire destroyed most of it. The fact that it still stood was a surprise.

Is this where he killed her? They'd found Sam's car here, but that was the extent of Katie's knowledge. The building loomed larger as she and the officer approached the entrance. It was an eerie place, now that she'd gotten a good look at it. The doors were charred and hung loosely on their hinges. It would take some finesse not to knock them off completely, so she carefully pushed open one side. Muted echoes reached her ears; the sound arose from farther back into the building.

"Ms. Reid, please stay behind me." Miller extended his arm in front of her to slow her pace. "Detective Avery? Agent Scarborough?" His words ricocheted throughout the empty building.

The voices silenced and soon, footsteps could be heard in their place. Around the corner, Marshall and Agent Scarborough emerged.

"Kate, what are you doing here? I thought you were with your folks?" Marshall asked.

But before she could reply, Officer Miller jumped in. "She insisted on coming down here. I thought Chief would have called to tell you."

Marshall checked his cell phone but had no missed calls. "Reception in here is terrible."

"This is where they found her?" Katie gazed at the derelict surroundings.

"No. Just her car; she was found at a rest stop on the outskirts of Rio Dell. We believe it was the killer's intent to get the chief and, by default, us involved. We've got forensics here examining the car and this was as good a place as any to set up and not be discovered by the media," Scarborough replied.

"That didn't appear to go over very well this morning, the conference." She stepped toward Marshall. "Listen, can I talk to you a minute?"

"Sure. We can step outside." Marshall followed her back through the entrance where she dared not move the doors again, only carefully slide between them.

"What's going on? You okay?" he asked.

"Chief said the FBI is pushing you to get me out of here."

"They are. I'm starting to think it's a good idea, Kate. I know it's not what you want..."

"You're right. It's not. Do you think you could convince them to set me up with—what did you call it—a protection detail, at the Victoria? They're already staying there anyway. I was thinking maybe I should stay there. My parents can't go through any more of this. And I know Sam's family shouldn't have to either."

"I don't know. I just think we're dealing with something that's going to get a hell of a lot worse before it gets better. He's deliberately screwing around with us. He's after you and God knows I don't want anything to happen to you." Marshall gently tucked her hair behind one ear. "I couldn't stand it if something happened to you, Kate."

She felt his eyes take in every part of her. He was afraid for her and it was frightening to witness such vulnerability. This was not a game and Sam had already paid the price for Katie's obsession. "There was something the chief said earlier before I came out here. I don't think he meant for me to hear it, or he let it slip out in frustration. Whatever it was, he said that I didn't know what I'd done. Implying that I'd brought the monster out of hiding and terrible things were about to happen, or rather, have happened. It scared the hell out of me, Marshall. He's not telling us something; I'm sure of it."

"You think he's hiding something from us?"

"It makes sense, doesn't it? I thought it was because he felt threatened by you or by the FBI, but now I'm not so sure."

"Let's just deal with one thing at a time. We're waiting on DNA to come back from the blood we found in the car."

She recoiled at his words. His matter-of-fact tone was intolerable to her right now. She'd heard enough already and it took every ounce of strength for her not to collapse in a puddle of tears again.

"Once we get that back, we can try to match it up with the case in Portland. If we get a hit, then we know we're dealing with the same man, without a doubt. It'll change everything, Kate. We'll have DNA and your description of him. We'll enter that into ViCAP and hope for a match with not only Portland but other cases as well. We're getting close, I swear it."

"But I thought they didn't have any DNA evidence from that case?"

"Well, that's what I thought, but a few years back, that department set up technicians to enter old case files into ViCAP. They were able to pull hair from the victim's clothing they still had locked up in evidence. After ruling out that it may have come from the victim or anyone related to the victim, they entered it as the unsub's. They've been waiting, hoping someone else would eventually enter evidence that would match. That's what we're praying for right now."

"You're starting to sound like one of them." An inadvertent chuckle escaped her.

"What do you mean?"

"Unsub? Unknown Subject? Isn't that the term Scarborough uses?"

"I guess you're right."

"And this is exactly why I need to be here," Katie continued. "You are getting closer to finding him and I still think I'm the only one who can get him to put that final nail into his own coffin. Marshall, do you think they'll agree to the hotel?"

"I'll talk to Scarborough. He's taking a lot of heat on this too. They don't want to risk any more lives."

"I don't either, but I can't go. Don't let them send me away."

"Let's go back inside before they start wondering what we're doing out here." He fell behind, letting Katie take the lead. "I think we should keep our relationship quiet for now, all right? They'll send you away for sure if they think I'm compromised."

"Are you?" She turned briefly toward him.

"You're damn right I am." Inside, Marshall spotted the agent. "Scarborough? I think we might have a solution for Kate."

Katie shrank into the background, letting Marshall take the lead on this one. She knew anything that came from her would be dismissed as reckless disregard for her own safety. He stood a better chance of going at it alone.

The two stood several feet away and Agent Scarborough glanced at Katie as he seemed to consider the proposition. "I don't know, Avery. I don't think they're going to buy it. They want her out of here before something else goes bad." His eyes shifted between the two of them as though suspicious of Marshall's motives. "I'll run it up the ladder, see what response we get. It'll take more resources. We'll have to have a team at the hotel, at her parents' house, and with Samantha's parents. We can't take any chances. It's going to bring lots of attention our way, overrunning a small town like this. I have to think he's close, Avery. All this..." Scarborough surveyed their surroundings. "He's making it too easy for us."

"Let's just find what we can for now," Marshall began. "I'm going to send Kate back with Miller to her parent's house." He started toward her, looking pleased. "Kate, pack your things. I'll call you when I know where you're going."

She agreed and followed Officer Miller back to the patrol car. But Katie had something else planned. "Would you mind taking me back to the station first?" she asked.

"I'm supposed to take you home, Ms. Reid."

"I left something there. I'll only be a minute."

He grunted in disapproval and opened the car door for her.

No sign of media vans or reporters remained when they arrived back at the station. She wondered where they had all gone, especially Aguilar. He wasn't going to stop and she knew he'd be in trouble if word got out where she would be staying.

"I'll only be a minute or two," Katie said, stepping out of the car.

Miller followed her inside and waited in the lobby, talking with his colleagues. Katie slipped away quietly and disappeared to the back.

She searched for Chief Wilson, but he wasn't in his office; an anticipated outcome she welcomed. While his door was closed, she peered through the window blinds and a sliver of what appeared to be an empty office was just visible. Katie opened the door enough to discreetly slip inside.

His desk was littered with files and paperwork which appeared to be concerning Sam. Among the clutter, Katie spotted the corner of a picture just visible from beneath a manila file folder. She pulled it out. It was a crime scene photo of Sam's body lying naked on the ground. A few twigs and leaves rested on her; the blood mixed with dirt matted her once caramel-colored hair. It was as if the killer flattened her into the wooded floor, her body having sunk deep into the soft, wet soil. From the report in the file, it seemed she'd been found about a hundred feet behind an abandoned rest stop on the outskirts of town.

California was hard hit by the economy, and in an effort to save money, closed down several lesser utilized rest stops. Unfortunately, these abandoned buildings were magnets for drug deals and other crimes. It was only by the grace of God that Sam had been found when she was. The thought of her out there alone for days or weeks nauseated Katie. According to a statement from a man named Lyle Hernandez, his maintenance crew came through once a month to do a safety check. He was the one who found her.

Katie continued to sift through the other photos. She didn't know what she was looking for and regretted what she'd seen, but something drove her to continue. Sam's abandoned car showed evidence of a struggle, as Marshall pointed out about the bloodstains. She had been taken to the rest stop, already half-dead. He finished her off there, according to the gruesome pictures.

Katie couldn't bear to look anymore. Her heart raced, but she had to maintain control. She was there to find out why the chief had said what he did. What was she looking for? She had no idea but would know if she came across it.

The sound of voices in the corridor caught her attention. She tried to arrange everything back the way it was. His computer was on but password-locked. It was too late now anyway; she'd spent too much time looking at Sam's file.

The muffled sounds in the hall became clearer as they approached the door. She quietly tiptoed to the file cabinet and tried to hide behind it. Just as the voices could be heard clearly, as if they stood right in front of her, her phone vibrated. Katie squeezed her eyes. *Please don't come in.* She pressed the button on her phone to silence it.

The voices became weaker and footfalls trailed off in the distance. They were leaving. Katie involuntarily let out a cry of relief and immediately covered her mouth. *Wait.*

When she was sure no one was left in the hallway, she softly stepped toward the door, peeking out of the slats in the blinds. They were gone. Katie slipped out as quietly as she had slipped in and emerged around the hallway, back into the lobby.

"I was about to come looking for you. I thought you got lost back there. Find what you needed, Ms. Reid?" Miller asked.

"Yes, thank you. I'm ready to go now."

Katie followed Miller to the car and slid into the front passenger seat. She pulled out her cell phone and noticed that the call earlier had been from Marshall. He left a voicemail message.

"Why aren't you answering, Kate? Where the hell are you? We got the okay. I'm going to arrange it with Miller to get you where you need to be."

His message was ambiguous, leaving Katie to wonder where the officer would be taking her. "Where are we headed?" she asked.

"Back to collect your things and then off to the Victoria in Fortuna."

Marshall must have reached Miller while she was busy snooping for information in the chief's office. Fortuna was only about twenty minutes from where her parents lived. Sam's work was in Fortuna. Another small town, but it had a business district. People from the surrounding area commute there every day. They wouldn't stand out as much staying in a place like that.

"Okay, Ms. Reid. I'll wait for you outside. Try not to be too long." Miller shifted the car into park as it came to a stop in the driveway of her parents' home.

Deborah was already holding the door open.

"Hi, Mom." Katie kissed her cheek. "They're sending me to a place outside of town, but I don't know where yet." She wasn't sure who was supposed to know her location but figured the fewer people, the better. "I'll know more after I talk to Detective Avery. I wanted them to bring me back here first so I could tell you that they're putting me under the FBI's protection detail."

"Chief Wilson already came by to talk to us. He said the FBI suggested it and that it would be best because the media wouldn't be as inclined to come here. But I don't care about that; I just want you to be safe."

"Does he know where they're taking me?" Katie asked.

John emerged from the kitchen with a cup of coffee in hand. "If he knows, he didn't tell us. Said they'd keep in touch to let us know you're okay. It sounds like it's for the best, honey. As much as I hate for you to leave my sight, I know the FBI and Detective Avery will keep you safe."

Katie rushed to her father, wrapping her arms around him. She loved him so much; loved both her parents so very much. All the time she wasted being angry, pulling away from them; wasted years. Keeping the secret from her was hard to forgive, but in their minds, they were trying to protect her. She was beginning to see that now. The harsh realities of her own loss had set in and she wouldn't waste any more time being angry.

Soon, with the bag tossed over her shoulder, Katie moved down the staircase, sliding her hand along the railing to steady herself from the extra weight. As she reached the bottom, John and Deborah said their goodbyes and helped her to the door.

"I'll make sure they keep you updated, okay? Please don't worry. I'll be fine and I'll contact you as soon as they let me."

John did his best to soothe his anxious wife.

Katie opened the door and said goodbye one last time.

Officer Miller was still talking to the patrolman out front. "You ready to go, Ms. Reid?"

"Yes."

20

It had been three hours and no word from Marshall. An agent was posted outside her hotel room door and Katie was starting to feel like a prisoner, but it was still better than the alternative. The worst part, though, was that it was the first time the case was moving forward without her and it wasn't sitting well.

She had already paced the room countless times, wondering where he was, and what was happening. Again, she walked to the sliding glass door that led to a small balcony in this fourth-floor room. Two weathered chairs and a side table were all that could fit in the confines of the deck. The agent out front advised her against going outside and since they were there to protect her, she resisted the urge. If they couldn't control her here, she knew what would come next.

The hotel was decent enough; not the Ritz, but what was around here? They were letting her stay on and that was what mattered. She peered through the curtains, beyond the balcony and sparsely populated parking lot to the river on the horizon. The highway was opposite the hotel's front entrance and she wouldn't be able to see Marshall coming from where her room was situated. So she watched the river flow, its dark waters heading downstream, eventually leading to the coast, and waited.

Meandering her way to a chair that had been crammed in the corner of the room, Katie grabbed the remote control and turned on the television. Nothing new; about Sam, or anyone else, for that matter. They kept playing snippets of the news conference from this morning, repeating the same thing. Everyone should be vigilant, but no one was in any danger. *Easy for you to say.*

The knock on the door startled her away from the television.

"Kate, it's Marshall." The sound of a key card sliding in the lock; click, and the door opened. "Thank you, agent," he said to the man outside.

"Why haven't you called? I've been waiting here for hours."

"I'm sorry. I didn't plan on taking as long as I did. But, we've got a match."

She stepped back. "A match?" A glimmer of hope sounded in her words.

"The man who killed Sam is the same one who killed Angela Richards. We got a hit."

"What does this mean?" she asked.

"It confirms our suspicions that we're dealing with a serial killer, one who's spanned decades. This is going to allow us a hell of a lot more leeway on this investigation. The FBI will send more agents. More agents mean the ability to follow up on more leads. We're about to ramp this thing up, Kate."

"I'm just sorry it took the death of my best friend to make it happen." She sat down on the edge of the bed, the images of Sam's body still in the forefront of her mind. "I snuck into the chief's office today after I left the warehouse." She looked up at Marshall to gauge his reaction, but he had the same deadpan expression he always had when he was waiting for the other shoe to drop.

"I saw the crime scene photos of Sam." Her emotions were rising, but she steadied herself.

Marshall moved next to her. "Why would you look at those? What were you doing in his office?"

"They were just there, strewn out all over the desk. I saw what he did to her; how he left her." She turned away and stared through the window. "I want to kill him, Marshall. I swear to God, I want to kill him."

"Come here." He pulled her close. "You've been so strong through all of this. I honestly don't know how you manage to keep it together some days, but your strength; it scares me sometimes. Staying here, not wanting to go into protective custody; it worries me that you're in this deeper than I am. And why were you in the chief's office? Is this about what he said to you, about not realizing what you'd done?"

"You didn't see his face when he said that, Marshall. He was afraid."

"Of course he was. We all are; afraid for you, for your family, and for all of us trying to solve this case."

"No, it was more than that. It was like he knew something that we didn't."

"Like what?"

Frustrated, she pulled away from his embrace and stood. "I don't know. I can't explain it, but something's not right."

"No, none of this is right, but you have to know that we've got the full force of the FBI on our side now. The chief? He's not a player in this anymore, not to any real degree. Hell, I'm only hanging on because Scarborough feels for us, for you, and what you've been through."

"The funeral's tomorrow. I can go, right?" Katie asked.

"Of course. I'll come with you. I'm concerned your presence will be a distraction, though. This is all over the news now, Kate. So it's probably best to stay in the background; let the family grieve in peace."

"He's going to take that away from me too? I can't say goodbye to her?"

"You already did. That will have to be enough."

THE MORNING of the funeral brought with it dark skies that threatened to unleash a downpour. The lightly woven cardigan Katie draped over her shoulders was scarcely enough to keep her warm and the chill grew more intense the closer they got to the gravesite.

Earlier, Katie stood in the church where Sam had been married, attending her funeral. It didn't seem possible. Marshall advised her to stay at the back of the church and she did. She listened to the same pastor who married Sam and Jarrod talk of her untimely death. No media was allowed in the service, but a few hung around outside, waiting to devour the family as they emerged.

Two policemen flanked either side of the entrance and another waited on the street to begin the procession to the cemetery.

They were the third car back. Clouds still filled the morning air, but on the horizon awaited blue sky. A few vague memories of the night before drifted through Katie's mind. Marshall's strong arms, which held her bare skin next to his; deep passionate kisses that made her forget, for just a moment, about what lay ahead. With a blink, the memories were gone, only to be replaced with the pain and sickness of her broken heart.

As the procession arrived, the cars lined the winding drive that led to the field of manicured grounds. Fresh flowers lay at the foot of most of the gravestones. They walked along the green grass, Katie's heels sinking with each step. The ground was soft and still covered in dew.

In the distance, she saw the pastor standing tall but somber. She was chilled to the bone now; nothing could warm her. Finally, they were there. Katie had never seen an open grave before and hoped never to see one again.

The pastor's final words were followed by each family member releasing a handful of dirt onto the casket. First, it was Jarrod, then Sam's parents.

"Please, let me say goodbye," she whispered to Marshall as they stood in the background.

"Wait until they start to leave. I'm sorry. It has to be this way."

The mourners were on their way back to their cars when Marshall finally allowed her to toss her handful of dirt onto Sam's beautiful casket. Its grandeur was meant to complement the beauty it held within.

"You have to let her go now, Kate, but she will not be forgotten; not by any of us." He led her away and back to the waiting car.

Her unsteady legs struggled to carry the heavy burden of Sam's death. Nothing would ever completely release Katie of that load, but watching the man responsible die at her hands would be a start.

Marshall drove on and made his way back to the hotel. Under the porte-cochere, he opened the passenger door for Katie and she gracefully stepped out in her high heels and calf-length black dress. Before yesterday, the only black dresses she owned were for parties or nightclubs, and they were still at her apartment in San Diego, tucked away for a time when she could think about such things again. She turned her face upward and looked at the sky, watching the rain fall in sheets. Katie was grateful to Mother Nature for waiting until her best friend was buried before she wept for her.

"Let's get you inside." Marshall led her through the lobby and up to her room, nodding to the agents stationed at various strategic locations to ensure Katie's safety.

She flopped onto the bed and fell back, staring at the ceiling. Exhaustion overcame her and all she could think about was sleep.

"Do you want me to order room service?"

"I'm not hungry," she whispered.

"Please, eat something, Kate. You haven't eaten all day."

She turned her head toward him, her face stained with dried tears. "I'm not hungry. I just want to sleep."

The vibration of her cell phone startled both of them. Katie sat up and opened her purse to find it glowing and rattling the contents around it. She didn't recognize the number and quickly looked to Marshall.

He sat down next to her and motioned her to answer it.

Raising the phone to her ear, she said nothing. On the other end, she heard the rush of cars passing by, the wind howling through the receiver. Whoever it was had been standing outside.

"You looked beautiful today, little Katie."

Her heart ceased as the person on the other end needed to say nothing more. She already knew who it was. And, gauging by his quick leap off the bed, Marshall realized it too.

He reached for his cell and dialed Scarborough. "She's on the phone with him now," he said, speaking under his breath.

"Why did you kill her? She had nothing to do with this!" Rage at what this monster had done filled her grief-stricken heart. Katie demanded answers.

"I warned you to leave it alone, didn't I? It's your fault, you know. You made me do it. And I so hate the grown ones; much harder to control. She put up a hell of a fight."

Katie grew nauseated by his words and then it dawned on her. "You were there? Today?" She trembled from the rush of adrenaline that shot through her body. "You saw me? You're such a coward. I swear to God I'll find you!"

"Calm down, little Katie; I got what I wanted from her and gave her back to you. Why so upset? She had a beautiful trinket that I've added to my collection. Now I just need one more and that'll have to come from you. My set won't be complete without yours. And if you won't give it up, then I'll have to find more to collect until you do."

The phone went dead. He was gone.

"Did you get it?" Marshall asked Scarborough, who was still on the other end. "Damn it!" He threw his phone on the bed, striking the pillow. "He was using a burner. They can't as easily track those phones. Even though they're monitoring your phone, it's still hard to get a location." Marshall inhaled a calming breath. "He's going to send the data to Vance, and see what he can do with it."

Katie sat still, although her heart still raced. She'd been able to confront the monster; let him know he didn't have control over her. "What are we doing here, Marshall? We've got the FBI helping and they can't even track him down. We just keep letting him screw with us and kill people along the way. He's not finished. That much he made very clear. Who's next? My parents? You? Maybe I should just give myself up to him now; save everyone the trouble."

"Stop. I know you're suffering, but that's not going to happen and you know it. We're finally getting ahead of this now with the new evidence."

Katie scoffed, knowing what that evidence had cost her, and so many others.

"It won't be long before we find him. Like I said before, his incredible arrogance is what's going to get him caught."

Katie rose from the bed and once again pushed the window curtains to one side to get a wider view of the parking lot below. Outside, she noticed a maintenance man throwing away some trash in the dumpsters that had been walled off from view. But from where she was on the fourth floor, she could see it well enough. A thought occurred to her as she watched him toss each garbage bag into the bin. "Do you think it's strange that Sam's body was found behind that rest stop only a day after she went missing?"

"Strange in the fact that the rest stop had been closed for the past two years. Strange that the maintenance crew happened to be out there that day," he replied.

She turned to catch just a flicker of suspicion in Marshall's eyes. "You want to rethink what I said about the chief?"

21

CHASING THE DREAM

I t was the pounding on the hotel room door that shook both of them out of their sleep. "Hang on! Hang on!" Marshall yelled as he searched for the time. "It's 5:30 in the morning, for God's sake." He pulled on his pants and ran his fingers through his hair. "I'm coming."

"Who is that?" Katie asked.

Marshall reached for the door and looked through the peephole. Agent Scarborough stood outside, appearing distorted through the fish-eye lens. He yanked open the door. "What the hell is going on? It's 5:30."

Scarborough made his way inside, not waiting for an invitation.

Katie was already sitting up and had only just been able to slip on her robe before he barged in. If their relationship had been a secret before, it wasn't any longer.

Scarborough, an acutely perceptive man, seemed unmoved at the sight of the two of them having shared a bed. "We need to get Katie out of here."

"What?" She jumped up, clutching her robe together, although her modesty had gone unnoticed. "Why? What happened? Is my family okay?"

"Yes, they're fine. I've been ordered to get you into protective custody now. Grab your things; we're leaving in ten minutes."

"Wait, hold on. What the hell happened?" Marshall asked.

"Chief Wilson arrived at the station about twenty minutes ago. He found a package that was left around the back entrance," Scarborough replied.

"Oh God." Katie eased back down onto the bed. It was the dreaded other shoe that was about to hit the floor with a great thud.

"Katie, it was your friend's wedding ring. There was also a note inside. It said he wanted it to go to you, as a reminder of what happened."

"We need to get down to the station and run it for prints," Marshall said.

"We're already on it. I don't expect we'll find prints." Scarborough turned to Katie. "He's here and we need for you not to be. This isn't coming from me, although I concur; it's coming from the top and you have no choice now."

She looked to Marshall, her eyes pleading for him to object, but she knew he wouldn't; not this time. He only started to gather her things. "Where are you going to go?" She'd hoped he would come with her, but that wasn't who he was. Marshall would see this through to the end.

She waited for him to respond, but he didn't, or couldn't. Either way, she knew she wouldn't see him again until all this was over. "When am I leaving?" she asked Scarborough.

"The arrangements are being made now. We'll go down to the station as soon as you're packed and ready. Then, I'm guessing you'll be leaving sometime this afternoon. I'll be down in the lobby. Get down there as soon as you can." Scarborough shot Marshall a judgmental glare and left the room.

"What kind of look was that?" Katie asked.

"The kind that says I should know better than to sleep with someone I'm supposed to be protecting."

"That's absurd. Everything you've done has been to protect me."

Marshall moved closer, standing just inches in front of her. "He's right. You should have been put in protective custody weeks ago after he contacted you again. I've been playing a dangerous game because I wanted to keep you close to me. I kept telling myself you were an integral part of the investigation and needed to stay. But in all reality, I've been the one putting you at risk. I'm sorry for that."

She tried to speak, but he raised a hand to stop her. "I'm in love with you, Kate. I realized it a long time ago. I know there've been times when I saw the look in your eyes; you wanted more from me, but I stopped myself. I knew it wasn't right. I didn't want to take advantage of your vulnerability."

"What changed?"

"I don't know. Sam's death; the pain I saw in your eyes. I wanted so badly to make it go away."

"That was the only reason? To make me feel better?"

"No, of course not; I love you and I knew you cared for me too. I wanted to be with you."

"You know I don't just *care* for you, Marshall. After everything we've been through? I love you too."

Scarborough pounded on the door again, destroying all momentum that was about to lead them somewhere she desperately wanted to go.

"Let's get a move on!" he shouted.

The fantasy they were living in was about to end. She would be hidden somewhere, God only knew, and he would stay and help the FBI until they found the killer.

"Will you know where I'll be?" she asked.

"Well, after Scarborough caught us in the same room, probably not. And he'd be right. If things start to go south; if I don't know where you're at, the safer you'll be."

She returned to packing her things, not wanting to acknowledge the fact that this could all end very badly; she couldn't bear the thought of losing someone else she loved.

After running a brush through her hair in the bathroom, she emerged, dressed and ready to leave.

Marshall was sitting patiently on the edge of the bed, watching the news. And there it was. A picture of Sam flashed on the screen. They both stared at the television in silence, waiting for the reporter to speak.

"Samantha Hansen of Arcata, California was found dead behind a rest stop just outside of Rio Dell. Samantha was twenty-eight years old and a newlywed. Police recently held a local press conference, brushing aside any claims that this case is linked to the well-known Katie Reid investigation. The victim of a childhood kidnapping more than twenty years ago, Katie Reid recently came forward with a sketch of her abductor, having memories of the traumatic event resurface less than a year ago. Police have dismissed any connection between the two cases, though, sources say, it is suspected that her abductor kidnapped and murdered several other children in 1989. Samantha had been a long-time friend of Katie, but police dismiss this as unrelated. The FBI is now involved and sources say the investigation has escalated since the tragic murder of Samantha Hansen."

Marshall turned off the TV. "Son of a bitch. That was the national news. We're going to be hounded by them now. Maybe Scarborough was tipped off and that's why the big rush to get you out of here; their profilers did a threat assessment and they want you gone."

"Why didn't he tell you?"

"I don't know, but we need to go—now."

HINTS OF DAYLIGHT's arrival were evident in the birds chirping and the few remaining night creatures scampering away, back into their burrowed holes. It was still early when they arrived at the station.

It wouldn't be long before the media converged on this small town. And the package? The one Scarborough rushed in to tell them about? Sam's ring and a note. The killer would no longer be able to sneak around here unnoticed, assuming that was what he was doing. Not with the FBI in full force and the press breathing down their necks. He would be forced to take more drastic measures to get her attention; more drastic than killing her best friend. This was the real reason why the FBI wanted her taken somewhere safe; away from everyone she loved in order to protect them too.

Scarborough, Marshall, and the others filed inside; Katie followed closely behind. One of the agents kept looking around like he was waiting for someone to take a potshot at them. Did Scarborough know more than he was letting on?

"We're going to hold a briefing to get everyone up to speed, including the agents who will be handling your transfer," Scarborough said.

Katie realized she was about to get the chance she needed. After the FBI began their meeting, she'd make her move. There were several agents, more than expected, and the entire Rio Dell police department, which consisted of about eight people. The only space that could hold everyone was the main bullpen area just opposite the entrance. Katie was not asked to participate, but to remain in the lobby, which was fine by her.

They didn't take any notice when she slipped out to the back. She told the dispatch officer, the only other person not involved in the briefing, that she was going to use the restroom. He only grunted acknowledgment, since he was trying hard to listen to Scarborough speak.

Approaching the chief's office, she ensured no one was around and jiggled the door handle; it wasn't locked, so she walked right in. "Now what?" she said, scanning the room and looking for something; anything that would stand out and scream "I killed Sam." But did she really believe he killed her? No. But she did believe he knew something and wasn't talking.

His desk was still covered in paperwork. "How the hell does he even work in this?" She then proceeded to scatter the papers in hopes of revealing something of meaning. She was forced to view the heart-breaking crime scene photos of Sam again but pushed them aside. She had precious little time and couldn't afford painful sentiments right now.

What was she looking for? How was it that Sam was found by a maintenance crew that only showed up once a month? She began pulling open the file cabinet drawers, the old metal rollers screeching on their drawer guides. *Nothing.* She rifled through the files on the credenza, then the files on the bookshelf. *Nothing.*

Time was ticking away as she scavenged through his office. "What is it that you're hiding, Chief?" She opened the pencil drawer and a sticky note with the word "Caltrans" was scribbled on it. Just below was a phone number and some dates.

Caltrans was short for the California Department of Transportation. *They'd be the ones who would maintain the rest stops, wouldn't they?* She thought.

Katie wanted to dial the number, but her phone was being monitored and if she picked up the chief's landline, would the dispatcher see it light up on the switchboard? In the end, she decided her phone would be the least noticeable, in the short term. Everyone who mattered right now to the investigation was out front.

She punched in the number and the automated operator answered. *Damn, it's not even eight o'clock yet. I bet they're not open.* But what struck her the most was confirmation that the number had in fact been for the maintenance department. The menu indicated that by pressing 2, she could reach highway maintenance. "Oh my God, did he schedule the crew, or know someone there who would do him a favor?" Katie was struggling to connect the dots completely, but it was starting to become clearer. The chief knew Sam's body was there. But if it was an anonymous tip, wouldn't he have shared that information? No, it had to come from someone he knew, someone he didn't want anyone else to know about. She disconnected the call and, for a moment, stood there, processing her theory, trying to make sense of it. But she was running out of time.

She started flipping through the files again in the tall cabinet, looking for anything else that would help her piece this together. She reached the back of the bottom drawer and spotted a file that had no label and lifted it just enough to bend it open. Inside were the chief's personnel files, at least, some of them. Katie scanned through, looking for anything of relevance, but she only read that he had been a detective with the Sacramento PD since 1980 and the files indicated he applied for the detective's position with Rio Dell in 1989; the same year of her abduction. She knew he had been in charge of her case during that time. He told her that he knew of her case and wanted to be involved, so he applied to relocate and head up the investigation. At that time, the Rio Dell Police Department consisted of about four people: the chief at the time, two beat cops, and then they had an opening for a detective because of Katie's case. Wilson applied and was transferred soon after.

There must have been cases that were more exciting in a big city like Sacramento; why did he have such an interest in hers? He would have probably soared in the ranks of that department, maybe even made Commissioner by now. But he chose to move his family to this hick town where nothing ever happened, except when three kids went missing in the summer of 1989.

She jotted down his badge number with Sacramento PD. It was the only identifying piece of information she could find. No social security numbers, no home address, nothing else. His badge number was the only place to start looking. Katie knew enough people in the San Diego PD who could help her pull information based on that alone. Her only problem now? She was about to be yanked from society; hidden away. No social media, no contact with anyone, not even Marshall. She would have to convince them not to put her into custody. Would a Caltrans phone number or the chief's personnel file be enough? Not this time; they were under too much pressure. The only solution would be to find a way to remove herself from this situation if she wanted answers. The information was hardly enough to warrant an investigation into Wilson. The likely scenario was the one that made her pulse rise at the mere thought of it. Execution was now the key.

She peeked out the window, expecting someone to come walking down the hall, looking for her, but the corridor was empty. She could slip out the back. Her purse was with her, so she had her cell phone, ID, some money—not much, but there were credit cards. It was too easy to trace those, but not if she withdrew as much money as she could in town, then not use them again. Keys? She needed a car. A patrol car certainly wasn't the best choice; she knew she wouldn't get far in that. Marshall's rental was parked out front. How was she going to get out of there?

Marshall would know what to do, but he couldn't be involved in this. It would cost him his badge and she wasn't willing to risk it. He was too vested in her now; he would want her safely in protective custody, insisting he could snoop around the chief more diplomatically than she could. But what would he find and would it put him in danger? She didn't know how long it was going to take for her to find answers, or even if the answers would be what she needed to hear. This had to happen without him.

Her pulse quickened to the point that she was feeling lightheaded. This was by far either the dumbest thing she was about to do or the smartest. *It would only be a few days, maybe a week at the outside. Then I'll come back with something or nothing and they can do with me what they will. Marshall would have no culpability.* She was rationalizing to the nth degree. It was the only way to convince herself she was not taking a ridiculously stupid risk with her own life. No protection from the killer who was after her. "It's only a few days, then I'll come back."

If she was going to leave, it would have to be now.

22

"**K**eys, keys, there** have to be some keys in here," she whispered, frantically searching Wilson's desk drawers. Someone would come looking for her any minute; there was no time to waste. How long had she already been gone? Fifteen, twenty minutes?

The top drawer of the credenza against the back wall; there they were—the keys to the chief's Chevy Tahoe. She snatched them up and rushed to the door. Opening it slowly, she peered around the still-empty hall and stepped out. Quiet, undetectable steps carried her quickly to the back exit, where she pushed the metal bar to open the door and slipped out. The back parking lot had few cars in it, so spotting the chief's navy-colored, late model Tahoe was an easy task. Emblazoned on the front driver and passenger doors were the Rio Dell police emblems, big as you please. She could have laughed at her own recklessness.

Katie pressed the remote keyless entry and jumped in. One thing had gone her way; the only windows at the back of the building were in the kitchen, the copy room, and two small windows from each of the men's and women's bathrooms. No one in the front of the station would be able to see her leave.

She started up the SUV and it roared with its great American raucous engine. Was she really doing this? No time to think; just do. She pulled out onto the road, turning left, opposite the station. Her hands shook and her heart was pounding against her chest. She felt like a convict escaping prison. Of course, she realized she would probably end up in prison for stealing the chief's car.

Sam and Jarrod's house; that was where she would go. It was only fifteen minutes away. Would he even be there? He had been staying at Sam's parents' house, but for how long, she didn't know.

With her phone being tracked, no calls could come in or out, or they'd find her for sure. There was a convenience store on the way; she'd have to buy a pay-and-go.

"That'll be forty-one dollars and sixty cents."

Katie handed the money to the cashier. The man looked like he was stoned, which seemed a little odd, considering the still early hour.

"Does this have a charge, or do I need to plug it in first?"

"You probably got enough juice for a couple of calls, but you're supposed to charge it up first," he said in a manner that confirmed her suspicions.

"Thanks," Katie replied.

After he gave her the change, she walked to the ATM and plucked as much money as her two credit cards would allow. Five hundred dollars; it would have to do.

She tossed her purse onto the passenger seat and ripped open the cell phone package, powering it up. The cashier stared at her through the window, his eyes squinting as if straining to see what she was doing. *Shit, I gotta get out of here.* Stoned or not, it wouldn't take long for the guy to realize she was in a car that didn't belong to her.

The torque of the engine launched her forward, but then she threw it into reverse and backed out. She was again on the main road and headed to Sam's house, punching her number in from memory. One of the few she could actually recall. For a moment, she imagined Sam picking up the phone off of the foyer table where it sat next to the bowl full of loose change. Instead, only the sound of her voice on the answering machine came through. He hadn't changed the message yet.

Jarrod's cell number was stored in her own phone and she would have to turn it on to search for it. So far, no missed calls, but that will soon change. Maybe ten more minutes, at best, and they'd know she was gone. Searching her contacts, she found his number and dialed it on the burner.

"Please pick up, please pick up," she chanted, worried he wouldn't recognize this unfamiliar number.

"Hello?"

"Oh, thank God. Jarrod, it's Katie. I don't have time to explain, but I need your help. I need to borrow your car."

"What? Why? What's going on, Katie? Where are you?"

"I'm sorry. I promise I'll explain when I have more time. Are you at home?" she asked.

"I'm on my way, why?"

"I'll be there in about fifteen minutes. Can I meet you there and borrow your car?"

"Borrow? For how long?"

"A few days; a week, tops."

"Are you in trouble? Where's Detective Avery? Isn't he supposed to be in charge of your safety?"

"I know you've got a million questions, but I just need to get out of town and I can't do it in what I'm driving now. I stole the Police Chief's SUV." As the words left her mouth, she could hardly believe it herself; let alone what Jarrod would think.

"For God's sake, Katie. What the hell were you thinking?"

He had every right to question her, but her frustration was growing, as was apparent in her unsteady voice. "Please, Jarrod. I really need your help."

There was silence on the other end and she was sure her plan was about to fall apart.

"Okay." His tone was almost perfunctory. "I'll be home in five minutes. Meet me there and I'll give you my keys. I've been meaning to get my motorcycle fixed anyway. Guess now's as good a time as any."

"Thank you, Jarrod. I promise I'll bring it back safely."

"I just want *you* to come back safely. The rest will sort itself out."

The line went dead.

He was going to help her. After everything, he was still on her side. A great wave of relief passed through Katie, but the moment was short-lived when her cell started buzzing from the passenger seat. She glanced at it to see the caller ID. *Marshall.* She quickly turned it off and continued driving. They'll be looking for her now.

JARROD WAS STANDING on the front porch of the house he had once shared with his wife when Katie drove up in the colossal SUV. He was shaking his head in disbelief. That was pretty much how she felt, too.

She jumped out and began walking toward him; a sheepish look masked her face at the audacity of her actions.

"You know," he began. "I woke up earlier this morning, after—well, not really sleeping at all and had a strange feeling. I wasn't planning on coming back here today. I was going to stay with Sam's parents for another day or two, but something told me to come home. She must be watching out for you, Katie." He dangled the keys in front of her. "Here you go."

"I know she is. Thank you and I promise this will all make sense soon. They'll be calling you, I'm sure. Just tell them the truth; that you let me borrow your car, but you had no idea where I was going."

Jarrod's subtle acknowledgment was enough. "Be safe, Katie."

She stepped into his car; a non-descript Honda Accord, very

suburban. "Tell them the keys are still in the SUV," she shouted from the driver's window. "I expect they'll be here within the hour."

She turned the ignition and the engine whirled and trembled softly. She backed out of the drive and onto the quiet, tree-lined road that lay ahead. The morning sun, now bright in its full glory, shone through the driver's window as she headed south. All signs pointed to Sacramento.

Marshall would be very worried by now, but she needed more distance before calling him back. However, if she waited much longer, the entire FBI would end up on the lookout for her, issuing an all-points bulletin. For all they knew, the killer had caught up to her.

No, it couldn't wait any longer. She'd have to make the call now if she stood any hope of her plan succeeding. But, not from her own phone; if Marshall knew where she was, he'd come after her.

"Marshall?"

"Are you okay? Where the hell are you, Kate? Why haven't you answered your phone? Whose number is this?"

She finally had to interrupt him as he hurled a thousand questions her way. "I'm fine, Marshall, I swear. I had to leave. They were going to put me in custody and if they do that, then I'll be useless."

"What do you mean, 'useless'? Kate, we talked about this. It's the best thing for you. You'll be safe. Now come back, please."

"I have to take care of something first, then I promise I'll come back. I'll only be a few days."

"You're not safe out there by yourself, Kate; you know that and you can't just take off in the chief's car. You need to come back now. What is so important that you need to take care of?"

"Please, Marshall, just keep looking for him, okay? Keep working with the FBI and find him. I'll stay off the grid; he won't find me and I'll be back in a few days or so. I promise to keep in touch so you know that I'm safe but don't come looking for me. You need to focus your efforts on helping the FBI. And I'm not in the chief's car anymore. Just talk to Jarrod."

"I thought we were working together to find him?" He was pleading now.

"I can't help you with anything if they send me away. I'll be sitting around every day, wondering what the hell's happening. Look, I don't have that many minutes on this phone. I just wanted to tell you that I'm safe and I'll be back soon. I promise I will explain everything. I just don't know what it is that I'll be explaining yet."

"You're not making any sense, Kate. Come on back now."

"Goodbye, Marshall. I love you."

She threw the phone out the window. If she'd learned anything about tracking a killer, it was never to use the same cell phone twice.

Midday was approaching now; she would be in Sacramento soon, maybe another forty-five minutes or so. How long had it been since she'd actually driven anywhere by herself? The past few months, she'd been shuffled around by others, monitoring, controlling, every move she made. She convinced herself it had all been for her own good, but now, the fog was lifting with each passing mile. As much as she'd trusted and loved Marshall, she had given him control of her life, taking a back seat to much of the investigation.

Yes, he kept her involved to a degree, but just enough not to expose her to the true horror of what this killer had done. After seeing what had happened to Sam, she was truly lucky to have made it out alive. Although sometimes lately, she wished she hadn't because that meant Sam would still be here.

The Sacramento exit off the I-5 South was approaching and, from the map, she knew she wanted Freeport Boulevard from there. A few more minutes down the road she spotted an old motel; the SkyRacers Inn. It looked like a place that was within her budget and it was close enough to the Sacramento Police Station.

It looked like it might have been a Travel Lodge at some point in the past, but it was the sign on the lobby door that made her think twice about her decision. *"No prostitution, no drugs, and no hot plates!"* She went in anyway.

The second-floor room smelled of mustiness and decay. The wallpaper that was once maybe a soft pastel blue with floral accents was now yellowed and peeling from the many smokers that had stayed over the years. When she turned on the air-conditioning unit below the window, it sputtered out a stale cigarette odor. Fortunately, though, cool air eventually replaced the stench.

"A couple of days... I can handle it," she said. Her stomach was rumbling, realizing that the cheese Danish she had snatched off the tray on the way out of the Victoria was the only thing she'd eaten since about six this morning. No clothes, no toiletries; she would need to buy a few things as well.

More importantly, making contact with the only person she thought could be of any real use to her now had to be first on the agenda. Time on the road had given her the chance to lay out clearly the next few steps in her plan. Contacting anyone at the San Diego PD would be a mistake. With news of Sam's death and everything that was happening, any of her friends there would question why she was on her own. At the very least, they'd tell Captain Hearn.

So, who was left? She didn't know anyone in the Sacramento PD and walking in there and asking questions would raise a lot of red flags. Her face was all over the news; she couldn't be seen. No, the only person who could help her now was the one person she'd hoped never to have to deal with again. Marc Aguilar, Channel 9 News.

He had been following her around for more than a month, ever since she came forward with the sketch. He didn't believe her story, tried to discredit her, but she thought she had enough compelling information now to entice him to help. If it meant breaking a bigger story, he was the type to be all in.

Last she knew, he was in Rio Dell at the press conference the other day. He was on the six o'clock news broadcast every weeknight, so he would have made it back in time to be on the air.

It was two o'clock on a Monday; her best option would be to try the news station and see if they'd contact him for her. It was a long shot, but she'd have to say it involved the Reid case without disclosing it was her. That would probably do it.

She ran down to the local pharmacy to pick up a couple of new disposable phones, some toiletries, and t-shirts and sweat pants. "I'll take this too," Katie said, tossing a bag of chips and a soda from the stand next to the checkout.

Katie handed the lady sixty-four dollars. At this rate, she'd be through her money in a matter of days. The dodgy-looking motel cost seventy-five dollars. Did everyone in Sacramento forget that California was nearly bankrupt? Worst case, her parents would wire her money if she needed it.

Back at the motel, she loaded up the minutes on her new cell and called Channel 9. "I'd like to speak to Marc Aguilar, please."

"May I ask who is calling?" the operator on the other end said.

"I have some information about the Katie Reid case he's been working on. I think he'll want to speak with me."

"One moment, please."

That was easy. She waited on hold for several minutes, getting annoyed that they were using up her time. "Come on, come on!"

"Marc Aguilar speaking. Who is this?"

"Mr. Aguilar, we met not too long ago. I think you know who I am."

"Ms. Reid. This is an unexpected surprise. What is it that I can help you with?"

"Can you meet me in Sacramento? No one can know who you're coming to see."

"I don't understand. Aren't you in Rio Dell, working to find your best friend's killer? What are you doing in Sacramento? It seems you've got the FBI handling things for you now."

"I need your help with some background information regarding Chief Robert Wilson. He used to be a detective with Sacramento PD and I need access to his files."

"You think I can get access to that information? You give me too much credit, Ms. Reid. I might have some pull here in San Diego, but those guys don't know me from Adam."

"Look, you only have to tell them you're expanding the story to include the original investigation and why Wilson transferred to Rio Dell. Do I need to tell you how to do your job, Mr. Aguilar?" His reluctance was unexpected; she would have to work harder and tossing insults at him was probably not the best way to achieve that.

The silence on the other end meant that he was either about to hang up on her or accept her proposition.

"Where do you want to meet?" he asked.

She hadn't blown it. "There's a diner a block from the police station. Can you meet me there tonight? How soon can you get here?"

"I'll have to catch the next flight. I can probably be there by eight tonight. I'll have to tell my boss where I'm going, but I think I can spin the whole background story idea. I'll call you when I'm near, but plan on eight o'clock at the diner. You'd better have something good."

DURING THE SEVERAL hours before their meeting, Katie had time to organize her thoughts, to figure out exactly what she wanted Aguilar to dig into. Funny thing was, it was the first time in months she'd actually felt truly safe. No one knew where she was and if no one knew, then he didn't know either. She only hoped that her disappearing act wouldn't come with consequences beyond that of her own.

Would Marshall forgive her for leaving? Maybe; if she came back with something significant. But he would probably still be pissed she didn't come to him first; have him look into this, when in fact, she had. His reaction to her initial concern seemed dismissive, like she was grasping at straws while he was trying to follow real leads. What she knew for sure was that she'd better come back with something real.

23

———

Katie pulled into the parking lot of the diner. The faded backlit sign barely illuminated the building's entrance and the sky was almost completely dark now. She checked her watch; it was eight o'clock on the nose.

It didn't seem quite as cold in the middle of the city as it had been farther north in Rio Dell. She had never spent much time in Sacramento and now remembered why. The economy had left several of the adjacent buildings abandoned, tagged by thugs. The police station was only a block away, but she supposed they had more important things to worry about than some graffiti sprayed on an abandoned shoe store.

She glanced around the parking lot to see if anyone was watching her, but at this time of night, she couldn't see much. The streetlights were few and far between. She had parked as close to the front of the diner as she could.

Katie opened the glass door and went inside. It wasn't one of those cool old fifties-style diners with mini jukeboxes at every table. This place was rundown with red vinyl booths, most of them torn, chipped blue laminate tabletops, and a linoleum floor covered in black scuff marks. At second glance, she might have chosen a better meeting place.

Marc Aguilar stood out like a sore thumb with his perfect hair, tanned skin, and scary, bright white teeth. She wondered if he had tried to disguise himself because he was dressed in a Sacramento King's t-shirt and plaid board shorts. He looked like a lost surfer.

"Pick that up at the airport, did ya?" She approached the table where he sat.

He mumbled something snide as she slid into the booth.

"I guess you're wondering why I called you?"

"The thought had crossed my mind. You do have the FBI and Detective Avery at your disposal. I've been trying to figure out all day why you need me."

The waitress approached with perfect timing. "Can I take your order?"

Marc deferred to Katie.

"I'll have the jalapeno green chili burger with a side of seasoned fries and a large Coke." She was famished and didn't care what he thought, even if he was trying to hide a smile behind his menu.

"I'll just have the chicken salad and an iced tea. Thanks."

The waitress shuffled off, leaving them alone once again.

"Glad to see a girl who actually eats. You don't see that much in my line of work," he said.

"A salad? Really?"

"I ate on the plane. So, why don't you tell me what this is all about and why you dragged me away from my beachfront condo to this—place? I only just returned from that podunk little hometown of yours, after watching the chief try to dismiss your friend's death as an 'unrelated incident.'"

His use of air quotes was getting annoying.

He scratched his head and cleared the frog from his throat, or rather removed his foot from his mouth. "I am sorry about your friend; I don't mean to sound disrespectful."

"Don't worry about it." She didn't want to give him the satisfaction of knowing just how much pain she was really in. "Listen, I'm pursuing another angle the FBI doesn't know about and I'd like your help."

"Why can't your detective help you?"

"Because he isn't sure I'm on the right track and he wants me to go into protective custody, which is where they were about to send me today. I sort of took off without anyone knowing about it."

"I see. Does he know where you are and that you're safe?"

"He knows I'm safe; that's all."

"Okay. What do you need from me?"

"I'd like to get some background information on Chief Wilson. He used to be a detective with Sacramento PD. I'd like to know how it came to be that a detective at a big city police department decided he wanted to take a position with Rio Dell PD to lead the investigation of my abduction case."

"I'm listening." His expression brightened at the thought of a potentially juicy story.

"Before we go any further, I need to know that I can trust you. You're a reporter and our history hasn't exactly been an amicable one. I know you've never put any stock in my resurfaced memories; that you think I made up all this stuff about remembering who took me."

"Now, just wait. I'll admit, your story was hard for me to swallow, but I'll be the first one to say I'm sorry because after what happened to your friend, there's no question that someone is after you. It's very clear, to me anyway, that there is a connection, whether or not the FBI will admit it. And you're right; I wondered why the memories surfaced twenty-odd years later. I mean, how could you be so sure that was what the guy looked like? It could have been any random person you had seen at any given point in your life, but you were so confident that he was the one who took you."

"I can't explain it, Mr. Aguilar, but I know it was him. And I need to know you get that now and will help me."

The waitress came back with their food, which was a good thing because Katie felt as though she would faint if she didn't eat something.

Marc pierced a dry piece of chicken from his salad and continued. "So what's this thing you want to know about the chief, then?"

She assumed that was his way of agreeing to help her. But the smell of that burger was making her mouth water, so before continuing, she chomped down on it; the green chili dripping onto her chin. She didn't care; it tasted damn good. Katie was beginning to feel like she could now go on. "Sam was left behind the rest stop on the outskirts of town and a maintenance crew found her the next day."

"Yeah, so?" He crunched away on his iceberg lettuce.

"Don't you think it's a little coincidental that a maintenance crew showed up the very next day after she disappeared? That crew was only scheduled to go there once a month. By all rights, she shouldn't have been found for weeks. Don't get me wrong; I'm grateful her body wasn't left there to rot, but it just wasn't sitting right with me. So, I had a look around the chief's office earlier this morning. I found a note with a Caltrans number on it. It was their highway maintenance division. And not only that, the chief's been really defensive lately, especially since the FBI got involved. And to be honest, he hasn't been all that helpful since I came forward with the sketch."

She took another bite and continued with a full mouth, "I don't know. I just feel like he's not telling us something, something big."

Marc looked at her blankly, waiting for her to continue. Maybe she wasn't presenting a compelling enough story and needed to elaborate to keep his attention. "I think he knew that maintenance crew would be there, or he scheduled it or something like that."

Marc placed his fork down on his plate and dabbed the corners of his mouth with a napkin. He then deliberately rested his forearms on the table and leaned in. "Are you saying you think the chief killed your friend?" His words were barely above a whisper, as if there were ears all around and he wanted to be sure no one heard this ridiculous accusation.

"No. I'm saying I think he knows who did. I think he's somehow connected to this individual and that's why he transferred to Rio Dell and that's why he made sure Sam was found almost immediately. He knew they would insist I go into custody if they thought there was a clear danger to me or my family. He wants me out of the way."

Marc no longer had the look of a child about to be handed a giant lollipop. He seemed deflated and uninterested.

"I'm sure this must sound farfetched, but I've been dealing with him for several months and ever since I was able to remember what my abductor looked like, he—changed. At first, I thought it was because Marshall—Detective Avery—had taken over and the FBI was involved, but I think it's more than that." She wasn't getting through to him and was starting to sound desperate.

"Okay, so say I help you find out more about Wilson's record; what do you think it's going to say that you don't already know?"

"I want to know about his family, his wife, children; all of it. When they got married, where, you name it. I need to find something that doesn't fit."

"Jesus, you realize you're asking a hell of a lot here. Sac PD isn't going to give me the guy's personal history."

"I know, but it's a start. Then I thought you could find the rest out through your contacts. You must have contacts with the city or state; someone who can pull personal records."

"Shit." He rubbed his forehead.

For just a moment, she thought about Spencer; he did the same thing.

"I guess I do, yeah. I can't believe you risked your safety to come down here and follow up on this. I gotta tell you, Katie, I'm not feeling it. But, as I'm here already, I'll give you a day. I'll get what I can tomorrow and after that, I would suggest you head back north and get yourself some protection. Let the professionals handle this."

His dismissive attitude got under her skin, but what choice did she have? His inquiries wouldn't raise eyebrows. He'd play it off like he was working an angle on the story. Wasn't that what investigative reporters did? And, he was good at his job. As much as this guy had been on her over the past month, he knew how to dig into a story. This was her one and only chance to get to the bottom of Chief Wilson's story and she wasn't about to let it go.

"Thank you." She began scribbling on a piece of paper. "Here's my cell and where I'm staying. I trust that you won't divulge this information to anyone else?"

"I give you my word."

"Good. Call me when you've got something."

"I'll call you *if* I've got something and if I don't have anything and the day's over, I'm sorry, but I can't justify hanging around up here to my boss. He'll start asking questions. We'll say our goodbyes and part ways; no one will know what we discussed."

"I appreciate that." She reached into her wallet and dropped two twenties. She didn't want him to pay, even though her cash would dry up sooner rather than later if she didn't watch her expenses. "Talk to you tomorrow."

KATIE ARRIVED BACK at her motel. It was nearly ten o'clock and she was exhausted. Having been awakened at the crack of dawn by Scarborough and then everything that had followed, she couldn't believe her legs managed to carry her to the bed. But before lying down, she pulled the bedspread down to the bottom. No way was she going to put her bare skin on that thing; not in this place.

I should call Marshall; tell him I'm okay. Her purse was on the table. It was too far to reach so she hoisted herself up one more time and grabbed one of the burners. She turned her phone on just to see if he had called. She couldn't leave it on for too long, they'd be able to track her.

Three voicemails; all from Marshall; each one sounding more desperate than the other. It had only been half a day since she'd spoken with him. He really was afraid for her, but she was safer there than anywhere right now. She turned it back off, then dialed his number on the throwaway. Only one ring and he picked up.

"Detective Avery."

"It's me."

"Oh, thank God. I've been trying to reach you."

"I know. I've had my phone off since I talked to you last."

"Listen, Kate; you need to come back—now. The FBI is looking for you. They want you in custody. It's not safe for you anymore; not after Sam."

"I'm not under arrest, Marshall. I haven't committed any crimes. I don't have to do what they want me to do."

"You did steal the chief's SUV."

"So, the FBI is going to arrest me for auto theft?" She had to calm her nerves; sounding defensive wasn't going to help matters. "I'm sorry, Marshall. I know you're worried. I can hear it in your voice. But, honestly, I'm fine. I'm only planning on being here another day, then I promise I will drive right back up to Rio Dell; right to the station."

"They want to know why you left."

"I don't know why; just tell them I freaked out or something. That I didn't want to be hidden away, useless to help anyone."

"But that's not it, is it?"

She wanted to tell him, wanted him there to help, but this was something she had to do on her own, to protect him, for once. "I will tell you everything when I get back, I swear to you. No secrets."

Hadn't she said that once before to someone she loved? It didn't hold much weight then. But this was different. She was keeping this from him for his own good; not because she feared an argument or hurt feelings.

"Damn it, Kate."

His frustration was waning, but she could still hear a hint of it in his voice. "I'll call you tomorrow, okay? I love you." The inflection in her tone made her words sound more like a question than a statement. And it was; she was asking for forgiveness and was waiting patiently for a response.

"I love you too."

The tension left her body as he said the words. He was upset with her, no question, but he did love her.

"Goodnight, Kate."

She ended the call and put both phones on the nightstand next to her bed. As she closed her eyes, a moment of fear passed through her, goosebumps rising on her skin. Maybe it was the creepy motel, or maybe it was a fear that tomorrow, she would find nothing and would return to face the inevitable. At some point though, her journey through the dark and imposing Redwoods would have to end. It seemed like a place she'd never really left.

A MAN and a woman argued outside, near Katie's motel room door. The muffled sound of obscenities being tossed around stirred her from what had been a pretty good night's rest. "Are you kidding me?" She folded the flat pillow around her head. But it was too late. She was awake. Katie rolled onto her back and looked up at the dingy popcorn ceiling. Today was the day. She would either drive back to Rio Dell, empty-handed, groveling for forgiveness or she would return, triumphant in her own investigative abilities. Like Marshall, she too had hunches and this one was strong.

But what Katie needed right now was coffee. She glanced at the wind-up alarm clock next to the bed and realized it was nearly eight a.m. The light seeping in around the edges of the blackout curtain was dull and suggested a much earlier hour. It was already the start of October and the days had grown shorter without her even noticing. Time had been standing still for so long, Katie could hardly decipher one month from the next.

One of the disposable cell phones began bouncing around on the nightstand, vibrating toward the edge until Katie snatched it up. It was the one with the number she had given to Aguilar.

"Hello?"

"You ready to get started?" The voice on the other end was immediately recognizable.

"What? I can't come with you," Katie replied.

"Why not? I'm not suggesting you waltz into Sac PD shouting, 'Give me Robert Wilson's files.' But you need to be a part of this too. I can't do this all on my own."

"Oh, okay. Yeah. I can meet you in twenty minutes?"

"Make it fifteen and meet me at the diner." Aguilar hung up.

Katie dropped the phone and began scrambling to pull herself together. Having managed a quick shower, she pulled her wet hair back into a ponytail, brushed her teeth, and was out the door.

Aguilar was sitting at the same booth from the night before. Only this time, he had some papers with him.

"I'm here; so what now?" Katie slid into the booth, clasping her hands as they rested against the table.

"I had a shitty night's sleep in my hotel room last night, but it did give me time to think about your suspicions. While I'm not totally convinced this is going to go anywhere, I'm sufficiently intrigued and have already begun to follow up on a few things."

Katie's eyes lit up at his suggestion that she might have something; that she wasn't crazy.

He pulled his laptop out of his carrier bag and powered it up on the table. "I've already put calls into some people I know at San Diego County Records; they can pull up files from just about anywhere in California, not that they're supposed to. However, there's a shocking amount of personal information online. So, that's where I started."

Katie had been this route before. Not pertaining to Chief Wilson, but she knew what anyone could dig up on the internet.

"Robert Wilson was married in 1983 to Sandra Sinclair, according to an announcement in the *Sacramento Bee*. That much, I found online. Then, I got an email reply early this morning from one I'd shot off in the middle of the night to my guy in Records. Seems the Wilsons lived in the suburbs of Sacramento and had a daughter in 1985 named Marisa. He joined Sac PD in 1984, where he started as a street cop and moved up to detective in 1988."

"So, the chief has a wife and daughter," Katie said. "That doesn't explain why he wanted to leave Sac PD for Rio Dell."

"That's what we know right now. The next step is to talk to someone in Sac PD, and see where that gets us."

"I can't go in there with you. My face is all over the news."

"Calm down; I know that. I'm going in there on my own right now. Why don't you go back to your room and I'll be in touch as soon as I get what I need. And, take my laptop. You can do some more research on your own and I'll forward any more files I get to this email address." Aguilar handed her a piece of paper with a Gmail account written on it.

The reporter who just a week ago had been her adversary was now her biggest ally. Marshall wasn't going to be happy about this new partnership. He trusted few people and even fewer in the media. But she suspected Aguilar would cooperate so long as he thought a big story was going to break.

"I'll call you later." Aguilar dropped a five on the table for his coffee and left.

Katie ordered some breakfast and scanned the internet for more leads on Wilson. Nearly an hour had passed when she heard her name and took her eyes away from the computer screen. She quickly looked around for the source and noticed the small flat-screen television hanging on the wall behind the breakfast counter. A headshot of Sam was on the screen next to the local news anchor.

"And in other news, the FBI has confirmed a connection between

the death of Samantha Hansen and the case of an eight-year-old Port-land girl, found twenty years ago. They have advised the public that they are on the lookout for this man. The FBI asks that if you know the identity of this person to please contact them at once. He is considered dangerous and should not be approached."

The sketch Katie released flashed on the screen. They were admitting to a connection and that wasn't a good thing. They wouldn't have released this information if they didn't believe the situation had gotten away from them.

Katie stowed away the laptop, hoisted the bag over her shoulder, and left the diner. She had to get out of there; her face might be the next one to show up on the screen.

BACK IN HER ROOM, Katie continued looking for anything she could find on Wilson and his family, but Aguilar seemed to have had better luck. The piece of paper with the Gmail address on it lay next to her. She opened up the account, but there were no new messages. The hours were ticking away and she had expected to hear from Aguilar by now.

She soon reached for the cell phone and held it in her hand, staring at it, debating the need to call Marshall and find out what was going on. He would only insist she come back, but what if he had more information? Something had happened overnight and she needed to know.

"Detective Avery." His tone was softer than before. He must have realized it would be her.

"It's me. I'm checking in."

"I was hoping it'd be you. Are you okay?"

"Yes. I'm fine. I just saw the news that the FBI admitted to the connection between Sam and Angela Richards."

"They did. Kate, I need you to come back here today."

Something was foreboding in his words, something that made her heart sink. "Something's happened, hasn't it? What is it, Marshall; what's going on?"

"There was another package, this time it was delivered to your parents' house late yesterday. I didn't find out about it until after we spoke last night. Miller called Chief Wilson and told him first."

"My parents' house? Aren't there cops protecting them?"

"Yes. But it was sent via courier. We're already working on who requested the delivery."

"What was in the package, Marshall?"

"It was a bracelet; a child's bracelet, like the kind a little girl would wear."

"Oh God, another child has gone missing? Who? When?"

"We don't know anything yet. But the bigger problem is that it was sent to your folks' place. Katie, we need to get you and your parents somewhere safe. We are getting close to finding him. The guys working in Oregon City may have finally turned up something. But we need you to come back and be with your family."

"What do you mean; what did they find up there?"

"I mean it's the little things that end up bringing down the bad guys, Kate. Scarborough's men tracked down a location in Oregon City. You remember the lead on the stationery store? Someone in the area knew the guy, said he lived in a small cottage on the edge of town. The FBI is there now, searching the place."

"Why aren't you there?" she asked.

"I'm supposed to bring you back and keep your parents safe. He knows where they live and until we hear of a missing persons' report that would fit, we don't know if he's taken another kid. Kate, I need you to come back now. Whatever it is you think you're accomplishing out there on your own isn't important anymore. If they find anything about his identity in that house, he's going to get desperate; start taking bigger risks. No one; not the FBI and not me, wants you or your parents around when that happens."

"Okay, I get it." And she did. She was scared, not just for herself, but for her parents. "I'll be back tonight, I promise."

"They know you're in Sacramento. You need to come back now before they come and get you."

"Wait, how do you know?" She suddenly felt betrayed. Had Marc Aguilar, Mr. Annoying Investigative Reporter, called her out? She knew she shouldn't have trusted him.

"Seems the chief still has some friends at Sac PD; someone called to tell him a reporter had been asking questions. I'm assuming you enlisted some help?"

"Shit."

"I need to tell them you'll come back voluntarily or they're going to send someone to come get you."

"Why am I being treated like the criminal here? Am I not free to travel wherever I want?"

"Normally, yes; but the last thing the FBI wants right now is for the press to realize you're out looking for answers on your own and that the FBI can't control you."

"So, it's not about safety, it's about controlling me."

"Not for me, it isn't. I want you back here with me because I'm terrified something's going to happen to you. But for them, yes; mostly it's about keeping a handle on the investigation and not having some rogue person out there thinking she can find the killer, especially as she's the only surviving victim."

"Marshall, I just need you to give me a few more hours. Okay? Can you just tell them we talked and I agreed to come back? I'll just have some 'car trouble' along the way, explaining the delayed return."

"Promise me it'll only be a few hours, Kate. I'm trusting that you understand what's at stake here."

"I get it. I caused the death of my best friend. I'm not going to be the cause of losing my parents too. A few hours, I promise." She hung up.

Katie began to wonder how much Aguilar was going to be able to find out. One of Wilson's friends either overheard him asking about the chief or was the one being asked. She was going to have to call him and find out what was going on. "Marc, it's me. Where are you?"

"I'm leaving the station now. I need to see you right away. I need to meet you at your motel. You said it was nearby?"

"It is. I'm at 6291 W. Freeport blvd. The SkyRacers Inn, Room 285."

"Fine. I'll be there in five minutes."

It was the longest five minutes Katie had ever waited to pass. She caught herself biting her nails; something she only did when anticipating bad news.

A knock on the door—"It's me, Katie. Marc. Open the door."

She walked over to the window and edged the curtain back just enough to confirm it was him and he was alone.

"Come in quick." She stepped aside to let Marc in. "So? What'd you find out?" She'd expected him to give her that pitiful look from last night. The one people give when they think you might be crazy.

"You're going to need to sit down, Katie." Aguilar pulled out his notepad. "Sac PD was a dead end. They shut me out the minute I started asking about Wilson's transfer."

"Yeah, I suspected as much. I talked to Detective Avery and he said someone called you out."

"Well, if it hadn't been for a call I got from my guy over in Records, I'd be coming to you with nothing. I got the big fat run around at the station."

"So what is it? What'd you find out?"

"Chief Robert Wilson, formerly Detective Wilson, used to be in the system."

She had no idea what he was talking about.

"The foster care system," he explained. "He had a brother and a sister, all in the system. Wilson isn't his birth name. It's Hendrickson. He was born to Elise and Frank Hendrickson in Eureka. Seems the parents hit hard times, split up, and the mother couldn't afford to care for the kids. She committed suicide and the three of them went into foster care because no one could track down the father. Wilson was five, his brother seven, and his sister was two."

While this was an interesting bit of information about the chief, Katie couldn't yet figure out why it was she had to sit for this one.

Aguilar must have sensed this and sat down at the edge of the bed next to her. "Wilson went on to be adopted by a nice family in the suburbs of Eureka."

"What happened to the other two? Katie asked.

"An accident killed the toddler."

It began to dawn on her why he had instructed her to be seated. "What happened to the sister, Marc?"

"She drowned in a tub at the children's home about six months before Wilson was adopted. Joseph, the older brother, claimed it was an accident; said she slipped under the water while he was getting her a towel."

"Oh God."

"Joseph's file was sealed after that. The only other information my guy could find was that he had, at some point, been placed in a mental hospital. He tracked down a couple of letters from a hospital in Eureka sent to the state, suggesting that Joseph Hendrickson not be released until the age of eighteen. The guy's been pretty much a ghost since then."

Katie stood up and began pacing the room. It was starting to make sense now. She had taken the chief at his word when she and Spencer first met with him. Saying he was going to talk it over with the DA and see if he could get the case reopened. That first letter sent to the station; a warning for her to stop digging around.

The chief tried to get her to drop it; tried to persuade Marshall to convince her to let it go. But she didn't; she kept pushing for answers.

Everything changed after the last letter was sent to her apartment in San Diego six weeks from the time Wilson was contacted. Looking back now, it seemed so obvious. Why hadn't she seen it before?

"Jesus, Katie, you don't know what you've done." Wilson's last words to her before she left.

Katie stared at the cheap oil painting hanging above the bed, her head reeling with this new information. She finally looked down at

Aguilar. "It's his brother, Joseph. That's why he transferred to Rio Dell. Somehow, he knew his brother was involved in the missing children cases. I don't know how he found him, or maybe Joseph tracked Wilson down. Either way, the brothers found each other again and Wilson must have seen what his brother had become. I don't understand why he didn't stop him the first time. What could have happened to make Wilson look the other way?" Trepidation began to rise in her. "I have to get out of here. There are far too many unanswered questions." Katie rushed around, throwing what few things she had into the plastic laundry bag, which hung in the closet.

"I'm going with you," Aguilar said. "You owe me that much after coming all this way."

"You can't release the story, Marc; not until we know more. It'll only jeopardize the investigation."

She knew if this got out now, everyone she loved would be in even more danger. Joseph already killed Sam. *He has a name.* She stared at Marc; begging for his cooperation.

"Okay. But I'm going to see this to the end. You understand that, right? I get the exclusive."

"First thing we need to do is get back to Rio Dell and talk to Marshall." She grabbed her purse and opened the motel room door. "You coming?"

24

Katie hardly said two words to Aguilar as they drove north. Her mind was racing with all the things that had happened between her and the chief. It was all so damn clear now.

Somehow, the chief had been able to keep his brother under control, keep him from killing again. Her relentless pursuit of her abductor only fueled a fire the chief had managed, up to that point, to hold at an ember.

She wanted to purge the rage that was welling up inside her. Wilson knew all along who had killed the children and had done nothing about it. He tried to protect an evil, hellish monster. He could have stopped it, brother, or not. He could have turned him in.

But what if she was wrong? It made sense, but she had no proof. The only way to know for sure was to find a picture of Hendrickson. Like Aguilar said, the guy had been a ghost, completely off the grid. Scarborough would be the only one who could get the records at the mental institution unsealed. There would be a picture in his file—an old picture—but they could run it through facial recognition software and compare it with her sketch.

She slammed her open palms against the steering wheel of Jarrod's Honda Accord. Aguilar was startled by the noise. Katie caught a glimpse of him opening his mouth, but when she turned to him, he said nothing. She could see he felt for her. "I'm sorry, Marc. I've just wasted so much time, been through so much pain over all of this. If you knew who I was before, you wouldn't recognize me now. For the past several months, my life has revolved around fear and death. I've been driven to find a man who destroyed my childhood and my family. And to know now that all of it could have ended so long ago... I just can't tell you what that feels like."

"I wish I could say I understand, Katie, but I couldn't possibly. I'm just sorry that I didn't believe you before now." He looked through the passenger window, the blur of trees whipping past. "As soon as we get there, you are going to tell Detective Avery, right? He has to know. In fact, I would suggest we approach the FBI first. We have to stop him before he kills again, Katie."

"I understand." She couldn't risk someone else dying because she wanted to be the one who found him; wanted to be the one to kill him. "I'll call him now. You're right; we need to tell them now." She picked up her own cell phone and turned it on. It buzzed several times with pending messages. She held the phone up to her ear to listen to her voicemail.

Aguilar was watching her intently, but she only glanced his way as if to say, "No news."

"It was just Marshall. He's making sure I'm on my way back."

"So, what exactly is going on between you two?" Aguilar asked.

Katie slipped up and, being a reporter, it didn't take him long to figure out why she had taken to calling Detective Avery "Marshall." "He's been with me through this whole thing; always supporting me and keeping me going."

"So you two are a thing now, I take it? Is that why you broke it off with your fiancé?"

"Figures you would know about that. But for your information, no it isn't; that was something completely separate and happened well before this." She had said that enough times that she actually started believing it herself. "This thing with Marshall; it just kind of happened."

"You realize that puts him in a bad position? He's supposed to be finding your abductor, not spinning his wheels looking after you and worrying about you."

"Yeah, I get that. I know I've risked too much by coming down here, but we have answers now. And, he'll understand that when I talk to him."

"Then I guess you'd better call him."

She held the phone up to her ear once again as it began to ring.

"Kate! Where are you?"

"We should be there in about half an hour."

"We? Who's with you?"

"Marc Aguilar from Channel 9."

"The reporter?" His voice raised to the point that Katie figured Marc must have heard.

"What the hell, Kate? What's going on?"

"Just please calm down, Marshall. Listen to me; I need to tell you something." She couldn't tell if he was angry or jealous or a little bit of both. "He was helping me get information on Chief Wilson."

"So he was the one asking about him in Sacramento. I thought we talked about this. That little stunt raised a hell of a lot of eyebrows around here. What is it about Wilson that's got you so freaked out?"

"Marshall, he has a brother."

"Who? Wilson? Okay. What's that got to do with anything? I've got a brother too."

"I know. Please, just hear me out." She was getting increasingly frustrated by his tone. "It's a long story and I'll fill you in when we get back, but for now, you have to do something for me. You have to tell Scarborough to look at the chief's brother. His name is Joseph Hendrickson. Marc's source could only get so much information, but it seems like he may have killed their little sister when they were in a group home. The guy pretty much disappeared after he was released from a mental hospital when he was eighteen. At least, that was as much as the California records showed."

"A group home? So, what, the chief was an orphan or something?"

"Yes. After his sister died, the brothers were split up, and he was adopted by a family whose last name was Wilson. Hendrickson was sent away to a mental institution. No one knows anything after that. You have to tell Scarborough, okay?"

"You think Wilson's been protecting his brother all this time? That he knew what he'd done and sat back and did nothing?"

"I think maybe it was a little more than that, but yes. I think he's been protecting his brother. He must have known what his brother did to me and the others and that's why he wanted to be transferred; so he could protect him from getting caught. It all makes sense now, Marshall. Why the chief's been so uncooperative." She didn't tell him about what she'd found in his office.

"Look, just get back here and we'll talk more. I need to understand what it is Aguilar found out exactly. If Wilson's in on this, I need to see what he's got before I go accusing the Chief of Police of conspiring to commit murder."

"I don't think he was helping him take the children. I just think he was keeping him from getting caught. Until I figured out who took me, he would have been able to keep it that way. But now, I think he's lost whatever control he had over his brother and he doesn't know what to do."

"Just get back here. Fast. I'll meet you back at the Victoria, I've got to go. We're down at the station now. The entire Bureau is over here, Kate. This thing is bigger than both of us now." Marshall ended the call.

"He doesn't believe you?" Aguilar asked.

"I don't think he knows what to believe right now. Sounds like the FBI's taken over everything."

"He'll understand and he'll be behind you on this. I only hope his delay doesn't cost any more lives."

Marc was right. Marshall wasn't going to tell Scarborough anything until he had a full understanding of the situation. She just didn't know if they had that kind of time.

The closer they got to Rio Dell, the worse the weather had become. The rain was coming down hard on the highway. The oil on the asphalt mixed with the water that had collected on the road. It glistened in streaks of blue and purple. The wipers couldn't go fast enough to clear the windshield for her to see through. She found herself pressing harder on the accelerator, needing to get back to Marshall as fast as she could.

"Uhhh, Katie, you wanna slow down a little bit?" Aguilar was gripping the arm of the passenger door until it turned his knuckles white. "Katie!" he shouted. "Slow down!"

"What?" She glanced at the odometer; it read 85mph. "Oh my God!" She lifted her foot, allowing the car to decelerate. "Jeez. I'm so sorry, Marc. I was somewhere else."

"Clearly. I'd just like to get back in one piece if that's all right with you?" His grip loosened only slightly and the blood began to return to his fingers. "Do you want me to drive?"

"No, no, I'm fine now. I really am sorry. Things are just—catching up to me. I feel like I'm trying to outrun them. I need to get back home and make sure my family is okay. I need to see Marshall."

"I get it. But I don't think anyone's going to benefit from you getting in an accident. We're almost there."

Soon, the rain began to slow to not much more than a drizzle. Once again, Mother Nature took her cue, bringing a calm over Katie. They were nearly there, only about ten minutes outside of town.

"I need to get this car back to Jarrod," she said, not realizing she'd said it out loud.

"Jarrod? Isn't that your friend, Samantha's husband?"

"You mean widower? Yes. You know, I always thought of him as kind of quiet, maybe even a little boring. But she loved him. And I know he loved her very much. He's a good man. I hope he'll forgive me one day."

"Katie, I don't think he blames you for anything. You don't help someone you think was responsible for taking away the love of your life. I think you're the only one who blames you."

The Victoria was finally in sight. There were several black SUVs in the parking lot, definitely FBI. Who knew how many were at the station? The whole town was in upheaval.

One thing was certain. It wouldn't matter what she had on the chief. They were going to put her in protective custody, by force, if they had to. The media attention was too great now. They couldn't have their only witness running off on her own tangents.

Katie pulled the small car into a spot between the great big government vehicles; the only gold Honda in a sea of black.

The two stepped out and walked toward the hotel lobby. Inside, Katie saw several agents milling about; on their cell phones or tablets. She took a deep breath as Marc opened the door.

Almost at once, they turned to look at the only two people not wearing FBI jackets. She spotted Marshall making his way through the crowd. Agent Scarborough wasn't far behind and he looked pissed.

"What the hell were you thinking, Katie?" Scarborough asked.

"Just wait a second. I think we all need to go someplace a little quieter." Marshall tried to herd everyone toward the office of the hotel manager, who'd long since lost his spot when the FBI rolled into town.

"You know Chief Wilson's pretty pissed off that you took his Tahoe," Scarborough went on to say. "Do you know how much danger you put yourself in?"

"Before you go on, we need to talk about something." Katie glanced at Aguilar, who gave a quick nod for encouragement. She looked back at Marshall, who seemed less than pleased by the exchange. "Agent Scarborough, I—we have reason to believe that the chief may know who the killer is."

Scarborough widened his stance, swinging his arms behind his back, on the defensive. "Would you care to elaborate on this theory?"

Aguilar jumped in. "Katie asked that I help her find out a few things about Chief Robert Wilson. She believed he had been behaving somewhat defensively of late and a comment he had made gave her cause for concern. And it seems there may have been some coordination between Wilson and Caltrans relating to the discovery of Samantha Hansen's body."

Marshall cut Aguilar off. This latest revelation seemed to catch him off guard as he shot a look toward Katie. "These two have been digging around Wilson's past and discovered that he has a brother who spent several years in a mental hospital. They believe this brother, Joseph Hendrickson, is Kate's abductor and the suspected serial killer."

"But it's more than that." Katie felt like she was drowning in the sea of testosterone. "Look, I know this sounds crazy, but I truly believe there's something to it and we need to know more about this brother. Wilson was adopted around the age of five. His younger sister died, it's believed, at the hands of Wilson's brother, who kept the family name of Hendrickson. We need to know what happened to Hendrickson and where he was around the time I was taken. Doesn't it seem a little suspect that Wilson would request a transfer to Rio Dell to head up the investigation of my case? How so little evidence was found and that there was never any link between Ashley Davies and the other cases when there so clearly is now?" She took a deep breath, realizing she was getting herself worked up. "Nick, please, if we could just see what the brother looked like, that would put this whole thing to rest. Can you give me that much?"

The agent's stance softened at her request. Maybe she had piqued his interest just enough that he'd look into it for her. "Give me some time with my team and I'll see what I can find. In the meantime, keep quiet about this. Avery, I'd like you to stay with Katie; make sure she doesn't make another run for it. She takes off again and we're all out of a job." Scarborough pushed his way to the door of the cramped office and disappeared.

Katie was left standing between the two men who obviously

disliked each other; a result of her own doing. Of course, up to that point, Aguilar had been a thorn in her side. But Marshall hadn't just spent the past several hours with a man who had flown up to meet her in Sacramento based solely on her hunch. It would take some convincing on her part to get Marshall to see that Aguilar had become their ally.

"It's been a long day. I'd really like to go get cleaned up and changed. Can I go up to your room?" she asked Marshall.

Marshall seemed shocked by her lack of discretion.

"It's fine; he knows about us." Katie held out her hand for his key and once it was in her grasp, she left the room, leaving the men staring at one another with little to say.

THEY WERE to meet with Scarborough back downstairs in only minutes. The quick shower and sparse makeup were enough to make Katie feel human again. Now it was time to find out if her little disappearing act had been in vain and if she had jeopardized everything only to find nothing.

The elevator in the old hotel inched along and Katie could think of nothing to say to Marshall that would make him understand why she left on her own. Standing inside, they both turned their gaze upward to the floor numbers as they lit up. The uncomfortable silence could not be broken.

The doors parted in the lobby to reveal Aguilar checking into a room at the front desk. It appeared he wasn't going back to San Diego anytime soon and Marshall's expression confirmed to Katie that he was displeased. Nevertheless, she would not try to sway Marc otherwise for the sake of Marshall's feelings. They were well beyond that now.

"Avery, over here." Scarborough waved them over and Aguilar wasted no time in joining the team.

They followed him into the small dining room that had been transformed into a mini command center.

"Is anyone left at the warehouse?" Katie asked Marshall.

"They've still got a small team running evidence over there, but here and the station are the primary posts. You wouldn't believe what's been happening around here in the twenty-four hours since you left, Kate. Your disappearance brought in all the big boys."

Scarborough took a seat at a small table and the others followed. He opened his laptop and slid a photograph of Joseph Hendrickson out of his files and toward Katie.

She gasped at the face of the teenager in the picture.

Scarborough then showed her another picture. "This just came in from Oregon City."

An older version of the teenager; this photo was of a man everyone could see was a match to the one in Katie's sketch.

"That's him," she whispered.

"You were right. You both were right," Marshall replied.

"We're tracking down the chief now," Scarborough began. "Last anyone saw him, he was at the station. I think we should head over there and have a talk with him. Katie, you should have come to us with this. It would've saved us a lot of grief and we could have been a day closer to finding the killer."

She wanted to defend herself, tell him that she'd tried, but it didn't matter now. "What's going to happen to Wilson?"

"He'll be booked for questioning. We need to understand what he knows if he knows where his brother is. We have to give the guy a chance to explain why it was he didn't tell us he suspected his brother and said nothing."

"Do you think it's as simple as that? You don't think he was working with the brother?" Marshall asked.

"Based on what we know of Wilson right now, I'd say no. But he's known, I expect, since the beginning. Brother or not, he's been protecting a killer."

Inside the Rio Dell Police Station, a chaotic scene had erupted. Marshall, Katie, and Marc Aguilar, who'd inserted himself as a member of the team, waited for Agent Scarborough to make his way inside, hoping he could shed light on what was happening.

Scarborough raced past them. "He's gone. Wilson's gone."

"Son of a bitch!" Marshall chased after Scarborough, leaving Katie and Aguilar to catch up.

"What happened?" Marshall asked the agent.

"I don't know. He caught wind we were coming down here to talk to him. Someone opened their goddam mouth."

They ran into Wilson's office. A few file cabinet drawers had been emptied and his computer was gone.

"What the hell? Did no one see him do this?" Scarborough shouted.

Katie could hear him yelling as she and Aguilar approached Wilson's office. "Oh my God. He can't be far, right?"

"Call his wife! Find out where the hell he is!" Scarborough barked orders to another agent.

"We need to get to his house now." Marshall took Katie by the hand and dragged her through the hordes of FBI agents crowding around.

She looked back, but couldn't see Aguilar. No time to worry about that now. She saw Scarborough emerge through the crowd and push his way out the door just in time to get into Marshall's car with them.

"He lives about a mile from here, off of Harrison Street. Go!" Scarborough shouted.

Katie knew where Harrison Street was and directed Marshall where to turn. Within minutes, they raced up the driveway of Wilson's home. Marshall jammed the car into park and they jumped out and sprinted toward the front door.

"Kate, stay here!" Marshall said.

Upon reaching the door, Marshall and Scarborough forced it open and Wilson's wife screamed from the living room.

"Where is he?" Marshall yelled.

She cast her reddened eyes toward the kitchen.

The men moved forward, guns drawn.

Katie would not be made to wait inside that car. She had to see him for herself. She had to ask him why he did it, why he protected the monster. She approached the front door and stepped inside.

Marshall and Scarborough continued their approach, stepping into the hall, not realizing that Katie was only feet behind them now. Mrs. Wilson remained frozen, standing inside the living room.

An absolute hush overcame the home. Katie advanced toward Marshall. He'd spotted her now and shook his head. He wanted her to stop.

Scarborough was the first to break the silence. "Chief, put the gun down. We just want to talk to you."

Wilson sat alone at the kitchen table. "It's all my fault. I tried to stop him. I stopped him before, but this time, he was different; determined to find Katie. God, if only she had listened to me. I warned her so many times to stop. Stop digging around, stop looking for him."

"Where is he, Chief?" Marshall asked.

"He just wasn't right, you know?" Wilson continued. "Our parents knew it. I know my mother killed herself because of him. He would threaten to hurt me when we were kids and my sister—my baby sister. They shouldn't have left him alone with her. I tried to tell them, but they didn't believe me." Wilson rested his elbows on the table, waving his gun around as he spoke. "After I became a cop, I tracked him down. He seemed—changed; better. It wasn't until we had Marisa that I knew he hadn't changed at all. She was just a toddler and I saw the way he looked at her. He looked at our sister the same way."

Katie caught just a glimpse of Wilson, but Marshall stepped in front of her.

"We need you to tell us where he is, Chief, before someone else gets hurt. You know it's the right thing to do." Scarborough had been an expert negotiator before he worked in the FBI's Behavioral Analysis Unit.

"Is she here?" Wilson tried to peer around the men who were pointing guns at him.

"No. She's somewhere safe."

"You're lying, Agent Scarborough." He looked again toward the hall. "Katie?"

She began to move out from behind Marshall.

"No," he whispered to her.

"I'm here, Chief."

"I'm so sorry, Katie. I wanted to stop him when you were taken. He'd already killed those other children. He didn't admit it, but I knew. I could see it in his eyes. That's why I moved up here because I had to control him and stop him from hurting anyone else."

"Why didn't you turn him in, Robert?" Katie's eyes filled with tears at his admission.

"I abandoned him. I left him to spend his childhood in a mental institution while I went on to have a good life with my new family. It's my fault; I should have been there to help him. All that damn hospital did was turn him into something evil. And I was afraid. Afraid of what he might do to my little girl if I turned him in." Wilson dropped his head and began to sob.

"Please, tell us where he is," she pleaded.

"I warned you, Katie. I warned you to stop and now look what you've done. I can't control him anymore. Why couldn't you let it go? You had a good life, too. You were the lucky one. I was able to keep an eye on him here; keep him under control. But then you came to me and I knew if he found out that your memory was back, he would revert to the monster he was."

"Did you tell him she remembered what happened?" Marshall asked.

"I didn't have to. He already knew. He'd been watching her for years. But I didn't know it. He called me and told me he knew I'd been hiding it from him. That's when it all changed and I couldn't stop it. He threatened my family, my daughter. And when she came forward with the sketch, I sent my daughter away, someplace far, where he couldn't find her, because I knew it was only a matter of time. And now, here we are."

"How's this going to end?" Scarborough asked. "You help us now, Chief, and they'll take into account your family history. It doesn't have to end badly for you, but only if you tell us where he is. You can make things right."

Wilson laughed. "It'll never be right. I'm responsible for my brother's actions. I'm responsible for the deaths of those children." Wilson closed his eyes and wiped the tears that had run down his cheeks. "He's here, in Rio Dell. I was supposed to tell him when Katie was going to be transferred into custody and tell him where he could find her before she left. If I didn't, he threatened to kill my wife. He's at the vacant cabin our parents owned; the place where he took the children, including Katie. It's north off Highway 101, just before the Arcata exit."

"Did you know he was going to kill Sam?" Katie battled for control of the anger that raged inside over what Wilson had done.

"No, I swear. He called and told me where she was. I made the arrangements for her to be found."

Katie closed her eyes and wept.

"I'm so sorry, Katie," Wilson said.

Marshall and Agent Scarborough began to yell when the loud crack of a gunshot rang out and Katie's eyes flew open again. It was the thump of Wilson's head hitting the kitchen table that made Katie scramble to see what had happened. Marshall held her back, but it was too late. She saw the blood pouring from him, running off the table and pooling onto the floor.

Katie grew dizzy as the ringing in her ears worsened and the sound of Mrs. Wilson's screams echoed in her head. Marshall yanked her from where she stood and dragged her out of the house. Everything around her was spinning; she leaned over the porch rail, retched, and then collapsed onto the deck. Marshall's voice was muffled in her mind. Her eyes opened as he tapped her cheeks to revive her.

"Kate, wake up. Come on, babe. Wake up."

His face came into focus. She was being propped up by him as he knelt on the ground.

"You're okay. You're okay," he said.

She could hear Scarborough talking on his phone, barking more orders. Mrs. Wilson cried hysterically. Two police units screeched their tires as they raced up the driveway, the men running by her into the house.

"Hold up! Hold up!" Marshall yelled at them. "It's over. Go see Scarborough." He brought his tone down again to speak to her. "Come on and sit up now, Kate. You can do it; you're all right."

Amid the confusion, she soon reared herself up and the sobs came harder than ever.

Marshall pulled her toward his chest. "It's over. You're safe."

"It's not over. He's here and he won't stop until he kills me."

"He won't hurt you, Kate. I swear to God, I won't let that happen." He continued to hold her as she cried without acknowledging the chaos that surrounded them.

Sam was dead and now the chief was dead. Katie knew she was next, regardless of what Marshall said. The monster would find her before they would find him. This was far from over.

The sirens grew louder as the ambulance and more FBI units approached Wilson's house. Two paramedics ran onto the porch where Katie still sat, unable to stand on her own, fearing she would hurl once again. Her ears were still ringing, but she heard Marshall tell the EMTs to take her to the hospital to get checked out.

"I don't need to go to the hospital. I'm fine," she said as they began shining lights in her eyes and strapping a blood pressure cuff to her arm.

"They just want to make sure, okay? Let them take you in and I promise I won't be far behind."

Inside the ambulance and lying on a stretcher, Katie recalled Wilson's final words. The abandoned cabin; where was it? They had traversed that forest months ago and found no signs of any homes. How far had the six-year-old version of herself run before being found along the roadside? A mile? Two miles? She would have had no real concept of distance at that age. But now that they had the birth name of Hendrickson, they could locate whatever properties the family might have owned.

For a moment, she felt sorry for Robert Wilson. He had a mother who had committed suicide and a brother who had "accidentally" killed his baby sister. She wondered how he had managed to lead a normal life after realizing his brother had become a killer. But who knew the nightmares he faced every night when he slept? They must have been far worse than her own.

None of that mattered now. The killer was near and he would find out about his brother soon enough. He wouldn't stay at the cabin; he was too smart for that. He'd eluded capture with the aid of his brother up until now. She was convinced he'd find a way out of town. Or, he would resign to the fact that he wasn't going to make it out of town alive and do whatever it took to get to her.

Rio Dell didn't have a hospital—only local practices—and so they had taken her to Arcata, to the same hospital where Sam's body had been taken.

They wheeled her inside. She could probably stand on her own without any dizziness now that the ringing had subsided. But when she attempted to rise, the paramedics insisted that she lie down while they talked to the Attending.

The doctor approached her and took her wrist to check her pulse. "How are you feeling, Katie? Any dizziness, nausea?"

"No, I'm feeling much better now. My ears are still ringing a little, but no more nausea."

"Good. I think I'd like to just get you checked out and then you'll be free to go home."

"Uh, doctor?" One of the EMTs approached. "Can I talk to you for a minute?"

The two moved several feet away and Katie couldn't hear what he was saying. However, based on the look on the doctor's face, she figured the EMT filled him in on the situation.

The doctor approached her again. His face was changed and a look of pity replaced what had previously been just a medical concern. "Okay, well, I think the best thing is to keep you overnight for observation."

She suspected this was Marshall's doing. "Can I have my cell phone?" Katie asked.

"I'll have your things brought to your room once we get you admitted." The doctor led the EMTs away.

Katie watched as they continued their conversation. She was going to be there for the night, by all accounts. It was probably the best place for her. But she was desperate to know what was happening with Marshall and if they'd found the cabin.

Soon after getting her into a room, a nurse brought her things to her. "Thank you." Katie rummaged through the bag in search of her cell phone. Her mind replayed the scene over and over. Wilson's head on the table and his wife's screams. The sounds pierced her ears like an ice pick.

Her phone revealed no messages. Why hadn't Marshall called to check on her? She had to know what was happening. She'd expected him to be at the hospital by now.

His phone rang, once, twice, then to voicemail. She disconnected the call when the nurse leaned into the doorway.

"You have some visitors," she said, leading Katie's parents into the room.

"Oh, thank God you're okay!" her mother said, rushing to Katie's bedside.

"I'm fine, Mom, really. They're just keeping me here for observation."

"We heard what happened at Chief Wilson's house," her father said. "They've blocked off all the roads out of town and patrolmen are everywhere. Is he in Rio Dell, Katie?"

"They think so, Dad. I'm pretty sure that's why they're keeping me here tonight."

"Well, why the hell aren't there any officers posted out front here?"

"I'm sure they're on their way, Dad. I'll be safe here. They'll find him. I'm sure of it and this nightmare will finally be over."

Deborah reached around her daughter to embrace her as best she could. "It'll finally be over for all of us, sweetheart."

Katie had almost forgotten the toll this must have taken on her parents. They'd been living with this for so long. To have it finally nearing its end must be indescribable. Then, there were the families of the other victims. She could only hope that when they did catch Hendrickson, he'd tell the cops what he did with the others and let the parents finally bury their children.

"Thank you for coming to see me, but I think it's best if you go back home. They've still got someone there at the house?"

John nodded. "One of them brought us down here."

"Good. I'll be fine. Marshall will be here soon. We just need to let the FBI do what they need to do." Only now, during this hellish nightmare had she finally wanted to relinquish control of the situation. She realized there was nothing more for her to do. She did what needed to be done to get this far. It was time to let go.

"Will they send you away tomorrow?" John asked.

"Hard to say, Dad. Hopefully, this will all be over after today. They know who he is."

"They know who took you? Who killed those other children?"

"Yes."

He choked back his tears, wiping his eyes with the back of his hand. Deborah handed him a tissue from her purse. These were not tears of relief, but tears of anger. "Someone from town?"

"No. It's a long story, but the chief had a brother. They know it's him."

"For Christ's sake. They'd better find that son of a bitch before I do, then." John turned away to shield them from the growing rage.

"I'm glad you're all right, honey, and that you're back home. Marshall seemed very worried when you left on your own yesterday," Deborah said.

"You know about that?"

"He asked us if we knew where you were. It just about sent your dad off the rails when he found out. You scared us all, Katie."

"I'm so sorry. It's just that—I needed to do something, something important and I know in my heart that I did the right thing."

"We could have prevented all of this," Deborah began. "And it's something we'll have to live with for the rest of our lives."

"Mr. and Mrs. Reid?" Officer Miller appeared at the doorway. "I think we'd better get you two back home now. Katie will be safe here tonight. They're sending an agent over now to stand watch."

"Contact us as soon as you're able, okay? I know you'll be safe and it won't be long before we can put this behind us." Deborah took John's hand and followed Miller out.

The room was quiet after her parents left; in fact, the entire hospital seemed quiet. Arcata wasn't much bigger than Rio Dell and this seemed to be the norm. Still, the silence made her feel uneasy. Nothing from Marshall and it was starting to get late. Officer Miller did say an agent was on his way, but it didn't stop her worrying.

A nurse pushing a patient in a wheelchair along the corridor appeared out of the corner of her eye, distracting her from her own thoughts. She looked at the man, wincing at his appearance. His face seemed to be badly burned, although she couldn't see much through his bandages. Katie quickly turned away when the nurse caught sight of her, embarrassed by her lingering stare at the suffering man.

The buzz of her cell phone offered a welcomed diversion. She swiped it off the tray table after seeing that it was Marshall on the caller ID. "There you are. It's been hours. I was getting worried. Are you okay?"

"I'm fine. More importantly, how are you doing?"

"I feel okay. My parents came to see me. You must've told them I was here?"

"I called the officer standing watch at their house and had him bring them over. I didn't want you to be alone."

"Thank you. But when are you going to be here? What's been happening? Have they found him?"

"One thing at a time, Kate. I'll be down to check on you soon. Scarborough and his men are tracking down the location of the Hendrickson's cabin. They've got barricades set up at the highway onramps and Route 53, leading out of town. We've been able to keep wraps on the local media since it's only a couple of guys at the paper, but I don't know how long we'll be able to hold off Aguilar. He's anxious to break the story. Fortunately, Scarborough's boss is here now and he's put the fear of God into him if he leaks it. They don't want anyone scaring off the killer or getting more press coming in and causing trouble for us."

"So, you think he's still there?" Katie asked, already knowing the answer.

"I think you need to rest for now. Scarborough is sending an agent down there soon to keep watch. I'll come see you as soon as I can, I promise."

"Okay. I love you."

"I love you too, Kate."

The call ended and she held the phone close to her chest as if she were holding a part of him. Her exhaustion caught up to her and she soon drifted off to sleep.

~

THE PUNCTURE that stung her arm ripped Katie from her rest. She saw a needle being pushed in. Adrenaline rushed through her veins as fast as a scorpion's venom, attempting to counteract whatever had just been injected into her. She reared her head up to see who was responsible for this pain. It was the man whose face had been burned and bandaged. Her heart was beginning to slow and her mind was growing hazy as it dawned on her what was happening.

Moments later, her body became limp and he tossed her over his shoulder. She was losing consciousness and fast. The scream that was building inside her escaped as barely a whimper. It wouldn't be long before she was out cold.

The hospital still had functioning windows in the rooms. He only had to open one and climb out onto the fire escape. He was a big man. Her vision was blurred, but she could see his girth.

They descended the two flights of stairs and by the time they reached the bottom, a single thought soared in her fading mind: It was him and he was going to kill her.

25

LITTLE KATIE

The fog was beginning to lift as Katie's eyes fluttered. Her vision was still clouded, but she could start to make out her surroundings. She tried to brush the hair from her face, but soon felt the restraints that shackled her arms behind her back. An aching head and an empty stomach lent themselves to the waves of nausea that whirled through her.

Her clarity soon improved at the realization she wasn't alone when the large figure perched on a stool opposite her began to shift. The true horror of this disturbing image began to sink in when she noticed the bandages hadn't concealed all of the raw, burned flesh. Exposed too, was part of his charred scalp, which was bright red and blistered. From her vantage point, the man was not burned any other place on his body. But no matter how grotesque, there was no doubt in her mind who this was. And when he spoke, the familiar voice infiltrated her entire body. It had been twenty-three years, but there was no doubt that this monster was Joseph Hendrickson. A ferocious impulse to scream arose from deep within her.

And, as if he could read her mind, he began shaking his head and placed his index finger over his swollen lips. "Don't scream, little

Katie. No one will hear you, certainly not your precious Detective Avery."

This was not the cabin, nonetheless, the place was familiar. She was sitting on a metal chair with a padded seat and backrest. The floor was concrete and a single light hung from the high ceiling, its light, casting a circle onto the floor in front of her. Two windows were boarded up and one smaller window remained uncovered, revealing the darkness outside. How long had she been out? They must have known she was gone by now.

"Where am I?" A groggy, muttering voice sounded; a result of whatever drug he shoved into her arm.

"You don't recognize this place? I'm surprised. I thought you were here helping the FBI and Detective Avery with the evidence I so kindly left for you all."

It registered with her now, only it didn't look like the same place. "The warehouse?"

"Where else would we be? Certainly not the cabin. I had to torch the place, thanks to my brother. And I so loved it there. All the fond memories of the times we had together and not just you; the other children too."

"Is that how you burned your face?"

"As a matter of fact, yes, but I admit it was somewhat intentional. I had to figure out a way to disguise my appearance since you revealed my face to the world. Thanks for that, by the way. Painful as it is, it was worth it. I got what I came for. My brother didn't even recognize me when I showed up at his house today. He wasn't going to give you up and I knew he was thinking of talking to the FBI, so I had to convince him that he had no choice. How easy it would have been for me to find his daughter after I murdered his wife."

Tears rolled down Katie's face as she listened to the sickening words coming from his mouth.

"I knew he couldn't handle it anymore—the guilt. Seems as though you pushed him over the edge, little Katie. But I had to work fast because we both knew what was happening. He found out about you and the reporter poking around Sacramento PD. Robert called and told me it was only a matter of time and that the FBI would be on their way soon. That's when I knew the cabin was going to have to go and I had to find a disguise. You know, I could hear you upstairs. I was hiding in the basement, listening to every word, even the gunshot that finally put my brother out of his misery."

Hendrickson lifted his weight from the stool and slid to within inches of Katie, leaning into her ear. "How does it feel knowing that everyone around you had to suffer because you just couldn't let it go?" he whispered. "How are you going to live with yourself?" He sat back and folded his arms across his wide stomach. "I guess you won't have to worry about that for much longer. You should be very proud of your handiwork. Without you, I would've continued to live a life of solitude and boredom in Oregon City. Everyone was so friendly there. The mothers, walking their children to school. Oh, it was tempting, but I didn't have the same fire in my gut that I have now. No, once you came forward, everything changed. And I'm so much happier now. Of course, I thought you'd stop looking once I took Samantha away from you. But not even losing your best friend was going to make you stop, was it?"

The harsh reality of his words breached her soul. She wanted nothing more right now than for him to stop, but this was what he wanted, wasn't it? Demoralize her to the point of giving up? "They will find me here. You have to know that."

His open palm came at her and landed with a stinging slap, knocking her head hard enough to tweak her neck. She reeled with dizziness for a moment until finally, she regained her senses. Her cheek was hot and throbbed in pain.

"Of course they will, once they realize the cabin is gone. That's the whole point of this. Oh, to see your Detective Avery's face as he watches you die; what a moment that will be. I imagine it'll be the last thing I see, but it will all be worth it. I'll finally have the one thing you took from me, little Katie; the absolute joy of stripping away your shiny veneer; revealing the dirty little cunt you really are."

She studied the room in search of an opportunity to escape. They weren't in the main warehouse, but a smaller office somewhere at the back of the building, near the loading bays. The big corrugated metal doors that opened for the semi-trucks were just visible. She would have to overtake him in order to even hope to escape. Right now, that didn't seem a likely scenario. She'd fended him off once before, but she doubted he would take any chances this time.

"What did you do with the other children? How many did you kill besides your sister?" She wanted him to get angry; give him cause to attack again. It was the only way she could attempt to strike him. From the look on his face, she saw that she had succeeded.

"My little sister? I see my brother didn't fill you in on all the sordid details. She was the reason my father left and my mother killed herself. There was barely enough to go around with just the four of us, but Robbie didn't remember that. Then she came along and we had nothing left. That little unexpected 'gift from God' tore my family apart."

"So you drowned her in a tub?" She continued to provoke him further. *Come on, hit me again.*

He stood and moved toward her, but then just smiled and left the room. She struggled to free her arms, which were bound at the back of the chair. He'd zip-tied them together. She tried to wriggle her wrists and tore her skin against the hard plastic teeth of the ties. Blood ran down her hands, dripping onto the cold concrete floor. She tried to stand, but his footfalls were drawing nearer.

Once inside again, Hendrickson set a box down on his stool, marched over to Katie, and shoved her to the ground. "I knew you'd try to leave. I made it easy enough for you. But you didn't think I'd be gone for long, did you? No, I just wanted you to think you had a chance at escaping, but not this time, little Katie. He kicked her in the gut as she lay on the ground. Her knees pulled up, trying to shield herself from another blow, but he aimed for her head this time. The last thing Katie saw was a large black boot rising above her face.

SHE HAD no idea how much time had passed, but her brain was pounding against her skull and the dried blood on her face cracked with each grimace. She was back up on the chair, feet and hands bound.

When the room came into focus, she raised her head and saw him sitting on the stool across the room once again. He was holding a small wooden box, maybe a cigar box, she thought. The first thing that came to her mind was that Marshall hadn't found her yet. What was happening? Wouldn't they think to come back to the warehouse? It was pitch black outside now; it must have been the middle of the night.

"I was wondering when you'd wake up. I've been sitting here for almost an hour. I'm sure you won't try that again, will you?"

She only looked at the box in his hands.

He lurched forward and screamed. "Will you?"

"No."

"Wondering what's in this box?" His cool voice and calm temper reappeared; a terrifying transformation from only a moment ago "I guess you could call me a collector, of sorts. I like to keep little mementos from my past." He put his hand in the box, and swished its contents around, the sound of clinking metal rising from it. "You might remember this. I gather that's what has forced our paths to cross once again." He pulled out the heart-shaped pendant necklace from the missing Arcata girl, Ashley Davies.

Katie's eyes welled up and spilled onto her face, the salty tears stinging as they fell into the wide gashes on her cheeks. She had no idea how many injuries she had sustained, but the vision in her left eye was diminished. The lid had swollen to the point that only a small slit remained open. But she recognized the necklace instantly.

"I have such beautiful little trinkets, except one from you." He eyed her entire body. "I don't see that you have anything for me to keep. Samantha had that interesting ring. I wanted to keep it, but I thought you might make better use of it. I did expect you to be wearing it now."

"They gave it back to her husband." The excruciating pain with each spoken word brought more dizzy spells, nonetheless, she would not reveal her agony to him.

"That's a shame. I was hoping to get it back. I don't know what it is that I'll get to keep from you today, but I'm sure I'll find something. Oh, and one more thing." The hospital bag that contained her belongings lay a few feet away. He walked toward it and opened it up, retrieving her cell phone. "I thought you might like to listen to your beloved detective's voice. He seems very worried about you. You know, you might want to consider adding a passcode to your phone." He held up the phone and played the voicemail.

"*I know you have her, you son of a bitch. I swear to God, if you hurt her, I'll fucking kill you! There's no place for you to hide now, Joseph. The roads are blocked and we all know what you did to your face. It's only a matter of time. You should give up while you have the chance because when I find you, I won't take you into custody. You'll be dead.*"

"It sounds like he loves you very much. Is he the reason you broke off your engagement? I was sad to hear Spencer was gone. He seemed like a good man. I think you may have traded down." He continued looming over her. "Well, I think I've had enough fun for one night. It's clear they aren't coming to save you tonight. I think you ought to try to get some sleep."

Once again, his hand connected hard with her face. This time, it was a solid fist that knocked her out cold.

SUBTLE MORNING LIGHT shone through the narrow, dirty window in the room where Katie remained alone. How long had she been out this time? Two, maybe three hours? It couldn't be but about seven o'clock in the morning and she was cold. The warehouse was only a shell since the fire and held absolutely no heat.

Her arms were numb from the forced position in which they had remained for too long. But it was her head that had succumbed to the brunt of the pain. The swelling of her left eye had reduced enough that she could freely look left and right, but with each movement, her brain ached. Hunger and thirst were beginning to take control of her. Where was Hendrickson? She'd expected him to be waiting; his burned face and purple lips curled up, smiling at her. He was not there and only the small wooden box remained where he had sat only a few hours ago.

Katie skimmed the room in search of the bag with her cell phone in it. Of course, he was smart enough not to leave that lying around for her to make a quick call to Marshall.

The door swung open with wild purpose and the monster was once again in her presence. "How did you sleep? Well, I hope. It seemed so when I came in to check on you earlier. You really can't take a punch. I should be more careful; I don't want you dying on me before it's time. Get up now." He walked over to her and grabbed her elbow.

The needling pain of her sleeping arm shot through her as he raised her off the chair. Her legs were weak and swollen from having remained in a seated position. They trembled under her weight. "Where are you taking me?"

"I thought we might go for a little ride today."

This was it. He was going to take her somewhere and kill her, just like he did with Sam.

"I've had a change of heart. I don't want to make it too easy for your boyfriend to gallantly come to your rescue, well—your demise. So, I think we'll spend some quality time together on a little road trip. Thought maybe we'd go up north."

"The roads are closed and everyone knows who you are. You can't really believe you'll get out of here alive."

"Oh, we won't be going far and not really out of town. I've been monitoring the police scanners, so I know where the roadblocks are. And besides, with the media helicopters hovering everywhere, broadcasting the FBI's every move, I think we've got the advantage here. There's one more place I'm pretty sure the FBI doesn't know about, not yet anyway. I think we'll be able to spend some time there for a while." He placed his hand on her head, his touch causing even greater pain to her already throbbing skull. His hand slid down her long dark hair, eventually caressing her back. "I miss being with you, little Katie. And I'm very curious to see how much you've learned over the years."

Her mind flashed back to visions of him, caressing her in the same manner. Younger, thinner, but just as terrifying, especially to the child she once was. She began to feel the same fear that ruled her younger self, running through the forest.

He yanked her arm and she dragged her feet until she was able to catch up with his quick pace. He was in a hurry, which meant to her that he knew they must be close. What was his plan?

The doors opened and the light poured into the warehouse. Katie's eyes squinted at the brightness, her swollen eye now in searing pain. The hospital gown she was still wearing allowed the cold air to penetrate right through to her bones and the paper-thin white camisole she still had on beneath offered only a little more protection.

When they reached the car, she noticed her bag lying on the back seat. The front passenger seat contained a grocery bag filled with bloodied bandages. There was another bag that had a hat and a few other things in it, but she couldn't see what they were. He wasn't leaving anything behind.

He shoved her into the back seat and walked around to the driver's side when he paused and looked back at the warehouse. She watched him stand there for a minute and then he looked at her again, like he was thinking he forgot something. He stepped back around, pulled open the door, and dragged her back out. "You got me worked up so much, I almost forgot my most treasured possession."

Katie knew it was the box. It still sat on the stool. Her pulse began to race the closer they got to the back room where it remained. Would he notice? He released her arm long enough to take hold of the box. Then once he held it securely against his chest, he gripped her arm again, squeezing hard.

She winced in pain, but it was nothing compared to the pain in her head.

They raced back to the car; she was tossed into the backseat like a ragdoll. When he jumped into the driver's seat, bringing the engine to life, he sped out of sight of the abandoned warehouse.

Katie looked through the rear window, the building shrinking in the distance. He hadn't noticed, not yet anyway, but that was fine because there was nothing he could do about it now. She managed the briefest of smiles, remembering the heart-shaped pendant lying on the floor, behind a leg of the chair where she had been bound.

During the night, awakening briefly, she had managed to drag herself and the chair to the wooden box. He was just outside the door, blocking it, asleep and snoring. It was a struggle to maneuver the box with bound hands, but she removed the pendant, opened it, and placed a scrap of her hospital gown that had snagged on the fire escape into the locket. She carefully placed herself in exactly the same position, the blood drops from her hands in the same spot in relation to the chair. She tucked the locket behind the back chair leg.

It wasn't much, but Katie hoped it would be enough for Marshall to know that she was still alive, for now.

"Your clothes are in that bag. Get changed," Hendrickson said.

"I can't. My hands are still tied."

"Goddamn it!"

He was agitated and becoming increasingly short-tempered. Did he really have a plan?

"Pull your legs up and through so your arms are in the front."

She did as he asked and managed to slip on the jeans she was wearing when they took her to the hospital. The bag still had everything in it, except for her cell phone.

His face still appeared badly burned, but he'd changed his

bandages, removing some entirely, leaving the least damaged areas exposed. He was wearing the hat now and he cringed when he put on the sunglasses, no doubt from the pain of the burns.

"Where are we going?"

They seemed to be heading east, from what she could gather. What was there? She wracked her brain. The nearest place was Bridgeville. It was about as small-town as you could get in this area, even smaller than Rio Dell. The back country roads could easily be overlooked.

Marshall wouldn't overlook anything, not as long as he had a say in finding her. But who was Scarborough taking orders from now? The FBI had completely taken over, so who was in charge? Katie had to keep up hope that they'd go back to the warehouse, find the pendant, and realize she'd been taken someplace else. There had to be a way to contact Marshall. Wherever Hendrickson was taking her, they weren't likely to find her before he'd had his fill.

There was nothing between Rio Dell and Bridgeville; not even a convenience store. If that was where they were going, it was only about half an hour or so away. The best Katie could recall, not many people lived there. Maybe some cabins dotting the green hills, a mom-and-pop grocery store, maybe a fast food place by now. She'd only been there once when she was thirteen. It was a perfect place to hide. Find an abandoned home on a couple of acres. It wouldn't be that hard.

Katie saw the sign pointing toward the 36, but he continued going straight, down a single-lane road. No one else was in sight. A sinking feeling started to settle in. She began to doubt her ability to come out of this alive. She would be gone and he would escape, once again. She couldn't let that happen.

Closing her eyes, she leaned her head back on the seat. In her mind's eye, Marshall was standing in front of her, his body inches from hers. She remembered his kiss, his firm arms wrapped around her as they embraced. At that moment, her mind jumped to a scene she couldn't explain, but one which compelled her to act.

Katie launched forward, threw her still zip-tied arms over his head, reared back, and began choking him. The car swerved on the country road. He slammed on the brakes, propelling her forward. Katie was halfway over the front seat now. He reached behind her head, his hands digging into the back of her neck, and pulled her over the rest of the way. She scrambled to get her legs out in front of her and began kicking him in the side. Her arms were stretching too far now and started to ache. He pushed her head back with one hand and tried to lift her arms with the other. Her own strength caught her by surprise. Though he'd landed a few good blows, she'd managed to keep hold of him. The car was out of control and heading for the shoulder of the road.

A moment later, both of his feet pounded on the brake. They spun around; Katie flying wildly between the dash and the passenger seat, pulling his head along with her. When the car finally came to a stop, he pounced on top of her, the weight of his body knocking the wind from her lungs. He easily tossed her arms over his head and was now free of her.

He pummeled her face and then started choking her. "How does that feel, Katie?" He laughed.

She struggled for breath, quickly bringing her elbows in toward her sides, using her hands to loosen his grip on her neck. The taste of blood filled her mouth and the pressure behind her eyes made them feel as if they were about to explode. He was choking the life out of her, right here, right now.

But then he stopped, releasing his hands from the death grip around her throat. She inhaled a great deep breath to refill her lungs quickly before she passed out; a terrible gasping sound escaped. She instinctively leaned over onto her side and spit out copious amounts of blood from the severe beating her face took once again.

She could hear him laughing. Had she even left a mark on him?

"Are we done here?" He wiped the blood from his lip.

Apparently, she'd connected at least one hit. His bandages were bleeding through. She looked at his neck. She had done some damage, but it was far from enough to stop him.

"Get back there!" he shoved her back over the seat with ease.

For the rest of the journey, she remained still and silent. He tossed one of his clean bandages at her and told her to clean off her face. Glancing back at her in the rearview mirror every minute or two ensured she wouldn't make another stupid attempt. It had been stupid and almost had cost her life. And although she hadn't hurt him to any great degree, she did accomplish what she'd set out to do.

Before her emboldened attack, she caught sight of her cell phone sitting in the center console in the front seat. The scene that flashed through her mind was of the attack. Once in the front seat, Katie had to figure out a way to take the phone and she had. Kicking him with her legs she positioned herself in such a manner as to snatch it up while he was busy protecting himself. She'd slipped it into the pocket of her jeans, beneath the hospital gown. He had no idea she'd taken it.

So Katie remained quiet, waiting for her chance. A sign appeared ahead and soon came into focus. "Bridgeville 10 Miles."

26

———————

Bridgeville **was one** of those towns that if you blinked, you'd miss it. Hendrickson drove slowly down to the main street, then veered left, presumably in search of someplace to stay.

Katie feared what he would do to whoever happened to be occupying a place he found suitable. She needed him to leave her just long enough to call Marshall to tell him where she was. Had the FBI already been to the warehouse? If so, they would be searching for tire tracks in order to track down this car. Having worked with Marshall this long, she'd learned a lot about tracking evidence. But if she could just call him, this would all be over.

"This'll do," Hendrickson said.

The small A-frame home was old and tucked back away from the street and its neighbors. From the outside, it didn't look as though anyone lived there. She prayed that was the case.

Hendrickson pulled up along the dirt driveway. It was barely nine a.m. and the sun still sat low enough in the sky to shine through the windows of the home. By the looks of it, no one had lived there for a long time. He leaned toward the passenger seat, opened the glove box, and pulled out a gun. Then, he opened her door and yanked Katie out of the back seat. She had no idea he had a gun. He must have gotten it from Wilson's home yesterday.

She knew he hadn't expected to survive this time. Was the gun for himself or for anyone who tried to rescue her?

They approached the front door. Hendrickson looked through the curtains of the front window that had been partially open; just enough to get a glimpse of the inside. He pounded on the rusted screen door. No answer.

He pulled her around the side of the house and toward the back. There were no fences or gates. No one out here needed such security. In fact, Katie suspected the front door wasn't even locked, unless the owner happened to lose it to the bank. The bank might have locked it up tight.

The backyard was overgrown and weedy, with scraps of trash and old rotted wood lying around. A rusted trike was under the makeshift aluminum cover that passed as the patio roof. Katie wondered what could have happened to the family that lived there and thanked God they weren't there now.

He dragged her back to the front of the house and tried the door. "No one's here," he said, opening it.

A stale odor floated out. This place had been empty for a while, it seemed. Some furnishings were still in place, old and torn. Hendrickson wouldn't let her out of his sight while he searched for any signs that someone might show up. When they walked past the bathroom, he caught a glimpse of himself in the mirror. Katie's handiwork didn't escape notice. He saw that blood had seeped through some of his new bandages after they'd struggled. His face looked just as hideous as it had when he had appeared at her hospital bed.

Any person who would go to such extremes to get what they wanted was beyond insane. He was obsessed; obsessed with her, even more so than she had been with him. The part that frightened her the most was that she wanted to kill him as much as he wanted to kill her.

With his fingers, he lightly pressed at his face. "Look at what you made me do to my face." He pulled her close so she could see his reflection in the mirror. Her face hadn't looked much better. The bleeding had stopped, but her left eye was black; the swelling worsened by the struggle. A gash that started just above her left eye, where the boot had made contact, extended down her temple and stopped at her cheekbone. She would never look the same again.

"We look like quite the pair, little Katie, both of us scarred by this. Maybe the only saving grace is that we won't have to live with it for long."

She shuddered, knowing that he had already resigned to his death and there was no doubt he was going to take her with him.

He led her back down the stairs and tossed her onto the worn, dilapidated couch. "You'll be here for a while; might as well get comfortable." Hendrickson walked into the kitchen and turned on the faucet. There was water, probably from a community well, but no electricity.

They had no food and only half a day's worth of light left. Darkness would set in by about five-thirty. On this sparsely populated street, there were no lights, no restaurants with illuminated signs; nothing but black, and the occasional porch light that might be left on to guide a loved one home.

She had to figure out a way to call Marshall. So far, Hendrickson hadn't noticed the missing phone, but she knew it was only a matter of time. As soon as he went back out to the car to gather his things, he'd know it was gone. He would do one of two things: beat the hell out of her again or shoot her, neither of which seemed a desirable solution.

"Can I use the bathroom?" she asked, pain shooting through her jaw with each word she spoke. "I'd like to clean up my face and I have to pee."

His distorted features looked even more gruesome as he approached her. "We were just upstairs. Are you trying to play games with me?"

She squeezed out a few tears on demand, although the stinging sensation they created brought about actual tears. "I just need to go to the bathroom, I swear."

He towered over her, lifting her from the couch. "Don't think for a second I'm going to let you go up there alone."

She had to make that call; she was running out of time. "Can I close the door, please?" she asked as they stood in front of the bathroom.

"Just get in there." He shoved her inside and slammed the door. "I'm listening and I'd better hear you pee."

There was a small window above the tub, too small even for her petite frame. Not to mention, she was on the second floor, and jumping from that height would cause injury enough to keep her from running. No, her focus was on calling Marshall. She only had to last a few hours before he would find her if that. But how to make the call with Hendrickson listening?

Her hands were still bound and so removing her jeans took some effort. She did have to go, that much was true. She'd removed the phone from her pocket and turned it on. He must have switched it off when he took her, knowing they'd be tracking it.

The phone seemed to take forever to boot up. When it did, the battery showed fifteen percent. It was enough; that was all that mattered.

"I don't hear anything," he said.

She managed to sit and finally, a stream started. A last-second decision, she called 911 instead. Given the amount of time she had, it was probably the better course of action.

"Hello, 911, what's your emergency?"

She cringed, wondering if he'd heard the voice on the other end of the phone. She was finished going and knew she couldn't speak.

The 911 operator asked again, "What's your emergency?"

She cupped her hand over the phone to quiet her words. "Bridgeville."

"Ma'am?"

She disconnected the call, shoving the phone back into her

pocket. She'd hoped that the operator would dispatch the police and, by turning on her phone, the FBI would pick up a trace. This was all she could do now: hope.

"I'm coming in there!" he shouted.

"I'm done and I'm coming out now." Katie kept her head down as she walked out of the bathroom. To look him in the face might reveal what she had done. Casting her eyes downward would serve as reassurance that he was in a position of power. She had no question in her mind to the contrary.

Her heart pounded fiercely against her chest. At any moment, he could go out to the car and she feared that would be the end. *Please, Marshall, please find me.* It was by far the riskiest thing she'd done yet and he wasn't likely to give her any more warnings. He was playing a game with the FBI but knew that his time was running out. And, if she'd spoiled his plans, there was no point in keeping her alive.

Hendrickson forced her back onto the couch and remained towering in front of her, his large frame completely blocking her view. He began removing his bandages; peeling each one away from the burned, oozing flesh. The burns had been severe and covered nearly half of his face.

She kept her head down, not wanting her empty stomach to turn. At this point, it would not take much for the bile to rise.

"Look at me!" he shouted. "Look at what you did to me!" He bent down, his face within inches of hers. His eyes were brown and bulging out of their sockets, but pristine white flesh remained around them. They moved up and down her body, scanning every inch of her. Could he see the phone in her pocket beneath the hospital gown? He reached his hand out toward her, but rather than strike her again, he placed it on her breast.

What thin clothing she was wearing allowed for little modesty. The heat from his cupped hand easily penetrated the gown and camisole and she could feel the slightest movements in his fingers.

He began pushing and squeezing hard, but she refused to show pain. She knew he wanted nothing more than to watch her suffer and she did not give him that satisfaction. He pushed her chest, grunted, and finally released her.

He turned away in anger. When his back was toward her, she released the breath held firmly inside, wincing from the pain that now pulsated in her breast.

She heard the front door open and the screen door bouncing against its frame as it closed. *Oh God, he'll know the phone is gone.* Katie was starting to panic. *Where are you, Marshall? Where the hell are the police?* Her throat tightened as a lump rose high. She tried to swallow it back down, forcing herself to find calm.

The rusty screen door slammed shut once again. Hendrickson was back.

She could hear his heavy footsteps in the hall, approaching the living room where she sat helplessly on the couch. He was getting closer and a single thought popped into her head. *Throw the phone under the couch!* Katie thrust her hand deep into the front pocket of her jeans and ripped the phone out. It was still on. She shoved it as far beneath the couch as possible.

As she reared back up, he was standing in the arched opening. If any sort of human being had ever existed inside this monster, he was long gone now. She recognized the look on his face. It was the same look she saw as she ran away from him; the twisted, murderous look.

"Where is it?" His monotone words chilled the room in an instant. Underneath his arm was the little wooden box. The hospital bag and his grocery bag hung in his right hand.

She wondered, for a moment, if he'd been asking about the phone or the pendant necklace, but she dared not answer.

The bags hit the floor and he opened his box of trinkets. "Where is the necklace, you stupid little bitch?"

Katie felt almost relieved, but that didn't last long. "I don't know. It must've fallen out in the car."

He threw the box at her, its contents spilling out, clinking and tumbling toward her feet. She knew each piece had come from a victim and they all lay at her feet. There must have been nearly ten.

She stared at his collection, shocked by the number of them. She raised her head, her heart filled with a hatred that surpassed anything she'd felt before. "My God, how many children have you killed?"

Hendrickson laughed. "Recently? None. These are all from my younger days, mostly before we first met. Save for Samantha's ring, which I selflessly returned to you. No. It was you who brought me back to life, little Katie. You were the one who rekindled the fire. But, oh, when I saw Samantha and I knew that she would help me get to you, well, I just couldn't resist.

"The funny thing was that she knew right away who I was. Of course, you had broadcast my face all over creation, so, not really that funny, I guess. And as soon as I saw that look in her eyes, the fear that I caused—damned if it didn't make me want to cum right then. I couldn't hardly control myself."

Katie felt the bile rise in her throat and fought hard not to let him see her disgust.

"That's when I knew I was back. I felt like the old me again. And boy, did she give chase. But, she was wearing those high-heeled shoes and she just couldn't get any speed. I caught up to her, pushed her to the ground, and I was so damn excited that I just fucked her right then and there on the soft wet ground, covering her pretty mouth with my hand. She struggled for a while, till I jammed my knife into her side. That quieted her down.

"Then, when I was finished, I dragged her back to my car and threw her in. She didn't have any fight left in her by that time, so the drive out to the rest stop off the 101 was pretty quiet. I took her around the back of the building. No one was around, of course, since it had been shut down. I called my brother after it was all over and told him where he could find her. I wanted to be sure that he knew I wasn't fucking around anymore and that he'd better get on board or risk losing his own family.

"I did have a little more fun with her though, but it started to lose its thrill. You see, I do prefer the little ones; so much more delicate and they don't fight back so much. My favorite part was watching the knife slide into her gut like butter. Over and over, her blood splashed up on my mouth and it tasted so sweet."

Katie trembled; she couldn't bear to hear anymore. He started touching himself as he went on about killing her best friend. "Shut up!" she screamed.

He moved in closer, knelt, and started sifting through the jewelry spread out on the floor. "So many wonderful memories. And to think, I put all that pleasure on hold for so long."

"What did you do with the children?" Her voice cracked through the sobs.

He stood back up and smiled. "Well, that depended on where I was living at the time. When you and me got acquainted, I had been having a heck of a time traveling up and down the North Coast. Mostly, I just buried them in the woods. Of course, the girl in Portland I thought I'd have some fun with. I put her somewhere I thought they'd find her right away. It still took a year before some hiker saw her and I think that was only because of the rains that summer washing away the cover. I didn't have a lot of time to bury her properly.

"I couldn't let myself get caught though, so I buried the rest of them around my folks' cabin. I imagine they'll find them soon enough. You know, I still can't quite figure out how it was you got away from me. It was like you had the power of God running through your little body that day. Took me by surprise, that's for damn sure. You were slippery, and I don't just mean when you got away from me."

He lurched over her, pulled her up, and dragged her to the banister. She lost her footing and felt a snap as she went down. Her arm was contorted to the point that her shoulder had dislocated. The pain was unbearable and only made worse when he stretched her arms up over the railing. If anyone was within fifty yards, they'd have heard that scream.

Hendrickson yanked an already loose spindle free and drove its blunt end into Katie's gut. "Shut up!"

Her arms hung on the finial so when she instinctively tried to double over, it stopped her. He pulled the gun from his waistband. Her eyes widened at the sight of it. He placed it on the ground and kicked it away. Hendrickson clawed at her front, tearing the hospital gown and even her camisole. He pushed his lips onto hers, trying to force her mouth to open, but she clenched her teeth as hard as she could. The blood that had seeped from his wounds smeared onto her face, her own cuts reopening by the force.

"I told you I'd get you, didn't I? The best part about it was that you suffered longer than any of them. You suffered your whole life. I bet you wish you would have died the first time around. Oh, I think we're going to have lots of fun now, little Katie Reid."

He released her from the rail and she fell to the ground; her knees withdrawing quickly to shield her. The welt on her stomach increased in size and began to darken. The blow had been so severe she wondered if she was bleeding internally.

Hendrickson went into the kitchen. He was out of view, but upon his return, he held a tape recorder. "Remember this?" He pressed play.

It was the song. The same song he'd played upstairs while she was in the basement. She remembered it now; an old, soft tune from the '60s, but she couldn't recall the singer.

"This was my mother's favorite song. She was listening to it when she pulled the trigger and splattered her brains out all over her bedroom. Dear old Dad had already gone away. And the only thing I could do was try to stop the fucking baby from crying. I guess it stuck with me ever since. They'd let me play the record in the home until they sent me away. Then, they took everything from me. My brother was gone, living the good life with a loving family, and what did I have? Three pills a day and a room with nothing in it but a bed. I guess they thought they were helping me."

"You killed your baby sister!" Katie couldn't yell and her voice sounded small, wounded. "My God, she was only a baby." The tears wouldn't come; not because she didn't feel the pain, but because dehydration had taken hold. There were no tears left to cry.

"She wouldn't shut up, just like you! Just like all the other little shits. I did their parents a fucking favor!" He shoved her again, straddled her, and forced her knees down. Just then, a buzzing sound came from beneath the couch. They were both taken by surprise as they swung their heads to see where the noise was coming from.

He quickly snapped his head back, his frame still resting on top of her. The look on his face changed as he realized what it was. "You goddam whore!" He jumped off of her and raced toward the couch, throwing it up as if it weighed next to nothing.

There it was; her phone bouncing as it vibrated with an incoming call. He looked at it and smiled.

She knew it had to be Marshall.

He picked it up and answered. "Detective Avery, so good to finally hear from you."

Katie realized the depth of his insanity. He'd gone from a crazed, violent psychopath to a civilized human holding a conversation in the span of thirty seconds. But more importantly, what was he going to do now?

"I don't think I can let you talk to her, detective. But I can promise you that she is fine. In fact, we were just about to play a little game. And based on this call, I can only imagine that you and your team of FBI grunts will find us soon enough. I'll tell you what; I'll keep her in one piece until you get here, okay?"

Katie could hear Marshall screaming at him on the other end of the line. A moment later, Hendrickson disconnected the call.

"That was either very smart of you or very stupid, Katie. I'm sure there will be sirens heading our way soon since I know they've been tracing your calls. And leaving your phone on? Nice touch. I didn't see that coming either. I had to take great precautions when I called you myself. But that was a fun game, wasn't it? After all, it brought you back to me. The only problem is that now we'll have to postpone our game. We may not be able to play it at all. I might just have to kill you instead." He threw her phone against the wall, smashing it to pieces.

The song on the cassette player stopped and only static could be heard. He stared at her, seemingly trying to figure out his next move. A moment later, he turned and walked into the kitchen, reemerging with a glass of water and a knife. Not a kitchen knife, but a large pocket knife that he must have been carrying all along.

His gun was out of reach, near the wall that separated the kitchen from the living room. She glanced at it, his eyes immediately following hers.

"You think you can get to it before I can?" he asked. "Go ahead. I think we should make this a fair fight, don't you?"

He wasn't going to let her get anywhere near that gun, she knew that. She remained seated, her arms crossed over her chest. "They'll be here soon. What are you going to do?"

Provocation was not her intention. Katie wanted to understand if she was about to die or if he would continue to torture her. She preferred the former.

"Oh, I don't think we're done yet," Hendrickson said, a determination like she hadn't yet seen. He lifted her off the floor. "We're going to play a little game of hide and seek with your detective. It should be fun." He led her down the hallway and out the back door.

She was cold and terrified; exactly how she felt before. Only this time, he wasn't chasing her. They were about to be chased.

27

___

She tried to keep up as they ran into the woods toward the stream. They were at least half a mile away from the house when she heard the sirens. They grew louder as they approached the house. There must have been ten of them screaming down the quiet street. What lay ahead was quickly approaching; the stream that led to the river.

Hendrickson continued to pull her along. Intentionally stumbling over the river rocks only made him yank harder on her already dislocated arm. Then the sirens stopped.

The stream widened and led them closer to the river. And, almost as if they'd spotted the place at exactly the same time, he turned sharply toward the derelict shack that might have once been a bait shop, her steps following closely behind.

He busted in the door with his foot. It had been barely hanging on its rusted hinges and gave way with ease.

The atrocious smell of rotting fish bait nearly knocked her down. The place was empty except for a standing refrigerator that housed white Styrofoam containers with what had probably been live worms inside. That must have been where the smell was coming from.

There was no electricity. The place was clearly abandoned, like so many of the small town shops.

Hendrickson pulled her around like an unwanted child whose father was searching for a place to punish her. That was exactly what was happening. Katie was different. She was being punished by him for escaping. He had little, if any, deviant sexual interest in her; like he said, he preferred children. He wanted to hurt her for leaving him, not letting him achieve the satisfaction he so desperately desired. The only sexual gratification he needed, she kept from him long ago.

"I think this will be a good place for us to spend some time, don't you, Katie?"

They stood in front of the store's cellar door. *Not again*, she thought. Images of the dark place he kept her before flashed through her mind. She felt like the helpless little girl again. "They're not far. What's the point? Why don't you just kill me already?"

He leaned into her. She could feel his hot breath against her neck and could smell his burned flesh. Had her stomach not been completely empty, she'd have lost whatever remained inside it. His wet tongue left a trail of saliva along the side of her face as he slowly tasted her dried blood.

"I could have killed you a thousand times over, little Katie. But I need to teach you a lesson first. You don't get to decide when you die —I do." He shoved her inside the storage area.

She nearly tumbled down the stairs and grabbed the rotting handrail to steady herself. It gave way and she fell to the ground. The concrete floor was wet and muddy, like the place had recently been flooded.

He followed her down, his steps were more cautious. "Well, I think this will do just fine."

"You know they're going to search every building in this town."

"Oh, I'm counting on that. Though it might take them just a little while to find this place. It's pretty far off the main road. I expect we'll have enough time for me to get my point across."

"Can I at least get up off this muddy ground? Can I sit over there on that crate?"

"What's the matter? Don't like getting dirty? I thought all you whores liked getting dirty." He pulled her up by her good arm and led her to the stack of crates a few feet away. He flipped one over and set it down, tossing her onto it.

Katie sat quietly, waiting for him to make his next move. She could feel the swelling in her eye calm down just enough to gain full peripheral vision again. But she felt weak. It had been almost two days since she'd had anything to eat or drink.

The grotesque man before her seemed to be suffering from the same. She watched as he carried another crate and moved slowly away. He seemed a little unsteady.

"I need some water." She watched his expression as he considered her request. Katie noticed his bandages had grown darker with fresh blood. He would need to treat them soon or risk infection, if there wasn't one already present.

"Stay here." He grunted and moved toward the stairs again.

Where am I gonna go?

He disappeared and she looked around for anything that could be used as a weapon. Her hands were still bound and her arms ached, even the good one. But there must be something she could use. Short of launching a plastic crate at him, nothing else remained in this abandoned cellar. Katie felt as if her luck was about to run out. They had no place to go. How much time did he have before Marshall and the FBI showed up? There was no doubt in her mind that his plan was to kill her in front of Marshall. But they had guns.

She had no idea what weapons he still possessed. They'd run out of the house so quickly, that she couldn't recall seeing him pick up the gun. The knife was probably still in his pocket. He could certainly do enough damage with that alone.

A moment later, Hendrickson reemerged. He held one of the Styrofoam containers from the refrigerator. "Don't confuse this gesture with kindness. I need you to stay alert and conscious long enough for me to kill you in front of the FBI and your detective." He thrust the container to her lips and proceeded to tip it into her mouth.

She wanted to spit up whatever that filth was. It tasted like it had come from the river. But thirst was powerful, so she swallowed the dirty water. "Thank you." Never before had she stared into a man's eyes to see such evil. She was nothing more to him than a possession; one of his shiny things. And she was growing tarnished.

He pushed her off the crate with a hard shove that nearly took the wind from her lungs. "I told you not to mistake anything I do for kindness." He dropped the container and water spilled out in front of her, leaving a small puddle inches in front of her face. He pulled out his knife and laid the blade against her bruised cheek.

The pain hit as he pushed the flat end of the blade against the purple bruise. Its sharp edge pressed into her flesh just enough to draw blood.

He reached into his pocket with his free hand and pulled out his own cell phone. "I think it's time we speed things along here. Call him!"

Her trembling hands reached for the phone. She swiped to turn on the screen and began entering Marshall's phone number. The only reason she'd remembered it was because she had been calling him from the burners in Sacramento. Otherwise, there wasn't a chance in hell she could have recalled it. Her numbers were stored, as were most people's, by name. The phone rang only once before the call connected.

"Detective Avery."

"Marshall, it's me." She began crying immediately. Just hearing his voice, for what she believed could be the last time, was enough to bring all her emotions to the surface.

"Are you okay?" He sounded just as desperate as she had.

"Mostly, yes."

Hendrickson snatched the phone from her, scraping his nails against her cheek. "Detective Avery, how are you? I have no doubt you're nearby."

"It's only a matter of time, Hendrickson. Why don't you make things a little easier on yourself and tell me where you have her?"

"Haven't I made this easy enough for you, detective? Or, rather, Katie has made things very easy for you, hasn't she? Tell me, how was it that you arrived at the house so quickly? You must have been somewhat close."

Katie couldn't hear what Marshall was saying, but knew he wouldn't tell him anything that might jeopardize her safety. Hendrickson only nodded as he listened. His face was vacant of all expression.

"I did expect to have more time with our Katie at the house, but then she went and left that damn cell phone on." He glared at Katie and an evil grin crossed his face. "Not to worry. I'm sure I've got some time left for fun with her. But, detective, I wouldn't wait too long."

"Let me talk to her now!" Marshall shouted loud enough for Katie to hear this time.

"Marshall! I'm in the...."

Hendrickson disconnected the call. "Now that wasn't very smart, was it? I can't have you giving away our location too quickly. They'll find us, but not yet. I just wanted to give them some encouragement." He turned off the phone and slid it back into his pocket. "Seems the detective and his team of merry men were at the warehouse when the signal from your phone registered. They all came blazing down here to try to find you. Must feel pretty good knowing the whole damn FBI and police force in Humboldt County is out looking for you. I'm guessing your face is all over the news too, just like mine, or at least, how mine used to look." He touched his right cheek; the bandage was wet with blood now. "That stunt of mine may have gone a little awry, but I was becoming a desperate man. And you know what desperate men are capable of."

He got down on his knees, leaned back, and rested his weight on his heels. Katie was still on the ground, lying on her side, and balled up into a fetal position. Hendrickson brushed her hair away from her face and traced her wounds with his knife.

She closed her eyes as the knife moved closer.

"Almost feels like before, doesn't it, little Katie?" He ran his hand along her leg until he reached her waist, and then he moved it down until he brushed the outside of her groin.

All the things Katie had done to find this man only brought her back to the same place she had tried so hard to escape. All the pain she had caused her family by forcing them to relive the trauma, losing her best friend, and even losing Spencer. All to be in this very same spot where she was convinced she was about to die.

Hendrickson began unbuttoning her pants, slowly pulling down the zipper when the sound of cars approaching made him lean back and take notice. "I think this party's about to get started." He looked back at Katie. "Oh, and I'd think twice before opening that sweet little mouth of yours." The knife was now pressed against her lips.

He stood up and walked toward the stairs, leaning his head in the direction of the door. "Sounds like we got some visitors." He rushed back toward Katie, picked her up from the ground, and shoved her in front of him. He held her by the waist, pulling her close enough that she could feel his heart pounding in his chest. Her back was against him. He held the knife to her neck, waiting. Waiting until the moment when he could see Marshall. Then, it would be over.

She knew he would slice her throat and Marshall would shoot him dead. The scene played in her head over and over.

The footsteps grew louder. It didn't sound like more than two or three people were walking around. Where was everyone else? She'd expected an army of officers and FBI.

They both heard the handle turn and the door latch release as it opened. Hendrickson was breathing heavily on the back of her head as she felt the knife press harder into her neck, so hard she couldn't swallow. He'd broken the skin and Katie looked down to see streams of blood falling down her chest, her torn clothing absorbing it like a sponge.

Appearing on the steps were shiny black shoes. They were not

Marshall's. As the unidentified person continued down the stairs, he revealed himself to be Agent Scarborough.

"Let her go, Hendrickson. You won't make it out alive if you take her down."

"You must be with the FBI. Agent?"

"Scarborough. Now why don't you put the knife down and let her go."

"Where's the fun in that, Agent Scarborough? In fact, I'll do you one better. I'll let her go if you put your gun down."

"I'm afraid I can't do that," Scarborough replied.

Marshall emerged just behind him.

"Go back upstairs. I got this," Scarborough said, diverting his attention.

When the agent turned to look at Avery, Hendrickson reached behind his back and retrieved his gun, dropping the knife.

Katie knew the situation had just gone from very bad to a hell of a lot worse.

"He's got a gun!" Avery shouted.

"Didn't think I had any tricks left up my sleeve? I almost forgot the gun in the mad rush to leave the house."

The knife bounced next to Katie's foot and finally settled a few inches in front of them.

"You've got nowhere to go, Hendrickson," Marshall said.

"Yes, I believe Agent Scarborough just relayed the same piece of information. I'm well aware of the fact, Detective Avery and I have no plans of making it out of here alive and neither does little Katie."

He pointed the barrel of the gun against her bruised temple, pushing hard. She squinted at the pain. That was where his foot had landed and it hurt like hell.

"Let her go or I'll take you down, you son of a bitch." Marshall was losing control. His face turned red from the rising anger.

Scarborough must have noticed. "Go! I got this!" he demanded.

"That's right, Detective Avery. You heard the man; he's got this."

Hendrickson angled the gun square against Katie's temple and, in an instant, flashes of light illuminated the dark cellar.

Katie was deafened by the sound of the guns, bullets whizzing around, ricocheting off of the cellar walls. She watched as chaos erupted.

Marshall's lips were moving, but she couldn't hear him. Everyone seemed to be yelling and she fell to the ground. Searing pain pierced her side.

Scarborough and Marshall ran down through the rain of gunfire. She couldn't focus, she was losing consciousness.

Her body moved in what felt like slow motion when she tried to grab her side. The last thing she saw was Marshall's face in agonizing pain as he fell to the ground only a few feet in front of her. They locked eyes for just a moment. Her vision began to blur and her eyes grew heavy, then darkness settled all around.

"Katie, wake up!"

The muffled words sounded in her ears, but the ringing was still too loud for her to decipher them. She felt the sting of someone slapping her battered cheek. Her eyes fluttered open, but her vision remained fuzzy. The outline of Agent Scarborough began to come into focus. His identity was confirmed by the letters on his windbreaker. She looked around and saw a scene very similar to the one at Wilson's house. People running around, seemingly without purpose.

"Marshall?" she whispered.

"Katie, he's been shot and so have you. Paramedics are on their way to take you both to the hospital," Scarborough replied.

She turned her head to the right and saw Marshall. His eyes were closed and other officers were around him, stripping the clothes off his chest. She turned the other way and saw Hendrickson. No one was near him. He lay on top of a pool of blood that could be from no one else.

Katie looked back at Scarborough and began crying. "Is he dead?"

"Yes, Katie. He's dead. It's over."

Her side throbbed even more as she cried harder. Katie pulled her hands back and saw the blood covering her palms. Panic-stricken, she looked to Scarborough.

"You're going to be fine, Katie. You and Detective Avery will be fine." He pulled out a pocket knife and cut the zip ties from her hands.

She again watched Marshall. The other officers had removed his shirt and were pressing on his rib cage. "Marshall. Marshall!" With each word, she winced in pain.

Sirens sounded in the distance. "You see? Everything's going to be fine," Scarborough said.

But when Katie looked into his eyes, he was watching Marshall with deep concern.

Hendrickson was gone, that much was true. The officers were taking pictures of him, but no one touched his body and they stepped carefully around the blood pool.

It was over; he was dead. But was she about to lose Marshall too? She began to feel weak again.

"Stay with me, Katie. The ambulance is coming." He pressed her side where the blood was spilling out of her like someone had forgotten to turn off a faucet.

She was getting very tired and everyone around her was moving so quickly. She watched them work on Marshall, his eyes still closed. *Please, God, don't let him die.*

A team of people in white and blue shirts rushed down the stairs, holding cases. One ran to Marshall's side, another rushed to hers. She could hear Scarborough explain the scene to the man.

"Katie, I'm Hank. I'm going to make sure you're all right. Can you hear me?"

She nodded only slightly, but it was enough to confirm she remained conscious.

"Okay, good. We're going to get you upstairs and into the chopper, okay?"

She was starting to drift, the man's face moving in and out of focus. More people rushed down with stretchers.

"Don't let him die," she said to the paramedic.

The man glanced at Marshall. "I'm sure he'll be fine, ma'am. I'm concerned about you right now."

Scarborough moved to Marshall's side where he and another EMT began talking. Katie couldn't hear what they were saying, but the look on Scarborough's face terrified her. The situation felt like a dream. Hendrickson was dead, Marshall was, at the very least, severely injured, and she had no idea what was going to happen next.

"Ma'am, we're going to lift you onto this stretcher. Do you understand me?" The paramedic took her pulse as he spoke.

Slowly, she blinked her eyes, indicating she understood. They hoisted her onto the stretcher and the two men rose in unison until she was off the ground. Scarborough jumped back over and spoke to them, too quietly for Katie to know what he was saying.

Scarborough held Katie's hand. "You'll be just fine."

"Don't let him die," she replied.

When the paramedics got her outside, she noticed a helicopter descending and several others overhead. Was it the media? Had the story gotten out already? But the one chopper descending finally landed. The door opened and she was led toward it. They loaded her inside. She lay there for a moment, wondering why they weren't taking off. Then, as she turned her head toward the opening, she saw the men carrying Marshall out. They were going to airlift them out together, which must have meant that he was still alive.

She watched them bring him in. He was unconscious and they had a manual respirator on him; *bagging him*, she'd heard it called before. But he was alive and she prayed to God that he remained that way.

The helicopter lifted off the ground. It was shaky and bumpy and nothing like being on an airplane. She screamed as the EMT began pouring a white powder-like substance into the wound.

"I'm sorry Katie but this will help stop the bleeding." He then rotated her just enough to do the same thing to her back.

She soon realized the bullet must have gone right through her. "I'm freezing," she whispered.

"Your body is going into shock." He grabbed her foot to confirm that her skin had become cold and then proceeded to rip open a plastic bag that contained a blanket. He draped it over her, bringing her some relief. But it didn't last long when he pushed hard on her wound. She moaned again in excruciating pain.

"I'm so sorry, but I need to keep pressure on this to help the QuickClot work." As he continued to apply pressure, he managed to also get her started on an IV and injected her with morphine.

It didn't take long for the worst of the pain to begin to subside. As she began to feel more alert, partly due to the IV restoring hydration to her body, the paramedics started shouting at one another, giving orders. It was so loud in there that she couldn't understand what they were saying. It wasn't until she saw the paddles that she knew what was happening. *Oh God, he's dying.*

"Help him, help him!" Her voice was too weak and she tried to sit up.

One of the men eased her back down, but she resisted. "Katie, you need to lie down. Let them do their job."

She couldn't watch him die right in front of her. Her screams grew louder. "Save him!"

A moment later, she felt very tired and heavy. She turned her head to see the paramedic removing a needle from her IV line. He'd injected something in her. Those were the last words she remembered speaking.

28

The room appeared in fuzzy waves as Katie's vision shifted in and out of focus. Nausea set in almost immediately. She rose on one elbow and prepared for the worst when a plastic bowl was shoved under her chin just in time.

"That's the anesthesia. It makes a lot of people feel sick afterward," the nurse said. "Katie, do you know where you are?"

Her head was pounding still and to try to turn to answer was nearly impossible.

"You're in St. Joseph's Hospital in Eureka. You've just come out of surgery for a gunshot wound. The surgery went well and you are in recovery right now."

"Where's Marshall?" The raspy sound that escaped her throat took her by surprise, as did the resulting soreness from the intubation.

"The doctor will be in soon to check on you. With everything you've been through, you really ought to rest." The nurse glossed over her question.

Katie knew that was never a good sign. Someone had better tell her what was going on with Marshall before she went into an outright panic attack.

No doctors around, only other nurses tending to their patients. Where was Scarborough? He would know about Marshall.

Still fading in and out of consciousness from the residual anesthesia coursing through her veins, Katie struggled to stay alert and get some answers. "Nurse?" she asked, barely above a whisper.

The woman turned around and walked back toward Katie's bed. "Yes, Katie?"

"Agent Scarborough? I need to talk to him, please."

"I'm sorry, but you're still in ICU recovery and visitors aren't allowed in here. Once you're moved to your room, visitors can come and see you." The nurse took Katie's hand. "I'm so sorry about what happened to you and I truly wish I could help, but it is crucial that you rest. It won't be much longer, I promise."

Katie leaned back onto her pillow, defeated, panicked, and unsure of what the hell was going on. One thing was clear; she wasn't going to get any answers as long as she was in here.

The doctor stood at her bed, holding her chart, but it wasn't until he spoke that she was roused back to consciousness again. She hadn't even realized she drifted off except that it was now two hours later, according to the clock.

"Katie, you're awake," the doctor said. "How are you feeling?"

"Better." The soreness in her throat was fading, but no less dry. But more importantly, her head was gaining clarity. "How long have I been in recovery?"

"About four hours in total. You're doing well enough to be moved, so they're getting your room ready now."

"Doctor, can you tell me about the other man who came in with me? Marshall Avery? Is he all right?"

"I am aware of the patient, but I'm afraid he's not in my care and I've not been informed as to his condition."

Anger was brewing inside her now as she continued to get the runaround. The doctor must have known of Marshall's condition. "Can someone around here please tell me if Marshall Avery is alive or dead?" Her voice escalated to the point that she caught the attention of a few of the other patients. It hurt like hell, but she got her point across.

"Just give me a moment, please, Katie, and I'll do my best to get some answers for you. In the meantime, these gentlemen are going to take you to your room."

"Thank you, doctor." Katie refused to apologize for her outburst after what she'd been through.

The nurses wheeled her bed down the corridor. She watched the ceiling tiles pass overhead and from the corner of her eye caught sight of a few Rio Dell cops and some FBI agents she didn't know. Why were they hanging around? Hendrickson was dead and as far as she knew, Scarborough had escaped unharmed.

When they got to her room, the nurses pulled the gurney parallel to her bed, grabbed the corners of her sheet, and lifted her onto it. It was at that moment she realized the pain meds weren't as effective as she thought and any movement was still excruciating.

"Is this comfortable for you, Katie?" one of the men asked.

"Yes, thank you." It wasn't, but the only thing that mattered to her now was hearing of Marshall's condition.

"Press this button if you need help and this one here, attached to your IV, is for pain. It does have a limit, but if you find that your discomfort level is too much after the limit's been reached, just call for a nurse and they'll see what they can do."

Discomfort level? she thought. No amount of medication was going to help her through this pain. "Thank you. I understand." Her patience was growing thin. Where was Scarborough? She needed her phone but then remembered it was lying on the floor of an abandoned house, having been smashed against the wall. What was worse was that she was starting to remember everything, including seeing an unconscious Marshall lying next to her in the helicopter, men scrambling to save his life. She tried to squeeze her eyes shut, but it hurt too much.

"Knock, knock." A weary-looking FBI agent was standing at the door.

Oh, thank God. "Agent Scarborough, please come in." Before she let him say a word, she pounced on him, begging for answers. "I need to know; they wouldn't tell me anything. Is Marshall alive?" Her heart raced with anticipation.

"Yes, Katie. He's alive, but he's still in surgery."

"Still in surgery? I've been out for hours. Nick, what happened to him?"

"He was shot in the chest, just below his heart. That's the good news."

At this point in the conversation, all she cared about was hearing the words, "He's alive."

"But Hendrickson used hollow point bullets, meaning that there are several fragments still in his chest. It damaged a lot of tissue, which, unfortunately, is exactly what it's supposed to do. The doctors are working very hard to repair that damage."

"But I got shot too. Why am I not in as bad a shape?"

"It was dark in that cellar, Katie. The situation escalated too quickly and Hendrickson didn't shoot you. I did."

"Oh." This was new information for which she was unprepared.

"I'm so sorry, Katie. It was my bullet and you were caught in the crossfire. Hendrickson had his gun on you, then just pointed it at Marshall and started shooting. When we returned fire, he pulled you directly in front of him, using you as a shield. I think that was his intent all along, to have one of us, ideally, Marshall, be the one to kill you, not him. He figured that would cause the most pain, I guess. He was a sick son of a bitch. Anyway, I thought I had a clear shot, but he moved you too fast and my bullet struck your side. Fortunately, it was a clean hit and went straight through you. Thank God. I can't tell you how sorry I am, Katie."

"You saved my life. It would have ended very badly for me if you hadn't shown up when you did. I know I'd be dead right now."

"Thank you. I tell you what, though, you're a hell of a tough lady. He gave you quite a beating." Scarborough took her hand.

"Hendrickson is dead, right?"

"Yes. We got him. He won't hurt you or anyone else ever again."

Her eyes started to tear up at the thought of what he'd done. She raised her other hand to her face, touching the stitches on her temple. "Should leave a nice scar, huh?" Her voice quivered as the tears fell.

Scarborough handed her a tissue but said nothing, only continued to offer his hand until she was ready to let it go.

A few minutes later, she took a deep breath, ready to speak once again. "When will we know more about how Marshall is doing? Did they tell you when he'd be out of surgery?"

"No. I don't know much right now, but I'll go find someone and get an update. Will you be okay?"

"Yes. I just need to know what's happening with him. I can't lose him, Nick. I can't."

"I'll see what I can find out." Agent Scarborough turned to leave.

She was alone for just a few minutes when Deborah and John stepped into the room.

"Oh God, Katie look at you!" Deborah broke down.

"I'm okay, Mom."

"We didn't know what the hell was happening for two days. They just kept telling us they had all their resources out looking for you," John said. "They should be sued! Leaving you alone at that hospital when there was a goddam killer after you."

"Dad, please. It's over now and I'm going to be fine."

"Thank God, you're all right," Deborah continued.

"It's over, Mom. It's really over. He's dead."

Deborah erupted into tears as John took hold of her. He took Katie's hand, struggling to hold back his own tears.

It was as if they'd both finally been released of the terrible secret they forced themselves to keep; a secret that almost destroyed their family.

"I'm sorry to interrupt." A doctor stood at the door next to Scarborough.

Katie gently wiped her face with a tissue. "No, it's fine. Please come in, doctor. Can you tell me what's going on with Marshall Avery?"

"I'm Dr. Ross, the cardiothoracic surgeon here at St. Joe's. I understand you both are Ms. Reid's parents?"

"Yes," John replied. "Nice to meet you, doctor."

"Very nice to meet you."

"Dr. Ross," Katie interrupted. "I don't mean to be rude, but please, I need to know what's happening with Marshall."

"Of course, I am sorry. Agent Scarborough suggested I come in and tell you myself. Detective Avery is out of surgery and recovering in the ICU. The surgery was successful, but it's going to be a while before he stabilizes. He's suffered a great deal of trauma to the tissue in his chest. If the bullet had fractured any closer to his heart, I'd be in here telling you a much different story."

"But he'll be okay?" Katie asked.

"As of right now, we are cautiously optimistic. We'll know more in a few hours. Now, Mr. and Mrs. Reid, it is still very important that Katie rests, so if you can, please see to it that she does."

"Of course doctor, and thank you," John replied.

"Agent Scarborough, can I have a word with you outside?"

Dr. Ross and Scarborough left the room and Katie was once again alone with her parents. But she wondered if Dr. Ross was telling her everything.

"Is there anything we can do for you right now, sweetheart?" Deborah asked.

"I wouldn't mind some water. My throat is so dry. And maybe a toothbrush?"

"Of course. Your father can get some water for you and stop by the nurses' station. I'm sure they'll have toothbrushes there." Deborah looked at John, who did not hesitate to take heed of his wife's wishes.

A few minutes later, Scarborough returned. "Dr. Ross said he'd keep us updated as much as possible on Marshall's condition, but did warn that it is touch and go right now. They had a hard time stopping the bleeding."

"I understand. I'm just grateful he's alive," Katie replied. "Mom, could you give me and Agent Scarborough a couple of minutes?"

"Certainly. I'll go see what's keeping your dad. He probably stopped at the gift shop."

"Thanks." Katie waited for Deborah to leave, then looked at Scarborough. "I know where he buried them."

He leaned into Katie. Her voice was still hoarse and difficult to hear.

"He burned down his parents' cabin."

"Yeah, we know about that already," Scarborough replied.

"They're on that property, most of them, anyway. He said it was the best way to keep them from being discovered. No one knew about the cabin."

"What about the Portland girl found on that trail?"

"He got her after he moved to Oregon City. Nick, he killed a lot more than we thought. When he held me at the warehouse, he had a wooden box. Inside the box was a bunch of jewelry. They belonged to his victims."

"Jesus Christ," Scarborough replied.

"There must have been at least ten pieces of jewelry in that box. Including the pendant I remembered."

"Marshall found the necklace. You put it under that chair, didn't you?"

Katie nodded.

"That's what kept us going. He knew you were still alive. Of course, turning the phone on was the real kicker, but when he found that necklace, well, let's just say I never saw that much hope in any man's eyes before."

"We need to find those children, Nick; give their parents some closure. I don't know if we'll find them all, but it's a start. And maybe we'll find more evidence linking him to other disappearances."

"We'll get on it now, Katie. I promise."

"I want to help. I want to be there to tell the parents that their children will finally be able to rest and so will they."

"Let's just take one step at a time. You need to get better first. But in the meantime, we'll search the property, that much I can do. And Katie, Marshall's gonna be fine."

"Thank you. One more thing, Nick. Did anyone else get hurt back there?"

"No. Marshall put Hendrickson down pretty quickly, even after he got his shot off."

"What's going to happen now? I mean, with Wilson's wife and the department?"

"They questioned her, but she didn't know anything. The last she'd seen Hendrickson was when her daughter was just a toddler. Wilson went to great lengths to keep his brother's activities a secret. So far as I know, she has a sister in Washington and I guess she'll be taking care of her and Wilson's daughter for a while. As for the Rio Dell Police Department, the FBI will finalize its investigation, finish talking to the rest of Wilson's staff, and close the case. Everyone's in shock over all this. No one thought he was capable of helping a serial killer, not even me."

"Well, we don't know what we're capable of until faced with a situation, do we? I think he believed he could control him forever."

"None of this is your fault, Katie. You were the one responsible for his capture. Those families will be grateful to you. You did a hell of a job playing detective. Ever thought of being one?"

Katie snickered with what little energy she had. "Marshall said the exact same thing to me not too long ago."

"You should give it some thought. Of course, we're always looking for good recruits, too." Scarborough squeezed her hand one last time. "I'll check in on you later."

29

The nurse checked in on Katie several times in the night; taking her vital signs and changing the bandage from the gunshot wound that still oozed blood. She never really allowed Katie to rest as the other nurse had been so adamant about earlier.

"How are you doing this morning, Katie?" the nurse asked.

"Sore." The swelling in her face must have reduced somewhat because she was able to see clearly out of both eyes again.

"That nausea all gone now?"

"Yes."

"Good." The nurse was quiet for a moment as she watched the clock, counting Katie's pulse. "You're looking better," she continued. "I was just told by Dr. Ross that if you'd like to see Detective Avery in a bit, you can."

A rush of elation gave rise in her, the likes of which she hadn't felt in months. He made it. He was still alive. "Yes, please; I need to see him."

"Okay, then. Let me go and get you a wheelchair. I'd like you to start trying to stand on your own anyway. Later, we'll have you up and walking around."

The nurse returned with a wheelchair. She helped Katie swing her legs to the side of the bed and both Deborah and the nurse raised her to a seated position.

Her side throbbed wildly at the change of position and Katie felt woozy, but it soon passed. Nothing would stop her from seeing Marshall. She carefully put her weight down on one leg, holding Deborah's arm for balance. The nurse positioned the chair to ease her into it.

Katie was steady on her feet for only a moment when she grabbed the arm of the nurse, who helped her down into the chair. They headed for the door. "Wait. Can I just take a look in a mirror first?" Her face had been badly beaten by Hendrickson and she had no idea what she looked like now. She prayed the swelling had gone down enough so that she at least was recognizable.

The nurse pulled out a hand mirror from one of the drawers in the bathroom and handed it to Katie. "Here you go."

Katie held it to her face. She was taken aback by the severity of the bruising. The swelling in her left eye had reduced, but the once red and puffy contusions were now much larger and had turned purple. The stitches were dressed as were the other cuts that criss-crossed her face.

"These are all wounds that will heal with time," the nurse said, taking the mirror. "Come on now. Let's go see Marshall." She continued to push Katie through to the corridor and into the surgical recovery unit, where Katie had been just the day before.

Her face would heal, but she would never look the same. Hendrickson had left his mark on her, inside and out.

The automatic door opened wide, allowing the nurse to push Katie in and down the aisle between the rows of beds, some with pulled curtains, some empty. And then she saw him.

Marshall was hooked up to all sorts of machines. He had oxygen tubes in his nose and heart monitors stuck to his chest, beneath his gown, and looked to still be sleeping.

Katie was now beside his bed. "I don't want to wake him," she whispered to the nurse.

"He's been in and out. Just give him a few minutes. I'm sure he'll open his eyes. I'll leave you here and come back to check on you."

She couldn't help but stare at him. From head to toe, she wanted to see the extent of what had happened to him.

"You're starting to creep me out a little, babe."

Startled by the sound of his voice, she gasped and clamped her hand over her mouth. "Oh God, Marshall. I'm so sorry."

"For what?"

"For all this; for getting shot, for risking your life—everything."

"Shhh, stop now. Don't you dare start blaming yourself for what Joseph Hendrickson did. For God's sake, I thought I lost you. I should have never left your side. Look at what he did to you." Marshall slowly raised his hand to her face, brushing it gently. "Baby, I'm so sorry."

So much had happened, the extent of which was just beginning to sink in. "He's dead now; that's all that matters." Katie reached for his other hand, which lay still over his stomach, and rested hers gently over top. "Have the doctors talked to you yet this morning?"

"They've been in and out most of the night and say I'm going to be fine, but it'll take some time to recover. I suppose that goes for you too."

"Scarborough told me what happened about me getting caught in the crossfire. He feels horrible about it."

"I know. I heard him yelling at the paramedic that he'd shot you. It wasn't his fault. Things got outta hand. It was so chaotic. I thought you were dead."

"I thought the same thing about you. I've been so scared, Marshall. They weren't even sure you would make it through the night."

"Are you kidding? I wasn't about to give up this collar." A short, small burst of laughter escaped him until he winced in pain. "We're gonna be okay."

NEARLY TEN DAYS had passed and the hospital was finally about to let Katie go home. She was walking on her own and all of the bandages had been removed from her face, except for the one covering the stitches. She was starting to look like herself again.

"They're letting me go home in a little bit."

"That's great news, Kate. I should be getting out of here in three or four more days, so I won't be far behind you."

"Scarborough and his team are at the Hendrickson place, or what's left of it, anyway, excavating. They found two of the victims so far," Katie said.

"Which ones?"

"The boy from McKinleyville and a girl they haven't yet identified."

"How many more?" Marshall asked.

"They don't know yet. But he's picking me up and we're going to head out there this afternoon."

"You think that's a good idea? You're just being released from the hospital after major surgery. I'm not sure you should go, Kate and I'm a little surprised Scarborough is letting you."

"Letting me?" She didn't mean to snap, but that was how she'd just come off.

"Sorry, but it's true. I don't want you to push yourself. It won't be easy and you know it."

"It won't, I know. But I asked him if I could be there. He had the box run through evidence, checking whatever was in there for other prints or hair or anything else that might help us find more victims. I'm going to return every piece of jewelry and the child it belonged to back to those parents. I have to do this."

"Kate, I know you do, but you need to take care of yourself first."

She leaned over his bed, her arms bracing either side of him. "This *is* me taking care of myself." Katie kissed him softly on the cheek. "I'll be fine." Rearing back up, she continued, "I'm going to come back down here every night to see you. Now that you're in a regular room, they'll let me stay the night."

"Okay, but I'm going to tell Scarborough he'd better keep an eye on you, and make sure you're not pushing yourself too hard."

"What's that you're gonna tell me?" Scarborough strolled in with his hands in his pockets and a haughty grin on his face.

"I was just telling Kate how you need to look after her. I'm not thrilled that you're taking her out to the cabin."

"Don't worry, Avery. She'll be fine. She's just going to be observing, nothing more." He turned toward Katie. "Ready to go?"

She nodded.

"Come on, then. Let's get you checked out of this place."

"I'll be fine," she reassured Marshall again, but his eyes conveyed concern beyond what he was expressing.

THE BURNED-DOWN remains of the home where Hendrickson took his victims appeared in the distance. The hour-long journey hadn't given her enough time to prepare for actually seeing the place again. A shell of what had once been the basement she recalled so clearly now was all that remained. Standing at the edge, looking into the blackened hole in the ground, Katie was immersed in visions of a daring escape from the man who was about to kill her, not once, but twice.

Scarborough approached quietly from behind, his shoes squelching in the mud where the water used to fight the fire had saturated the ground. He reached out toward her, resting a comforting hand atop her delicate, rounded shoulder. "This was where he kept you?"

A subtle nod was all she could manage at this moment.

"If this is too much, just…"

"No," she interrupted. "I need to be here. I need to help you find the other children."

"Katie, they're hand-digging all around here. We're covering a half-mile radius of this place, looking for anywhere else he might've buried them. Unless you have some kind of map, I'm not sure how much more help you can be. I agreed to let you be involved in this because, as far as I'm concerned, you're the one who solved this case, but if it gets to be too much, you need to let me know."

"We need to find Ashley. It's because of her that we're here today and Hendrickson is gone."

A charred metal cot with stuffing from a blackened mattress, presumably the same one Katie was forced to lie on for three days, was tossed on its side in a corner of the room. The place itself didn't look much different from what she had been able to recall, except for the furnishings being mostly reduced to ashes.

She glanced over at the staircase, where only a couple of steps remained attached to the floor balustrade. She saw her younger self who'd managed to gather enormous strength against tremendous odds, to escape from a monster who had already done unspeakable things to her. And he would have buried her along with the other children for which they were now searching.

"We need to find her so her parents will know that her death meant something. If I hadn't remembered that little girl's necklace, we wouldn't be here right now. We might never have found him."

"We'll find her, Katie." Agent Scarborough wrapped his arm around Katie's shoulder and gently piloted her from the edge of the basement.

The two walked out into the woods and everything came back to her in a mad rush of memories. She leaned on one of the giant Redwoods to steady herself, reliving the horrifying escape.

"Katie, are you okay?" Scarborough asked.

"Yeah. Just give me a minute, if you would." She took a few deep breaths, reaching for her side as a brief outburst of pain passed through her, and then shifted her weight back onto her feet. "Okay, let's keep going."

Shouts could be heard in the distance. Then, Scarborough's phone rang.

"We're heading down!" he replied to the person on the other end.

"What is it?" Katie asked, trying to keep up with his too-quick pace.

"They found another one."

Scarborough ran for several hundred more feet before spotting the fifteen or so men standing around a single spot where the soil had been upturned. Katie couldn't keep up but made it down with the assistance of an agent who had just arrived.

"Agent Scarborough, over here!" Another agent waved them over.

"Wait here, Katie."

She gave Scarborough the same look she would give Marshall whenever he tried to tell her not to do something he knew damn well she was going to do anyway.

"Fine," he said.

They approached the circle of men, who parted immediately at their approach to reveal what had been discovered.

Only a few fragments of human remains were exposed, but it was enough to know that extreme caution would need to be the protocol for excavating this unknown victim.

"This is Number Four," a member of the team spoke up.

"Okay, let's find out who this is," Scarborough said.

Katie and Agent Scarborough moved away to allow the forensics team to do their job.

"How long before we have an identity?" she asked.

"Hard to say; it depends on what they find. I'm not an expert in that field, but I can tell you that the men over there are the best at what they do, so I have no doubt they'll figure out who it is."

"How do you get used to this, Nick?"

"You never get used to it; you just accept it."

It was clear he was trying to make the situation less tense than it was, but Katie was staring at the remains of a child. She doubted that she could ever accept it.

"You just learn to, Katie. Otherwise, this stuff will destroy you. It's not easy coming face to face with the dark side of humanity, but you eventually get to the point that you realize you're not doing it for any other reason than for justice." He paused for a moment and glanced around at the scene: the mounds of dirt, the yellow tape, the people walking around. "I'll tell you one thing, Katie. I've never met anyone like you, driven, verging on obsessed. What do you think you're going to do after all this is over?"

"I don't know, Nick. Go back to San Diego and live my life, I guess. Whatever that means."

"What about Detective Avery? You two seem to have gotten pretty close."

She smiled just hearing his name. "Yeah, you could say that. I don't know. It's a little strange. Our entire relationship has evolved as a result of this—situation. I'm not sure how you go back to normal."

"I don't imagine 'normal' is in the cards for you two."

"Probably not," Katie replied.

There was only one reason for her to be here right now, watching these people do a job she could scarcely imagine. Katie needed to let it go, finally, really, let it go. The nightmare was over and it was time to stop. She turned to Agent Scarborough. "Thank you for bringing me here today."

30

Katie sat down in the chair next to Marshall's bed. She exhaled as if she'd been holding her breath for years. It was finally over and she didn't know what to do. She looked at Marshall, and raised her hand to her face, lightly running a finger over the stitches on the left side. "Do you think Scarborough will still let me come along when he talks to the parents of those children? I need to be there for them, Marshall."

"I know you do. I think he'll let you do what you need to do to get closure on this."

"Before we go home, I'd like to say goodbye to Jarrod and thank him for what he did."

"That's a good idea, although I can't say I agree with him letting you go like that. But you're so damn stubborn, I probably couldn't have stopped you anyway."

Katie leaned in and kissed his lips, which were dry and chapped, but that didn't bother her. "I think I'll go back to my parents for a few hours and come back this evening. They say you'll be able to leave tomorrow, based on the tests they ran today, so that's good news."

"That's what they say, but Scarborough needs me for another few days while they wrap up the investigation. Do you want to stay?"

"Of course. I'll see you in a few hours."

THE NEXT MORNING found Katie aching after an uncomfortable night on the hospital's pullout bed in Marshall's room. She pulled back her hair, twisting it into a bun, mindful to pull her bangs over the stitches and splashed some water on her face. She went down to the cafeteria to get breakfast. On her return, Marshall was awake and was no longer alone.

"Agent Scarborough? You're here early," Katie said. "I'm sorry, I didn't realize you were coming or I would have brought you some coffee as well."

"Don't worry about it. I wanted to come by before heading back out to the site."

"How'd it go yesterday?" She handed Marshall his coffee.

"We're still searching, but I think that'll be winding down soon. We discovered a pattern to his burial locations and I think we may be on the verge of finding all of his victims."

"How many?" Marshall asked.

"Six in total; so far."

"God, that's less than we thought, at least," Katie said.

"Yes. We'll need to identify the remains, but preliminary forensics suggest that a couple of the bodies had been there for quite some time, longer than the others taken when you were abducted, Katie."

"So he'd been active well before 1989," Marshall replied.

"Looks like it. We'll know more in a few days. There was one other thing I came here for." Scarborough looked at Katie. "We have identified one of the bodies found a few days ago. It was Ashley Davies."

Katie lost her breath for a moment.

"I was wondering if you'd like to take a trip with me to talk to the parents today."

Katie looked to Marshall for his approval, although she didn't need it. He would have no objection. "Yes, I'd like to go with you, please."

"Okay, we'll have to stop at the station and pick up a few things, then we can head out. You ready to go now?"

She raised a finger to pause and then cut away to the restroom to fix herself up. Her heart raced with fear and sadness and excitement; everything was balled up in her chest. She felt like this was her chance to gain forgiveness from the parents whose children didn't make it home. It was that need that drove her to obsession. The guilt was overwhelming at times, but this was her chance to find some relief. "Okay, let's go." She snatched her bag and tossed it over her shoulder. "I'll see you later, okay?"

Marshall agreed and instinctively glanced at Scarborough.

"It'll be fine," he replied to the question Marshall didn't need to ask.

KATIE WAITED PATIENTLY in the lobby of the Rio Dell station while Agent Scarborough spoke with members of his team. There was protocol to be followed so the coordination was a necessary task.

After several more minutes, Scarborough emerged, briefcase in hand. "Okay, let's go." He held open the lobby door for Katie as she led the way to his car.

She was grateful to have had a chance to eat a small breakfast. Her nerves were on edge and an empty stomach would make matters worse. She'd met with the Davies family before, but now she would be meeting them to bring closure; after all these years, they would get peace.

They headed northwest on Highway 101, the Redwood Highway, back toward Arcata.

"The necklace?" Katie asked.

"It's in the case." Scarborough didn't take his eyes off the road and continued along the quiet highway. "Katie, I'd like to ask you something."

"Yes?"

"I was talking with my supervisor back at the station."

Katie knew of this man and had seen him a few times, but he never approached her. She waited for Scarborough to elaborate.

"Handling this job requires a certain type of person." He glanced at her for just a moment, then returned his gaze to the road ahead. "You've been vital to this investigation and everyone knows that. We're all convinced that if you hadn't pursued this to the extent that you did, well, Hendrickson might have remained free for the rest of his life."

"And my best friend would still be alive," she interrupted.

"But the fact remains that you were the one who brought him down and Wilson, who, honestly, got what he deserved. So, in my opinion, you brought down two very bad men."

"If it hadn't been for Marshall's support, I don't think I'd be here now. He kept me from falling apart many times, Nick."

"He's a good man, Katie, that much is obvious. But, going back to being that certain type of person. Well, I've got to say, you're just about as close to that type as anyone I've come across in a long time. My supervisor tends to agree. A little impulsive, bordering on care-less, but that can be reeled in with the right training."

"What are you saying, Nick?" She was beginning to suspect where this was headed.

"We'd like to have you come work for us in the Washington field office of the BAU, with me." Scarborough looked at her for a reaction.

Surprised by the invitation, she measured her response. "Don't you need to have a degree or something?"

"Well, I understand you have a BA in Social Sciences from UCSD."

"Why am I surprised you know this about me?"

He grinned. "The recruiting process means you'd have to go through training at Quantico, then specialized training geared toward work in the BAU. It'd take a couple of years and mentoring, but Katie, I'm telling you, this is who you are. I read the file about everything you did to get here."

"Look, I appreciate it, but I've got to piece my life back together first. For the past nine, ten months, I've been living and breathing this nightmare. I'm not sure what I'm going to do now that it's over."

"Come work for us."

"I don't know; I'd need some time to think about it. Don't get me wrong. I'm honored, but I really need to sort out my life, fix myself."

"We can help you. No one can go through what you've been through and not be damaged. The point is to fix the damage and keep the drive. Look, this probably isn't the best time to talk to you about it, but I wanted to see where you were at, what your plans were, and get a chance to present this to you without anyone else around."

"You mean without Marshall around?"

"I'm inviting you to start a career, one that you were made for. I just thought it'd be best to present it to you when you weren't looking for someone else's approval." Scarborough sighed. "I saw how you looked at Avery back there. Seeking his approval; wondering if he thought it was a good idea for you to come along with me this morning. Now I'm not saying that's what he expects. My guess is, he doesn't. But that's how you are when you're around him. You are much tougher than you know, Katie Reid."

They made a right turn onto the quiet street. The third house on the left; that was the one. She remembered it from a few weeks ago. Was it only a few weeks? It felt like months had passed.

"Okay, we're here. Now there are a couple of things I'd like to mention. First of all, I'll address them initially. Once I've had a chance to ease them into the conversation, I'll let you say what you want to say and return their daughter's belongings to them, okay?"

She tipped her head in agreement and stepped out of the car.

The cool breeze made goosebumps rise on her arms. Katie took a deep breath, breathing the clean pine-scented air. She began to shiver but wasn't sure if it was from the cold morning air or nerves. Her stomach tightened into knots. The only thing that calmed her down was closing her eyes and envisioning the moment she would hand them their daughter's necklace.

Scarborough stood on the front porch, waiting for Katie to approach. "Are you okay?"

A smile of acknowledgment briefly appeared when she joined him, but soon faded as they waited.

The door opened before he could knock. In this small town, when a black SUV pulled into the drive, it was obvious that the person wasn't from the neighborhood.

"Mrs. Davies? Agent Scarborough with the FBI. We met before?"

"Of course, agent. Please come in."

Nick turned to Katie, placed his arm against her back, and led her in ahead of him.

"Ms. Reid, nice to see you again. What happened to your face, dear?" Mrs. Davies asked.

"Oh, nothing. I'm fine." Katie wondered if they hadn't known what happened. That she'd been kidnapped by Hendrickson. Maybe after all these years, they just didn't bother listening to all the terrible news on television, that they'd heard enough in their lifetime. She didn't bother to explain the marks on her face.

"I believe my office contacted you, Mrs. Davies?"

"Yes, sir. They said you were coming down. Please, follow me. Mr. Davies is in the other room."

The smell of the house reminded Katie of Sam's parents' home; warm vanilla, so wonderfully inviting. She swallowed hard against the lump that was rising in her throat.

Mrs. Davies led them into the family room where her husband sat perched at the edge of his armchair, holding a folded-up newspaper. Had he known about Hendrickson? When Katie greeted him, she realized he had.

A forlorn but compassionate smile lifted his hollow cheeks. It was clear that Ashley had her father's looks. Katie imagined what he must have looked like as a younger man when his daughter was still alive. From the pictures she had seen, Ashley had similar facial features: high cheekbones, wide-set eyes resting above a narrow, but slightly bulbous nose. Seeing through his now middle-aged features, he was once a very handsome man. Ashley would have turned into a beautiful woman.

Although devastating for both of the parents, Katie thought it might have been even more so for Mr. Davies. She remembered how her own father reacted when she was returned. It was often the mothers of lost children who were the ones who gained the most sympathy, but she believed it might be the fathers who bore the heaviest burden. Are all children not raised to believe their fathers are their protectors? Katie would still have to work to mend her relationship with her father, but she was lucky to have that chance.

"Ms. Reid, it's very nice to see you again," Mr. Davies started. "I'm so very sorry for what has happened to you, yet again."

"Thank you, Mr. Davies, but I am fine now."

"I'm sure you are." He looked at Scarborough. "Agent Scarborough, nice to see you as well. Please, both of you come and have a seat."

Katie and Nick sat down, once again, on the floral-printed sofa. Mrs. Davies had expected them and set out a basket of fresh pastries and muffins. Coffee and juice flanked either side of the basket.

"Mr. Davies, I don't know if my office filled you in on the purpose of our visit, but I'm guessing you are aware that we have eliminated the person responsible for the abduction and murder of your daughter, Ashley."

"Yes, sir, we are aware of the circumstances surrounding our daughter's murderer." He looked directly and knowingly at Katie. "I'd like to thank you, Ms. Reid, for all you've done to help find the man who took our little girl. There hasn't been a day that's gone by we haven't prayed for this outcome. Mrs. Davies and I are religious people." He cleared his throat. "But we've been waiting for this for a very long time."

"Of course you have, sir," Nick replied. He placed the briefcase on his lap and opened it.

Katie looked inside to find a small white box. Nick lifted it from the case and handed it to her. She knew what was inside.

"Mr. Davies, we were able to retrieve this from evidence and I have to tell you, sir, that this particular item was the one thing that made it possible for me to continue searching for the truth. For whatever reason, be it from God, or the souls of those taken from us, somehow the memory of this stayed with me, buried deep in my subconscious, but it was always there. And, it's the reason I'm here today." Katie handed the box to Mr. Davies.

He turned to his wife, his eyes growing red. She motioned for him to open it and so he lifted the box's cover. Suddenly and without warning, years of anguish and grief rose to the surface, shaking the once-stoic man's body. As he raised the silver chain from the soft white cotton on which it was cradled, the heart pendant gently swung from its center.

Mr. Davies' hand quickly rose to his eyes, wiping them clear of the tears that had spilled over. Mrs. Davies took her husband's hand from his face, her own tears falling down her cheeks and squeezed until her knuckles turned white.

"She's home, honey. She's home."

Katie had to turn away, hardly able to control her own emotions, but when she glanced at Nick, his composure remained unaffected. Not hardened, but not moved. He wasn't married and had no children, but that wasn't the reason for his lack of emotion. Katie knew it must have been due to the years of facing parents or wives or husbands in this very same manner. Telling them they would never see their loved ones again, or in this case, handing over all that remained of them. This would be how she would learn to react over time if she chose that life.

"Thank you, Ms. Reid, for returning this to us. I can't tell you how much it means," Mrs. Davies said.

"That necklace saved my life—your daughter saved my life."

"We'd better be going and leave you two alone." Nick pushed off the sofa and offered his hand to Katie to help her up. "The local police will be working with you from here on out, but if you need anything, please give me a call." He handed Mrs. Davies his card.

"When will we be able to put her to rest, Agent Scarborough?" Mr. Davies asked.

"Soon, I'm sure. I'll inform the local department that we've spoken and let them know to be in touch with you as soon as possible regarding the return of your daughter's remains. Thank you both and I hope we've been able to help bring closure for you."

Mr. Davies shook Nick's hand, then turned to Katie. "May I give you a hug, Ms. Reid?"

Katie smiled and opened her arms.

"I know your heart is heavy," he whispered. "But you need to live a good and happy life, Ms. Reid. It's the only way we win."

Katie sat in the car, her hands clasped in her lap. It was silent, save for the wind washing over the car as it rolled down the highway, disrupting the otherwise still surroundings.

"Are you okay?" Nick asked.

"Yeah." She turned to him, unveiling a thin smile. "Nick, can I ask how you came to work for the FBI?"

A brief, knowing chuckle escaped him. "Nothing traumatic happened to me. I had a good childhood and my parents are still married." He glanced at her. "Not all of us are here because of a need for answers. Sometimes you just grow up wanting to put away the bad guys. That was me. I was raised in Lincoln, Nebraska, was a Cornhusker—that's what those of us who went to the University of Nebraska are called."

"Yeah, I figured." Katie was a little offended he assumed she knew nothing of college football. It may have been close to nothing, but that was beside the point.

"Then I decided to become a federal agent. I'm good at what I do, Katie. That's how I know you'd make a good agent someday."

"Do I have time to think about it?" she asked.

"Of course. Hell, you could come to me in a year's time and I wouldn't have changed my mind about you. It'd be a waste of a year, but if that's what it takes. Look, maybe you're right. I'm sure taking some time away from this would be a good thing. But honestly, I don't think that's who you are. I think this is the stuff that makes you tick."

The hospital soon revealed itself against the horizon. "What's the next step?" she asked.

"With this case? We'll continue identifying the remains, secure the site, remove any other evidence, and release it to the locals to condemn. We'll contact the victim's families, just like we did today and eventually, this case will finally be closed."

"Will they need me for anything else or am I free to go back to San Diego?"

"I think you've done your part, but there may be a need to stay in contact. I'll still be the agent in charge, so if I need you, I know where to find you. Does this mean you're going home soon?"

"I don't know yet. Marshall mentioned you need him for another few days. I may stay until we both can go home together."

MARSHALL'S HOSPITAL room door was closed, so she gently knocked, not wanting to wake him if he was asleep. "Marshall, it's me. Can I come in?"

"Yeah. Come on in."

She opened the door and saw Marshall sitting on the edge of the bed, pulling his gown back up as the nurse held his chart, writing something down on it.

"Looks like you'll be able to get out of here tomorrow, Mr. Avery," the nurse said.

"No sweeter words have ever hit these ears," Marshall replied.

His charm knew no bounds and Katie couldn't help but smile. "Finally, I'll be able to get a good night's rest. No more sleeping on this couch." She walked to Marshall, reached for the ties at the back, and tied the gown for him. Her hands brushed his shoulders and slid down his arms. She missed touching him, lying next to him, feeling his warm breath against her cheek. More than ever, she wanted to go home and just be with him.

They'd grown close because of all of this. She wondered how to build a relationship out of it. But when she looked into his eyes, she already knew the answer.

"So how did it go this morning with Scarborough and the family?" Marshall asked.

"It was hard, but I think we did a good thing for those parents."

"I think it was a good thing for you too, Kate. I wasn't convinced, but you seem the better for having done it."

The nurse put his chart back at the end of the bed and left the room. They were alone.

"You sure you're all right? Looks like you want to say something," Marshall said.

"No. I'm just anxious to get out of here."

31

———————

Their final night in Rio Dell. It had been a long two weeks, but they were both ready to go home. Katie stepped out onto the front porch of her childhood home for what would be the last time, at least for the next few months. "Goodbye, Mom. Thanks again for dinner."

"You'll be back here for Christmas. You promise?"

"I promise. Bye, Dad." She waved a final time and stepped into the driver's seat of Marshall's rental car. He hadn't yet been released to drive, so it was up to her. It was a small thing, but Katie felt that she was regaining control with the responsibility of the simple task of driving. It seemed that with each passing day since Hendrickson's death, she'd begun feeling more and more in charge of her life again.

Katie pressed the button on the door to lower her window. It was late and the air was cold and damp. The smell of the trees mixed with the soil. It brought about visions of the tall redwoods that were nearby. Her hands firmly on the wheel, she breathed in. "What happens when it's over, Marshall? Why do I feel so empty?"

"Because your entire life has been affected by what happened to you and now it's done—over. I can only tell you from my experience.

The only thing that can make that feeling go away is to move on to the next case."

Katie examined every feature of Marshall's face with intense scrutiny. The lines that made him appear older than he was had grown a little deeper. His eyes seemed just a little wearier. But the difference now was that in those penetrating green eyes, she saw a reflection of herself. Not as she viewed herself, but as he viewed her: strong, controlled, determined.

The tires rolled over the crushed rock with ease as they pulled around the circular drive and onto the paved road. The headlights illuminated only small sections of the road in front of them, leaving what lay ahead unknown, except to those who had traveled the road enough times to remember its twists and turns, which were still shrouded in darkness.

"Aren't you cold with that window down?" Marshall asked.

"No." The goosebumps pressed hard against the sleeves of her light sweater. "It feels clean, you know?"

THE VICTORIA WAS EMPTY. No FBI, no police. It was a far different scene from just a couple of weeks ago; another sign that it was over and another reason for the emptiness in Katie's chest to grow larger.

"Wow, this place really cleared out."

"Scarborough said he's only got a couple of guys left to wrap things up, apart from the forensics team." Marshall retrieved his card key and slid it into the slot, waiting for the click.

The minutia was burning into Katie's mind. It was as if this was a moment she was supposed to remember forever.

Once inside, Marshall moved to the bed and sat gingerly upon its edge, his wounds not yet healed. "You've been different today, distant. I don't blame you after what you've been through, but something happened. Something that is pulling you away from me; I can feel it and it scares me."

He knew; of course, he knew. That was why he was so quiet on the drive back. Why would Scarborough tell him? "You know?" Katie sat next to him on the bed.

"I know something's not right."

She realized from his response that Scarborough hadn't said anything. Marshall was good at reading people; something she recalled discussing with him when they first met. "Agent Scarborough asked me to train with him—well, his department—at Quantico. Says he thinks I'd make a great agent someday and he talked to his supervisor about it."

"And what did you tell him?"

"Nothing yet."

"What do you want to tell him?"

"I don't know, Marshall. I've been trying to figure out what I'm supposed to do now that it's all over. Do I just go back to San Diego, keep working for the department, and eventually become a cop? I don't know. And then, what about us? We haven't talked about it at all, really. Not that there hasn't been enough going on around us lately, but I can't tell what it is you want from me, or from us."

"I guess I've been trying to figure that out myself. But I know that you and I can have a normal life. Live together, maybe; leave the door open to the future. And as far as work goes, I think you could have a hell of a career with the department in whatever role you choose."

"Do you think Scarborough's right? Do you think I could do well as an agent?"

"Of course I do, Kate."

"What if you came with me? He's worked closely enough with you to see how valuable you are."

"He thinks I'm a good detective and he's said as much, but, Kate, I've got ten years on you. I'm not looking to change careers. I'm happy where I'm at. He is right about you though; your potential. I've known that since that day you followed me into the parking lot, asking about cold cases and investigations." He smiled as if the scene had just replayed in his mind. "That seems like a lifetime ago. I love you, Kate, but you need to decide what's best for you; not me, or anyone else."

Katie knew he wouldn't stop her if she wanted to go, even if it meant never seeing her again. He just wasn't that way. But it didn't have to be like that. It wasn't like she'd be gone forever, or that they couldn't travel back and forth to see each other. Why would it have to mean the end?

She unbuttoned her shirt and slid it down her shoulders, revealing the stitches that remained and would eventually be the scar that was Hendrickson's final mark on this world.

Marshall reached out to touch her shoulder. He shook his head as he looked at the line on her face where there had been stitches and the yellowed bruise on her cheek. He kissed her gently but with great passion.

THE PLANE TOUCHED down in San Diego. She always dreaded that part, especially at this airport where the approach was steep. As they walked down the corridor and past the other gates, they approached the baggage claim area. They had been on an early flight and so it was just now coming up on 2:00 on this cool October day. Katie was glad to be home again.

She and Marshall stepped onto the escalator and began to descend. She noticed his expression fall as he looked on ahead of her. Confused, Katie turned to see what had caused this change and as they continued down, she saw for herself.

Bulbs flashed and a mob of reporters pushed their way through the travelers toward the two of them. As soon as they reached the bottom of the steps, Marshall jumped in front of Katie, shielding her from the looming horde.

The whole country had been following the story. It broke after Hendrickson was caught, but Katie had been protected up to that point, thanks to the FBI. No one had been allowed access to her and her only contact with the press had been a text message from Marc Aguilar, ensuring she was all right. Turned out, he had kept his word and didn't leak the story ahead of time. Once they got the killer, however, it was open season for the media.

In the sea of reporters, Aguilar emerged. Everyone shouted questions at her, asking if she was okay, if she felt responsible for her friend's death, how she felt now. Marshall tried his best to keep her behind him as they pressed on, but then she stopped and looked at Aguilar.

"Mr. Aguilar, did you have something you'd like to ask me?" she said.

Marshall swung back at her in surprise.

"It's okay; I can do this."

He lowered his arm and let her emerge from behind him.

"Yes, Ms. Reid. First of all, I would like to apologize for our slightly adversarial past."

Katie smiled and waited for him to continue.

"Can you tell me, Ms. Reid, are you sleeping better now that this is over?"

"Yes, Mr. Aguilar, I sleep just fine now. Thank you for your concern." She motioned to Marshall, who then continued shielding her as they made their way out of the airport and jumped in a cab.

"I don't expect this will go away anytime soon, Kate."

"Neither do I, but I can handle it."

THEY HEADED STRAIGHT to Marshall's apartment and on arrival, he called Captain Hearn.

"He wants to see us first thing in the morning," Marshall said.

"I'm sure he does. And, it's probably not to give us any promotions, I bet."

"Not likely, after some of the stunts we pulled—or, I pulled. After all, you're a civilian. At least, for now."

It didn't take much to catch onto his meaning. He was right, though. She was going to have to decide what to do. Scarborough had sent her a couple of emails with information and questioned whether or not she'd made a decision. The fact of the matter was, she hadn't yet. "I'll be right back." She walked into the bathroom, turned on the cold water, and dampened a washcloth that had been folded up on the shelf above the toilet. Katie pressed the cold cloth against her face, then remembered how much makeup she had on to cover what remained of her healing bruises. Oh well, what did it matter now? She was home, away from the curious stares of the other passengers and the media that were anxious to pounce on her until they bled her story dry. It was just her and Marshall now. She breathed in moist air through the weave of the cloth and then lowered it from her face.

She heard Marshall answer his cell phone, but couldn't quite make out what he was saying through the closed door. But one thing was certain, he was pacing the floor. The sound of his footsteps on the tile traveled down the hall. She quietly turned the handle and pushed the door just slightly ajar.

"I'll tell her. Thank you for the call."

The conversation ended and soon she emerged from the bathroom, although she behaved as if she hadn't known he'd been on a call.

"I just got off the phone with Agent Scarborough."

"Oh? What did he want?"

"Just making sure we arrived safely and asked if we were planning on going into the station today. I told him we'd be in first thing in the morning."

"That was nice of him to check in on us," Katie said as she moved toward the couch.

"I imagine he wanted to know if we were going to see the captain," Marshall said.

"Why would that matter?"

"My guess is that either Scarborough or his boss has already been in contact with Captain Hearn."

"Probably. Since the case crossed jurisdictions, I'm sure there's some inter-agency coordination going on." She was trying to deflect what he was getting at.

"Somehow, I don't think that's what it was about. Senior agents like Scarborough don't generally deal with those kinds of details. Come on, Kate. You can't pretend not to know what this is about, can you?"

Marshall wasn't angry; he wasn't being sarcastic. He was concerned and she knew that. In her gut, she supposed she already knew the answer, not just about knowing Scarborough's inquiry, but to the bigger question; the one that loomed over every word they spoke.

The refrigerator had no food in it, but still had a couple of bottles of water. Katie grabbed them from the fridge. "Do you want one?"

"Sure."

She was stalling now and that wasn't fair to him. "Here you go." She handed him the bottle and stood just inches in front of him. This man would do anything to keep her safe, but she no longer needed his protection. So what would remain of this relationship that had been built from her desire for vengeance?

"Whatever you decide, I'll support you, but I need to know where we stand, Kate. I've been trying not to put any pressure on you..."

Before he could finish, she pressed two fingers against his lips. She set their water bottles on the table next to them and held his gaze for what could have been an hour, but was really only seconds. "I know who I'm supposed to be now, Marshall. If you had said to me a year ago that I'd become this person, I would have said you were crazy. But now—well, everything's changed and I'm different. I believe you're different, too. And, while I think working for the FBI would be pretty amazing, I know that I can still be pretty amazing here—with you."

"Before you go on, I don't want to be the reason you choose to stay, if that's what you're saying. This has to be your decision and yours alone."

"You can say that Marshall, but you can't expect me not to consider you in all this. I'm thinking about my life as a whole. Not just what I do for a living, but who I choose to share my life with. You've made me a better person, whether you want to believe it or not. I discovered who I am because of you." Her eyes brightened. "You want to know where we stand?" Katie took Marshall's hands in hers and raised them to her chest, pressing hard enough for him to feel her heartbeat. "I stand with you."

THE END

ABOUT THE AUTHOR

Robin Mahle has published more than 30 crime fiction novels, many, of which, topped the Amazon charts in the US, Canada, and the UK. Most recently, she has delved into the world of psychological thrillers.

Also a screenwriter, she has adapted some of her works into teleplays, which have gone on to place in film festivals nationwide.

From detectives to federal agents, and from killers to corruption, her page-turning tales grab hold and refuse to let go. Throw in tense action and thrilling twists, and it becomes clear why her readers come back for more.

Robin lives in Coastal Virginia with her husband and two children.

If you enjoyed Ms. Mahle's work, please share your experience by leaving a review on Amazon.

ALSO BY ROBIN MAHLE

The Kate Reid FBI Thriller Series (17 books)

The Chef (stand-alone psych thriller)

The Man in My Attic (stand-alone psych thriller)

The Compound (standalone psych thriller)

The Remy Fontaine Fugitive Hunter Thrillers (4 books)

The Det. Rebecca Ellis Thrillers (5 books)

The Allison Hart PI Thrillers (5 Books)

The Lacy Merrick Thrillers (4 books)

**Sign up to receive <u>Robin's Newsletter</u> so you can stay up to date on her new releases, events, contests and even exclusive new material!